THE KING'S TRAITOR

Doris Leslie

SAPERE
BOOKS

THE KING'S
TRAITOR

Published by Sapere Books.

24 Trafalgar Road, Ilkley, LS29 8HH

saperebooks.com

ISBN: 978-0-85495-061-4

BOOK ONE (1537-1541)

Vivunt in Venerem frondes, omnisque vicissim felix arbor amat.

The leaves live for love, and every happy tree loves in his season.

Claudian

ONE

It was nearing sundown when he came to Wymondham, and another twelve miles to go. A gale had stormed up over the woods flanking the level common land, where black-faced sheep grazed undisturbed by the tug of the breeze at their wool.

His way lay along the road to Norwich, between serried ranks of dwarf fir trees planted against the force of the winds and called 'wind-breakers' thereabouts; and here was the Oak — gnarled and stunted as the firs, yet none the less sturdy for that — which he and Will Kett had used to climb and fight to be King o' the Castle. The tree looked to have grown stouter, broader, but no taller in the year he'd been away. Its brittle leaves hissed in the boughs like voices boding mischief, and, torn from their dying clutch in one last savage wrench, spun madly round to fall in heaps of autumn gold where shapes of things, unconformable and ugly, and not to be imagined, crouched unseen.

Philip crossed himself and shivered, breathed a prayer to Mother Mary, just in case; for you could never tell what lurked within those shadows to credit talk of witches' revels held on Hallowe'en about the Oak.

He shifted his seat in the saddle to give ease to his right buttock; his left was sorely chafed after sitting on it the better part of three days' hard riding to save the bruise he had got from that kick. Jesu! What a send-off! But well worth its pains, for this unlooked for exeat — or not? His breeks were plastered cruelly to his galled backside, grazed and bleeding from the burden put upon it, for all that he weighed light.

'John!' Halting his horse he shrilled across his shoulder to his servant, riding glum and gaunt behind him. 'Here! I'm stuck. I'll have my breeches off and a patch o' pig's grease on or there'll be no skin left to me.' He dismounted, swearing broadly as he had learned how from his betters, and from no less than the King himself. 'Come on!'

John came on and came down, hitched his mare's reins to a branch of the Oak, and tended, none too gently, his young master.

'Hell's torment!' Philip yelled. 'You've peeled me raw! Now where's that grease?'

That grease was in the baggage bound to John's saddle and brought forth with contumely to effect that 'twere better to suffer one half-hour more of peeled hide than arrive at the house of his father in breeks dark-stained and stinking. 'For,' quoth John, ''tis a powerful penetrating stuff and rank as any laystall.'

'Do as you're bid,' said Philip through his teeth. 'Had you suffered as have I these three days past, you'd care naught for a stain or a stink.'

Then John set to with a surly will, rubbing balm on sore places from the pot of unguent offered by the innkeeper's wife at the hostelry in Newmarket where they had lain the night. She, good soul — remarking on Philip's discomfort, and to his shame — had stripped him bare and marvelled to see the great bruise he carried, big as a hoof. She had asked how he had come by it, guessing his age to be no more than ten, with a bum so pink and tender as a babe's, to shame him the more for his smallness, and he turned twelve this Michaelmas! Nor was he disposed to tell her how he came by it, even though he might have bragged a bit — for not all could say they'd been kicked by a king — only that he found her mightily fat and ill-favoured, with a smell about her when she hugged him to her bosom, as of a dead rat encased there, and other sorts unseemly. Then she had crammed his mouth with marchpane, gave him a pot of grease from a boar of her own killing and said he must apply it to him daily with a pad. 'So pad me,' said Philip, 'and let us get on.'

John dutifully padded him with grass.

Up again in the saddle Philip sighed his content. 'Here's a pair of clotpolls that we are!' cried he. 'I'd have spared myself this hurtsome scraping of my hide had I thought of a handful o' grass.'

It was darkling when they clattered through the empty streets of Norwich, but in the marketplace a great concourse was gathered where a bonfire was lit; and around the doors of houses were hung boughs of the birch and russet garlands twined with flowers and the berries of the rowan. Some of the shops displayed, over their painted signs and half concealing them, branches of wrought iron containing a goodly show of lamplight. Here and there were rows of coloured candles, and all about a coming and going and a pushing and a shouting and a ring-a-ring o' roses of the lads and lasses, and a jingling of bells from a group of Morris dancers, and a man on stilts. 'Even here, you see,' Philip excitedly stood in his stirrups to watch, 'as so it has been all the way, do they joy for the birth of a prince.'

'Time, too, that we had him,' growled John. 'There's none wants a queen to rule in England as never has had one before.'

'We *have* had one before then!' Philip contradicted. 'But she made herself Queen and caused a mort of trouble. Her name was Matilda. I've a Grand-Aunt Matilda. She's a nun at Carrow

Abbey. I went to visit her at Carrow with my mother.' A little crease appeared between his eyebrows as he spoke of his mother, whose face, strangely, he could sometimes see as clear as he could see his own in the Queen's Venetian mirror, and sometimes he could see her not at all ... 'Yes, and my Grand-Aunt, Dame Matilda, she kept a he-goat with bells round its neck.'

'Which,' said John, 'has since been devoured.'

'What!' giggled Philip, 'the goat?'

'No.' Never was so stolid, so humourless a John. 'The Abbey of Carrow and other holy houses, along with the New Learning.'

'Me, I love not the New Learning.' And, having uttered the unutterable, he glanced askew at John to see how he would take it. He took it like a deaf-mute. Philip slipped him a grin, clapped heels to Crispin's sides and rode ahead.

Dangerous talk, no question, was this voicing of his elders overheard in quiet ways about the gardens of Hampton or Greenwich. John might or might not be of the Faithful, so Philip had better keep a guard upon his tongue and hold his peace on matters that were no concern of his. Yes, in this twelve-month at Court he had gleaned much of dire happenings retailed by his fellow pages. Why, Harry Neville had told him how three of the holy Carthusian friars had been charged with high treason and died on the gallows for refusing to name the King Head of the Church. Harry, then in attendance on the King's unlawful son, the young Duke of Richmond, had been greatly favoured to witness that which was done to the Charterhouse monks. Cut down while still living, their bellies ripped open — so Harry with gusto related — and their guts oozing out, all twisted, like a purplish mass of bleeding snakes. And the stench! Harry said he was hard put to hold his vomit. The Duke could not, and had to be revived with a pomander.

From these grisly visions Philip edged his thoughts to things more pleasant: this week's great event that was bringing him home, and no news of it yet to his father, for what use to send a courier when he could come as quick ... was it only five days since?

He saw himself at Hampton Court with his fellows in the anteroom outside the Queen's bedchamber. He and Tom Wroth were in attendance to fetch and carry at the order of the midwife, who every so often would poke her head round the door to send them for basins of warm water or fresh towels.

He and Tom, to pass the time, were playing pitch-and-toss with silver farthings and an eye for the back of Sir Francis Bryan, Master of the Henchmen, who stood at the window drumming impatient fingers on the pane. In muted voices the King's pages laid odds on or against the pending birth; they too had an eye for the Master, stiff as a ramrod in red velvet slashed with yellow.

'Two nobles for a knave!'

'Three,' Harry Neville capped it, 'for a girl!' He had nobles in plenty to lose. All the King's pages were older and grander and richer than Philip or Tom. Then had come from within an agonised shriek in a sobbing crescendo to curdle the blood. Philip's spine crept and Tom paled. The King's pages exchanged looks. Sir Francis ceased his tattoo on the window, turned sharp about, made as if to speak, said nothing, strode away. And from the Queen's chamber, after those sounds had dwindled to moans, were heard grave murmurs, and the King's voice, strong, 'By Holy Cross, the child! I can take another wife...' And a long silence.

Tom and Philip slid their farthings into their pouches. The King's boys smoothed their sleeves, and, arms folded, waited at attention, while Harry whispered from a corner of his mouth, ''Tis hoped Her Grace had swooned before *that* came to her ears.' The silence deepened drearily, until the door was flung open with a shout to shake the rafters, followed by a whimper as of a drowning pup.

The King, his feet wide planted, padded shoulders squared, his face a-gleam and bursting with smiles to show his small stained teeth, bellowed the news that circled all the palace: 'A prince! A prince is born to us. Praise be!'

Thereafter a ferment of confusion; a hurrying, scurrying and shoving of Philip on this side and that by gentlemen he had never seen before nor likely would ever see again: foreigners, ambassadors, and purple-robed physicians, and a tripping to and fro of maids of honour, chattering like magpies and ogling the men; and the coming of the Lady Mary, the one familiar face of all to Philip. But even she; to whom he owed his office here at Court, since his mother before marriage had attended her at Hunsdon, had not a glance for him. She swept on and into the chamber; nor was it his place to pry at keyholes, though Harry Neville, not so squeamish, did … O, and the christening next midnight! That was something, truly, and Philip's first glimpse of the heir to the throne.

His sister Mary, Godmother, received him at the font. The four-year-old Elizabeth, his second sister, followed him. Wakened from her sleep to be arrayed in robes of state, she held the chrisom, perilously waggled, while the Queen's long-faced brother, Edward Seymour, Lord Hertford, clutched her in his arms, striving to hush her squawks of delight at this peep-show. There, too, was her grandfather, father of that Never-say-What Nan Bullen, with a towel about his neck; and

Sir Francis Bryan, Sir Anthony Browne and others known to Philip, all of them with towels about *their* necks, crowding to the silver font, awaiting the arrival of the chief participant who, despite the soothings of his nurse, Mistress Jackson, howled lustily throughout the whole performance.

Borne in a litter in the wake of her son, with a page attendant on her either side, came the Queen; and while the archbishop dipped in holy water the urgently protesting prince, the organ thundered the *Te Deum,* boys' voices sang it, and Philip joined his shrill treble, woefully flat but luckily unheard, to theirs. Then, amid a sycophantic chorus from the bishops that 'A John the Baptist is come among us,' Garter-King-at-Arms proclaimed that yelling, scarlet, squirming atom, latest scion of the Tudors: 'Duke of Cornwall, Earl of Chester, most dear and entirely beloved son of our Dread and Gracious Lord and King Henry the Eighth. May God Almighty grant good life and long to the Right High, Right Excellent and Noble Prince Edward,' who by this time had looked, so Philip believed, to have screamed himself into a fit.

She who had brought this joy-dementia to England lay propped on her cushions, fever-flushed, her restless hands picking at her jewel-encrusted gown and the necklet of pearls at her throat; which, she may have thanked her Lord and Master — and her God — still supported her reeling head upon her shoulders.

Incense filled her nostrils with aching pungency. The chanting and the shouting, the trumpeting, the prayers, clashed in her ears to her heart's wild throbbing. Her body, still wracked from the torture of travail, lay drenched in a sickly sweat. Candles on the altar blossomed like fiery great tulips; light from two hundred torches haloed her son's bald head;

and, from her shrine, the tender compassionate face of God's Mother gazed down to dissolve her in an all-pervading peace.

Philip, beside her, had seen her eyelids sink, her face ghost-white against the crimson damask pillows, and whiter than the coverture of lawn, gold-threaded, that he had feared for her and thought her gone, and sidled close, with whispers — 'O, Madame, O, Your Grace...' — and touched a finger to her chilly wrist. None observed his daring — nor his fright, nor her pallor — save Tom, following behind, who had squeaked, 'Shall I call the gentlewomen?'

But at that moment a trumpet-blast, louder than any, resounded through the chapel; the Queen's eyelids fluttered open to show a filmy streak of blue; a feeble hand stretched, groping. Philip took and held it fast in his to give it warmth. He had seen her thin lips move in the flicker of a smile, heard her breathe his name: 'Philip Pugh...' And his chest swelled.

Three hours later, still in attendance, and while still the trumpets blared for Her Grace's Benediction on her newly baptised babe, the King, red and jubilant with feasting, came from his wife's couch to the anteroom, and seized the nodding Philip, who by this time was half asleep.

'Queen's Page! You, Pugh. Hooh! Phooh!' Puffing and playful, the King caught him up by his belt, swinging him round and off his feet. 'You're not wanted here. You can go.' The King belched; Philip blenched. What was this? His dismissal?

It was, with a mighty kick at the whirling youngster's seat to speed him.

'Sire! How, Your Grace,' he gasped, 'have I offended?'

'Hey? Offended?' The small flat eyes crinkled into laughter. 'Off with you, and home with you. Offended? Yes, an you stand upon your going, so will we be, i' faith! The Queen is pleased to grant you leave of absence in reck-hic-nition of good service. Take a week, a sennight maybe. Off you go!' And His Grace, well advanced in celebration, belched again, strong-smelling, dropped him, grinned to see him sprawl, served a parting kick to his behind and, guarded by his gentlemen, went lurching down the corridor to spill his drink in the rushes. Philip asked no second bidding to be gone … and here he was, bone-weary, sore, and barely a mile from home.

Setting his horse to the gallop he bent to whisper in his ear, 'For this last lap over Mousehold, good lad, and a feed of oats to bed you down.' Tossing his head as if in answer, Crispin leapt to his stride, picking his way, unforgotten in a twelvemonth, along the tussocky grass track fringed with furze and thorn and clumps of the late blackberry. Up behind him, ambling on his grey half-winded mare, came John Locke.

A grape-bloom mist rising from the river shrouded all the heath. Low in the sky swung a young crescent moon trailing tattered cloud-scarves. The wind had dropped; and there in a hollow, with a glow of light in its windows, chimney-stacks smoking and a welcoming whinny from the stables — 'That's Bess!' cried Philip. 'She's heard us —' lay Sprowston Hall, his father's house. 'And who's to know we're coming?'

In at the gatehouse, round to the yard he rode, slipping from the saddle, with a broad 'Hola!' and a smack to Crispin's sweat-streaked rump to send him head-on for his stall.

'Why —' At the buttery door old Andrew stood peering, holding up a taper to the darkness — 'what's to do?'

The first thing to do was to see the horses fed before he sought his father. He found him in the hall with guests at the board that looked to be cleared of a banquet: empty flagons, oyster shells and capon bones, the carcass of a goose, a haunch of beef, a salmon soaked in wine, stuck with cloves and half demolished; dishes piled thick with sweetmeats, a sugar-loaf and every kind of fruit, while sundry titbits flung to his father's two Irish wolfhounds lay strewn amid the rushes. Sighting Philip, they relinquished their share of the feast to fall on him with boisterous greeting.

'Down, Douce — hey, Doran, enough!' Laughing, he dodged them, who, on their hind legs to lick at his chin, stood half a head higher than he. As his father, sitting back to the screens, turned to enquire the source of commotion, his narrow face, lengthened by its buff-coloured beard, was bereft of all expression save bewilderment.

Mild-mannered, with the stooping shoulders of the scholar and, unlike his chubby son, tall and lean as his two hounds, was Geoffrey Pugh. Shaken from his customary absent-mindedness at the sight of the travel-stained Philip, whom he was inclined to mistake for an apparition come to warn him of disaster, he got upon his feet and, dazedly remarking, 'Good — good life!' approached, with timidity, to take him by the hand for reassurance that this was indeed his son, and in the flesh. 'How come — how come you here? Have you supped?'

'No, sir, not a bite.' Reminder of four hours' emptiness widened a hole in his belly.

'Then sit — sit you down and fill yourself. There's not — there's not much left, I fear.' His father's speech, slightly impeded by a repetitive hesitancy, was as if apologetical for giving voice at all.

Philip sat, tenderly, in the place of honour indicated by his father, a chair elaborately carved and used only by the master of the house. The three guests, his neighbours, sat on stools and, bringing one of these set around the great log fire,

Geoffrey seated himself, plied his son with wine and bade him eat.

Scarcely pausing between mouthfuls to answer the volley of questions hurled at him by the gentlemen, who were garrulous and wordily explosive as his good father was not, Philip readily gave his account of the christening. News of the birth had already reached them, passed lip to lip through every town, every village, and from every spire pealing joy-bells all the way from London; but none had a story, first-hand, to tell, and Philip, full of drink, was nothing loath to tell it, and may have somewhat embroidered as he went along.

Yes, the Queen had been taken with a seizure during the baptism, and had he not been in attendance beside her — when all eyes were fixed on the font and none on Her Grace — she surely would have died. And because he revived her he had been granted of Her Highness this sennight's leave of absence, which being unexpected had given him no time to —

'Is't true,' came high-pitched interruption from Sir Roger Wodehouse of Kimberley, four miles beyond Wymondham; he, who for his lack of inches was dubbed the 'Little Knight' — Philip prayed he'd be less dwarfish at Sir Roger's age — 'is it true that the King was asked by the doctors to decide which life, hers or the prince's, should be saved?'

'Come now, Sir Roger.' It was Robert Kett of Wymondham who spoke, his dark brows shelving to meet across his monumental nose. 'The lad can surely not be apt to answer that?'

'Yes, sir,' Philip nodded, 'I am. For as I waited in the anteroom outside Her Grace's chamber, I heard —' He stopped abruptly. No. Better not blab of that which he shouldn't have heard: 'The child! I can take another wife.'

So, warmed with Malmsey, he smiled at the 'Little Knight', quaffed his cup, foraged in the carcass of the goose for its liver, and tongued the fat from his fingers with relish.

'A fearful decision to make,' went on Sir Roger, undeterred by Kett's frown, 'and worse still when concerning the birth of an heir to the throne.'

'Yet all's well, as it chanced.' This from Tom Aldrich, the third of them. Twice Mayor of Norwich, elderly, balding, he exuded opulence from every pore. His black velvet doublet was sable-edged, pearl-studded; his sleeves were bolstered and slashed with white satin. He wore rings on his thumbs and index fingers, and round his neck a chain of wroughten gold. 'Shall we,' heartily suggested Mr. Aldrich, 'let it go at that, Sir Knight?'

But Sir Knight, thirsty for gossip as any old wife, would not let it go at that. 'They do say the King sets more store by Queen Jane than ever in her heyday for Queen Anne, even to a reconciliation between himself and the Lady Mary.'

'Such store, sir,' Kett took him up, sharp, 'that despite she was down on her knees to the King praying him for restoration of the abbeys on behalf of the rising in Lincoln and Yorkshire last year, His Grace sends fifty thousand horse and foot —'

'Ten thousand, as I've heard,' put in Sir Roger. 'Numbers swell by repetition.'

'— to scatter the Fenmen, poor wretches,' Kett doggedly pursued, 'and bind them to serve and obey with life and land.'

'Such insur-insurrections,' ventured Geoffrey Pugh, 'are infective as the plague to overrun and devastate the right of — right of law and order.'

'Pah! Law and order? Confiscation,' declared Kett, 'by persons of low sense and less repute who batten on the spoils of monasteries made forfeit to the Crown. What of our worthy neighbour — himself a man of law, if not of order — who strips the lead from the roof of Wymondham Abbey's Church and carries off the freestone from the Chapel of Our Lady? Is *that* law and order, or vandalism legalised?'

'Have a care, Master Kett.' Sir Roger shot a doubtful glance at the wall behind him. In the wavering light of the logs, the tapestry, patterned with armoured men and wimpled women of bygone years, seemed to quicken and crowd close as if they had ears for that which should never be spoken. This loud-voiced Kett was a notorious firebrand and one with whom it was wise to be wary. 'We have no proof, more than village gossip, that our good neighbour, Serjeant —'

'Reform,' intervened Master Aldrich, blandly steering the talk to less personal drift, 'is parent to a new school of thought which, in the progressive sequence of events, must replace age-old traditional doctrine.'

'The cause of events,' timidly suggested Geoffrey Pugh, 'is, as Cicero has it, ever more of interest *semper causae eventorum magis movent quam ipse eventa* than the events themselves. Take the Pil — the Pilgrimage of Grace, for ex — for example, which, alas, has gone the way of —'

'Reform, yes!' Kett was at it again with scant regard for his host's contribution to the argument, 'but not if its cause must lead to legions of homeless monks and nuns cast out to go a-begging door to door, they who gave of holy charity. So much —' a fleck of spittle lodged upon his lip — 'for your Reform!'

'Sir...' Philip plucked at his father's sleeve. Having eaten his fill and mixed enough of Malmsey and ale to bring to his head a buzzing as of bees, he could make no point of such discussion, and nor, to judge from his father's abstracted look as he crumbled bread on his platter, could he. 'Sir, may I go to bed? ... Mass!' added Philip on top of a yawn. ''Tis a wearisome long ride from Hampton Court.'

His father smilingly nodded. 'Yes, to bed. You have not — have not forgotten where you lie?' He brushed his son's cheek with his cool, dry lips. 'Sleep very well, my dear, and so — goodnight.'

Unnoticed by the others, still loud in their debate, Philip slipped away.

The staircase leading to the gallery that gave access to the lodgings was in darkness. He groped for and found the door of his room, to be met by the gleam of a candle, dead almost down to its socket, and a strong fetid smell that was certainly not of burnt wick. Closing the door behind him, and as, cautiously sniffing, he unbuckled his belt, something shaggy and cumbersome sprang from out obscurity to butt him in tenderest parts. He doubled, squealing with the shock and pain of it: 'Pardie! First my back and now my front to be disparaged!' And, hands fisted, striking blindly, he fell forward, half impaled on a pair of horns.

'Now the blessed saints preserve us,' he yelled in a rare fright, 'if 'tis not the devil himself!'

At which, from the bed, further to scare and convince him he was set upon by Satan and his imps, came eldritch shrieks.

Clammy of palm and weak-kneed, Philip, gabbling a Paternoster, backed to the door and was about to turn and bolt when a voice, urgent with terror but thankfully human, stayed him, crying, 'Help, help! Robbers! Thieves! Have at him, good Benedict — have and hold him fast!' Then, in the feeble light of the snatched candle, he perceived himself to be at closest quarters with...

'God's Mercy!' he panted, 'a goat!'

'Who are you?' Somewhat less terror-tinged was the voice that now shrilly demanded, 'How durst you break so unmannerly into my chamber?'

'And who are *you*?' retorted Philip, panic rapidly subsiding when he saw, scrambling out of his bed, nothing more to be feared than a girl in her shift, and greatly more frightened than he.

'I'm Jocosa, and that's Benedict, sick of the colic from eating of the arras. I've had him with me in my chamber these two nights past, dosing him with physic. As for you —' she continued, gathering courage as she saw Philip a-grin, 'if you've come to steal you'll find naught to steal from me.' Saying so she aimed a naked foot smartly at his shins. 'Get out! Or I'll have you in the stocks.' At which his giggles, swelling, surged in laughter, to bring her at him in a fury with her nails. 'There's a saucy snite you are!' She clawed his cheek to leave a bleeding scratch upon it. 'That'll learn you to make a mock of me. Benedict! Help! Murder! *Thieves!*' And again she let forth in a torrent of screams, while Benedict, turning his back on the pair of them, unconcernedly chewed at the rushes.

Philip fled.

Stumbling down the stairway he collided with his father at the foot of it. His guests had departed and, disturbed by the noise, he was preparing to investigate.

'Sir!' Philip flung himself upon him. 'Why didn't you say there's a girl in my room — and a goat? Or is the house possessed of demons?'

'Possessed?' his father echoed mildly. 'Not so far — so far as I know. As for demons — tush! The nightmare. You ate too much of goose-liver, dear child.'

'Sir!' Philip danced impatience. 'I have been most abominably used by a horned beast — goat or devil — and stinking to high heaven, that attacked me in my — well, and there it is!'

'A beast? What beast?' parrot-wise his father queried. 'Ah! The goat. Yes, she would have it in her chamber, believing it were dying — which unhappily it is — is not. A most destructive animal. That reminds me — the arras in the hall must be repaired, if it be not past repairing. I was not advised on the arrival of your — of your Grand-Aunt Matilda that a — '

'What?' ejaculated Philip. 'My Grand-Aunt Matilda? Is *she* here?'

'Yes.' Myopically his father peered. 'I laid my tablets somewhere. I've work to do upon a poem based on the Hippolytus of Euripides from which I was — I was disturbed by the coming — having disremembered that they were invited — of my neighbours. Yes, my aunt, Dame Matilda, is here from Carrow, since that the abbey was confiscated these three — these three months past. The young maid, Jocosa, came with her. I could not refuse her sanctuary, she being my kin — my kinswoman, daughter of the Sow … Now, where did I lay my tablets?' He held aloft a lighted taper, glanced anxiously about and broke into smiles. 'In the hall. I left them in the hall. Take this.' He handed the taper to Philip. 'Go fetch them. Yes, 'tis an in-insalubrious habit to harbour a goat in the house. You recollect — or maybe you were too young — how that her father, my cousin, the Sowerby of Drayton, died of the Sweat — and his wife — leaving her orphaned. She was a scholar at Carrow, and with the — with the Dissolution — ah, so here they are!' The squire's narrowing gaze widened in surprise to rest upon the tablets lying on a stool. He took them up and wandered off, murmuring, 'Tomorrow you shall meet your cousin once — or is it twice — removed?'

'Father!' Resignedly Philip followed after him. 'Where am I to sleep?'

'Sleep?' His father rounded vaguely, and in some concern, to say, 'Is not your bedchamber made ready for you, child?'

'No, not,' Philip gritted his teeth, 'while that girl and her pestilent goat are there in "sanctuary". I'd best take me to the stables.' He turned huffily away and was caught back.

'Why — but why the stables? Go you to my bed — I had forgot the girl was in it — I'll be writing until dawn.' Holding him at arm's length his father searched his face, remarking: 'Are you — are you hurt? You bleed.' And with a clutch of his breath, 'You grow more than ever like your — like your mother. I am joyed to have you here again and in such seeming health. Bathe it well. *Beata sanitas. Te praesente amoenum ver floret gratiis; absque te nemo beatus.* Give me the taper. I'll light you up the stairs.'

He kissed him on the forehead; stood to watch him out of sight. And Philip, fumbling his way along the gallery to the door of his father's room, entered it warily — any more goats? — flung himself fully dressed on the bed and slept the clock round.

The brothers Kett, of whom Robert, the younger, was squire of three manors, had acquired a fortune in trade; William, the elder, in 'butchery', so did the less successful designate his ownership of bullocks sold in Norwich market; the other in a tannery and the buying of raw hides stripped from his brother's herds. Be that as it may, and although William, it was said, had surplus interests as a mercer, the two held considerable property in land.

The family of Kett, spelt originally Cat, derived from the Norman Le Chat, claimed to have come over with the

Conqueror; but William and Robert Kett, Ket, Cat, or whatever, were a cadet branch of this ancient tree, and had been established in Wymondham little more than half a century. None the less they were accepted, and respected, as entitled to bear arms: *Or on a fess between three leopards' heads erased affrontés azure, a lion passant argent*, conspicuously blazoned above their porticos.

On a morning in October, some few days after his visit to Sprowston, Robert Kett, returning to Wymondham from Yarmouth where he had been to inspect a consignment of hides to be shipped to Flanders, came on a disturbance outside the Abbey Church. The townsfolk, with a fellow in their midst whom Kett recognised as one John Browne, a cooper, were in clamorous accord with his demand that the church, scheduled for destruction on the seizure of the monastery, be saved.

Halting his horse at the edge of the crowd, Kett grinned in his beard to hear John Browne declaim: 'My masters, I have here in my pouch a gold angel that never did me good, and that ye shall have between you an you support me in that ye all do make your mark to this petition, which I doubt me not the King, His Grace — and our Squire Kett —' deftly sighted on his tall white horse, 'will uphold and approve. So let us offer each his mite to this our cause that we buy back and restore unto us some part, at the least, of our noble Church and Our Lady's Chapel, robbed of its glory by persons or a person unknown, who —'

Yells of 'We know 'un! Ay! we know 'un!' interrupted the speaker, who, raising his hand and, with another look about him, away beyond the crowd, cried: 'Ay! we know, but 'tis not for us to name 'un lest we be named in — or out — of our turn!' Loud laughter greeted this sally. 'And so, sirs,' continued the cooper, 'are you for me in agreement?'

He was answered by a vociferous chorus of 'Yea!' with Kett's voice breaking in louder than any. 'I'll back you all — full measure!' And down among the bobbing heads he flung his purse.

An ugly scramble followed of hurtling bodies fighting to grab it where it lay trampled in the dust, amid a hubbub of oaths, of shouts and curses, and the terrified shriek of a woman.

'So!' cried Kett, 'is this your "noble" enterprise? You, who prate of desecration to God's House, and yet yourselves will rob the Church of largesse offered at its gates? Shame on you! If this be your protest against despoilment of that we should have to hold and cherish in the honour of our Faith, then go you — join the ranks of the despoilers!'

'Hold hard, Master Kett.' The ringleader elbowed his way through the muttering throng, who, subdued by Kett's outburst, sheepishly fell back to let him pass. 'Bludgeon this whoreson knave as he deserves. 'Twas he who set example for these poor fools — like apes — to mimic.' At which Browne's disciples, in loud assent to their vindication, flung themselves on the offender, a swart, black-bearded clod alive with vermin, and dragged him forward, profusely bleeding from the nose.

'Sir,' declared John Browne, thrusting his captive under the head of Kett's horse, 'we ask no more than honest right to guard our church, with heart and life if need be. As for this devil's dung —' he raised his fist and, to the onlookers' howls of delight, drove it squarely at his victim's underjaw with such force as to dislodge his two front teeth.

'An' here be Squire's purse,' held on high by a tow-haired yokel in a shepherd's smock, and recovered from unsavoury concealment between the ragged shirt and jerkin of the scapegoat.

'Then you can give it back to me,' said Kett. 'It will be fairly dealt again when — or if — the petition be granted. Not before. Come on, now! Hand it up.'

Constrainedly, the purse was handed up and returned by its owner to his pouch; then, glowering down on the sullen group around his saddle, 'There's not, I'll warrant me, a barleycorn to choose between that hank o' gallow's meat —' Kett flicked a finger at the sanguinary object to whose unkempt beard clung two greenish-yellow fangs — 'and the whole scurvy pack o' ye!'

Leaving glum faces and ominous murmurs behind him, he walked his horse away, but had not gone half a furlong when he was overtaken by one who came hurrying after on foot.

'Master Kett!' The newcomer, red as from an apoplexy, hailed him with gasps. 'I stood unnoticed on the — fringe — of that — disgraceful — exposition. A moment, pray you —' he held his heaving side — 'I've a formidable stitch.'

Kett pulled up, a smile slanting. 'How now, Serjeant Flowerdew, why such haste? We are none of us so young that we can outrun the winds, if not my good gelding here — at crawling pace.'

Puffing, blowing, mopping sweat from his brow with a handkerchief, he, thus addressed, recovered breath to demand, 'May I speak — freely — Master Kett?'

Turning his head but not his eyes in this stoutish gentleman's direction, Kett laconically replied, 'By all means, sir, speak freely, if speech in our land still be free. You would say…?'

The serjeant, as befitting a lawyer from London turned squire to hold accumulation of his clients' fees in the Manor of Hethersett, forensically said what he would say.

'May I suggest, Master Kett, without Prejudice, and in your Interest entirely, be it understood, that you refrain from Interference in this wild-goose Scheme of the rustics hereabouts to raise money among themselves, that they may buy back a Moiety of the Abbey Church? Albeit, I was much relieved to see you reclaim your Donation.'

A short, squat, shaven man was Serjeant Flowerdew, round of face, pot-bellied. He wore a doublet of green Flemish cloth and a cap and outer coat of rich blue velvet, wonderfully slashed and embroidered. His apparel, indeed, savoured rather of Court than of country.

'Such Procedure, I fear, would result,' he continued, 'in some repercussion were it told in High Quarters. We look to you, sir, as our Prop and Stay —' if his smile, exposing many teeth, were intended to ingratiate it lamentably failed; Kett was busy with the buckle of his belt — 'to uphold Authority,' Serjeant Flowerdew proceeded on a somewhat higher key, 'and not to be misguided by, shall we say, False Sentiment?'

'We can say sentiment,' Kett pleasantly replied, 'if sentiment it be, and false, to preserve and treasure that which is sacred to God and to our Faith, if not sacred to the King.'

'Sir!' The serjeant exhibited shock. 'Curb your tongue. All that is God's is Sacred to the King His Grace. But —' protestingly he spread his hands — 'a leaking roof and beams, worm-eaten, a few relics of Idolatrous Images carven from wax to enforce Superstition? Let us not, in our Enlightenment, treasure such as these, but a Sense, Master Kett, of Proportion.'

Ponderous, fruity, was the speech of Serjeant Flowerdew, with an emphasis on capitals and an upward look from eyes like boiled gooseberries at Kett, who, slightly inclining his head, made no reply to this, more than a curt: 'My way lies to the right, yours, sir, to the left. I will bid you a very good day.'

And wheeling his horse he trotted on out of the town.

The afternoon was drowsy with furtive sun, half hidden in a curtain of low cloud; but there was blue enough between the sluggish drifts to lie reflected in watery mud-ruts left by recent rains. His road, ill kept and straggling, wound through open fields, yellowed with the stubble of reaped harvest, and, beyond them, meadows girdled by thick encroaching woods.

Slowing his horse Kett let his eyes wander, marking the tarnished rust and amber of autumnal trees, the distant oxen patiently drawing a plough, a shepherd with his flock, limned like figures on a frieze against the black-browed pastureland. Then, as he looked, a smile dwelling in his eyes as a man may look on a loved mistress, noting with pride of ownership the gracious curve and gentle upward sweep of these, his fruitful acres, he saw — his smile deepening — a boy and a girl, she leading a goat, he striding ahead ankle-deep in the razed corn and seemingly oblivious to her abuse, of which Kett caught the words: 'Jobbernowl! Pig's offal! Philip — *Philip* — wait for me. Why won't you answer? I only want to know —'

'And know too much.' This, savagely, was flung at her with a half-turn of the head as, sighting Kett, he ran to greet him. 'Sir! Well met and timely. I had thought to call upon you at your house, not having opportunity on the night of my arrival to hear what news of Will. Is there any likelihood of seeing him before I return to Court?'

'Will is in Flanders,' he was told. 'I have sent him there as 'prentice to a wool merchant in Antwerp.'

'Flanders? So,' Philip said, chapfallen, 'I'll not see him here before I go.'

'May be. He journeys to and from Yarmouth every two-three months, and should be due this week.'

'Who is Will?' The girl, dragging her reluctant goat, had joined them. Philip scowled at her in silence, while Kett, twinkling, answered for him.

'My son, William. That's a fine well-favoured goat you have there, Mistress Jocosa.'

'He's been sick nigh to death o' the colic. He can't stomach half he eats, being no common goat but nobly bred at Carrow from the abbey's herds. Dame Matilda, she reared him by hand on mare's milk, his dam having died when he was a newborn kid, and when the commissioners came to turn us out, the prioress gave him to Dame Matilda, but 'tis I who tend him. She's too old, she says, to fetch and carry for a goat. He's so wise, you'd not believe — a true Benedictine, named for our patron saint. How old is your son, Master Kett?'

'Fifteen.'

'I'm twelve. Three months younger than Phil but taller for my age than he. Look.' She stood back-to-back with the reddening Philip, who sourly shrugged from her. 'Sheep's bladder, you!' She pulled a face at him. 'Blown out with high conceit to burst yourself. Marry! I'll say they learn you courtly manners in the King's house. I've seen as good in a sty.' Her eyes, dark as sloes with an uplift of curling lashes to her eyebrows, peeked round at the much-amused Kett. A long-legged child, thin as a rail, creamy-skinned and with a mouth as red as it were painted. But she went poorly clad in a drab-coloured gown of monastic severity, and was not, Kett remarked, over-clean in her person. Her hands were filthy, her small heart-shaped face was streaked with dirt; and her hair, thick and matted, would have been the better for a curry-comb. Yet she was like to be a beauty, he decided, were she washed.

To Philip, however, trim, immaculate beside her, she represented everything he loathed.

'Will your son come to Sprowston if Philip isn't there?' she persisted, gazing up at Kett as he gazed down.

'To visit you, mistress, I've no doubt,' he replied; doubt uppermost for all that, since Will, as reported by the Fleming with whom he had placed his son to learn his trade, had already found his budding manhood in the alcoves of Antwerp. And, hastily, he added, 'He'll scarce have the time to pay visits, for he comes and goes within a day and night.'

With a wave of his hand he went on his way, spattering mud kicked up from his horse's hooves.

Jocosa leapt aside, but not soon enough to avoid a mouthful of slush. Disgorging it with splutters she yelled after him: 'Here's a fine gentleman, you — to befoul me! Yes!' She rounded on her escort, who found her case side-splitting. 'Laugh! Mighty comical, is it, to see me eat dirt? Well, take a bellyful on't — spiced for flavour.' And, releasing Benedict, who shambled off with attention to a thistle, she scooped up in her hands the droppings of oxen on the cart-track, darted forward and daubed Philip's face with the muck. 'That'll learn you,' she panted, 'to make game of me!'

'A murrain!' emitted Philip. 'You hell-cat!' He caught her by the wrists, but stayed his fist from assault upon her ear. One could not, howsoever sorely tempted, hit a girl. He let her go, though with violence enough to send her sprawling, and without another word or backward look he too went on his way.

We must allow him cause for grievance. Bad enough to be deprived of bedroom to make shift on a straw pallet with a log for his pillow, in an attic set by for the lackeys; worse still to find his home infested with a young and an old maid.

Dame Matilda would alone have been a trial. Near on seventy, uprooted from the convent where she had lived sixty years of her life, she, in her three months' installation at Sprowston, had taken to herself full charge of the household, its master, its servants, and — since Philip's arrival — of him.

She had it firmly he was heading for perdition, consequent upon his contact with the Court. Even in her cloister talk had come to Dame Matilda of the King's divorce and unsanctified marriage with his 'concubine, the Bullen', who had supplanted the one and only Queen to meet with her well-deserved fate. That Philip's appointment as page to the King's third wife was sponsored by the Princess Mary did, in some degree, condone his situation, but nothing could convince the holy lady that, despite his tender years, he went untainted by anti-Papalism, fornication, heresy, and all the seven sins.

No wonder, then, that Philip's vacation offered endless opportunity for the dame to pump him dry regarding his activities in the household of Queen Jane, and his — if any — spiritual guidance. Who was his priestly instructor? Or was the holy custom of Confessional abolished with all else of the True Faith? Did the King's Lord Privy Seal, the maleficent Cromwell, sit in the box, as was said, to hear the sins recited by each man of his own neighbour? Did the King carry God's finger mark in the shape of a running ulcer on his leg as token of Almighty disapproval, in that His Grace had raised the serpent Cromwell from the dust to kill by torture saintly martyrs and battle with His Holiness the Pope?

Philip's unready response to such or to similar catechism may have convinced the good nun of his damnation, when, throat-sore with shouting in the lady's ear, for she was sadly hard of hearing, he told her, inexcusably: 'Madame, go ask the King or my Lord Privy Seal or the Serpent himself of these matters, but lest your tongue be ripped out in the asking, it were better you do not ask me!' The most of which, however, went unheard, but enough to hurry the dame to her prayers for the soul, past redemption, of Philip.

Yet he might have more readily accepted his grand-aunt as a fixture in his father's house than the girl, Jocosa. While the dame was an irksome, if necessary encumbrance, Jocosa, his distant cousin, was a curse. She too would be forever plaguing him with questions concerning the King and the Queen and the Court; and would pepper her discourse with abuse of himself in language to raise him a blush. 'Such ruttish speech as yours,' he said, 'would shame a Wapping fish-fag. Is that what you learned from the Ladies of Carrow?'

'No.' She poked her tongue at him. 'I learned it from the cook.' And, with a giggle, enlarged. 'Our prioress, she fed us — the boarders — so niggardly we went always with a sinking in the stomach, and the cook he would sometimes give us broken meats and pies if we begged at the door of the kitchen, and if Dame Margaret, the Cellaress, was not about.'

This conversation took place in the orchard where she had followed him who sought refuge from her there. She was seated in the fork of a gnarled apple tree while he, armed with a basket, lifted the windfalls. Most of the fruit had been picked in this last month, but there were still some of later sort russet-ripe for gathering.

'Ha! But I could tell —' Jocosa grinned with impish reminiscence, digging teeth white as almonds in an apple — 'I could tell a thing of Dame Margaret, too, for she was not so holy, neither. Once on a time I saw — from the dorter window — Father Anthony, the nuns' priest, walking in the garden with the cellaress, and you'd not believe,' she took another bite, 'what I saw the —'

'I'd liefer not hear what you saw,' Philip interrupted, but with slightly less conviction than his words implied.

'I saw,' said Jocosa, shying the core of her apple at his nose, 'the Father with his hand on Dame Margaret's — *ow!*' A piercing scream terminated further revelation. 'I've been stung by a wasp!' She leaned from her perch, wrist bared of its covering sleeve. 'See,' she whimpered, 'how I'm swollen.'

'Suck it,' Philip unsympathetically advised.

'What! And suck the poison in? O, misery me, it hurts like the devil.'

'Come here,' he commanded, 'get down.'

Nimbly she got down, her face pain-puckered; and he, taking her hand with disgust for its dirt, raised her wrist to his mouth, sucked and spat, and sucked again, and pushed her from him, saying, 'Now, if one of us is poisoned it'll be myself — but not from the sting of a wasp.'

Whereupon she flew at him, pommelling his chest. 'Pig! Filth! You pig-faced filth, may you be stung by scorpions. Will you have it I am poison?'

'If the cap be fitting,' Philip said, 'then wear it.'

'So!' She snatched his cap from his head and stuck it on her own. 'I'll wear your breeches too and make a better boy than you — who should have been a girl.' And wickedly she aped his voice in accents ladyish and drawling — 'If the ca-ap be fitting wa-arh it. Huh! I'd liefer be rude and downright in my speech, which is bred in my bones and my blood from the soil of Norfolk — as yours should be were you not puffed up to split yourself with London pride — than walk and talk so finical as a Jack-pudding at a — *gah!* St. Joseph!' she screeched, her wrist to her mouth, 'how it pricks! This wasp must be a hornet! Will you suck again?'

But he struck her proffered hand away and left her standing there in the leaf-chequered sunlight, with his velvet cap raffishly aslant upon her head and her mocking laughter on her lips ... and he hated her. All of her he hated. Her hair, black as a witch's; her eyelashes like spiders' legs; her scoffing jeering ways and sly narrow looks at him that induced a perturbation in his middle, not unpleasant, but which only made him hate her more, and with a hatred, most disturbing, that drove him to seek her were she not already seeking him. For despite she was vexatious as a tick he, for his confusion, could be happy neither with her nor without her. A hundred times a day he wished himself returned to Court and quit of her — a wish to be speedily granted, but in circumstances not as he had willed.

In the solar Dame Matilda Graby sat checking the monthly accounts. Most of the food consumed at Sprowston was produced from the home farm, but such items as salt and dried fish to be eaten during the winter and Lent must be bought, besides all condiments and spices. Fresh fish, too, for Fridays, must be purchased from John Ball, who, father and son, for generations had supplied not only the Ladies of Carrow, but the chief manors of Norfolk, journeying back and forth from the coast by way of the River Wensum.

Dame Matilda, who at Carrow had charge of the feeding of never less than twelve nuns and as many boarders, and aware that the Squire of Sprowston had as little idea of the value of money as any one of his own sheep, had made it her business drastically to curtail much waste of food and extravagant wages. Here, for example, was the sum of eight shillings and fourpence per year paid to Elianore Richmond, assistant dairy-maid — assistant, forsooth! — who did no more than skim the cream and drink the most of it. And here also one Joanna

Coke, the so-called 'housekeeper', received *twenty* shillings —
great heaven! — per year for her board and keep, and two and
fourpence special 'catering' fee, whatever that might mean,
although Dame Matilda shrewdly suspected it went to make
provision for her three children by several fathers. Yet to turn
her bastards adrift, the good dame had not the heart to do.
She, who for the past fifty years had been the Bride of Christ,
and who was now deprived of all that she once held in fee for
God, knew what it was to be homeless. But, as she sat, her
calm brow furrowed over the list of items to be ordered for the
coming week's consumption, and making a marginal note —
*too much of mutton ate. Sheep should be kept and valued for their wool,
not eaten piece-meal in the kitchen* — none to see her would have
guessed that she nursed in her bosom a bitter revolt against the
monstrous decree of the King, or of his apostle, the villainous
Cromwell, who had cast her from her cloister to be the guest
of charity. Nor that neither prayer nor penance, nor the
constant reminder of the hair-shirt pricking her withered
breasts, could pluck from her heart the seeds of mutiny.

Her task was done; the goose-quill laid aside, the inked notes
sanded, the parchment sheets gathered and bound together
with a cord, when a clatter of hooves in the forecourt below
and a voice calling: 'Hola! Who's within?' sent Dame Matilda
stalking to the window.

A lad in leather jerkin and red hose, astride a tall white horse,
was looking up as she looked down. At sight of her coiffed
head and black habit he snatched off his cap — a jaunty scarlet
cap stuck with a pheasant's feather — and from the saddle
reverently bowed. In the voice of a man that belied his
beardless chin, he asked, 'Madame, is Philip at home?'

'What?' Dame Matilda inclined an ear. He, bawling, repeated his question. 'I know naught of Philip's whereabouts,' was the rejoinder, 'nor, young gentleman, do I know you.'

'William Kett, Madame, at your service, son of Robert Kett of Wymondham,' came the prompt reply, with a grin to split his face: a handsome nut-brown boy with hair bright bronzed and gold-tipped where the sun had caught it. 'I am just returned from Flanders and have heard Philip is here.' His bold glance raked her with an uplift of his eyebrows, as if he would have added, *and what do* you *do here?*

And interpreting that unspoken insolence the dame, in the high-pitched tone of the deaf, answered tartly, 'You had best go seek him if you want him, for I am not his master.'

'Nor,' the urchin, grinning wider, said, 'his mistress.' Which remark was fortunately lost. 'My thanks to you, Madame. Good-day.'

Dame Matilda slammed the casement; then, as she turned from it, she heard in her good ear the sound of running feet and a glad, 'Why, Will! Well met! I'd despaired of seeing you before I must go back to Court.'

Glancing down again, her lips compressed, Dame Matilda saw that William had dismounted to be engulfed in warm embracing. Her long nose twitched. Kisses! Yet she had heard how in the world, men — and boys too, seemingly — kissed each other for welcome. And now came Jocosa — for once goatless — to put Dame Matilda in a state. Would the creature be at the arras again? More than likely if let off the leash. But the goat was of less concern to the dame than the girl.

She had always been a problem. When, some six years before, she had been placed at the convent by Lord Sowerby, her father, who was also a kinsman on the maternal side of Dame Matilda, she and the prioress had hoped that the child would ultimately take the veil, to which end her parents, to be rid of her, would not have been loath to consent.

Lord Sowerby and Agnes, his wife, from talk gleaned at Carrow, were worldlings attached to the Court of the King and his 'concubine', for by no other name would the Ladies of Carrow acknowledge Queen Anne Boleyn, to whom Lady Sowerby had been distantly related. According to Dame Matilda, the Sowerby of Drayton had married beneath him, since Geoffrey, forbear of the Boleyns — or Bullens — and 'prentice to a mercer, had acquired wealth enough in trade to become Lord Mayor of London. Therefore, the faults and failings of Jocosa — froward, hoydenish, spirited as a young filly to curb — were attributed to her lowly Bullen connections.

The Sowerbys between them had squandered a fortune, leaving their daughter penniless save for a pittance, barely sufficient to clothe her. Thus, but for Geoffrey Pugh's acceptance of the child in his house, she would have been destitute indeed.

So here she was, and another survey from the window assured the dame that the maid was making the best of opportunity to force herself upon the notice of young Kett.

Hastily descending, the good nun was chagrined to see Jocosa mounted pillion on the tall white horse, with her arms round the waist of Master Will. It was lucky perhaps for Jocosa that the dame could not hear her urging him, 'Hurry! I'll be catched before we start if that old Pokenose comes prowling. Get *on*, will you! Phil can follow when he's saddled Crispin. Be quick. O, Jesu, she's there — at the door.'

And before Dame Matilda could stay them they were gone, out of the forecourt, out at the gates, with Philip hell-for-leather after them on Crispin.

They crossed Mousehold Heath at a gallop, entered the city by St. Austin's Gate, went on past the castle and, turning east through the Gate of St. Stephen, came to the outposts of Carrow.

'Pull up!' Jocosa shouted in Will's ear. 'This is the abbey where I was schooled. O, how it is lonely and lost, poor soul. Look, O, look! They've been hacking down the chapel. I must go and see.' And as Philip joined them, glowering, on Crispin, she detached herself from Will, slid from the saddle, and ran to explore. Brambles caught at the hem of her kirtle, tall nettles stung her as she passed along the weed-infested cloisters, awed by their empty silence and the pervading desolation where once the gentle tread of nuns, the rustle of their habits, and their hushed voices had blent with the chime of vesper bells. Climbing the circular stone staircase that led from the south transept of the Chapel of St. John adjoining the Chapter House, she paused, her mouth agape.

The great columns supporting the vaulted roof had been partially destroyed, and one of the east windows cruelly mutilated. Broken pieces of stained glass lay scattered on the stone seats circling the walls, amid a heap of fallen masonry.

Jocosa crept forward to gather in her hand those sparkling fragments: red, topaz, purple, blue. 'They'd make a handsome necklace could I string 'em,' she decided; and the sound of her whisper in that ruined silence set her in a tremble so she needs must drop her findings, all but one, a jagged edge of ruby; and where her fingers clasped it, oozed a thin trickle of blood. 'As if,' she said, 'it wept red tears.' But to take and keep this relic as memento could not, for sure, be stealing, since the murderers of Holy Church had done their worst already. And from that place of quiet desolation with a smell about it, to her scared fancy, as of death, she fled to the refectory and up the octagonal turret stairs, and so to the dorter where she had used to sleep with other boarders, all deserted now save for scuttling mice and spiders. And, her heart beating hard against her ribs, Jocosa hurriedly retraced her steps down that oaken stairway, shrouded in grey dust when once it shone with beeswax, and out into the sun-lost mist of the October morning to hear Philip impatiently calling, 'Come on! Must we dally here all day for you?'

She ran to him where, beneath the well-remembered walnut tree on the south side of the cloister, he bestrode the fretful Crispin who was chafing at the bit and in a quiver to be off.

'I had to have one look again at where I used to live,' she told him, breathless, 'and see here — what I've found.'

She held the red glass up to him, her palm still scarlet-streaked.

'You've cut yourself,' said Philip, unconcerned.

'No.' She shook her head. ''Tis a bit of the Chapter House window that weeps for the poor wounded abbey — tears of blood.' And licking at her hand she asked, 'Am I now to ride pillion with you?'

But he only scowled at her for answer and turned his horse down the road to the entrance gates of Carrow.

'Up then!' cried Will, cheerily, and leaned from the saddle to help her mount. 'You'll have to make do with me.'

Light as a bubble she hoisted herself up behind him with her arms round his waist and her cheek between his shoulder blades, the ruby glass still clutched in her fist. Relishing the mingled scent of leather, boyish sweat, and hay and horse dung, she said, 'I like your smell,' and sniffed it deeply, 'and I think that I like you.'

She sensed the smile in his voice as he replied teasingly, '*Like* is too poor a word, Jocosa, for the way that I like you!'

She raised herself in the saddle, to bring her mouth on a level with his ear and nibbled at it, saying, pleased, 'Kind you are — gallant you are! Not sour as curds and despising as Philip. Is it true you're no more than fifteen? You talk like a man.'

'I'd do more than *talk* like a man —' laughing, Will slewed his head round at her, lips pursed to kiss, not her mouth that he aimed for, but the air as she drew from him, startled — 'an you were also fifteen.'

Well!

One hand clamped to the front of his belt, the other still clutching, despite the hurtful prick of it, her precious piece of glass, Jocosa was encouraged to think he might one day be minded to marry her.

'Philip,' she shrilled, 'on to Wymondham! I want to see Will's father's house.'

So now Philip and they were riding abreast, but Will spoke no more to her nor of her. It was all of this and that — 'and the damage done,' said Will, 'by those ruffians to the Church —' and of a petition and people, unknown to Jocosa: Sir Roger Wodehouse, Serjeant Flowerdew — 'a pretty name,' she panted to Will's unresponsive back.

'Who,' said he across to Philip as they jogged, 'besides that he has stripped the lead from Wymondham's Abbey Church, has enclosed much common land, and there'll be trouble with the peasantry, my father says, in cause of it.'

'Your father, and mine, too, have done the same,' retorted Philip. 'There's not land enough in Norfolk for every man to graze his sheep.'

'Which,' said Will doggedly, 'some time or other will raise a hornet's nest among the commonalty, mark me!'

Jocosa thumped his shoulder. 'O, look — the Oak! Can I get down and climb it?' Her words passed him by, unheeded, and less than the hum of a gnat above the steady clip and clop of hooves. She thumped again and yelled at him, 'I said I must get *down!* Your saddle's too hard. I'm sore in my seat. Won't you stop?' But he and Philip were still talking together; and with no more regard for her 'than as if I were a maggot,' she muttered, as they rode on past the Oak without so much as the wink of an eyelid at it.

Jocosa sulked.

The mist that had lain sodden on razed cornfields and meadows was lifting; and in the sky, mournful with low cloud, a gleam of sun peered out between blue clefts to gild the level road ahead whence, presently, two horsemen approached in a swift canter. They halted at a horse's length, and one, a long-faced gentleman in sombre black, demanded, 'Is this, sirrahs, the road to Sprowston Hall?'

'Straight ahead for some ten miles,' Philip answered, 'and through Norwich.' Then as the gentleman, with curt acknowledgement, made as if to ride on, Philip asked, 'Have you some business with my father, sir?'

'Your —?' The gentleman enquiringly paused. 'Is your father Squire Pugh?'

'Yes, sir.'

'And you are —?'

'Philip, sir, his son.'

The stranger dismounted, and, handing the reins to his servant, said, 'This saves us loss of time if we would be at Hunsdon on the morrow.' Glancing from the staring Will to the wide-eyed Jocosa, and back again to Philip, he added, 'I have to say with you, young sir, if you will kindly step aside.'

Philip got down from his horse, his arm through the bridle, and wonderingly obeyed. Why these doleful trappings? Even the servant went gloomily in black. And why Hunsdon, the home of Princess Mary?

Then, shock-blinded by a rush of tears that he could not, for the life of him, withhold, he heard that the Queen, his well-loved mistress, was dead … and that the King's Highness commanded his presence to attend the obsequies of Her Grace.

TWO

Surrounded by his gentlemen, all dutifully in black, the Royal Widower at Hampton Court sat grief-bowed, lost, dejected, too stunned to rail at the monstrous fate that had deprived him of the only wife whom he had truly loved.

Forgetful of his all-absorbing passion for 'that accursed and venomous whore' who had cuckolded him with Smeaton and half a dozen others, including her own brother, he was writing tear-blotted pages to Francis, the French king: *Divine Providence has mingled my joy* — in the birth of his son — *with the bitterness of death.*

Hands were raised to hide the whispers, beards were stroked to hide the grins of his attendants. How long before this travesty of sorrow would turn to joy again in the chase of a fourth wife? Yet there were those from whom memory shied to recall how, on that May morning, not eighteen months since, he had waited to hear the deep-throated guns from the Tower announce Nan Bullen's doom and his release; and that her life's blood was still wet in the straw of the scaffold when the then-happy widower had rode off to marry the girl now lying in regal state, dead of the longed-for heir she had borne him.

Not a few sentimentalists were moved to pity for the stricken father of that puny morsel, scarce two weeks old, on whom was showered an almost maniacal devotion. Heartbrokenly sobbing, refusing to eat — but not, it was noted, refusing to drink — the bereaved Majesty, gigantic in his mourning purple, nursed in his arms the pale babe, his one solace in this welter of woe. And to the accompaniment of explosive belches and a deluge of tears — a lachrymal capacity he had handed to his elder daughter — Henry, the King, would croon in a quavering voice to Edward, the prince, the song — his song, and his wife's favourite — of 'Greensleeves'. Most affecting.

So, for quite a week, he retired 'to a solitary place to pass his sorrows', while, in Hampton Court's chapel, Mass was daily solemnised around the guarded corpse. But these melancholy rites were not attended by the King. Leaving his daughter Mary as chief mourner in his stead, he betook himself to Windsor with his infant son, whose clamorous protest against his own personal loss was comforted by proxy at a stranger's breast. Yet neither he nor his father were the sole sufferers of that cruel bereavement.

Accompanied by her ladies and members of the dead Queen's household, Princess Mary knelt at the head of the coffin. She had a raging toothache and had caught a streaming cold. The November nights were raw with fog, the chapel walls were damp, and the flagstones beneath her knees chilled her to the bone. Her jaw swelled. She went in torment.

The death of her father's third wife may have been a greater loss to Mary than to her infant brother or the King. Jane Seymour, her best friend, had been a tactful mediator between herself and her father. Brutally threatened by Cromwell and Henry's relentless comissioners, Mary had been forced, after weeks of resistance, to surrender her will to the King, renounce her title of princess, and admit her mother's marriage null and void. Ill, weakened by persistent bullying, she had at last given in, to perjure her soul by signing the articles that confessed her a bastard and false to her dead mother's faith. But with the coming of Jane, it was as if a heavy pall had been lifted from her life. The two were almost of one age, and Jane, loyal to the memory of Queen Katherine, to whom, before the advent of Anne Boleyn, she had been maid-in-waiting, received the King's daughter with the deference due to her as second lady in the land.

So for one year, despite that she must for ever carry with her the scar of her remorse in that she had not been strong enough to hold fast to her beliefs and resist the King's supremacy, the lonely girl had found, if not happiness, the ghost of it. And now the Queen to whom — after her mother — Mary had given all her love, was gone, and she left to the untender mercy of her father.

What, she wondered, as, cramped with kneeling, the ready tears pouring — what of emptiness more would the future hold for her? What hope of marriage? Any man, a commoner, were he of the Faithful, would be welcomed. Her starved womanhood yearned for fulfilment, her heart for affection, and all her mother instinct, stirred at the first sight of her baby brother, was awakened to the longing for a child of her own. True, she had been courted — not for love, but as a means to her father's political ambition. When barely six years old she had been formally betrothed to her young cousin Charles, King of Spain, Emperor-to-be of the Holy Roman Empire. That had come to nothing; and she, who could remember the most powerful potentate in Europe only as 'that ugly man' who had given her a box of comfits and a kiss for dancing to him 'prettily', had been offered to another cousin, James V of Scotland, and again rejected. And now, in an age of child marriages, she was a spinster still, unwanted and unwooed at — twenty-one.

Her praying hands covered her face. The princess wept into them, sneezed, and applied to her dripping nose the crumpled ball of her soaked handkerchief. One of her ladies signed to a black-velveted torch-bearing page. He tiptoed to her side and was commanded in a hissing whisper: 'Go find the Lady Mary's woman — a clean handkercher.'

Glad of even a moment's release from this endless lugubrious vigil, Philip leisurely went on his errand, to return with a silken square. The princess smiled wan thanks as she took it, and he, back in his place beside the bier with another two hours yet to go before his supper-time, surreptitiously rubbed one foot against the other to relieve the itch of chilblains.

Those three weeks of the obsequies were dreary days for Philip. He and Tom Wroth took turn and turn about in attendance on the mourners in the black-swathed chapel. The Lady Mary's sneezes were infectious; Philip caught her cold and was allowed no leave to nurse it.

Shivering, red-nosed, he and Tom — both exactly dressed alike in brand-new black and led by the King's eldest daughter mounted on a white horse — rode in the funeral procession from Hampton Court to Windsor. Then, when all was thankfully over, Philip, Tom, and other, less important members of the late Queen's household were rewarded by the Lady Mary with the gift each of a rose noble for past service.

As neither Philip nor Tom had been advised if their future service would be needed, they went in daily expectation of dismissal. Ever since that startling summons on the road to Wymondham, when the King's messenger had hurried Philip off to Hunsdon where he had lain the night, the burning question *What will they do with me now?* had persistently nagged him. He had not been permitted so much as a moment's farewell to his father. Will Kett, with Jocosa up behind, had been bidden to make all speed for Sprowston to tell the sorry news, while Philip, tearfully subdued, had journeyed on to Hunsdon and thence to Hampton Court.

And now a month had gone by and he was none the wiser as to royal intent concerning himself. Rumour gave it — and had come to him by way of Harry 'Know-All', as he and Tom dubbed the King's senior page, who had it from one of the Privy Chamber — that His Grace was in 'right good health and as merry as a widower may be.'

Certain it was that even if the King were not, his gentlemen and heralds, on the night of the Queen's wake, had been most decidedly merry and so continued for several days. Harry Neville, who knew everything, told with giggles how Clarencieux had all but broke his neck by falling down the stairs to land on Garter-King-at-Arms; that another had ravished one of the housemaids; and that every man of them stayed up until all hours, gambling, feasting, drinking, very merrily indeed. And that, though the King sat solitarily apart from these festivities, he was — according to Harry — already 'talking brides' with Cromwell and the French Ambassador.

'Francis,' Harry said, 'must sure split himself a-laughing to hear how England's king trots out girls as they were fillies to see which one goes best.'

Which one *would* go best? The elder boys laid odds together. Would she be another maid-in-waiting, or a Princess of the Blood? What blood? French blood?

Over in Paris, Cromwell's agents were dancing attendance on Mary of Lorraine, the young widow of Louis of Orléans, and daughter of the Duke of Guise, reported as comely but fat. 'All the better,' said Henry, his appetite sharpened — he had fasted too long — 'I'm a big man and I need a big wife to my bed.'

Francis, lips a-quirk, sent a brief polite refusal to his prospective kinsman. *Your Highness — my brother — regrettably this is impossible.*

'Impossible?' roared Henry, when the message was delivered by Marillac, the Emissary of France. 'Why is it impossible?'

'Because, Sire,' came the suave reply, 'the duchess is already betrothed to the King of Scotland.'

Henry took it hardly. Aside from the fret of his enforced celibacy, he had set his heart on a French alliance in the hope of dividing Charles, his daughter's cousin and his hated rival, from Francis, whom Charles was courting with a view to an end of their wrangles and permanent peace. This would never do. Two great Catholic powers, freed from war and united, would be a serious menace to his anti-Papal Supremacy. Marry he must, and this time with an eye to political advantage.

Word had come to him through Hutton, his ambassador in Brussels, of another young widow, the Princess Christine of Denmark, aged sixteen, whose husband, the Duke of Milan, had recently died without issue, and whose mother was sister to Charles V. A sweet revenge to capture her, bleed her uncle, the emperor, of a handsome dowry, and weaken the bonds of friendship with the loathly Francis.

Hutton reported the youthful Christine as of *competent beauty … and when she chanceth to smile there appeareth two pittes* (dimples) *in her cheeks, the which becometh her right excellent well.*

Henry was not proof against those dimples. He sent Holbein to see and portray them, and his secretary Wriothesley to woo her and verbally to paint her royal suitor in colours even more glowing than her own.

A rapidly rising young diplomat and crafty as a fox was Wriothesley. He had been one of those commissioners who had badgered Mary into signing her recantation; but for all his silken words he could not badger Christine. 'As God should help me, if he were no king, I think an you saw him,' purred Wriothesley, his eyes askance on those 'pittes' that deepened to her smile, holding laughter — at whom? at him? — 'you would say that for His Grace's virtue, wisdom, goodliness and gentleness of person, he could not be matched,'

Nor, it seemed, could the Duchess of Milan be 'matched' — with Henry Tudor.

'If I had two heads,' she replied saucily, 'one would be, I promise you, at His Grace's service.'

'God's Body!' uttered Henry, when with certain reservations Wriothesley brought his 'gentle' master word of this rebuff, 'a chip of Charles's block who speaks as she is tutored. The emperor knits one delay to the tail of another — and by Jesu, that baggage, she carries a sting in *her* tail that were she mine I'd twist it for her!' Then he let out a laugh to shake his chins, seized the Holbein miniature, gazed on it, his little eyes twinkling, and clapped a hand red as a ham on his secretary's shoulder. 'Enough of this heretical dominance!' he cried. 'Find me a Protestant bride.'

Cromwell was consulted, and Cromwell had in mind a substitute to answer all requirements: the sister of a Flanders princeling who was making an infernal nuisance of himself in his attempt to annexe the border territories of his small state of Cleves.

Meanwhile Henry, chagrined at his failure with royal princesses abroad, sought to salve his wounded pride in a series of bloodbaths at home. To be rid of all obstacles to his supremacy, he raised from the ashes of the Old Order a phoenix-like army of New Men standing solidly behind him to track down and destroy, by the axe or at the stake, all who denied his reformed faith and himself as the head of it.

Suspicious of his daughter Mary's submission to his will, she was again disfavoured, her household disbanded; and Philip, who had hoped to be Her Highness's page, was still kicking his heels in the corridors at Hampton Court.

His childish treble now rang the changes from a squeaking alto to a harsh, distressing croak. Though never likely to be tall he had broadened; he had outgrown his clothes and his awe of the King's pages. He had come to fisticuffs with Harry 'Know-All', who had called the Lady Mary 'that bandy-legged bitch', for which Philip had broken Master Know-All's handsome nose. He had kissed, under the mistletoe at Christmastide, Mistress Elizabeth Fitzgerald, more familiarly known as 'Geraldine'. A newcomer to Court, wooed — and later immortalised in verse — by the ill-fated Earl of Surrey, the 'Fair Geraldine' had returned his kiss with interest, to embarrass his dreams. On the strength of which, having received from his father an increase of his allowance, he bought himself three suits, one purple, gold-embroidered, one red velvet, embossed, and a third in yellow satin for high days and holy days. He also invested in three pairs of Spanish leather gloves, and spent much of his time regarding his reflection in the silver salver with which he served the King on bended knee; for although not officially appointed King's Page, he and Tom Wroth, son of a Groom of the Chamber, were called on to attend the King and his guests at state banquets.

From Sir Francis Bryan he earned approval for his Latin verse and a birching for his inability to cross the *Pons Asinorum,* when he was set to write five hundred lines served to him as penance. Under cover of these, when kept at his task while his fellows played 'Up Pig and Follow Me' in Hampton Court's maze, Philip wrote his first and, probably, his last poem to the 'Fair Geraldine':

Far, far beyond the rest, so much Belov'd
Is Beautie rare whereto my Hart is pledg'd,
And were't true as 'tis oft alleg'd,
Must brake in Twaine and burne within my Brest
To knowe thou'rt in promisse trothe'd to Surrey
Woe, woe that I, poore fool, am faine
To comfort me in dreameful Blisse
So I may live and dye againe upon … a Kisse!

Yet, despite this lyrical eruption, symptomatic of dawning adolescence as the pimples on his chin, time hung heavily upon him. He longed for a sight of his home, of the dogs and, in minor degree, of his father. But when he approached Sir Francis with a request for leave of absence on the plea that his grand-aunt, Dame Matilda Graby, who lay sick unto death — a monstrous fabrication — had expressed a desire to see him, he was curtly told that no exeat, by command of the King, could for this present be granted. He must await his further orders.

During this interim, and while awaiting further orders, he was accorded, and never in his life forgot, a glimpse of King Henry's might.

On a cold, blustering day toward the end of the year, Philip, attended by his servant John, went to London by water from Westminster Palace Stairs to buy those Spanish gloves. He spent the better part of an hour in the 'Habberdasher's' in the Chepe, as noted in his list of expenditure for that and every month, of which, doubtless prompted by Dame Matilda, his father demanded an accurate account.

The entry for December, and in especial the last item, may have caused the good dame some disquiet.

Toe my Taylore Tipcotte for doublet and trunkes: III Angels

Toe my Habberdasher at the Syne of the Catte and Parrotte for lethere gloves, Purpell, Bloue (blue?) *and crimsone: II Crownes*

Toe Pastrie Cooke in East Chepe for Marchpane and sugared Almondes: 10d

Ale for my man John Locke: 9d

Toe Mistress Fitzgerald's woman for red roses: 6d

As they emerged from the shop, Philip, turning to the right, was stayed by his servant who, pointing to the left, said firmly, 'This is your road, sir, to the quayside.'

''Tis early. I'll not go back yet,' replied Philip, luxuriously sniffing his perfumed 'bloue' gloves. These he had chosen to wear while John carried the other two pairs, along with a 'gyrdle', not entered in that month's account and reserved for a later date to be mendaciously listed in January under the heading *New Yeare's Gifte to the Master of the Henchmen.*

And much pleased with himself and his purchases Philip went swaggering along the narrow cobbled way from Bishop's Gate to the heart of the city.

The streets, even for that busiest time of the morning, were more than usually crowded. There were lean men, stout men, clerkly men and all sorts; purposeful merchants shoving aside any who hindered them to or from their business; a showman from Moor Fields with his troupe of tumbling dwarfs; a scraggy priest, limping in worn sandals, fingering his beads; a blind man, a beggar-man, tattered and high-stinking, who clawed at Philip's arm, thrusting his disease-scabbed face at him with whines of, 'Pity, gallant gentleman! Pity, sir, for Christ, His Sake — no food has passed my lips this seven days so may I die if 'tis not truth I speak. Good sir — my lord — I perish!'

'Mass! And so will I,' retorted Philip, dodging a strong effluvium of ale and raw onions, 'if you blow your plaguey breath at me. Get out!'

A scuffling aside and a volley of curses greeted this gentle admonishment, followed by a well-aimed kick, as on he went with John behind, disapproval stiff in every joint.

And now more and more people came pouring from houses, from alleys and shops, all hurrying in one direction — 'Where?' Philip asked the dour John.

'Nowhere for you, sir, to go,' he was told. 'Best return to the palace while you may.'

Which only piqued him further to enquire of a man with a cast in his eye and the blood-spattered smock of a butcher, 'What *is* all this to-do?'

'A raree-show at Smithfield,' came the answer with a chuckle and a leer, the squint-eye fixed on heaven and the other on Philip's blue gloves.

Imbued with curiosity and an indefinable excitement that seemed to possess all that scurrying herd, Philip signed to his servant and followed where they went.

He had pushed his way to the forefront of the crowd, and there stood wedged, unable to move so great was the press of bodies fore and aft to crush him, that he feared his bones would crack. He had lost John. He had lost his fine plumed cap, snatched by a cut-purse who had rifled his pouch; but this he did not discover till later.

And now he saw ... and wished himself ten miles from that place where all London had come to watch and gloat on the burning of a man alive.

If only he had heeded John, good John, who knew what he did not until he was here, within sight, almost within touch of the stake piled high with faggots, tarred with pitch and ready for the sacrifice of him whom the King himself had brought up for trial to be judged and condemned as 'a miserable heretical sacramentary'. Thus much, from talk about him, he had learned, with one name on every lip: Lambert, alias Nicholson, a priest turned traitor and schoolmaster who had instilled heresy into the mouths of babes, insisting that the sacramental bread and wine was but the spirit, and not the body and the blood of Jesus Christ. Furtively, Philip crossed himself and called in muted breath on Mother Mary to save him and all believers from the devil and his works.

The huddled crowd was silent now, as if its voice were frozen as the rimed hoar-frosted cobbles at its feet, when the sheriffs and officers came walking in solemn single file to that place of death — 'a raree-show!'

Philip glanced wildly around. Where, O, where was John? No exit; no way out. Here he was and here must he stay, clamped, to suffer torture with the damned who now appeared, borne by two stalwarts on a hurdle.

They loosed the ropes that bound him, raised him up and fastened a chain about his middle. *By this, as a beast to the slaughter,* so in a letter to his father Philip wrote of it, *and shorne of his shirte to his waiste was he tyed to the stake…*

Then, as the faggots were lighted to flare upwards in flames fanned by the nipping wind, a shuddering groan was wrested from those who dumbly watched.

Philip closed his eyes against the smart of smoke that seared his vision, that filled his shrinking nostrils, that turned his stomach sick. But when that awful sound rose up again his eyes could not stay shut, and, his horrified gaze riveted upon the stake, he saw the flames licking gaily at the wretched victim's feet, his legs, his thighs … There was a sudden howl of agony, as suddenly controlled, and a voice, ecstatic, from those blackened lips: 'Ye may kill my body, but only God can kill my soul and cast it into everlasting fire! To God alone do I answer for my sins. To God alone do I commit...'

The rabble roared for him; some howled at him, booing, throwing stones at him; some fell on their knees to pray for him. Philip stood rooted, stuck, mumbling foolishly, 'God ha' mercy, God ha' mercy. Jesus! Save, save, save...'

There was a mighty crackling and a smell in his nose of roast meat. A woman screamed; another laughed. Philip retched and tried to force himself out from that writhing, groaning, bobbing mass of onlookers and, his throat choking, eyeballs starting, he saw, through the belching smoke-wreaths, the shrivelled flesh fall in rags from its charred bones...

''Twas quickly done,' one beside him muttered. 'I've seen 'un burn for three hours or more.'

'Ay! That minds me of a witch's burnin' down by my home in Kent, when I was a lad in the old king's time.' This second speaker was toothless, hairless, scrawny, bowed with age. He launched forth on a tale of the witch's burning: how that the flames would not eat her, she having put her spell on them; of how her black cat had leapt to her shoulders and stood untouched, unharmed in the midst of the furnace, to cry in the voice of a man on the King of Hell to be revenged for this outrage to His Grace, the Devil; and how at the last she had dropped, screeching, into the blaze and was reduced in the wink of her cat's eye to ashes ...

''Twas a fine burnin', that was.' The old man chuckled and nudged an elbow into Philip's ribs. 'But I'd liefer see 'un hanged in chains. 'Tis slower and more hurtsome, to give 'un time for repentance.'

Then, with a coldness on his forehead, a sickness at his heart, and that smell of burnt meat still awfully about him, Philip slithered down and heard no more...

'Why, lad, come to yourself! All's over — well over.' A voice in his ear, an arm supporting him; a face bent above his own, paler than he was wont to know it, anxious, too, but cheerful; a hand firm and warm on his wet forehead. His eyes blinked and cleared to recognition.

'Will! Will Kett!'

Will Kett it was, and looking, Philip thought, a trifle green. He had seen, but could not reach him in the crowd, which had melted away even as the flurry of snow that fell to melt the flames feebly lapping at that black twisted thing still sticking to the stake.

'How come you here — in London?' Philip gasped; he struggled to his feet, ashamed. What an exhibition — like a girl — to swoon. But this stink! He fought against a surge of repetitive nausea, grinned in a sickly manner, and, with well-turned nonchalance, as if the burning to cinders of a man was an everyday occurrence to a gallant of the town, said, 'Walk with me to a tavern, Will —' though never in his life had he been inside of one — 'and we'll drink damnation to this cursed heretic. But first — to find my servant.'

John was found, and, long-sufferingly, trailed the pair of them to stand guard at the Sign of the Boar's Head in East Chepe, where his young master, arm-in-arm with Will, went in; nor, for some time, did he come out.

An overflow from the Smithfield crowd filled the inn parlour to capacity. Three seedy individuals in rusty black velvet and red hose plucked and scraped at their lute and viols while the company, with bawdy song and laughter, joined in the chorus.

Will found two vacant seats at a table near the fire that blazed merrily on the wide brick hearth, and, in lordly fashion, called for wine. White-aproned drawers ran hither and thither with flagons and tankards of ale, crying, 'Anon, sir, anon!' to Will's order.

The oak-panelled walls, the low-beamed ceiling, bore dark evidence of a century's smoke. The trestle table in the centre of the room was occupied by a company of merchants, 'prentices, women, highly dressed and highly coloured, at whom Philip gazed in admiring wonder. One of them blew him a kiss. He spread his chest and daringly returned it. Will laughed loud, clapped a hand on Philip's knee and told him: 'Faith! A prime doxy, but —' complacently he stroked the sprouting hairs on his upper lip, greatly envied by Philip as was also the russet down on Will's chin — 'she'd cost too dear, I'll warrant, for my pouch.'

Philip, on whom unaccustomed wine served, not only to dim the memory of horror just witnessed, but pleasantly to souse the smell of it still clinging to his nose, drained his bumper and beckoned a drawer with the air of a man well-used to drink — and women. 'Another flagon here. Fill the cups. God's Body!' at the top of his lungs he swore the King's oath, inviting more looks from the ladies, and more kisses from fingertips, doubly returned. ''Twas as good a burning,' quoth Philip for the benefit of her who smiled on him with a raising of her cup to her lips pursed above it, ''twas as good a burning as ever I did see. Ho, sirrah, did you hear me? Fill up!'

Over their second bottle Philip learned that Will was lodging with his uncle, William Kett, at the Sign of the Dolphin, being here on business. He had finished his 'prenticeship, 'and am now —' he, too, threw this out at the ladies — 'my father's right hand, journeying back and forth from Norwich to the

Pool of London to superintend the import of consignments from Muscovy. There's a mort o' commerce between the Muscovites and us,' he said, grandly. To which Philip's careless nod implied that he, as a courtier, had naught to do with trading merchants, even one so wealthy as the father of Will Kett.

'I am ing — ignorant,' said he, guarding a hiccup, 'of such means to the making of money.'

'Yet,' Will retorted, 'money-making, or the lack of it, is at the root of all evil,' his voice dropped, 'as the King's Grace knows full well. Hence the dissolution of the holy houses to fill the royal coffers.'

But this remark, if heard by the wine-mazed Philip, passed him by uncomprehended; and only when Will, tipping the dregs of the leathern flask into his cup, was off upon another tack — 'That wench, she grows apace —' did he bestir himself from a descending coma, to enquire, 'Who' she?' And staring cock-eyed at Will, whose face had oddly seemed to swell and divide itself, he asked again, 'Who — wha' wench?'

'Why, marry! Jocosa. I tell you,' Will confided with winks, 'she could put to shame the madames here — and heads above 'em. She's a beauty, believe me.'

'Beauty?' echoed Philip, almost sobered by the shock of this. 'Wha' — *she*? Uglyssin. Eyes li' two — pish — pitch-balls,' he pronounced with care, 'stuckinalumpadough. Whaff I've suffer',' he too was confidential, 'from tha' wenchessinsolence none'll ever … An' her nails! Madsapuss.'

'So be it.' Will glanced frowningly about him, mindful of those two dead flagons. 'She's gone, or is going, from Sprowston. Hi! Drawer!'

'Going?' echoed Philip, roused from astonished contemplation of the whizzing walls and upheaval of the room. 'Gone? Thass' good. Iss',' he asked, suspicious of his hearing which might well be as false as his sight, 'iss' true?'

'Am I a liar? A trivial passage of — shall we say arms — or call it a misunderstanding between Mistress Jocosa and — hey, drawer! Another flask.'

'Nofformee,' said Philip.

'A passage of arms,' Will emphatically repeated, himself a trifle fuddled, 'that led to high words, and so — here, drawer, you whoreson deaf-mute — did you not hear me call? 'Nother flagon.'

Philip unsteadily stood. 'I muss b'gone. I'm jewback a pal'ce.'

'A murrain on your going! Today's a holiday. We've seen king's justice done and must give it celebration. So why go?'

But Philip was hunting for his purse, his fingers all thumbs at his sword-belt that carried nothing more of use than a jewel-hilted dagger, and — an empty pouch.

''S'Blood!' he cried. 'I'm rob'! Lossmemon…'

Will, flushed with wine, grinned wide and drawled, 'A timely loss.'

For a second Philip's hand sprang to his dagger-hilt, and fell to his side, as, scarlet to the ears, he pulled himself together to retort: 'An you'll loan me the price o' these two bol — bol'tles I'll sen' my serv'n straigh' 'ith it to you.'

Will got upon his feet. 'No talk of price shall be between us, lad. I'll pay the reckoning, and gladly, for the honour,' mock-gallantly he bowed, 'of wining with a royal page. Hi, you! Drawer!' He flung a silver coin on the table. 'Well, Phil, an you *will* go…' His eyes strayed to a lady, plump and blonde, seated on a settle by the fire. Shielding her face from the heat of it, her hand touched her pouting lips and, as she tipped her rosy tongue at him, Will said, 'So shall I stay.'

'Fine doings!' muttered John Locke when Philip came staggering out; and since his young gentleman could not walk he carried him down to the barge.

THREE

Christmastide at Sprowston brought Jocosa little cheer, and in sore disgrace with Dame Matilda.

True, there had been some merry-making, mumming, singing, dancing among the household staff, and a masque which Jocosa was forbidden to attend and could only watch, on sufferance, from the minstrel's gallery in the great hall, that on Christmas Day had been given over to the servants, hinds, and any of Squire Pugh's tenants who wished to partake of the fun. And certain it is that had she not offered the squire a broad reminder of the time of year, she likely would not have received so much as the rose noble, strategically extracted on request that she might be allowed to ride over to Norwich to buy presents for him and Dame Matilda.

'Presents? Why — what presents? And why,' hazily demanded Geoffrey Pugh, 'would you buy a present for me?'

'Sir, for Christmas.' Jocosa raised her eyes; the uplift of her lashes touched her eyebrows, shaped like the wings of a bird in flight. 'Not that I have more to spend,' dolefully she apostrophised the rafters, 'than'll sit on a farthing.'

At which the gentle Geoffrey, greatly touched, had tendered her a gold piece saying, 'Go, child, buy some frip — some frippery that you may fancy for yourself, which will be gift enough for me.' Whereupon she had rioted in 'frippery': a pair of green hosen, a silver bodkin for her hair, a silk handkerchief, a pound of sugared almonds, and for Benedict a red ribbon to tie up his beard, which he objected to and subsequently ate. To old Andrew she gave a pewter cup, and to Dame Matilda she gave nothing, receiving in return, on Christmas Day, a jar of pickled walnuts and a lecture, for 'Better far,' quoth the dame, 'that you should give alms to the poor than squander money on your personal adornment, and ribbands — heaven help us — for a goat!'

Thereafter, and until an event of more moment offered her further food for reflection, Jocosa had naught to occupy her mind other than to brood upon her wrongs and to envy the lot of the goose-girl who, the gayest of gay at the masque, had been chased and caught and tumbled in the rushes by half a dozen oafs. And there, with her kirtle drawn up to her chin, indecently she lay, kicking her legs in the air and laughing loud to kill herself.

Seated in the winter parlour at her tambour frame, Jocosa's thoughts harked back to that occasion, and how she had stood alone and isolated in the gallery while the junketing below ran faster and more furious, and the masquers, in fearsome heads of beasts and demons, had snatched each a girl, every one of them gaily bedizened, as Jocosa, in her drab-coloured patched and mended gown was not; and how the men had pranced with them around the towering Christmas cake bedecked with a mighty holly branch and ablaze in its blue flame of Malmsey. And then, what a clapping of hands and a digging in the cake to search for embedded coins and trinkets, another triumph for the goose-girl, who had been the lucky finder of a silver penny and was hoisted shoulder high to chalk crosses on the screens to ward off evil sprites and devil's imps who might have lurked, disguised, amid the mummers. But none of this was for Jocosa — no, not even on Twelfth Night, when all the boys and girls had gone a-wassailing to sing outside the Great House and their neighbours' houses too, for cakes and ale.

Why, then, should she have been denied her share in Yuletide jollity?

Alas, she knew too well the answer. She was undergoing penance for having overstepped the bounds of modesty, and 'in such wanton wise', thus Dame Matilda's verdict, 'as to bring dishonour to her dead father's name'. And all this, Jocosa sullenly reflected as she plied her needle, in cause of that snite, Will Kett, who had made himself too free with her.

Will Kett...

Bent over her embroidery, her cheeks burning to a memory evoked and best forgotten, Jocosa reluctantly relived that day, last November, when Will had come upon her in the solar, unannounced.

She was seated then, as now, at her tambour frame — and how she abhorred this everlasting broidery fit only for spinsters and such like aged hags as Dame Matilda, Will, home from foreign parts, had been a frequent visitor at Sprowston, but always with his father, never yet alone. On such occasions Jocosa, guarded by the dame, would sometimes be permitted to dine with the gentlemen, but not until that morning in November had she exchanged words more than greetings with Will Kett.

He had grown beyond all knowledge, tall, broad, inclined to be plump, with a look in his eyes as they slyly raked her, to set her in a tingle from her ear-tips to her toes. She therefore was not disagreeably surprised when Will had come to Sprowston unattended by his father, and stood in the doorway, his cap in his hand, his hand on his heart, and in his eyes that same tingling look.

'I had to find you,' he confessed, 'and gained admission along with a barrel of smelts for the squire.'

Smelts! Jocosa bit her thumb, biting back her laughter. There was that about Will which always called for laughter, turning most commonplace words to a jest.

'Where,' asked Will, advancing nearer, 'is your Dame Dragoness?'

'My —? Oh!' Her laughter bubbled over. Was there ever such a droll as this Will Kett? But she sobered in an instant to tell him, 'In the still-room, pickling green walnuts. Shall I tell her you are here?'

'No, marry! I'm not here for her. I'm here,' said Will, 'for you.'

And how it happened she could not well remember, but between a second and a second she was on the settle with Will's arms about her, his hands astray over her breasts and under her kirtle in adventurous caressing exploration, until — 'I think,' he whispered, breathing hard, 'that I have lost my way!'

Her heart was racing, her head swimming, she was drowning, dissolved in a whirlpool of strangest delights. She sighed, and she slackened, lying limp within his arms, her face hidden, her rumpled hair divided in a dark cloud upon her nape. She heard him softly laugh and say: 'By God! If I could have and teach you more than just a taste of — this!'

'No!'

But that cry, wrenched from her, fear-sharpened, the instinctive revolt of innocence against forces too prematurely roused, had served only to inflame him past restraint. Heedless of her struggles — and she fought him tooth and claw — he seized and held her captive, his kisses hot and roving on bared neck, on mouth tight-closed against his seeking lips. And then…

'For pity's sake! What have we here? A bawdy-house?'

63

The strident voice of Dame Matilda had brought Jocosa to her feet and Will Kett to his senses.

'Madame.' Straightening his ruffled hair and wholly unabashed, he bowed low to Dame Matilda, while Jocosa, hate seething for him who had put her to shame, adjusted the slipped shoulder of her gown. 'Madame, you are come,' said Will, glib, 'at a most opportune moment. I was about to call on your assistance to revive Mistress Jocosa from a swoon. She appears to be, however, now restored —' turning swiftly he put his arm about her — 'but not yet in a fit state to stand. Sit you down again, mistress. Be easy.' And with a glance at the shocked nun, he winningly suggested, 'Pray, Madame, have you at hand a goose-quill to burn under her nose? There is no better restoration from a swoon than the smell of burnt goose-feathers, or, failing that, of hartshorn.'

At which the dame, whose face expressed nothing but incredulous disgust for this impromptu, only partly heard since it had travelled to her distantly through her deaf ear, pointed a finger at the door, saying, 'Out! Out of this room, sirrah — out of this house, before I set the men to hie you from it. Go!'

'But, Madame,' protested Will, 'I cannot leave the house until I am assured that all's well with this sick maid.'

'If she be,' Dame Matilda had said grimly, 'still a maid...'

Her mouth awry as if the taste of it were sour, Jocosa watched a log fall from the flaming pile to the bucks and lie smouldering in burnished ash amid its curl of smoke. And then she giggled, recalling how she had gone after Will into the courtyard, and before he could mount his horse had run behind to kick him in the rump, shouting, 'That's for you, Master Willy-Nilly Kett for bringing me to trouble with the dame. And if you've naught better of sweethearting to teach a girl than to buss and fumble at her like a swineherd with his mopsy on a haystack then — ooh — *aah*!' Frightfully grimacing, she had retched at him, 'That's all the thanks you'll get from me — and *this*!' And with a parting kick she darted back into the house.

Meanwhile Dame Matilda, greatly harassed, took her grievances to Squire Pugh. Wrested from his transcript of Euripides he heard, in a daze, the good lady's complaint.

'The girl is abandoned. A Bullen to her bones. Had I not come upon them in the nick of time she would have surely been deflowered. That young Kett is a danger and a pest — hot as an unserved stallion. And if she's not already raped, then, mark me well, Nephew Pugh, she will be.'

Nephew Pugh, wedging a finger in the open page, closed the book upon it, and, his quill at his lip, an ink-splash on his beard, wonderingly echoed: 'Raped? Jocosa? Not in — not in *my* house, Dame. No, no!'

'Yes, yes!' the dame insisted, 'unless you drive her from it. Let the Howards have her till this ill-breeze blows by. Is not the Dowager Duchess, Agnes Tylney as she was, kinswoman to Lady Sowerby who was Bullen on the one side with the saving grace of Tylney on the other? The responsibility of that riggish young leman about her is too much for me. Don't forget, nephew, I'm seventy. I did not think at my age to be harried with a strumpet on my hands.' She folded them; her faded eyes, set in a network of wrinkles, gazed through the mullioned window at the westering sun that sank, red as a holly berry, behind a dump of firs.

'At one time,' mused Dame Matilda, 'there were certain unsavoury incidents at Carrow among a few — a very few, God forgive them — of the younger nuns who stayed not immune to nature's call' A flush, that might have been the reflection from the glowing sky, tinged her shrivelled face. 'So that,' said Dame Matilda, straightening her back to ease a stab of pain between her shoulder blades — she suffered sadly from rheumatics — 'so that, then, is settled, is it not? We will send Jocosa to the duchess where, *Deo volente,* she shall remain until such time as Will Kett may be off again to Flanders.'

Yet, despite Dame Matilda's attempt to pluck this troublesome brand from its burning, Jocosa was still at Sprowston when, early in March, Philip obtained his long-desired leave. An outbreak of smallpox at Lambeth, where dwelled her kinswoman Agnes, the duke's second wife, had caused an indefinite postponement of Jocosa's visit.

Philip, whose journey was held up owing to a heavy snowfall, and had been compelled to lie two nights at Newmarket, arrived at Sprowston with fingers so numb he could scarce hold the reins. This time he was expected, his father eagerly awaiting him in the great hall with a feast prepared and neighbours invited to share it: Robert Kett, Serjeant Flowerdew, Sir Roger Wodehouse and Mr. Aldrich were there to welcome the son of the house. 'Grown to man's estate,' declared Sir Roger, who, Philip was relieved to note, stood now an inch shorter than he.

His father eyed him fondly. 'Not — not yet to man's estate. On the — on the border — shall we have it? — of his manhood.' Which was gratifying; and the more so for the attention of the squire's guests who, when full justice was done to the dinner, drew their stools in a circle round the fire to partake of nuts and wine, and hear Philip's account, colourfully rendered, of the King's most recent and fourth marriage to the Lady Anne of Cleves.

As Page of Honour Philip had followed the cavalcade headed by Sir Anthony Browne, Master of the Horse, that escorted the Lady Anne from Greenwich to Black Heath where a tent, wrought in cloth of gold, had been erected for the new Queen's reception.

'But,' Philip's voice held a giggle, 'talk is a-buzz in the Court that the King's first sight of the lady pictured by Master Holbein as a goddess, heaven-sent, struck His Highness dumb, not in admiration, for 'tis said —' this with an eye to Sir Roger who sat, hands on knees and lips parted in readiness to gulp every mouthful of this tasty gossip — ''tis said that the King was in such sorry case to see a lady so much unlike her portrait, she being sadly pitted with the smallpox and of dark complexion — yet wearing — as I live! — a yellow wig — that His Grace returned to Greenwich to vent his wrath on my Lord Privy Seal for bringing him to wed, as His Grace would have it, with a Flanders mare.'

At which all the company, save the dreaming host who had heard no word of it, and Serjeant Flowerdew, who had, and tut-tuttingly expressed his disapproval, were moved to uproarious laughter. 'And sirs, moreover,' well-pleased with this reception, Philip expanded, 'the King called a council to discover if 'twere possible to find just cause to release His Grace from his intended marriage.'

'The King will find *un*just cause enough,' broke in Kett, sprawling on his stool, legs outstretched to the fire, his hands stuck in his daggerless belt, 'to release himself — with the swing of an axe.'

An uncomfortable silence followed this remark. Tom Aldrich hastily buried his nose in his ale cup. Serjeant Flowerdew cast up his eyes and pulled down his lips; Sir Roger nervously wet his; and Philip, fearing he had said too much, curbed his tongue to quick denial. 'No, indeed, Master Kett. I have heard how the King is not ill-disposed to the Queen more than to her looks, but Cromwell they say is a marked man.'

'If that be so,' cried Kett, pounding a fist in his palm, 'then by God's Wounds, we have reason to bless this latest of Queen Consorts. Long may she last!'

'Amen to that,' chirruped Sir Roger. 'And so, sirs,' he raised his cup, 'here's a health unto the King, his Queen and to their issue of the future.'

The toast was drunk, the cups refilled, and Kett, frowning into his, remarked: 'There may likely be no issue of the future. For the present a sickly babe is all that stands between the throne and the Princess Mary, and she —'

'Woe Betide,' interrupted Serjeant Flowerdew, a sudden suffusion of red unbecomingly mottling his dewlaps, 'if the *Lady* Mary,' he markedly stressed the correction of title, 'should step into her Brother's Place, and — may God forbid — our Most Noble Prince of Wales should not survive his Father. Such a Misfortune would be Disastrous both to Church and State.'

'How so?' Kett's look, charged with belligerency, pinioned the pontifical lawyer. 'I do not hold with inconsistencies that make of Church and State a house divided. If that the Princess Mary should, in God's good time, become Queen Regnant, the spiritual welfare of our country and our being might then be joined again in unity, and not in controversial dispute between the old and the new faith.'

The company exchanged furtive looks. Serjeant Flowerdew, although more deeply flushed, replied with suave temperance, 'Sir, you walk not with but Behind the Times. Life — and by life I would include its Spiritual Aspect — must progress. These few years, since Wolsey's fall, have witnessed the Greatest Upheaval toward Enlightenment and the one and only True Understanding of our Saviour's Word, Who died that We might live.'

'That we might live,' repeated Kett; his eyes beneath his heavy brows held each a danger spark, 'and love, as our Lord Christ did teach us, our neighbour as ourselves. This being so, Sir Serjeant, let us now come down from heaven unto earth that I may ask why should your lands, my lands, and those of our good host here, to say nothing of Sir Roger's lands at Kimberley, be enclosed that there be no sharing with our neighbours — the Commons — of their grazing rights? Sirs, should we not, according to the tenets of our faith and for humanity's advancement, restore to the starving husbandman his ancient rights and liberties that we have thieved from him? Is that love? Is it justice? For, sir, if the King's honour, as it is said, stands for the good of his people, high or low, then we, the high ones,' his eyes came mockingly to rest on the combustive Serjeant, 'are the hinderers of the King His Grace's honour.'

'Master Kett,' the Serjeant magisterially stood, and, turning his head this way and that as if he were addressing a jury, 'it is my Bounden Duty,' he pronounced, 'to advise you — Take Heed. That which you have spoken here between these walls and beneath the roof of Squire Pugh, our host...'

Caught unawares in a yawn, the squire deprecatingly acknowledged this attention with a murmured 'Sir, you're welcome.'

As if stone deaf to this remark Serjeant Flowerdew went on, 'That which you have spoken, sir, if where else voiced might bring about some Fatal Consequences, Master Kett,' he added pointedly, 'to You.'

Philip sat in the fidgets; such talk as this, though sparsely understood, held sufficient of sinister meaning to put him in a fright. The memory of that martyrdom at Smithfield still smouldered. But Kett, undismayed by the Serjeant's rebuke, returned him an airy rejoinder.

'Come, Master Serjeant, you should know me well enough to know that what's on my lung must out on my tongue, and that nothing pleasures me more than a good argument.'

'*Argumentum ad judicium,*' murmured Geoffrey Pugh as, with propitiatory smiles, he rose to hand the wine. 'Sir Serjeant, pray seat yourself. The night is young, and this wine is of my — of my choicest. Sirs, to you!' He raised his cup; his guests brightened to respond, and Philip, whose head was somewhat reeling, he having drunk his full share of his father's choicest, made his excuses to the gentlemen and took himself to bed.

He was up early next morning, doused his head in icy water effectively to clear it and, calling the dogs, went down to the river to fish. He had not yet seen Jocosa, and hoped that by sneaking out betimes he might at least delay the inevitable meeting.

The harsh weather of the last few weeks had changed. A tardy sun flooded copse and meadowland with a fiery green flame. Spring whispered in the softly savoured breeze that brought with it the shy scent of primroses, starring mossy banks where violets crouched beneath their darkly shining leaves, but as he stooped to pick a buttonhole, he heard that voice he dreaded, shouting: 'Wait, Phil, wait for me!'

She had followed him, was breathless with her hurry, slight as a reed, and, for all her fifteen years, a child still in form and face. Nor was she clad as befitting her age: her dress of that same shabby brown she had worn when last he saw her, yet now its hem was a good twelve inches higher than her ankles, and she looked to be bursting from her bodice.

'How glad —' she gave a little hop and skip — 'how glad I am to see you.'

'You've grown,' he told her lamely.

'So,' she said, 'have you. I should think we are now of one height. Shall we measure?' And then: 'You've dropped your primroses.' She gathered them up and tucked them in her girdle, saying, ''Tis a sin to pluck flowers and throw 'em away. May I come fishing with you?'

Without waiting for an answer she swung along beside him.

'I'll be whipped for this,' she said, 'when I go back. I'm forbidden to talk or walk with you unless the dame be present to guard me as a felon and brand me as a bawd. She says I'm wanton. She says I'm to be sent away for having turned your father's house into a stew. You don't have to believe her.' Side-glancing, she caught his grin and threw it back to him with giggles. 'So *that's* off my conscience. Do you fish with a fly? Me, I tickle for trout. I took a haul of six last week, before the snows came. They were prime.' She smacked her lips. 'I know a pool where they breed like conies.'

He let her run on, seemingly regardless of his sulks. Her voice, with its slight Norfolk burr, so different from the clear, clipped accents of Court ladies, vexed his ears, yet he could not but admit that were she schooled and tamed and taught fine speech and manners, she could hold her own in comeliness with any maid of honour, excepting only one. And in the memory of that 'only one', who, these three months past, had ousted from his thoughts and heart the once fairest of them all, 'Fair Geraldine', Philip hotly blushed, and fiddled with the drawstring of his knapsack, slung across his shoulders, and was reminded how Jocosa had some kinship with this latest charmer who now held him in thrall.

'Your mother,' he said, with careful nonchalance, 'was she not related to the Howards?'

'Only of distant blood, by marriage, through the Tylneys. The Duchess of Norfolk was a Tylney, but my mother was kin to the Bullens, which is no credit, Dame Matilda says, to me. I'm to visit the duchess at Lambeth so soon as the smallpox there is over. Do you know the duchess? I'm told she's close-fisted, so mean with the food that the servants of her household and the ladies, too, go rooting round for acorns like the pigs. Would that be true?'

'Entirely untrue,' retorted Philip, 'although I'm not acquainted with the duchess, but —' he had to speak of her, for want of better audience, even to this coltish, uncouth wench — 'I am acquainted with Mistress Katherine Howard, who is a granddaughter — or rather,' he corrected, 'step-granddaughter, of the duchess, who was in charge of her until she — Mistress Katherine — came recently to Court, appointed maid-in-waiting to Queen Anne.'

Jocosa eyed him slantwise. 'Is she young or old?'

'Not old.' Philip wished he'd held his tongue. The girl was too inquisitive by far. 'Where is this pool you speak of?'

'How old? About my age? Is she fair? Is she pretty? Is she fat?'

'Certainly not fat,' was the terse reply. 'Thin, and fair — I think. I have not much observed her.'

'You look hot,' remarked Jocosa. 'Do I walk too fast for you?'

'You walk too slow.' He strode ahead. The dogs galloped on before him, and Jocosa, running to keep pace, caught at his arm to tell him, 'This way to the pool.'

He slackened speed, and hastily turning the talk to a less delicate subject, 'Where,' he asked, 'is your familiar?'

'My —?'

'Your bearded friend.'

'Oh, Benedict. Poor Benedict,' sighingly she said, 'he's old now and fat, if your girl,' she flung at him, 'is not. The dame has had him tethered in the orchard to eat the springing nettles, as she *says* — but 'tis done to spite me so's I don't have him in my chamber. Look! Here's the pool where you'll find a goodly haul. But I'll tickle 'em and lay I'll catch the most.'

'You won't,' said Philip, sharp, 'you'll stay still and keep mum — or go home.'

And mum she kept, obligingly, to watch him while he tied his fly and cast his line. The sun dappled the water, glinting through low-hanging boughs where yellow catkins drooped amid a beading of yellow buds. Very still she stood, until tiring, she sat, and clasped her knees while patiently he cast his line and cast his line again; and presently his patience was rewarded with a widening of ripples as a monster of a trout rose to the bait, and then — Jocosa sneezed.

He lost his prize and rounded on her in a fury. 'Why! You — ' His lips closed on the rageful epithet poised to hurl at her. 'You've frighted him. You'd best be gone. He'll not come up again, thanks to you!'

Sullen-mouthed, eyes clouded, she retorted, 'Well — I — could I *know* that I would sneeze? You're a fine fisherman not to pull him in when he's ready, jaws gaping, for his bite. A poor excuse to blame me for the loss of him. But since you turn so snarlish I'll be gone and gladly, Master Cross-Crab!' And with a poke of her tongue she flounced away.

Philip changed his fly. The pool was rich, as she had said, with fish in plenty lying in the shallows. Tall rushes, higher than a man, hid the far bank of the stream ringed round with reeds, but never a trout came up from his bed to snap at the fly, floated temptingly over his disdainful nose.

An hour passed in minutes slow and crawling, and at last a big stout fish, a very patriarch of fishes, cosily ensconced on his couch of weeds, bestirred himself to regard with some faint show of interest the gold-and-red-winged lure lying within three inches of his head. There ensued a short, exciting tussle, when, just as his speckled-bellied catch rose to take his feed, came a second catastrophic interruption. A cry, fear-fraught, screamed out from a near copse of larches: 'Help! Murder! Help, Phil, help! Come quick!'

Jocosa, at her tricks again to plague him for sending her away. 'By Cock,' he muttered, drawing in his empty line, 'I'll wring her neck for this, the jade!' To drag him from his sport, to sport with her! But when the dogs, noses pointing and a-quiver, darted off in the direction of those cries, Philip, softly cursing, flung down his rod and went after them.

Through undergrowth of bush and thorn the wolfhounds forged their way, and Philip, running now, and fearful of he knew not what mishap had overtaken her, was soon on the scene of the disturbance: Jocosa, struggling in the arms of one whom at that distance he could not recognise, but that she fought him frantically he saw. He saw, too, as he neared them — and, seeing, ran the faster — that her captor was none other than Will Kett. And Will had got her on her knees, with his full weight topping her to bear her down.

His heart like a drum at his ribs, Philip rushed madly on, calling to the bounding dogs — 'Go for him, Doran! Douce!' — who at his word were growling and snapping at Will's calves.

A fierce scuffle ensued, young Kett kicking out at his wolfish assailants, while Jocosa, dishevelled, her gown torn from her shoulders, wriggled free, standing back to cry in terror: 'Stop, Phil! Stop them or they'll kill him.'

'Go!' Philip bade her, 'go, I tell you — *go.*'

She went as if chased by the devil; and the dogs, at a signal from Philip, left their attack to go with her, on guard.

'Now you, Will Kett.' Philip squared himself. 'You shall account to me for this.'

'To you?' From wincing examination of his torn hose and bitten legs, Will looked up. 'By Holy Rood! When I lay hands on those brute curs of yours I'll slit their guts! And who are you,' he threateningly advanced, 'that calls me to account for a passing jest?'

'Kett,' said Philip, quiet, 'if what you did or would have done to her were passing jest, then take this to *you* as passing jest — from me!'

With which, though half a head the shorter and half a stone the lighter, Philip hurled himself at Will to land him a buffet on the jaw with all his strength behind it. For a second, taken by surprise at the suddenness of that onslaught, Will staggered, but in a trice had recovered his balance to return blow for blow straight from the shoulder.

It was a fierce if clumsy scrimmage fought in the dappled shadows of the copse where the sun's rays, dagger-bright, thrust through the budding trees, while mating birds, startled from their love songs, fell to silence, till those two, blown and battered — and with Philip much the worse for it — gave way.

Will Kett, the tacit victor, stood over him who sank to his knees holding himself below the belt.

'That'll teach you, my young bantam,' jeered Will, 'to meddle in what's no concern of yours.'

'Of mine it is!' Philip was up again and on his feet, having got his second wind. 'You've trespassed on my father's land to assault my father's ward, and if that be no concern of mine —' his words gurgled in his throat, choked by a gory flow that dribbled from his nose, and inwardly again he cursed the girl, Jocosa.

Will was one broad grin. 'Since when did you turn knight-errant? The maid was randy ripe and had you not come between us I'd ha' proved her — and I'll wager I would not ha' been the first.'

'You whoremongering scab!' In a blind rage of fury kindled from God alone knew what depths of passions primeval, as yet unexplored, Philip was up and at Will's throat; and how the battle might have ended, none could tell; for just at its peak, with their two bodies locked, legs entwined, in bitter contest, Philip was collared — not by Will.

'Master Philip — sir, for shame!' His servant John, his footsteps muffled on the yielding moss, had come upon them unobserved. 'Is this how you would settle a dispute — to fight at clapperclaws like any common town trash? Swordplay is the only play for gentlemen, though you fight not,' John said sourly, 'with one of your own kind. As for you, Master Kett,' his voice took rising impetus, 'I am come to bid you go from here nor show your face on this — the squire's land — again. The young gentlewoman, she —'

'Cock's Bones!' cut in Will, savagely, 'and would you heed *her* blab that holds as much sense or truth in it as in this pussy-willow?' which he snatched from where it dangled above his tousled head; and, slightingly, slung at Philip's spreading nose. And then he laughed, for all one eye was black, the other closing, and held out his hand. 'So, Philip, *pax vobiscum,* peace to you and let peace be with us.'

'No.' Philip put his hand behind his back. 'We've still a score to settle, and there'll be no peace with us until it's paid.'

Will Kett lost his smile. 'As you say and — as you wish.' Jauntily he turned, and, limping just a little from the bites upon his leg, he strolled away.

The upshot of that encounter, which was in every mouth, not only in or around Sprowston but beyond, to Wymondham, hastened Jocosa's departure. 'For,' quoth Dame Matilda, to whom this last shock had been one too many, 'while the girl is stalked on all occasions by that knavish whelp, she had best be placed where she'll not meet with interference.'

And thus it came about that two days later, in the early hours of the morning, one of the duchess's household from Horsham in Norfolk arrived to carry off Jocosa, who, it had been arranged, would be held there in safe custody until removed to Lambeth.

Philip, much disfigured, his nose half astride his face, was dragged from his sleep to see her go.

She stood beneath his window. Her shouts, having failed to waken him, were followed by a hail of pebbles on the pane. He rose from his bed, opened the casement and saw her there below it, cloaked and habited for riding. 'Come down. Won't you bid me Godspeed?' she demanded. 'Here's a churlish host you are!'

Unwillingly he clothed himself, scrubbed his face, and went to her who waited in the forecourt by the mounting block. The Duchess's man had brought with him a nag for her, while another servant was to follow with the baggage. 'Which,' Jocosa lamented, 'is little enough. I'm shamed to go visiting in reach-me-down rags.' She gave a flick with her riding crop to the rusty velvet of her kirtle, over which she wore a doublet, fashioned by Dame Matilda to fit her from one of Squire Pugh's — 'That you look,' Philip achieved, with a slow painful grin, since his lips were cracked and sore still — 'half girl, half Ganymedes.'

She went bareheaded, but her cloak of murrey cloth, slung across her shoulders, had a hood to it, and this she adjusted, tying its strings to imprison her hair.

'Well, so,' said Philip, foolishly, 'you're leaving us.'

'O, not for long. You'll not be rid of me so easy. The Duchess don't want me any more than do you or the dame or your father. I'll be back here when you come home again. That's a promise, or,' she told him saucily, 'a threat.' And, of a sudden, suspiciously bright-eyed, 'I'm sad that I mustn't take Benedict. None cares for him but me. I've given Andrew my one crown piece that he will see him fed and housed and —' a quiver slurred her voice — 'and treated fairly, though I have my doubts o' that.'

Disdaining Philip's preferred help, she mounted to the saddle; gathered the reins in her left hand, and bent to lay a soothing finger on his nose. 'Borne bravely in my cause,' she whispered to his reddening ear, 'and — hearken, Phil, I didn't tell John all that happened in the copse. I only said you were fighting because of words between Will Kett and you, and nothing more, so if the whole world knows the truth on't they'll not know it from me.'

'Nor from me, neither,' flashed Philip.

She smoothed back her horse's mane that the breeze had ruffled, saying with a spurt of laughter, 'Maybe Will has bragged a bit, not of what he did, but of what he *didn't* do.' Then, 'I wouldn't want to be the cause,' she said, 'of strife between you two. Don't think too hardly of Will Kett. He's as good as you are — and as bad as I am!' And as she leaned over him, her hair escaped its hood to brush his cheek; her lips hovered, teasingly, two inches from his own. He drew back, scarlet.

'Well, well!' Her laughter was a trifle shrill. 'At least we — you and I — are friends. Or are we not?'

To which he gave no answer more than a brief nod; and she, shrugging a shoulder, kicked her heel to her horse's side and trotted off; nor did she once look back.

From behind his swollen nose he watched her go.

FOUR

In the long gallery at Greenwich the Queen's ladies stood in weeping clusters by the windows that overlooked the Thames. They were taking their last sight of it on this day of their return to Cleves, by order of His Majesty the King.

All were dressed after the Queen's own fashion, thus Marillac, the French Ambassador, to his master, Francis, *which is so heavy and tasteless that even were they belles they would be frights!*

It is likely the French king, no less than the Emperor Charles, were vastly entertained by the reports of their envoys concerning Henry's fourth marriage to another Anne, who, talk had it, was a maiden still; and this despite that the day after the nuptials when Cromwell enquired of the King if the Queen had found favour in his sight, he was told savagely: 'No, not in sight nor touch neither; for by her breasts and body I knew her for no virgin — to strake me to the heart!'

And to 'strake' Cromwell also to the heart with fear of what might be the end of it for him, who had brought about Henry's latest fiasco.

Those two royal allies, Francis and Charles, were enchanted. If in such early days of marriage Henry kicked against the fetters that bound him to his whey-faced, yellow-wigged *Frau,* he would doubtless soon be quit of her — and, with any luck, of Cromwell, that cuckoo in the nest of the Old Faith. And good it was to know that Henry's first attempt to stamp his heel on these poisonous Protestant weeds had been to sack the Queen's Lutheran retainers and appoint a household composed of English ladies, the majority of whom were un-reformed.

So, on that April morning, three months after her marriage, Anne — an unlucky name she may have thought it, if she ever thought at all — bade farewell to her tearful 'frights', and, with Teutonic phlegm, accepted the bevy of nobly born matrons and maids assigned in their stead by her spouse.

The gentlemen of her brother's Ducal Court, who had escorted her to England, were in like manner deposed and replaced by equerries and pages of her husband's choice: among them Philip Pugh, Chief Page of Honour.

He had no reason to cavil at his elevation. The Queen, her *ja*s and *na*s and *doch*s and guttural ear-scraping English notwithstanding, was a kindly soul. She had a passion for sugarmeats, and would send Philip to ransack the shops of pastry cooks to buy her comfits, cakes and sugarplums, and, when replete, she would offer the surplus to be shared between her page and Mistress Howard, her most favoured maid-in-waiting.

And so it was that young Katherine and Philip were much in company together, called on to play Cat's Cradle with the Queen, to brush and tend her lap-dogs, or to join in the madrigals sung by the royal minstrels; and although the Queen was seemingly tone deaf, and Philip not much better, Mistress Katherine sang, he fatuously told her, 'sweet as a celestial choir'. She was equally proficient with the virginals and, when again extolled, she admitted she had studied music as a child while in the care of the Dowager Duchess of Norfolk, under one Master Manox; and why, he wondered, should she blush at the mention of that name which was often — too often for his liking — on her lips?

'Master Manox, he taught me this tune'; or 'Master Manox composed this song for me.' And then the Queen would ask for more and more of 'that so *schöne* singing', and would stuff Mistress Howard's mouth with marchpane as reward for it.

Always when the Queen was present at a banquet Philip would be required to attend her, serving silver dishes to Her Grace on bended knee, while the King strove to drown his distaste for his wife in an over-taste of Malmsey. He had grown more bloated, stouter, and more gross of late. His ulcerous leg caused him constant discomfort, was purulent and stank. He dressed outrageously in garish colours better suited to a stripling of fifteen than to the ageing corpulence of fifty. His swollen belly, emitting abdominal growls, swung pendulous and flabby above the jewel-studded girdle that offered it inadequate support. And, whether in self-defence or from self-conceit, he had now assumed the title of Majesty, the first English monarch to be thus addressed.

It is possible that Anne was as little taken with her husband's charms as he with hers. Yet, two tastes they had in common: the one their gluttonous delight in food, the other their delight in Henry's son. To Anne of Cleves, bereft of kin and kind, in a land of hostile strangers, the pale, flaxen-haired boy, England's hope, was her sole comfort; to the King the hub and centre of his life.

Those about him marvelled at his passionate absorption in that puny toddler, brought daily to the Presence by his nurse, Mrs. Jackson, 'Mother Jack', as, from the moment he could lisp a word, he called her. The name stuck.

There, face to face in their throne-like chairs, they would sit, those two; Majesty, immense and padded, glittering with priceless gems, his flat narrow eyes under their infantile brows embedded in folds of flesh; the small hard mouth beneath the gingery moustache, trimmed arc-wise to meet the sparse bristling beard that covered but could not hide the fallen dewlaps; and, absurdly dressed in similar magnificence, brocaded, jewelled, its hair like a cap of spun glass fitted close to its head, that pathetically old and elfin mite would return its father's doting gaze with a long unwinking stare. Never a smile greeted each ponderous clumsy enticement; the clapping of red beefy hands in time to the favourite bawled song of 'Greensleeves'; the dangling and rattling of baubles — a gold chain, a casket containing rings and things — 'all yours when you grow big enough to wear 'em.' Or a gaily spotted wooden horse on wheels, with shining scarlet nostrils. 'See here —' inwardly groaning with the pain of his leg, down on all fours, sweeping aside the scented rushes, went the King, to demonstrate the mettle of this highly varnished steed — 'now, Edward, you! Come, help His Grace.' A sign to Mother Jack. 'You, son, must pull him. Here's the cord. Now pull.'

And, raised from his chair by his nurse, Edward would be dumped on the floor beside his father, the cord placed in his dimpled fist. 'Pull! Pull!' roared Henry. 'See him go. One day you'll ride a-gallop on a horse, not of wood but of flesh. You'll like to go a-riding, Edward, won't you? *Won't* you?'

A judicious nod, a lisped 'Yes,' a sigh, a tired yawn, politely patted by fingers small and boneless.

'And,' his father persisted loud, as if to stifle a creeping doubt that anything so weakly would ever ride at all, 'you'll engage in jousts and lead in tourneys, as did I, when you're a few years older. You'll grow big and strong.to combat with the best of 'em. You will. Yes,' the King reiterated fiercely, 'you will!'

'Yes,' would come the echo with an upward look, half sly, half mischievous and wholly disconcerting.

'And one day,' the King stroked back a silken strand of hair that fell across the child's pale forehead, 'you'll mount higher than a saddle. You'll mount, my son, a throne — our throne — in place of me. Look, Edward,' into those massive arms he would be lifted, and carried to the window, 'see — there.' The King pointed to the sun-dazzled river where the bellying sails of merchantmen spread wide to the breeze like the wings of white eagles. 'There on the tide of this splendid waterway that is the life's blood of our kingdom, flows the wealth of our realm, along the trade routes of the world, across the seas to distant lands where sweet spices grow and the grape of the vine, and the fruits of the olive that give the holy oils with which you, my son, shall be anointed. And every day, in every week, that one of your ships sets sail is for her — and for us — a great adventure!'

A nod, a pursing of baby lips parted to show a gleam of tiny teeth. 'A great — a *bonaventure*,' said the prince; while those about the King, who heard him would lift hands and eyes to heaven, crying: 'Hark unto His Highness! A prophet, nay, a genius, to outwit Erasmus! Such a linguist to speak French at — three years old.'

And the King, rubbing his harsh beard against the shell-like wondering face, asked, 'Who taught you that word, *bonaventure?*'

'The Lady Sister Mary.' Edward's mouth puckered, his head moved; impatiently he wriggled. 'May it please Your Grace to let me — *go!*' His voice, high-pitched and querulous, held tears of rising temper.

'I'll never,' muttered Henry, 'let you go…'

But even the mutual bond of baby worship could not sweeten the King's embittered attitude toward his wife. On the contrary, when he discovered that the Queen besieged the nurseries at all hours of the day to stuff Edward with sweetmeats — 'and give His precious Grace the bile,' Mother Jack indignantly declared — the King forthwith removed him to his manor of Havering-atte-Bower in Essex. There was, however, yet another child to receive from Anne a lavishment of attention and sweets: the seven-year-old Elizabeth. And in her first recorded letter, a remarkable achievement if it were her own, she expresses her *impatient desire* to see her new stepmother and her reluctance to *disobey the commands of the King, my father, which prevents me from leaving my house till he gives me full permission to do so … In the meantime I remain with much submission Your Majesty's very dear Elizabeth.*

The King's 'full', if grudging, 'permission' for the Queen and her 'very dear Elizabeth' to meet, appears to have been granted in the New Year, 1540. Thus we find the prince and the two princesses gathered, all three, under one roof for the first time since Edward's birth.

It must have been an odd and rather touching little trio drawn together for those New Year celebrations. Mary, despite her inherent antagonism to the small red-headed sister born of that other Anne who had warped her girlhood, deprived her of her birthright, and debased her adored mother, was so made that she could not harbour enmity for long against one so young and of her blood, and who now was equally deprived of royal status as herself. And so we have it that she, always generous to folly and the depletion of her none too well-filled purse, gave 'a kirtle to my Lady Elizabeth's Grace', of a startling yellow, and to her small brother a crimson satin coat, pearl-embroidered, with golden clasps and tinselled sleeves to chafe his tender skin and cause a pandemonium of yells, with the Queen, his sister Mary, and Mother Jack around him in a fuss. Elizabeth, meanwhile, disregardful of the racket, paraded the nursery showing off her yellow kirtle to Philip and Mistress Katherine.

No other page nor maid-in-waiting was at this time in attendance; and Philip, having dutifully admired the Lady Elizabeth's new finery, spoke aside to Mistress Howard with a redness in his face.

'I — if you will not take it as impertinent — I have a New Year's gift for you, unworthy, yet I hope — acceptable.'

'A gift? For me?'

What could have been more gratifying than her eager response to this overture; her hand, that the love-sick Philip likened to a lily, outstretched to receive it.

'A necklet — a necklet of gold. O, Philip!' Never before had she called him by his name; it had always been politely, 'Sir' or 'Master Pugh'. 'Is this for me — this lovely thing?'

'A poor token,' he panted, 'of my regard.'

It had cost him a whole quarter's allowance, but he would willingly have forfeited his pocket-money for a year to gain such sweet reward as her rapturous delight in his 'poor token'.

'I thank — I thank you, Philip. Will you clasp it for me?'

From red to puce his colour deepened as she offered him her down-bent nape. 'Such a little slender neck,' he breathed, so low she scarcely could have heard him. Or did she? She swung round. Her eyes, quick-glancing as a squirrel's, lighted for an instant on the Queen's broad back and returned to Philip in delicious intimate conspiracy.

'I have a locket here,' she murmured, 'to hang upon your necklace.' And diving her hand into the bosom of her gown she brought forth a jewelled pendant. For an instant she opened her palm to show the device of a ruby heart shot through with a diamond arrow, and a fleeting impression of the initial H inscribed, also in diamonds. That minstrel fellow

— Manox, Philip remembered — she once, but only once, had spoken of as 'Henry'.

Henry Manox. H!

'I have had no chain on which to wear it, but now,' she said, on a note of elation, 'I *will*.'

Then back again in a hurry that symbol of love, spelling death and damnation to Philip, was replaced in its nest as the Queen turned from the howling Edward to bid her handmaiden: 'Katerina, go! In my chamber you will with my handkerchiefs find a silver — how you say — pomman — pommer —?'

'A pomander, Madame,' sniggered Elizabeth.

'*Ach, ja!* Lisbet, she always puts me *recht* when I am wrong. Go, Katerina, for His Highness bring it.'

His Highness ceased boo-hooing to say, 'Don't want a pomander,' and commandingly, 'Take off my coat. It scrapes me.'

'*Na, na!* Not this beautiful coat, *mein Herz*, the coat the Lady Mary has given? *Doch! So* —' slavishly the Queen unbuttoned him — '*Mutter* will take it off, *ja?*'

Edward, glaring, pushed her hands away. 'You are not my mother.'

'*Du Lieber Gott!*' The Queen's bovine eyes moistened reproachfully. '*Aber,* I love you as my son, *mein Herz!*'

'I am not your *Herz*,' sulkily said Edward. '*Herz* means "heart" in English. So how can *I* be your heart?'

'Darling!' Mary gasped, and to the Queen apologetically, 'Madame, I pray Your Majesty excuse —'

'*Na, na!* It is nothing. Edward, *mein* Edward —' the Queen's thick lips slobbered kisses on him — 'look then here, *mein Sohn,*' as Katherine approached, and, with a curtsy, presented the bauble. 'Give it to me. *So!*' Taking the silver toy the Queen swung it by its chain before the prince's button nose, which he wrinkled disdainfully.

'It smells.'

'*Ach ,ja!*' cried the Queen ecstatically. 'It smells. It smells good, not? And look what is written here, from the wedding ring that your father's Majesty gave me. *God send me well to keep.* See, Edward, here it is writ. And this pretty thing also for you, Edvard, is well, God send to keep. So laugh, *Mein Herz*, and happy be and no more angry with his *Mutter,* not? Laugh, *mein Liebling,* laugh!'

'Laugh'' echoed Elizabeth with scorn. 'All this baby talk is enough to make him cry, not laugh. Such a pack o' fools. Look, Edward, *this*'ll make you laugh.' She ran to him, grimacing, her tongue pointing between a gap in her upper milk teeth where two had vanished. 'I pulled 'em out myself, they were hanging on a thread. I'll pull out yours, too, when they're ready. See? Amn't I a comic without my teeth? Now laugh — to split yourself!'

She tickled him; he crowed and chuckled, pulled her hair, and they were at it together rough and tumble in high glee, until, 'Whooh! she pursed her lips to a whistle. 'This room's like an oven, and that coat of his has put him in a sweat. I'm in a muck sweat, too.' She rubbed her hand across her forehead, twirling round on Philip. 'Page, open a window and let in some air.'

But, as he hastened to her bidding, Mother Jack intervened with shocked protest. 'Sir, I pray you heed not my Lady. An open window! Madame, would you, God forbid, give His precious Grace a rheum?'

Philip hovered, undecided, halfway between the window and the prince. The princess hunched a shoulder.

'Very well then, let him bide — and let him stew. Here, page...' Beckoning Philip, she lifted her chin; a smile dawned, close-lipped, to hide her missing teeth. 'I know your face, but not your name. What is it?'

'Philip Pugh,' he bowed, 'Your Highness.'

'No.' She shook her head; one last ray of the winter's sun probing a leaded pane fell on her hair to make of it a copper-gold glory. 'I'm not a Highness. I'm a Lowness — the King's bastard.'

'Madame!' uttered Philip feebly.

Her smile widened. ''Tis true. And my sister Mary, she's a bastard, too. I thought all the world knew that. I've had it told me over and over and *over* again.' At each repetition of the word her voice rose shrill, and shriller.

The pinched narrow face of the King's eldest daughter — a face too old for her years — turned sharply, a frown between her lowered brows.

'What have you been told?'

'Something —' a spriteish look preceded the reply — 'something that Lady Bryan, my governess, is always saying, always calling me and you. Something that is nothing, after all. Dear Your Grace.' Spreading the folds of the thick yellow damask, she billowed low to the ground. 'I thank you, sister, for your gracious gift. I'd give you one in return, but that I've not two groats to spend, having spent my little all on a new cap for Edward.'

Mary's inscrutable eyes, dark with un-youthful shadows of sorrows repressed and silently endured, softened and lightened. She came close to cup in her hands the child's pointed chin and, gazing down: 'I'll take,' she said, 'the will for the deed — with a kiss to seal it.'

'Kisses,' scoffed Elizabeth, 'are cheap.' But the kiss was given and, fourfold, repaid.

And, in Philip's ear, to turn him dizzy, 'I'll owe you,' whispered Katherine, 'the same.'

In the following May Philip wrote to his father *It is said about the Court that His Majesty's Grace seeketh a divorce from the Queen, and that Cromwell will be brought before the Council for trial on several counts...*

The chief being Henry's own private count to be settled between himself and Cromwell, Cupid's Messenger: he who had rhapsodically reported the King's fourth prospective wife as of 'a beauty universally extolled and who in form and face and feature excelled all other aspirants to the high honour of the King's Consort, even as the golden sun excels the silver moon'. And lo! Buoyed on hope, his appetite whetted by fair words and the fairer portrait of Master Holbein — bribed no doubt, by the dastardly Cromwell to depict 'a very lively image' — the King found himself confronted with 'a Flanders mare'!

To repudiate the marriage at the eleventh hour would have been politically impossible. Henry dared not risk alienation of Anne's brother, Duke of Cleves, and all his princeling satellites in Germany, to lose him an alliance that might prove of inestimable value if Charles and Francis, those two sworn enemies of his, should jointly attempt an invasion of Britain. None of his council, nor Archbishop Cranmer, to whom he appealed after his first horrified glimpse of his betrothed, could suggest any alternative other than to 'Put my head in the yoke and,' Henry said heavily, 'marry her.'

But if his neck were in the yoke, Cromwell's head was on the block, or, as Henry, in his mind's eye, saw it. Such deliberate deception, such insult to injured Majesty could not pass unrevenged.

So, on a May morning, the King's Vice-Regent, Vicar General, Baron Cromwell of Oakham, Earl of Essex, who had sent to their deaths countless tortured victims of his 'Terror', was brought to the council chamber and, in his turn, condemned by his peers, crying: 'Traitor!' and 'Traitor!' again: the whole pack of them licking their chops to hunt down this wolf who had ravaged their folds, devastated their churches and battened — with his Lord and Master and his tool — on the spoils thereof. But his master's little greedy eyes had been opened, at last, to the truth. He had been duped.

Yet there was more behind the destined doom of Cromwell than a repugnant bed-mate forced upon the King under false pretences; more than Henry's accusation, through the mouthpiece of his council, that the Lord Essex had been 'counter-working against the King's Majesty's aims to divide the Church against itself'; a more vital, a warmer, more personal reason than any of these: the Eternal Cause, that blindly, microcosmically, pursues its same indiscriminate purpose with kings and with commoners and butterflies and cats...

So while the Catholic party, headed by Norfolk, snarled at the heels of their trembling quarry, Henry, the King, was rowed in his barge over the river to Lambeth. There, the septuagenarian Dowager Duchess of Norfolk entertained her royal visitor at an intimate gathering exclusive to her household, with feasting and dancing, and a girl in white and silver who wore a white rose in her hair.

'A rose without a thorn,' the King whispered, and was watched from her distance by the beaming duchess; and by one of her young ladies, a newcomer to her charge, of whom none took the smallest account. She had nothing but her youth to recommend her, was hoydenish and awkward, spoke with a country accent, had no manners, little wit. To school her, judged the duchess, for the post she had in mind — and if the Lord God willed it as in His own good time — would be a tedious, troublesome task demanding patience, which the duchess lacked. Yet the girl, though poor as an old shoe, was of Tylney blood, which, being thicker than water, merited promotion before one of other sort. And if her figure were unformed and, as a child's — unshapely, that with the years would improve — her years were young, fourteen, fifteen at the most, her eyelashes stupendous, and her mouth — the Tylney mouth — a tempting asset. The Duchess had experience enough of unripe virgins to appraise them at their face — and body — value.

The smiling glance of the duchess travelled to the far end of the hall where stood the King, his eyes gloatingly upon his prize, who, her back hard-pressed against the arras as if she would sink into it and lose herself, gazed up at him with something of the panic-held look of a rabbit in the coils of a cobra.

The Duchess closed her smile, turned her head and quacked, 'Jocosa!'

That other girl, of no account, who stood in fascinated wonder at this, her first sight of the King, 'come to honour me,' had said the duchess, 'with an informal visit', started at her name to bob a curtsy.

'Madame?'

'Don't,' hissed the duchess, 'stand there gaping like a gowk. Go, bid the minstrels play.'

FIVE

And now it is said, wrote Marillac, the French king's gossip, to his master in a letter dated July 21, *that the King is to marry a Lady of great beauty, a niece of the Duke of Norfolk. I cannot tell how far this is the truth.*

It was truth enough for all of Henry's intimates to know it, and to know that the wedding had been arranged to take place privately at Oatlands. For no sooner was Cromwell flung in the Tower than Henry set in motion those usual preliminaries to rid himself of Anne of Cleves that had so well succeeded with the first Katherine and that other Anne. The marriage was declared null and void, primarily by reason that 'the Lady Anne was pre-contracted to the Prince of Lorraine': this the first that any of those concerned with the King's petition had heard of a previous contract; and secondly, 'that the King, having espoused her against his will, had not given consent to the marriage which also he declared had not been consummated.' A committee of statesmen and clergy, including two archbishops and a dozen or more lesser divines, met to examine the case and pronounce their pre-arranged verdict. Henry, meanwhile, had packed Anne off to Richmond, 'concerned,' so he said, 'for the state of her health, the Plague being rife in and about London'…

'But,' chuckled Marillac, 'if the Plague were rife about London *Henri* would have been the first to flee from it.'

So, to Anne at Richmond, came three of the King's gentlemen to announce that by decree of Church and Parliament her marriage had been dissolved; at which the poor woman, convinced that this — as precedence had led her to believe — was the precursor of her death, promptly fell into a swoon, but at once recovered when assured that the King desired nothing more murderous than a divorce, and that henceforth he would adopt her as his 'sister'. Whereupon she all but swooned again, for joy.

And with that same macabre sense of the melodramatic as when he had dressed himself in bridal array to rush off and marry Jane Seymour, even while the death bells tolled for the murder of Anne Boleyn, so did the King choose the moment when the head of Thomas Cromwell was hacked from its trunk to wed his fifth, his youngest, and loveliest of wives.

For some three or four weeks the rejuvenated king wallowed in honeymoon bliss with his new toy before he brought her from Oatlands to Windsor, where, at a banquet attended by his 'Sister Anne' as guest of honour, Katherine Howard was publicly acknowledged Queen.

When, after the general exodus of the deposed Anne's household, Philip heard that Katherine had appointed him her Page of Honour, he was sunk. How to endure the anguish of propinquity with one so high above him as the angels, one who had led him on with acceptance of a 'token' and the promise of a kiss, to let him down!

H. Henry Manox? No. *Henricus Rex.* We may well believe no boy in Britain could have been in sadder case than Philip when he waited on his Lady at her wedding feast.

The King had arranged that this was to be no ceremonial banquet for ministerial grey-beards, but an assemblage of youth, of young Howards, the Queen's sisters and brothers and cousins, the sons of her uncle, the great Duke of Norfolk.

Henry sat between his two wives, past and present Anne, who, with somewhat disconcerting alacrity, had agreed to the divorce, was in high fettle and a costly if hideous new gown bought with the generous allowance — though he may have thought it cheap at the price — granted by her 'Bruder Heinrich'.

Philip, on bended knee to serve the Queen, saw how she had blossomed, never say stoutened, in these few weeks of marriage, but was still the more delectable for that. Her eyes rested on him kindly; she called him by his name. She took a capon's leg and gnawed at it with lusty appetite. The King leant over and across to grab and gnaw the juicy morsel in his turn; then passed the remains to his Sister.

'Here, you! Take a bite. 'Tis prime and fat and tasty, all credit to my cook.'

He held a drumstick for the 'bite'. Anne delightedly devoured it, rubbed her stomach in approval, and offered him the wing she had discarded. 'This also is good, *mein Bruder. Doch!* Eat, *lieber Heinrich,* with me.'

So, sharing the feast titbit for titbit, they guzzled and belched in unison and perfect amity together; while Katherine, with indulgent smiles for the pair of them, scooped from the dish the liver of the fowl, chewed it, smacked her lips, and wiped her greasy fingers on Philip's hair.

'You are now,' she whispered with her mouth full, 'my very own personal page,' to raise him up to heaven and fling him into hell when, seizing the King's red puffy hand, she played 'This Little Pig Goes to Market' on his sausage fingers, nibbled his thumb and said, 'I'd liefer stuff myself full o' *this* little piggy than of any fattened capon for my joy.'

'I'll stuff you!' roared Henry. 'I'll stuff you till you burst, with another son for me, my Rose.' He was drunk; he was maudlin. He blubbered. Tears of sentiment trickled down his sagging cheeks and dropped into his beard. 'Are you happy, heart's dream?'

'Happy?' Her gaze sped from the unlovely sight of him and went straight to the smoke-darkened rafters, 'So happy I could think I was dead and gone to Paradise.'

'Child!' Henry shuddered. 'Never say it. We live, we love, and now,' he bellowed to the minstrels' gallery, 'we'll sing!'

'I saw the new moon yester'een
With the old moon in her arm...'

Sweet and clear rose the voices of boy choristers, the King joining his rich baritone to theirs; and, as the song ended, he hugged both his wives to him and playfully knocked their heads together, saying on a gust of laughter: 'Here's my old moon and here's —' he snatched a kiss from Katherine — 'my new one!' Then, 'Come *on!*' he bayed above the twanging music, 'bring in the Morris dancers.'

They were waiting there in readiness behind the great carved screens, to rush in helter-skelter with a rollicking jingle of bells and toe-and-heel tapping on a space cleared of rushes in the centre of the hall.

The Queen stooped to tell Philip: 'Go, seat yourself at table, Master Pugh. You have ate nothing yet.'

'Your Grace.' He rose, he bowed, he backed, threading his way through that hurly-burly of clattering feet and madly leaping green and scarlet bodies strung with bells, to a vacant stool below the salt, among the lesser fry.

Lackeys offered him choice dishes: jellied lampreys, roasted breasts of peacocks, larks' tongues soaked in honey; but he ate sawdust and drank ink for all he knew, his fingers picking at this and that to leave the half untasted. Then, of a sudden, he became aware of a curious sensation, as if he were possessed by someone other's will, to draw him from himself and his eyes from his platter, staring at the end of the board where sat the Queen's maids, and —

'God's Soul!' The exclamation sprang from his lips, unheard by any. 'What's here?' Jocosa, or her double?'

No, not the Jocosa who rode off from Sprowston in her 'reach-me-down' habit; not she, that tatterdemalion tomrig of a girl, half boy, he had known, and had hated; but another, a changeling, bewitched, and — bewitching, with hair like black satin parted on her forehead beneath a small jewelled cap; a creamy-skinned girl with a mouth poppy-red and eyes darkly glowing, full of hidden laughter: a girl in a flame-coloured gown.

Philip blinked and hastily turned to a groom of the King's Privy Chamber next to whom he was sitting. 'Sir — Master Culpeper, do you know the name of that — of the young lady seated there among the maids of honour? The girl in the orange —' *was* it orange? — 'gown?'

'Orange?' Master Culpeper, debonair, graceful and blond, cocked a laconic eyebrow. 'Yes...' The reply was abstracted, his interest centred on an over-ripe peach, the juice of which had run down his chin and on to his white bepearled doublet. 'Here, sirrah, you!' he beckoned a servant, 'bring me a napkin. A pest on't! There's no stain, save a bloodstain, so hard to remove as that of fruit juice. You were saying?'

'The — that young — the girl over there,' stammered Philip.

'Mistress Sowerby? Yes, I know her. Jocosa, a distant kinswoman of mine.' He took the napkin from the attendant and dabbed at his elegant tunic. 'I've not seen her,' he added carelessly, 'since she was a child. She had little beauty then, and, seeming, has little more now. There's no shape to that filly. Too thin for my choice.'

The supercilious smile that accompanied this cool appraisement, suggesting connoiseurship far beyond Philip's experience, roused in him an unconscionable urge to smite that smile from the fellow's face; and, with his right hand in readiness fisted on his knee, he said, equally cool, 'She's also a kinswoman of mine.'

'Of yours?' Culpeper eyed him over, that smile still hovering. 'How?'

'On her father's side, and when you named her — I recognised —' and there he stuck, at a loss to explain why he shouldn't have known his own relative, and one who had lived in his home for three years. 'I did not — had not heard —' he floundered — 'that she had come to Court.'

'So?' Culpeper flung aside the napkin. 'No good. My man must see to't.' He helped himself to grapes. 'There's a bunch of relatives among us here today, the Howards high in evidence headed by Her Grace, the Queen,' his glance slid away, 'who is cousin-german to myself.'

This was news to Philip; he took to it unkindly, and was mortified to intercept, or maybe he imagined, a return of a glance that, to his fancy, lingered just a shade too long between Her Grace and her cousin Culpeper.

The evening sun, thrusting through the stone-framed window, shone on the squirrel-brown hair of the Queen, lighting it to rusty gold, lighting to rainbow fire the diamonds about her throat, lighting her amber-coloured eyes to fevered brightness, while, lips parted, she gazed blindly dazzled, at — whom?

Philip drank wine in too much of a hurry, choked, and set down his cup as the King staggered up from his chair, raising his jewelled goblet to toast the Morris dancers. 'Brava! Brava! Here's a health to ye, my masters!' His great voice rang through the hall subduing the music, the laughter, the din. 'Enough! Go feed yourselves. Come, all of ye...' gesturing the company risen to its feet, he dragged his pale Queen to hers. His arms engulfed her. 'And now,' he roared, *we'll* dance!'

Yes, he would dance, who had not danced since that 'accursed goggle-eyed witch,' his second wife, had danced into his life and into his heart, had danced to her end — with death. And subduing a shiver of gooseflesh he bent to suck kisses from his young Queen's shrinking mouth. 'My rose,' he gulped, 'my rose without a thorn.'

No thorn here to pierce his flesh that weighed heavier upon him than the creeping burden of his years, defied in the challenging glint of those little narrow eyes, in all that ruddy-cheeked and overblown magnificence, and in his exuberant shout: 'Come on! We'll lead a galliard.'

How Philip came to be paired with Jocosa he never quite knew, for he had drunk a trifle more than he could carry at fifteen; but when Their Majesties led off, followed by their gentlemen and ladies, and he stood apart to superintend the clearing of the trestle-boards by servants in green liveries, their chests emblazoned with the gold device of the royal leopards, he turned to find her edging up behind him.

'You didn't know me, did you?' Her mouth was tilted upwards in its faun-like teasing grin. 'You never thought to see me here at Court, a maid-in-waiting in full rig.' She spread her skirts to show the glittering flame of the brocade. 'Eight shillings an ell it cost, if a groat. The Duchess bought the stuff for herself and then said it made her look like putrid wax, so she passed it on to me. A fine gown it is, I'll say, and I'm grown fine to wear it, amn't I?'

'Very fine.' Philip agreed with a giggle and care for his speech, which was tripping. 'I muss' offer you my heart — my heartiest fel-felicitations on your —'

'Ouch!' She pulled a face at him. 'Cut the puffery — you're primed as a piper. Never did I see so much bibbing as since I came to Court. Shall we dance? I've learned my steps with the duchess if nothing else for my good, and I'll hold you up should your legs run away. Will you take me, or shall I take you?'

So she took him and steered him, zigzagging in and out that intricate maze of multi-coloured doublets and glittering jewel-flashed dresses. Through the dusty gilded light of torch-flares, figures moved in measured slow formality to the lilting rhythm. Philip found that she, surprisingly, could dance, and was glad enough of her support when, full of wine and giggles, he slipped, regained his balance, and laughed with her loud, at himself. Then, when the galliard was over, the King, dripping sweat and wheezing from unwonted exertion, called for the Antick Hay.

Fast and faster twanged the music; the young Howards and the choristers sang it, and Jocosa's voice shrilled tunefully above them all:

'She thumped it on her way
With a sportly hey de gay!'

The girl Queen smiled on her as she passed with the lumbering king. Directly behind them, guided by Culpeper, waggling her padded hips, squealing as she slipped and skated on the polished floor, came Henry's other wife, his 'Sister Anne'... Hands across, twice round, twirl about, two singles, set and turn and round again to face Their Majesties; then all that brilliant company billowed and bowed to the ground.

'On with the dance!' Mopping his wet face with the back of his hand, the King commanded his guests to 'Dance while you may and till you drop. But we'll to bed.'

With the Queen on his arm, beaming acknowledgement right and left to homage, this bloated, swag-bellied Silenus, triumphant in the capture of his nymph, retired to the nuptial couch.

Philip, if he would, could not be rid of Jocosa. Her fingers, entwined in his, clung; and now it was 'One Penny, follow me.' Up and down the staircase, past the grinning minstrels, trooped the young Howards, pages, maids-in-waiting, whooping, shouting for a game of Blind Man's Buff.

The Lady Anne, the Duke of Norfolk, and all the older folk had gone: Culpeper, too, in attendance on the King. And now, at last, Philip was divided from Jocosa. *Pouf!* He stood aside to clear his head and get his breath. Her caperings had winded him, while dizzily he wondered what she had in her rogue's eye to make him want to wring her neck or tumble her! And, at that thought, he, hot already, burned the hotter, to find himself chasing where she darted like a flaming dragonfly, right into the arms of the Blind Man. Philip paused. Who was this? A silken kerchief bound and hid the upper half of his face, revealing a chinless jaw that sprouted a nondescript beard. He was tall and lean, his spindle legs were encased in yellow hosen; he wore a doublet of carnation pink profusely broidered; and his hand, weighted with rings, fumbled at and fingered Jocosa from her breastless front to mouth and nose and hair, guessing her name three times, the third time rightly.

'You win!' She tore the bandage from his eyes to bind her own.

Philip knew him then; one Edmund Gynkes, a hanger-on about the Court and brother-in-law to the Solicitor-General, Richard Rich, who, though honoured with a knighthood, was a man of better brain than breed. Himself a tradesman's son, he had reverted, in marriage, to type, taking for wife the daughter of a wealthy member of the Grocers' Guild. Gynkes. Yes, Philip knew him, the Court butt, promoted through the influence of the King's Attorney to the unofficial post of Deputy Groom of the Chamber. And here he was, prinked out in jewels from the profits of his father's tallow grease and mutton fat, making sheep's eyes at Jocosa.

Having now passed from the giggling stage to the aggressive, Philip splenetically glowered at the overtures of Master Gynkes, mopping and mowing with a face like a cheese. He recalled how he had heard Robert Kett, in talk at his father's table, say that any upstart Jack-of-all-Trades could climb the Court ladder to land himself at the King's elbow, so be it his coffers were filled to overflow into His Grace's pouch …

'Ha! How goes it, Philip? Marry! You look about as joyful as a gammer who's been robbed of her goose.'

Tom Wroth was at his side. A fat boy, grown fatter, but still treble-voiced was Tom, whose recent elevation to the household of the King caused Philip further grievance; for although Tom's position as 'Server' savoured of an office little higher than a lackey, it gave him entry to the Privy Chamber with precedent above, and opportunity to patronise, a page.

'That cheesy fellow, Gynkes —' burst forth Philip, and paused, uncertain of what he would say.

'Cheesy!' Tom gave a squeaking laugh. 'That's good. So he is. I'm told his grandsire, who founded the family fortune, can be seen any day at his booth in Soper Lane, beguiling aldermen's wives with a ripe goat's cheese or prime flitches o' bacon.

Who's the girl hanging on to his sword-belt? If,' tittered Tom, ''tis catch-as-catch-can, it's she who makes bold to be caught.'

Which remark, in as much as it was vexing, could not be denied. Jocosa, though blindfold, appeared to pursue the hopping, skipping, mincing Mr. Gynkes with enough deliberation to raise a shout among the rest who dodged her. 'Hold hard! No cheating. You can see under the kerchief.'

'I can't — I swear I can't!'

'You can!' One of the Howard boys dashed up to tighten the handkerchief around her head and pull it down over her face.

'Hi!' She struck at him. 'You'll smother me.'

'Girls!' declared Tom, with fine contempt for the sex. 'Never trust 'em to play fair. She *was* cheating — or maybe she's partial to cheese.'

'Say that again,' Philip's voice was ominously quiet, 'and I'll ram your teeth down your throat.'

Tom's mouth fell open. 'Why, what have I said?'

'Something,' murmured Philip, 'that ill behoves one who calls himself King's Gentleman to say.'

'God's Lungs!' squealed Tom, scarlet. 'King's Gentleman may likely be more worthy of his state than Queen's Page, or — an you prefer it — than Queen's Codling.'

'And say *that* again,' repeated Philip, smooth as silk, 'and you'll swallow your words till you choke.'

Whereupon Tom sidled up to say it, jeeringly, again, when — and this was shocking — Philip's arm shot out, and they were at it in a brawl that brought a laughing, shouting group of youngsters to ring them round and lay odds on the winner. 'I'll back Tom Wroth — the heavy-weight!' cried one.

'Ah, but Pugh's the more nimble,' was the verdict of another.

'Go to't, Phil! Have at him!' Relieved of her bandage, Jocosa pushed her way to the fore, clapping hands in her excitement and jigging up and down on the toes of Master Gynkes, who stood directly behind her and whose corns suffered torture from the impact, unprotestingly endured. Then, amid shrieks from the girls, cheers and guffaws from the boys, and a stamping of feet and whistling on fingers and catcalls to raise the roof, came interruption, swift and stern.

'Young gentlemen, your names, sirs, if you please.'

Mr. William Grindal, Deputy Master of the Henchmen, fresh from Cambridge and very conscious of his duty, bore down upon to drag apart the two belligerents.

'This disgraceful misbehaviour in His Majesty's Court shall be reported to Sir Francis. In the meantime —' holding each by an arm, Mr. Grindal marched them off — 'you will go to your quarters and there remain in solitary confinement until further notice.'

Further notice duly given was, in equal proportions, dispensed to the backsides of both with twelve strokes of the birch. This chastisement resulted in a truce between the pair, born of mutual discomfort. 'Which only goes to prove,' quoth Tom, glumly, when in Windsor Great Park and too tender yet to sit, they lay face downwards in the bracken, 'that wherever there be girls there will be trouble. And the King'll find that soon enough — as so I've heard.'

But that which Tom may or may not have heard was as yet only spoken in whispers, loud enough, however, for Monsieur Marillac gleefully to seize on and report to Francis that: 'Henri has a *mal d'esprit*'. And this, in direct contradiction to a letter from Philip to his father, written while in attendance on a royal tour of the midland and northern shires.

The King, the Queen and all the Traine are exceeding merrie and the Queen wondrous kinde. She hath given me a gerfalcon which is so bolde and keene to the Quarrie more than at oure mewes at home that I am faine to present Her Highnesse's Grace with a dish of Partridge Pye for her supper my gerfalcon having catched me three fine Braice.

It was at Pontefract Castle in Yorkshire, the seat of Lord Darcy, and when Philip presented his 'pye', that he first came in contact with a Mr. Francis Dereham, the Queen's Secretary and general factotum. At one time attached to the household of the Dowager Duchess of Norfolk, he had joined the Court at Lincoln on its progress to the north.

Since the Queen, whose education admittedly was wanting — she could neither read nor scarcely write, and was in sore need of a scribe — Master Dereham's chance appearance was both opportune and timely.

So we hear that the blushful Philip, kneeling to offer his 'pye', had been graciously thanked for it. 'O! Baked to perfection —' by the King's head cook, who we may believe was well tipped for his pains. 'I can't wait to sup,' cried the Queen, digging fingers in the flaky crust, 'before I taste.'

She did more than taste; she gobbled, insisting that Master Dereham too must have his taste.

The Queen's damsels, primly smirking, eyebrows lifting, stood apart and watched Her Grace feed herself and Mr. Dereham, popping morsels in his mouth, as if he were her lap-dog. But to Philip and the ladies, none was offered.

Dereham … As he backed from the room Philip brooded on the person of this highly favoured gentleman so suddenly arrived upon the scene. Who was he to gain admission to Her Grace's privacy, to read and write her letters while her maids were bidden, 'Go. How can I dictate my correspondence while you stand about me gaggling? Go!' And at the stamp of her foot they went, no farther than the matting at the door, where, ears in turn to the keyhole, they listened, to hear nothing of dictation; nothing, indeed, but low-voiced murmurs, to cause more titters, eyebrow lifting, shrugs, and: 'What's this of a pansy?'

'Do you remember the silken pansy you gave me, broidered with a symbol of true lovers' knots?'

True lovers' knots! A symbol? Heads nodded, whispers fluttered. Here was a thing to wonder at. The pansy. Motto, surely, of the French King Francis worn at the Field of the Cloth of Gold, as retailed by those of Her Grace's maidens who had heard it from their fathers, how he and his followers went in purple velvet, worked with lovers' knots; and in the heart of every knot a golden pansy flower, circled with the words 'Think of Francis'. And Mr. Secretary Dereham's name was Francis. Think of *that*!

They thought of that to the exclusion of all else, encouraged by more whispers passed from mouth to mouth, of how Master Dereham had given something other than a silken pansy to 'Kat' Howard when she resided with her granddam, the duchess. There were tales told of midnight revels in the gentlewomen's dormitory while the duchess was sound asleep and snoring; and how Dereham had reigned as Lord of Misrule at these orgies where the young men of the dowager's household made free with the girls, romping together on their beds, exchanging tokens, kisses, and heaven only knew what else ... Yes, and how the thirteen-year-old Katherine had not been backward, neither, to lie naked between sheets with Master Dereham.

Naked, perdy! ... Yet seeing was believing, and some had sworn they'd seen too much to get themselves appointed chamberwomen to the Queen because, maybe, they *knew* too much. All, that is to say, with the exception of the duchess, blind and deaf to rigs beneath her roof.

The first hint of it came in a letter, unsigned, to tell of junketings between her gentlemen and ladies, and not a maid among the lot of them uncoupled — no names mentioned — save a broader hint of one *close akin unto Her Grace.* And this was found — of all places! — on the dowager's *prie-dieu* before the altar in her private chapel. None knew who wrote it, but there were some who guessed that the music master Manox, who played so sweetly on the virginals, was not so sweet at playing second fiddle.

Investigation forced upon her, the duchess rose up from her knees to swoop down and surprise the youthful 'Kat' 'in arms with Dereham, kissing'. Due punishment was meted right and left: a clout on the ear for Master Dereham; a slap in the face for one of the gentlewomen standing by to call *peccavi,* a minute too late; and a whipping for young Katherine, with the threat of instant dismissal to the three of them should any such disgraceful scene occur again. But not until the King was in hot pursuit of Katherine did the dowager send Dereham off — to Ireland. And from Ireland he had now returned to wait upon the Queen and bring her 'heartsease'.

Tom Wroth, who, with Philip, accompanied the Court on its travels, had it pat from those attendant on the King how that this Dereham fellow was bragging of a troth between himself and the Queen before her marriage. 'So,' Tom, grinning, gave a jerk to Philip's elbow, 'what now of heartsease — hey?'

But, 'Keep your filthy clack under your tongue,' retorted Philip, 'lest it hang out too far — to hang *you*!' For, although he had side-slipped, if not fallen out of love with his royal mistress, his fidelity to her remained unshaken. Yet it must be confessed that his rose-coloured sight of his lady had cleared to discover her figure not that of a sylph, her complexion not that of a beauty. Her hair, euphemistically described as 'auburn', was inclined to be mousy, her eyelashes almost imperceptible. Eyelashes ... Jocosa. What amazing eyelashes *she* had. Even Tom, who dismissed all girls as 'trash', admitted Mistress Sowerby had 'something'.

Vastly improved in looks and deportment was Jocosa. While her senior in age by barely three months, Philip felt to be immeasurably the wiser — elder-brotherly, in fact — toward Jocosa. He must allow her artlessness a refreshing contrast to the sophisticated wiles of the other maids-in-waiting, whose petty vanities and addlepated chatter made him sick. But Jocosa was not of the entourage attendant on the royal tour. She had been returned, *pro tem*, to the Duchess of Norfolk. Just as well, decided Philip in his new fraternal role, and in view of these recent appendages to the Queen's household, of Dereham and of Manox, the music master, who had also reappeared and, if Tom could be believed, 'lechered after anything in kirtles under forty'.

Manox. Philip burned to remember how that name had caused him, once upon a time, excruciation. Well, well! As Tom so rightly said, wherever there be girls, even though that they be queens, there would be trouble.

That note, for example, laboriously penned by Her Grace while at Lincoln on the homeward journey, carelessly folded and handed to Philip:

Take this to Master Culpeper, who I am grieved to learn lies low with a tertian fever. Say I will send my physician to tend him.

No harm, surely, in sending a note to her sick cousin, but the reception of it gave Philip to fear that the Queen played too trustingly with fire.

He found Culpeper huddled in blankets to the chin, his teeth a-chatter, and, despite the month was August, the room hot as a bake-house.

Politely expressing concern for his plight Philip delivered the Queen's message with the note, went to the door, was recalled.

'Here, what's-your-name? Pugh. Return to Her Majesty these words: I am as ever and always her — No. Say naught of this. Say only I send my warmest thanks unto Her Grace and that I will write my answer when I'm up from my bed. This low-lying cursed fenland has wrought its mischief on me. Pray you draw the curtains this side, to shield me from the window's light. It comes too sharp upon my eyes.'

'Can I,' ventured Philip, as he adjusted the heavy red damask hanging from the cornice, supported by four great carven posts, 'do aught else for your comfort, sir?'

'Dereham —' Culpeper raised himself on an elbow to turn over the Queen's letter — 'Dereham didn't write this. She,' he chuckled, 'wrote it herself. The only letter, to my knowledge, ever written by her hand. She says —'

'I do not wish,' interrupted Philip, standing straight, 'to hear what the Queen writes to you, sir.'

'God's Wounds! But you shall. She says, *I did hear you were sick and did never long for anything so much as to see you.* That's fond, and it's cousinly, yes? *It maketh my heart to die when I do think that I cannot always be with you.* And that, too, is right and proper to her kinsman.' Culpeper licked his parched lips and reached down for a sucked orange among a miscellany of phials on the stool by his bed. His eyes glittered strangely. Philip guessed him light-headed.

'Sir, may I not fetch the Queen's physician to you? Her Grace —'

'Faugh! No physician can heal me. I'm too far gone in, *that* she says, *which maketh my heart* — as hers — *to die. Be good,* she says, *to my man.* She honours you. Man! You are not near to manhood ... where's my pouch?' He rummaged under pillows. 'Find me my pouch.' Philip retrieved it from the rushes where it had fallen. 'This,' Culpeper offered him a crown piece, 'for your pains.'

'Sir,' Philip drew back, 'I am no paid servant in my duty to the Queen.'

''Tis her wish that you be paid, but if you won't take, I'll keep. I can ill spare it, who am given no reward for my duty to the King and his bad leg that rots to putrefaction. A fine bedfellow for — ha! What's here? Ho! Ha! Culpeper laughed a high cracked laugh. By Holy Blood, but this beats all. *I would you were with me now, that you moutte se what pane I take in writtin to you* ... '"Moutte." "Se." So much can Dereham teach her! I could, and I *will*, teach her better.'

With another burst of laughter he flung back against his pillows as Philip silently went out and closed the door.

It had been a most successful tour, and the King in his element at the enthusiastic welcome accorded him in Yorkshire by penitent resurgents, who, five years before, had caused such disturbance with their 'Pilgrimage of Grace'. No sign now of unrest, save here and there among the ragged peasantry that lined the King's highway to greet the royal cavalcade with scowling looks and mutters and spasmodic threatening cries:

'Pluck down the enclosures!'

'Fill up the ditches!'

'Lay open the Commons. Look at you — and look at *us*. We starve!'

Yet no more starved nor ragged than the outcast priests and beggars that littered London Town; nor could their voices carry strength enough to be heard above the trumpet blasts, the clatter of hooves, the gay jingle of harness and chorus of cheers and God-blessings for their hearty bluff and 'Good' King Hal.

So, home again; but poisoned talk of his young Queen had flown before him to buzz around the mitred eminence of Cranmer, who stooped an ear … to listen.

It was All Souls' Day and the King at Mass giving thanks unto God for his safe return, and 'for his joy in the good life he was leading and hoped to lead with his present wife after sundry great troubles of mind'.

The chanting of boys' voices rose and fell in crystalline cool waves of sound; the flicker of candles illumined the sumptuous robes of the officiating priests, struck diamond-sparks from the King's jewel-encrusted kneeling bulk. *'Deo gratias,'* he mumbled, clutching at his beads, weeping grateful tears for God's beneficence in giving him this rose of pure white loveliness, to have, to hold, for ever … until death. *'Beata aeternitas vel aeterna beatitude.'*

His pages got him on his feet. Clumsily genuflecting, he backed from the altar, and turned to find the archbishop at his side.

'Thomas! Father. Friend.' Fervently he raised to kiss with warm wet lips the Primate's pale knuckles. 'How am I blessed in you and in God's bounty.'

'Sire,' Cranmer's heavy-jowled face retained its wonted calm, but the low-lidded eyes were downcast, as into that flabby pawing hand he slid a paper, 'this, to my sorrow, I most sorrowfully render, having not the heart to tell by word of mouth what must be told.'

Katherine, her ladies and her gentlemen were gathered in one of the smaller State rooms adjoining the Presence Chamber, to hear the Queen's minstrels, in the gallery, with Manox in their midst, sing a madrigal; and as the last notes died, he, proficient in all instruments, took his recorder and gave them a sweet melody, impromptu.

'Delightful! Delicious!' The ladies offered rapturous applause, the gentlemen's approval more tepid. The Queen, looking up from her play with a kitten, cuddled in her arms, cried, ''Tis excellent, Manox! You must give it me again, but I have a fancy now to dance. Sirs,' she fluttered her fingers at a near group of courtiers, 'take each of you a partner. Cousin, you — to me.'

Leisurely, Culpeper detached himself from a cluster of girls about the fire that sent forth a fragrance of pine cones and spiced logs freshly sprinkled. The minstrels plucked their lute strings; the Queen rose from her great chair and handed the kitten to Philip.

He bowed and took it from her; it clawed at his shoulder and spat, scared of the movement and stir, and of this stranger who held it. Stroking the small arched back, Philip tucked the indignant bundle of fur under his arm and retreated to a window seat. There, remote from the weaving pattern of the dance, unobserved of any save one, paired with Master Gynkes — and who but he should have the right? — Philip held the now-mollified kitten on his knee and drew from his pouch a parchment. This, a letter from his father, dated some several weeks back, that he had found awaiting his return to Hampton

Court; and although he had it by heart, having read it at least a score of times, he needs now must read it again.

You will doubtless have heard how that the Dowager Duchess of Norfolk hath given consent to a marriage between our young kinswoman Jocosa to one Edmund Gynkes who I am told, is close related to Lord Bach, a recent creation, he being Solicitor General to the King His Majesty. I have not been consulted in this matter but am given to understand from the duchess as thus she writes me that the maid she be willinge and the gentleman worthie, much enamoured and of good estate.

Of his estate I know naught, but Sir Roger Wodehouse who is more cognizant than I of these matters, his brother Sir Thomas being of the Court who hath made recount to Sir Roger how that this Master Gynkes is a man of goodly fortune having acquired through his father dead and he an onlye son, some wealth from merchandise of what sort or parts I know not so the maid be willinge and well placed it is not for me to raise objection nor yet for your Grand Aunt Matilda albeit she opposeth the match.

My health is good but I suffer much discomfort from the Haemorrhoids for which Dame Matilda hath brewed me a soothing simple of the Pilewort. I had hoped you would have been home in time for the celebration of your XVI birthday in token of which I have instructed Sir Francis Bryan to increase your quarterly allowance by II nobles. The wedding of my young kinswoman Jocosa is to take place the last week in September which I am unable to attend since in my condition I cannot undertake so long a journey in the saddle nor can I spare the leisure from my transcript of the Aeneid of Virgil.

Haec scripsi non otii abundantia sed amoris erga te…

The last week in September! And this was the end of October. Married. Jocosa. And to such a one as *that*. Philip shot a baleful look across the room at Master Gynkes, prinked out in apricot velvet, silver-braided; bowing, scraping, partnering his wife. Jocosa. A protesting mew came from the kitten as Philip's fingers clenched upon its frail body.

And this, his first sight of her since his arrival and not a word exchanged between them yet. But last night the news had greeted him after he had read and disbelieved his father's letter; disbelieved, because such truth, if truth it were, was past all power of credence. He, her husband, that chinless, witless cheesemonger, that prancing popinjay ... Mother of God! How could she give herself as wife to such a...?

Blind fury seized him, unreasoning and unrecognised as the first instinctive revolt of the frustrated predatory male. Islanded in solitude he sat, nursing the kitten, whose offended tail uprose as if in sympathy and swelled, while hate — for whom? For that posturing ass, for Jocosa, for himself? — enmeshed him in a web of tension, taut to breaking point.

The music ceased; the dancers scattered. Philip left his seat to return the kitten to the Queen; and, despite the shapeless crowding of his thoughts, he saw from the corner of his eye, that Culpeper, conducting the Queen to her chair, had slipped a folded something in her hand; that she crushed and hid it quickly in the bosom of her gown, and, taking the kitten from Philip: 'My little cat,' she crooned, 'my sweeting. Look, cousin, is not this a pretty little face?' The Queen impudently raised her own. 'So like a pansy's face.' And there was no mistaking Culpeper's sharp impatient turn to her as, frowning, he stooped to whisper. All this Philip saw, and did not see, for a tugging at his heart that leapt and dived when he heard himself hailed.

'Why, Philip!'

That same clear upward lilt of her voice, that same hovering, mischievous smile.

'Is it true?' His words jumped at her hoarsely. 'It can't be true that you —' His throat closed.

'Yes. 'Tis true. Come here to the window.'

In a daze he followed where she led him to the seat he had just vacated; and there, side by side, shoulder to shoulder, just touching, they sat, she with her boyish slim hands clasping her crossed knees. She wore a dress of dark crimson, gold-threaded. She had pearls round her throat and rings on her fingers, but on the third finger of her left hand one ring only, to which Philip's eyes were drawn until, with a little breathless laugh, she hid that hand in the folds of her gown and said, 'You don't wish me joy on my marriage.'

'How can I — how could you? Why *did* you?'

At that cry, wrenched from him, unwilling and unwilled, all his tempestuous intangible bewilderments receded, were dissolved; and in the magic of this moment when adolescence, marking time on the threshold of young manhood, breaks bounds, is freed from youth's ingrowing painful crises, its suspenses, its impossible desires, he knew himself surrendered and revealed...

How long they sat together Philip could not tell, since time, in his bemused discovery, was non-existent. He let her talk; he scarcely listened till, with fleeting comfort, he heard that — 'the duchess, she it was who urged me to't since she could not, she said, keep me for ever, and me not having a dower would likely go short of a husband to find myself paupered and homeless.'

'Not,' he muttered thickly, 'while my father's home is yours.'

'Yes.' She sighed, an indrawn treble sigh, and, with that swift uplift of lashes to the slanting brows, she said, 'Yet I was never welcomed in your father's home — by you.'

He lowered his head, gnawing at his inner lip with a redness in his ears and a screaming in his heart: *Thrice cursed besotted fool I was! But how — how could I know?*

And as if she took that thought from him she laid her hand, for a second, on his. 'What's done can't be undone. And if I tell you —' she swallowed — 'that he's good to me and kindly? He gives me jewels and things and money, though I'm still in waiting on the Queen, not —' she caught back a giggle, 'as a maid. I'm a Woman of the Bedchamber, now that I'm a wife.'

'Are you,' he made his lips firm to say, and it seemed that his tongue was of leather, 'are you happy?'

'Yes.' Somewhat too emphatically she nodded. 'I'm happy — in a part of me that loves fine clothes and gewgaws as Her Grace's kitten loves cream. We had a grand wedding. You should have been there to dance at it — as had you not been journeying so far away you would have been, Phil, wouldn't you? You must tell me all you saw and did while on your travels. But first let me tell you —' And although she twinkled gaily her eyelashes were wet. 'We had a great feast and a bridal cake with a tall white sugar tower to top it. And the duchess, she gave me my bride's gown, but he paid for it — ten angels! And we ate and we drank, and then the relatives — so many of them — and Lord Rich's daughters, too, cow-faced girls they are, but kindly, they took me to the bridal chamber to disrobe, and when he came to bed —'

'Must I,' broke from Philip in strained agony, 'hear this?'

'Yes,' again that instant's pressure on his fisted hand, 'you must. It will make you laugh. Me, I laughed till I — till I cried. When he — my husband — came to my bed he was raddled to the hilt. He can't hold his drink. He's weak-stomached, and was sickly. The groom's men, they'd dressed him fine in a nightgown of yellow velvet lined with miniver that fadged shocking ill with his colour, poor soul, and would you believe? They'd dressed fine to match him — his ape.'

'His — *what?*'

She shook with silent laughter till the brimming tears ran down her cheeks. 'His ape. His pet monkey. He loves it. He loves all animals. He'd even have had Benedict to live with us — only that,' her voice faltered, 'he died. Dame Matilda wrote to say how he'd got eating again of the arras. I knew he'd come to grief if I weren't there. I'll warrant a nail got stuck in his belly, poor soul, and it — it killed him.' She went seeking in the pocket of her kittle for a handkerchief, and mopped her eyes and said, 'I've catched a plaguey cold. Will you come to visit me in our — in his new house? 'Tis a fine big house in Water Lane.'

Philip jerked his head in answer; he couldn't just then speak.

'The King —' went on Jocosa, with further application of the handkerchief to her pinkened nose — 'the King's at Mass. The Queen attended earlier this morning. My husband, he follows the New Order, but I'll not be reformed.' She vigorously wagged her head. 'Not me. I was born and reared in the Old Faith. You too, Philip, weren't you? But we mustn't speak too loud of our beliefs. Gynkes, for all he's simple —' she clapped fingers to her lips and hastily corrected — 'or not one of your prosy preaching wiseacres who know all and know nothing — well he, Gynkes, he says, if we give voice to our thoughts even to four empty walls, we'll find an ear in each of them to hang us. O, look, they're going to dance again. Come, dance with me.'

She sprang to her feet, holding out her hand in that half-imperious, half-coaxing, well-remembered gesture as when at Sprowston, she had used to drag him off to climb the apple trees and pluck the fruit to pelt him. But as he rose to follow her the folding doors burst open.

The King, head out-thrust, slow-moving side to side like a bull about to charge, eyes bolting, chest heaving, one fist to it clutching, stood there on the threshold. The leaping firelight gleamed on the gold and scarlet of his coat; on the bright brocaded doublet, on a jewel in his cap; on that convulsed empurpled face with its scant gingery beard; and on the small, sagged mouth.

The Queen, tripping to the music, her fingers in Culpeper's, stayed her steps, Culpeper his; the dancers theirs, as if an icy wind had chilled them; and, still in the gallery, the hidden minstrels played. Then, from those twisted lips, came a deep groaning sound as of a wounded beast; and all that staring company were petrified to silence while on a gasping breath the words gushed forth:

'Put up your lutes. Put up — put up! 'Tis time to dance — no more.'

BOOK TWO (1546-1548)

Quomodo lucem diemque omnibus hominibus, ita omnes terras fortibus viris natura aperuit.

As light and the day are free to all men, so nature has left all lands open to brave men.

Tacitus

SIX

Againe what a joie is it knowne
When men may be bold of their owne
 Thomas Tusser, poet, husbandman, grazier, 1527-1580

But men were not yet to be 'bold of their owne', as was evident to Philip when, in the autumn of 1546, he returned to Sprowston for two months' vacation by favour of yet another Katherine, the Queen.

He now held office of gentleman-in-waiting to Her Majesty, the King's sixth wife; and if in these nine years at Court from boy to man, from page to equerry, he had chafed against his calling, he made no attempt to free himself from its limitations.

None the less, it was during his sojourn at Sprowston that he first became conscious of issues more puissant than those progressive ecclesiastical doctrines with which the King, his prelates, and his ministers were constantly embroiled; issues that significantly stressed the difference between life lived, as Philip knew it, and as life envisioned by that Utopian martyr, Thomas More. And musing on these problems, he was dimly aware of a lifted new horizon beyond the protective colouration of his class that resignedly accepted monarchical omnipotence as one with religious or political upheaval, and its black-listed termination in horrific death.

Strange that the merciless end of Katherine Howard, whose youth's indiscretions, bared to the bone by carrion swooping to foul her young past, had not roused public sympathy so much for her as for her stricken husband. He had loved her; that twisted the hearts of all who heard and some, including Philip, who had seen his huge body shaken with sobs when the disclosure of his girl Queen's pre-marital 'base, voluptuous, carnal, vicious life', as judged by her inquisitors, had been made manifest to prove her guilt … 'Pierced with pensiveness', the King had 'cried a-plenty tears'; and his young wife's uncle, the thin-lipped, sanctimonious Norfolk, had cried with him to drive the sword home to its hilt in Henry's heart with the avowal, eyes to heaven, that Katherine, his niece, had 'prostituted herself with seven or eight others than those named.'

Not even her last breathless words, 'I die a queen but would liefer die the wife of Culpeper', could turn the King's loyal subjects from his bitter fate to hers. She had sinned past all forgiveness, 'to entice him by word and gesture to love her and to taint the Royal Blood … A whore, a wanton, far gone in fornication': Norfolk's mud-slinging to save *his* head was inexhaustible. And: 'Good people,' her fainting voice had barely carried far enough to reach the ears of those who stood around the block on Tower Green, 'Good people, pray for me? They prayed, but not for her; for their king, the hail-fellow-well-met 'Good' old Harry.

Only Philip, as, long afterwards, did he, to one, relate how, when they bore away the little bleeding body of the young slaughtered Queen, he betook himself on that same night to the chapel where they laid her to be buried; and there beside her rough-hewn coffin he knelt and prayed God's Mother intercede for her forgiveness and guide her soul to heaven.

Something of that sorrow, and the ache of it, was with him when, on an October afternoon, Philip, riding Crispin, took the road to Wymondham.

The day was fair and cloudless: the sky a clear flax-blue, and, on either side his way, the level pastureland and meadows lay unparched, still green from the rains of a wet summer; the trees still full and scarcely bronzed. At an easy pace he rode, eyes searching right and left in puzzlement to note, not having taken that same route until this day a week or so after his homecoming, how the aspect of the countryside had changed, as if a loved familiar face wore a distorted mask: a travesty of what it should have been, the features altered, the mouth widened, the brow creased, scarred, furrowed: not with age.

And as he passed the Oak which he, Will Kett, and one other, had so often climbed, straddling its sturdy boughs while she — on Philip's lips a smile came and went — plucked acorns to throw at him, he halted. On his left, as far as sight could see, the wide undulating sweep of land, with its dark wooded fringe, was chequered in a pattern of rough fences, ditches, hedges, newly planted, not yet sprung to height; for all the world, he thought, as it were a mighty chess-board. And in these confined spaces, unevenly measured, sheep grazed in their thousands, diminished by distance that the earth looked to be a-crawl and white with maggots; and burnt in or painted on the shaggy wool of nearer flocks, he discerned initials, red and black; here and there a brazen yellow. *Whose sheep? Our sheep?*

Standing in his stirrups Philip marked the letter P on one consignment; and beyond, enclosed, an F. Farther off, eyes straining, he deciphered a W and, confined again, a K. Now what could be the meaning of this? Hitherto these pastures, he remembered, had been shared between the squirearchy and peasants, where by tacit understanding the landlords, freemen, and villeins had been subject to an accepted policy concerning cultivation of the common fields. Under the manorial system these 'fields', overspreading vast acres, had been divided into strips, some broad, some narrow, yet each allotted to the ownership of peasants who, according to their means, might acquire twenty, thirty of them; but now —? Where the barley, where the rye? And why, in Satan's name, these ditches, hedges, fences raised that God's good earth must needs take upon itself another pattern?

Philip shook his head; the question was unanswerable. 'Let's on then to Wymondham,' he cried to Crispin and the cool October air. 'We'll call on Squire Kett. Maybe he'll explain this conversion.'

On they went; but when they came to Wymondham who but Kett himself should they encounter riding out as they rode in.

'Now 'tis said,' thus Robert Kett over a flagon of Malmsey, he having brought Philip to his house to partake of the excellent dinner provided by Alice, his wife, ''tis said that by confining a modicum of land or open village field, the portion of the humble is increased. I refute it!' Kett crashed a flat hand on the table to make the pewter cups and platters jump.

His wife, a shrivelled little woman with timid hare's eyes, jumped too; and Philip, mopping with his napkin a splash of wine on his tunic, said, 'How, sir, can you refute it? For, if by confiscation of common land converted to proprietary pasture, the landlords must employ paid labour, a hind may earn more in fair wage than the miserable pittance he can earn for himself by free grazing of a few sheep. Howbeit, 'tis understandable that the peasantry should stake a claim in their time-honoured rights, yet I think —'

'You think?' Contemptuously Kett quashed this stripling's argument. 'How can *you* think, nor wot of the evils that, like mildew on a crumbling wall, rot the sprouting seeds of endeavour to right these rooted wrongs? You, reared in the Court, strung about with music, poesy, tourneys, and the King His Grace's pleasures — and his gluttonies — how can you have understanding, more than a babe in the womb, of the parlous conditions imposed on these poor wretches whose forebears have left them one common heritage — the land — whereby to scrape from its soil a bare livelihood, now seized and taken from them. Yes! Seized by those in monied strength and with no word of 'by your leave' or 'prithee'. Confiscated and enclosed, hedged round. I tell you, young gentleman —'

'Sir,' Philip, who in silence, seething, had sat through this tirade made bold to interrupt, 'you say "hedged round," "enclosed," as, so I grant you, I have seen and, among the grazing sheep some branded with a scarlet K. Would these be your flocks, Master Kett, on common land enclosed?'

To which Kett's reply was a curt nod and, pointedly forsaking the discussion, he turned to his wife, whose part as hostess had to do with nothing of this talk more than unobtrusively to serve her good man and his guest. 'Before we speed our friend upon his way,' commanded Kett, 'go fetch a flagon of your especial cowslip wine and a venison pasty to take to his father.'

Flustered, she went to his bidding, while Philip, conducted by his host, strolled about the high-walled garden, admired the trim box hedges, the orchard with its white-washed apple barks, and lively bee skeps, for the day was warm enough to bring them out to work in late asters and Michaelmas daisies. 'But,' said Kett, 'there'll be little honey taken this year. The rains have soused the flowers, and watered the nectar. Your father, he keeps bees?'

'Yes.' So now it was all, pleasantly, of bees; and a jar of honey to be added to the basket containing Mistress Kett's 'especial' cowslip wine and her venison pasty. Only at the last as he mounted Crispin, the basket slung by its strap from the saddle, did Philip enquire, 'Sir, what news of Will?' And only then, without she was addressed, did Alice Kett give voice.

'Will's got himself a wife.'

'Will married?' Philip stared astonishment. 'Since when?'

This last month, he was told, to the daughter of a Fleming. 'Will does much business back and forth from Flanders,' Will's mother said with pride, 'but we've not seen his wife. He wrote us…'

She gave a timid glance aside at Kett who, nodding, added, 'Yes, he wrote, and mighty pleased, withal, he is, nor have I cause to quarrel with his choice, she being the daughter of a cloth merchant in Antwerp and no lack of means behind him. My duty to your father, Philip. Come soon again to visit us. You are always welcome.'

And all along the homeward way, while Crispin, heading for his stable, covered the ground at double the speed with which he had come, Philip thought about Will's marriage and wondered what the girl was like: another Anne of Cleves, a 'Flanders mare'? And then, as ever, when he heard how this one, that one, of his boyhood's friends were wedded or betrothed, came a digging in the region of his heart, for he would never marry. No. He saw himself — at twenty-one — a bachelor confirmed, unmated, despite promiscuous attempt to test his manhood and to brag a bit of conquests with Tom Wroth. Still, he was young: there was yet time, some day, somewhere, mayhap, to find that miraged haven sought in loneliness, in dreams, in messages unuttered between another and himself; or in a song, unsung.

Giving Crispin a free rein he cantered along the grass verge of the highway to Norwich, slowing through the town and out at its gates. And, eyes straight fixed between his horse's ears, he bethought him of the problems raised by Kett as to the common right of property; which, he decided, and as Kett had made clear, had naught in the world to do with him.

The King and Queen were at Whitehall when Philip returned to his duties that, although officially attendant on the Queen, were divided between herself and her ailing husband.

Henry, now a dropsical diseased grotesque and older than his fifty-five years, was so superabundantly swollen with fat that it took four men to carry him from room to room, and machinery to hoist him up the stairs; yet, with that same indestructible joy of living which, in his youth, had won him the adoration of his subjects and his discarded Spanish wife, he still clung with fierce prehensile tenacity to the last broken shreds of his life.

These past few years had been eventful, to refund him from his people some of their confidence, pride in and affection for 'old Harry'; and this despite the blood-tracks that led to the Tower and Tyburn, and those cindered ashes scattered round the tarred and smoking faggots at Smithfield.

Hailed as a conqueror he had come to grips with France and Francis, to win Boulogne, if only on a temporary lease. But he had sent the French fleet flying from the Solent when they dared to make a landing on the slopes of Bembridge Down. There had been some English losses; the *Mary Rose* was sunk along the Sussex coast; and England's victory, if such, proved inconclusive. Then came that clash of arms with James V of Scotland, when Norfolk threw the Scots˙ back across the border to follow up a fresh attack that brought death to King James, from a broken heart, it was said, to see his armies vanquished. No wonder, then, that all these alarms and excursions had taken heavy toll of Henry's health — and his exchequer — to force upon his people a debasement of the coinage. Henry's son, Prince Edward, would wed the baby Queen of Scots, so word ran in taverns over tankards; but by that time England's king had married his sixth wife, already twice widowed and young enough to bring him half a dozen princes more.

Yet, despite his risen popularity, dissensions and growls against Henry were afloat, on bated breath. None relished exchange of nickel coin for silver; nor the consequent cost of living that had soared to staggering heights, though the effect of it was felt by none save those of the King's lesser subjects who toiled in the once 'common' lands enclosed against them by their overlords; or in the shipyards, tanneries or those fetid ways where whining mendicants and outcast priests, with a horde of ravenous curs yapping at their heels, slunk like sewer rats from their holes in search of garbage to fill their starven bellies, and evoke a jeering chorus from the gutters:

'Hark, hark! The dogs do bark,
The beggars are coming to Town.'

It was on a day toward the end of November when Philip rode out from Whitehall with a list of royal names in his pouch for whom he must buy Christmas gifts: the Queen, the young Prince Edward, the Ladies Mary and Elizabeth, and one other of the Blood: that shy little super-intelligent girl, the diminutive Lady Jane Grey. But gifts to the Royalties, graciously received, gave very small hope of return.

At the sign of the Cat and Parrot in West Chepe Philip dismounted, and, handing the reins to John Locke, approached the booth where all kinds of trinkets, toys, gloves, rolls of tinsel stuff, ladies' hoods, caps, ribbands, girdles were enticingly displayed.

One there, with her handmaid at her side, engaged the shopkeeper in heated altercation concerning this 'dear-priced drossie rubbish which you may swear is silver but *I'll* swear is refuse metal of base coinage, melted down.'

Philip masked a grin; he knew that voice and, despite her back was turned to him and her shape hidden in a crimson cloak, he knew that voice's owner. The argument, high-pitched and clear on her part, had attracted others to it; a fish-fag from Wapping who balanced on her head a tray of smelts hawked beneath the noses of farmers' wives to whom sea fish was hard to come by; a few of these had paused on homeward way from market to outlying villages beyond the City's walls; and here a milkmaid with a pole across her shoulders, the empty pails swinging as she tiptoed, agape, to see and covet what she could never buy; and a black-faced chimney sweep, a blue-coated apprentice, a sauntering gallant who stayed to finger and discard a drinking-cup; a butcher's boy, his basket filled with hanks of fresh cut meat, all jostling shoulders for a nearer view of a free entertainment.

'Foh, sirrah,' she stuck to her point, 'would you bleed me, poor soul, who cannot add two and two, of one angel for this paltry thing? Well, then, I'll none of it. One's my limit. Take or leave. Come, Joan,' to her maid, 'we'll go. There's better shops than this in Chepe with fairer trade to deal me.'

'Nay, madame,' washing his hands, the vendor — that same 'habberdasher' whom Philip from his early days at Court had patronised — put a curb on his tongue, cringingly to wheedle, and not as he was tempted to offer the lady a taste of his mind, 'if I tell you, as God may be my judge, I am much the poorer to give away my merchandise far below its worth or that I paid for it to meet Your Ladyship —'

'I'm not Your Ladyship, and you can keep your nickel dross. I'll not take it an you give it. Now price me this.' She pointed to a little gilded leathern collar. 'This I'll have for my husband's ape, yet I'll warrant me its clasp is not of rubies but chips of coloured glass.'

'Nay, madame, on my oath, albeit they be not rubies at this price, but garnets, a rare if not so precious stone, yet, look you, even the most expert eye could never know the difference.'

'So! An they be not rubies, but garnets, so rare — as you say — and as I say no more rare than a peck o' dried peas, then price me your trumpery. What! Eight *shillings*? Not on your life! Six or nothing … Seven, then, and six too much at that. Joan, come on. We're holding up his trade with half London here to stare as at a peep-show. You should pay me, you rogue, as your 'prentice to bring custom.'

Loud laughter met this raillery and, as she turned to laugh with them who pressed about her, she sighted Philip a pace or two behind. 'Hey, Phil!' Her hand went up in greeting. ''Tis you now to be fleeced, and what's your fancy?'

His fancy was for nothing but to watch her gay young face with a colour risen at the meeting of their eyes, and a fading, gentle as the afterglow of sunset. Then, as those who loitered there passed on their way, leaving these two alone, he lightly said, 'My purchases can wait an I may walk with you. Do you go home?'

'I think…' She poised a finger to her lip, side-glancing at her maid. 'Do we go home? Or is there more to buy? What of those saffron cakes your master bid us bring him?'

'If madame would have me buy the cakes —?'

'Yes,' she nodded quick assent, 'go buy them, and for me a jar of spiced ginger, for yourself a pound of sugared almonds, and cobnuts for the ape. Here's my purse. We'll go ahead. You follow. Master Pugh will see me to the door.'

And with John Locke alongside, mounted and leading Philip's horse, they walked together through the crowded cobbled streets of a city unchanged since the time of the Plantagenets, save for the ruins of a shattered faith; ruins of monasteries and churches; of altar pieces, monuments, and statues; ruins of painted windows glinting in the dust and rubble where broken walls still bravely stood, crippled relics of Reformational storm. Yet, withal, a cheerful boisterous city.

The day was mild for November with a red sun peering over gabled roof-tops from a smoke-dimmed sky; for, in Henry's London, almost every kind of trade and craftsmanship was carried on within the city's walls: and every kind of smell, accordingly, rose up in mingled savours of melted tallow, glue; of brewer's yeast and malt; of roast meats and onions from the cooks' shops; of vegetables rotting in gutter-streams and laystalls where flung refuse awaited the scavengers, if starving dogs — and men — had not been there before them. And over and above this variety of smell rose stronger still variety of sound. From the narrow lanes and byways off Chepeside, in the workshops of blacksmiths, of armourers, and carpenters, came an incessant hammering, and clanging and whirring of wheels; a grinding and sharpening of knives and swords and daggers; from St. Nicolas Shambles the terrified lowing of doomed cattle; and everywhere persuasions of the 'prentices stationed in shop doorways to outcry one another in a deafening cacophony of: 'What d'ye lack? What d'ye lack?' offering neckerchiefs, hosen and feathers, pomanders — these much in demand by those less case-hardened to save their more sensitive nostrils: a motley collection of goods, quick and dead, from caged song-birds, white peacocks, live eels and hutched rabbits to minivers, sables, and foxes, ready for the skinners in St. Mary Axe; the sellers of pattens in St. Margaret Pattens; the turners of beads for prayers in Paternoster Row; upholsterers in Cornhill, the grocers of Soper's Lane, the shoemakers in Cordwainer Street; and always the patient plodding pack-horses and loaded wagons rumbling back and forth from Thameside with imports of foreign countries: Rhine wines, French wines, velvets, silks, and Brussels lace; and all of this in every street, crossing and conjoining, running parallel to fill the air with divers orchestrated din, as much a part of London as its prevailing stink.

'I like,' Jocosa said, 'to walk and see the sights, if not to buy beyond my purse, for you never know what you may hap on — for your luck. Yet I still feel I'm a stranger here to wish myself a cottage in the country, were it never so mean a little house, where one —' she paused to sniff and pull a face — 'can breathe. You've but just returned from Sprowston, have you not?'

He had.

'And is all well with your father and the dame?'

All was well, he told her. 'The dame, as ever, active, a trifle deafer maybe, but in full possession of her faculties —' a smile gleamed — 'and of my father.'

They talked desultorily of this and that, their speech guarded as their looks that flew like thieving birds between them, each conscious of a secret held and hidden from the other. Side by side, he guiding her, they went, his hand on her cloaked elbow, eyes up and alert for muck thrown from windows under rough-carved wooden gables; she, with laughter, to dodge a loudly grunting pig, fled from the slaughter-house, pursued by a butcher with a hue and cry behind him. 'Lord sakes! Look, Phil, he's 'scaped his sty, or maybe he knows what's in store for him at Christmastide, poor soul, and takes his leave.' Then, in a trice, she sobered for its fate, and grabbed at its twist of a tail. 'I've half a mind to take him home with me and save his head. My husband would welcome him. He's partial to dumb beasts. Would you believe, he rescued a poor bear, blinded from a baiting down by Hockely-in-the-Hole, where some villains had gouged out its eyes with their spiked staves. Yes, he saved it — and brought it home. And how it wasn't killed by those brutes I'll never know, unless St. Francis, his dear self, was watching over him. Phil, why is it you seldom come to visit us?'

He had been away, he said.

Yes, she knew that; and hunched a shoulder at him, ripe lips pouting. 'But before you went away — how many months or years is it? Two years since you have broken bread at board with me — with us. And why?'

Because his time ... Her Majesty ... he mumbled.

Ah, yes, the Queen, and all his courtly duties, banquets, tourneys, jousts, she understood must have first claim on his time to keep him from old friends while he made new ones. He would be at the butts? She had heard tell of his prowess as an archer and at tennis — in the tiltyard, too. Would he be attendant on Their Majesties at Christmas? And the Ladies Mary and Elizabeth, would they be at Hampton Court? Oh? 'But not ourselves. We are not commanded. Gynkes is seldom now required to attend the King as deputy to one or other of the household...' Nor was she, to wait upon the Queen and glad enough to be released from courtly duties having her own home to care for. 'Such a big house as it is and a staff of lazy servants. If only the dame were here to superintend, she'd not stand for their idleness…'

So, in some such fashion she sustained a sprightly chatter, with not much support from him more than was monosyllabic.

The house in Water Lane stood beyond Lud Gate, in a narrow rural way leading off the Strand down to the Thames: a fine house though not to Philip's taste, with too much elaborate woodwork carved in a bold design of fruit and garlands, and a newly acquired coat of arms, freshly painted to depict in gold, and red and blue as of *Gules, three Boars' Heads guardant on a Field azure.*

'You'll come in,' offered Jocosa, 'and drink a stoup of wine with me — with us?'

The unlatched door swung open at her touch. Philip followed her into the large dark panelled hall. On a raised dais stood a long oaken table spread with a Persian rug; two other boards in the centre were laid across trestles; some benches, a chair, and a few stools completed the furnishings. The chimney-breast and overmantel were emblazoned with the same heraldic pomp as that above the door and on the hall screens. Flemish tapestries adorned the walls; and a good array of silver cups and plates were displayed upon a dresser. The whole interior evinced its owner's wealth, with nothing in it, Philip guessed, of Jocosa's choice.

Bidding him be seated she went to order refreshment. He heard her calling from behind the screens, 'Bring wine and beakers, and take a tankard of ale to Master Pugh's man at the gates.'

A servant bearing pewter cups and a flagon of Malmsey on a tray, another with a dish of cakes, preceded her return. She was now divested of her cloak. At her heels, and eagerly, came the master of the house.

'I am right glad,' he said, 'to welcome Master Pugh.' His eyes, of so pale and empty a grey that the irids looked to be merged in their whites, rested vaguely on his guest who rose to bow. Jocosa poured wine; her husband hastened to hand it and invited Master Pugh to eat of 'these excellent caraway cakes made by my wife,' he nodded at her, smiling, 'for my pleasure. I am —' carefully he picked them over, to choose one of those with sugar icing — 'much addicted to caraway cake, albeit saffron is my favourite of all.'

'I have sent Joan to buy some,' Jocosa told him. 'I was making purchases in the Chepe when I met Philip out on the same errand. And here is what I've bought for you — and Jeremy.' She held out to him the little leathern collar; and, his smile spreading, he took it from her.

'Now is not this well done! She forestalls my every need, and Jeremy's. Only yesterday,' he turned to Philip, 'did I tell her, with no second thought, believe me, that Jeremy, my monkey — the pleasantest creature and so wise — had in mischief mishandled to break of his collar. So she buys me this. I thank — I thank thee, wife.' He came to kiss her. She offered him her cheek, half-turned. Philip drank wine and looked away. Jocosa looked at him and gently pushed her husband from her, saying, 'Is the poor bear still in pain?'

Dolefully Gynkes shook his head. 'Not so much in pain as wounded to his soul, poor beast. Sir,' to Philip, his eyes widening, he said, 'I have a bear. I saved it from wicked tormentors. Yes, I did. I gave it house-room. My men built me a hut of wood for it, and there it lives outside here in the court. It eats honey but naught else for all I bring it raw ox flesh, and 'tis so thin that its ribs can be counted through its fur. But a well-mannered, grateful bear for aught of kindness shown. Were I the King I'd pass a law to put an end to the baiting of bears. Once, indeed, when in attendance on His Grace, I spoke of this, so-named, pleasured sport of men, but he — the King — feigned not to hear, nor indeed, may not have heard me. Will Master Pugh be pleased to stay and dine with us? I would be honoured.'

This one-toned monologue was accompanied by a restless roving of those pale eyes, while he munched cakes, his fingers picking at the crumbs that he let fall on his scraggy knees, encased in green hosen. He wore a coat of yellow velvet over a doublet of amethyst satin. His sleeves, slashed with crimson, were lavishly embroidered. He was hung about with jewelled chains; yet despite his parrot-gay accoutrements, he gave somewhat the impression of a ghost with those pale eyes, that pale hair receding from an egg-shaped pale forehead; and the pale scranny beard that enhanced rather than concealed his want of chin. When he smiled, which was often, he showed unsightly teeth in a mouth that stayed always a little open with the jaw a little dropped.

Declining his invitation to dine, Philip rose to go, was urged by his host to stay a while longer. 'Wife, bring another flagon. What news, sir, of the Court? I am so seldom now commanded that I am out of touch with the...' He offered cakes. 'Prithee, sir, oblige me.'

Philip unwillingly obliged him. More wine was brought, and a refill of his cup not refused. Master Gynkes now turned the talk to the latest topic on everybody's lips, the imprisonment at Windsor of the Earl of Surrey: 'For making treasonable speeches,' he said, 'so as I'm told. The King loves him not in that he has quartered his arms with His Majesty's own. They say he'll be taken to the Tower, poor gentleman. A pretty poet. Such sad things come about among us of the Court, one never knows from day to day — ' His straying glance wandered from his wife's clouded face to Philip, who in that indeterminate presence, found himself at loss for words; but Master Gynkes had words enough for both; nor when a servant entered, leading a small monkey by a silver chain, did he stay his flow of speech longer than it took to lift the thing in his arms and fondle it. 'You shall have the gift thy lady brings thee, sweet,' said he, 'when our guest departs, which will not, I trust, be yet. I was saying — yes, I think —' A faint pucker creased his brow, 'the world is changing. There are ugly deeds afloat of which one dare not speak. Sir Richard Rich, my sister's husband —'

'No, not of him,' Jocosa swiftly interposed. 'Think not of him.' She glanced aside at Philip, and, while lovingly Gynkes mumbled to the monkey, her lips moved in a whisper: 'He can't forget. 'Tis on his mind — of poor Anne Askew's end. He saw her burn. He crept out against my knowledge.' And to her husband: 'See now if the collar fits.'

'Yes, indeed...' But he made no movement to the stool where he had left it lying. 'It does not do to dwell,' he said, 'on torture done to woman, man, or beast. I've witnessed — but my sister married him of her own free will. He has risen in the world to power, and in his power he and the new Lord Chancellor, Wriothesley, they racked her — yes, they racked her — for that she spoke too freely 'gainst the Mass. And they burned her at the stake. She took long — too long — to burn. I saw —' A shudder swept his meagre frame. The monkey twisted its neck to look up at him with dark mournful questioning eyes. 'There, there,' Gynkes lowered his lips to the tiny head, ''tis over, and her torment, too.' A tear welled and dribbled down his nose. The monkey, still gazing up at him, put out its little hand to clutch at a gold button. 'Brave she was,' Gynkes said, sighing deeply, 'brave. Unflinching. Sir, an you must leave us, will you not come see my bear before you go?'

So out through the screens they went, all three, and the monkey, to the courtyard, where white doves clustered picking at the fallen grain. Some, at sight of Gynkes, fluttered down to perch on his arm and around his feet, one on his hand. A mongrel dog leapt up to greet him on three legs. It lacked a paw.

'This sad little one,' Gynkes said with his wavering smile, 'I found in sorry case. A cart had crushed its foot. I brought him home and sent for my barber-surgeon who advised the foot to be cut off. He saved the limb, and at my request he doused him well with wine to benumb the pain of amputation. He goes hoppity and happily enough on three legs now, do you not, my dear?'

A delighted wagging of a ridiculous tail, longer than its body, gave reply to this. And Philip saw how that Jocosa's eyes, as they rested on her husband, held a look he had never seen in them before: a look — the thought stabbed him with sweet anguish — as of a mother who looks on her smitten child whose hurt she cannot heal.

The bear, morose and huddled in its hut, its head in a bandage, the eye sockets empty, one arm in a sling, sat on its stern, drooping and motionless. Only the spasmodic heaving of its ribs gave any indication that it lived. Master Gynkes put a finger to his lips. 'Praise be! He sleeps. We must not waken him. Let us tiptoe — quietly — away.'

Subduing inward laughter, half-hysterical, Philip 'tiptoed', as he was bidden, in the wake of Master Gynkes, round the back of the house to the front.

As he mounted his horse he carried with him a last lingering glimpse of those two: she bright-faced, though he could have sworn her eyes were wet; he with the monkey on his shoulder, and, for all his gay trappings, less like a man than the shade of one there at her side.

The King was sick, and weary of the pain that wracked his wakeful nights, that goaded to torment his days. Tended by his wife in the hushed quiet of his bedchamber he sat, his suppurating leg stretched across her lap while he submitted to her patient application of hot poultices and balm. He would allow none other but herself to treat him, for even his physicians shrank from contact with the reeking ulcerated poison he exuded; and although her gorge rose in repugnance, she performed her ghastly duty with unflagging outward cheer. Yet his fast-ebbing vitality returned in a tide-flow of vigour renewed when he went forth resplendent to prorogue his Parliament in speech 'so moving and so fatherly', they said, that he reduced one sentimental secretary to tears.

'Dear friends, we by God appointed,' he told them, 'have found such kindness in your hearts for us that we cannot but choose to love and favour you in all your ways.' Then, at his 'dear friends', unnamed — and at Cranmer, seated within eye-shot, his low-lidded face impassive — Henry darted a barbed arrow. 'Some of you, and some of whom —' that rich mellow voice, a trifle thickened with catarrh, rang out in all its old accustomed strength, to strike his listeners with wonder at the unconquerable spirit walled within the mortifying flesh — 'are so stiff in your old *mumpsimus,* and others so busy with your new *sumpsimus,* that instead of preaching the word of God you rail at each other in vain exposition of perverse doctrine.'

He was grieved to know and hear how irreverently was that precious jewel, the Word of God, disputed, rhymed, sung, jangled in every ale-house and tavern... This the prelude to more burnings of heretics, among whom was Anne Askew, a Protestant pioneer and friend of the Queen, for denouncing the Mass as 'an abominable idol'. At all costs must Henry, in these last years of his life, impress upon his people that while he allowed God's Word to be transmitted to them in their mother tongue by his Archbishop Cranmer, no mercy would be shown to those who preached against it, or did deny him and the tenets of his Faith.

The Queen herself had but narrowly escaped her predecessor's doom by her support of, and intercession for, the tortured Anne Askew.

It was all about the Court that Gardiner, Bishop of Winchester, chief instrument of Cromwell's fall and much in favour with the King, had endeavoured to impeach the Queen on the same charge as that of her martyred friend. There were some who said the King had tired of his sixth wife and was now seeking a seventh, to cause apprehensive flutters in the virgin breasts of maids-in-waiting when his little puffy eyes turned appraisingly on this one on the other. But Gardiner's scurrilous intrigue against the Queen was frustrated at the eleventh hour. The Bill of Articles framed against her, together with a warrant for her arrest, had been dropped — a providential accident — by the bearer in the gallery at Whitehall. One of the Queen's attendants saw the paper lying there, took it up, glanced at it and brought it, in terror, to the Queen.

There followed a commotion.

Katherine, whose bedchamber adjoined that of the King, 'fell', it was reported, 'in an agony', which was not surprising. So frenzied and so loud were her lamentations — with one eye on her royal spouse's door — that the King's physician, Dr. Lingard, sent a gentleman-in-waiting to tell her, 'His Majesty, greatly incommoded by the noise, must know the reason for it or entreat Her Grace to cease her cries.' Whereupon the Queen's physician, Dr. Wendy, summoned by her frightened maids, sent word back that 'much distress of mind had caused Her Grace's sickness'. Then, moved by conscience-guilt or by compassion, Henry was hoisted into a chair, carried to his wife's apartment, plumped down beside her, and, with no avail, strove to soothe. At length, when her physician had plied her with restoratives, the sobbing Queen mustered voice to tell him, and to stake her life on one strategical last stroke: 'If ever I have dared to differ with Your Majesty on this or that doctrinal point of religion, it was because I saw how such discussion did divert you from the path of your infirmity. If, therefore, I have erred in any such respect it was only for your comfort, Sir…' And so on.

The King was charmed; also he was mindful of her excellent good nursing. If he lost her he would never find another wife so willing, so adaptable and kind. The King shed tears; and she, who in this crisis and for all her sobbing had shed none, knelt with covered eyes to kiss his hand. He raised her up. He said, 'And is this so, sweetheart? Marry! then we are perfect friends again.'

He had quite forgotten the warrant he had signed for her arrest.

The next day, walking in the palace gardens, the King's arm lovingly about his 'sweetheart's' waist, occurred an incident of which we have account from Philip in a letter to his father:

I must tell you though it be my lot to witness much of His Grace's wrath yet seldome have I seen His Highness in so ragefull an ill humour as when Chancellor Lord Wriothesley with 40 of the Guard approached seeking audience unwelcome as it seemeth with His Majesty who in a moment of caprice for what cause I do not know did accost his Lordship roundly thus, Beast, Knave, Blockhead, Fool, you Arrant Fool, you Whoreson, Go, begone out of my sight. Then with his stick the King did ram at him the while my Lord he ducked his head and bibbled foolishly to say, May it please your Majesty I was mistook. Whereon the King bid him again to go and with his guards in haste his Lordship went ... I warrant me the Queen as all of us attendant are in fear that our Lord Chancellor hath brought upon himself some dire punishment for when Her Majesty did intervene on my Lord's behalf, the King with sorrow saith, sweet Kate you little know how evil he deserveth of thy Grace. On my word Sweetheart he hath been a very Knave to thee. And naught else was talked of for a week among us here since not I alone but other of the gentlemen and five of the Queen's maidens were present at this scene which had so comical an aspect we shall never have done laughing.

You tell me in your letter just received naught of happenings at Sprowston. What of Flowerdew? Does that old canker between him and Kett still feed on its own venom? I trust that you, my father, will not become embroiled in unneighbourly disputes anent these spreading grievances among the peasantrie who when all is said have certain cause for their complaint in that as Kett hath it their livelihood is taken from them. London teems with homeless vagrants cast adrift from the soil who come here to seek a living and find none since they know naught of city ways that they must steal or starve.

The latest talk that causeth much dismay is of Lord Surrey's attainder. He lies now in the Tower to await his death. Poor gentleman, I grieve for him. His father too, His Grace of Norfolk likewise is there detained under sentence. Truly these are troublous times we live in. One can never tell from day to day on whom the axe will fall, there being everywhere dissension and fanatical reversion with our Church a House divided and our Prayers in English read. More of this I must not write. Penned words are dangerous. I beg you, Sir, to burn it.

Since Christmas the King's health shows signs alarming to his Doctors and to us of the Bedchamber who are in close attendance. I sleep now in a room adjoining that of His Grace within call. The Queen hath requested me of this.

I have writ my quill blunt and my ink well dry hence these faint last words which I trust, Dearest Sir, you can decypher.

From the Palace of Westminster January XII.

By your entirely devoted and obedient son

Philip.

The palace lay hushed in a silence heavy as the smoke-shroud drifting from London's chimneys to wind itself about the sodden gardens of the King His Grace's House.

Propped on his pillows in his great canopied bed he lay, watched by grave-faced physicians who, hour by hour, marked that slow relentless sinking as of a gallant ship foundered on the jagged rocks of pain.

That extraordinary being, named by Erasmus 'a universal genius', once the idol of young Britain to challenge all comers in the tiltyard, was now met in mortal combat with his supreme last implacable enemy.

Those around him saw, and seeing, marvelled at the courage sustained in that palsied hulk beneath the purple, gold and scarlet coverlid; and in that swollen face, a travesty of its once buoyant youth, when he, a crowned boy king, had stood beside his Spanish Queen to receive the homage of his dazzled subjects. Nothing now save the burnt-out embers of that fiery spirit which, for eight and thirty years, had dominated England, was left, unyielding still, to grapple with those dark descending wings.

He asked for wine but could not swallow from the cup held by one of his gentlemen, Master Philip Pugh. Then, his lips moistened, he rallied, indistinctly to articulate: 'The Queen … send for her.'

Summoned from her couch, having snatched an hour's sleep, she hurried to his bedside to hear him tell her in a few brief words, 'It is God's Will that we should part.' He said he had bequeathed to her three of his manors, some of the Crown Jewels and certain silver and gold plate. Was it an intentional perverted sense of humour that caused him, when he gathered breath again to speak, to name one Thomas Seymour as a member of the council? For what had Thomas Seymour to do with her, his wife, more than that before her marriage to the King she had been betrothed to Seymour? And did those sunken eyes, fixed so narrowly upon her whitening face, glint sideways at her, slyly, as he said, 'You'll be well dowered…'? Then he curtly bade her leave him, and asked for his daughter Mary.

She came, she knelt, she wept to hear that thickened voice, charged with emotion, express — surprisingly — his sorrow in that he had not 'given her in marriage to cause her an infinite grief'. And he, who all his life had seen himself Chief Player on a stage elaborately set, may not have been unmindful of this dramatic curtain-fall on a tag to wring the hearts of all who heard him: 'Promise me that you will be a kind and loving mother to my son, your brother, that little helpless child.'

Choked with sobs she promised. Drenched in tears she kissed his hand inert upon the covers. With a feeble gesture of impatience he dismissed her. He never had been moved by women's tears, and Mary had always been prone to turn herself into a Niobe. His hand was wet. He signed for one to wipe it.

His physicians and his gentlemen stood by in a huddle, wondering what next?

Cranmer was next, brought by Philip, sent to fetch him from his country house at Croydon. The King slept; and woke, with a rolling of his eyes at the dark recesses of his chamber. He stared, as if he saw — and may have seen — a phantasmal procession of cowled figures resurrected from the haunting memory of disembowelled Carthusians, whose grinning skulls still mouldered in grim warning, spiked on the parapet of London Bridge.

'All is lost!' And on those words, with one groaning last ejaculation, 'Monks! Monks! Monks!' he fell into a stupor; nor when Cranmer prayed beside him did he know or hear him there.

In the corridor Lord Hertford and Sir William Paget, Secretary of State, paced back and forth awaiting the signal that would decide the fate of the Duke of Norfolk who, at dawn on the morrow, must die — if the King lived. But more than the fate of a heretic duke hung in the balance of time: the fate of a nation with the rise to highest power of Lord Hertford, Edward Seymour, elder uncle of the King's son, Edward Prince.

The torches borne by halberdiers, ranged along the arrased walls, flickered on the spectre-pale features of Lord Hertford, flung a stalking shadow of his tall spare frame. Sir William Paget, adapting his short legs to those long strides, eyed Hertford askance to hear him tell, below breath, of revolt threatened among the lower orders; of injustice done, of wrongs fermenting that must be righted to secure for those, tyrannically shackled, a freedom of speech, of thought. 'Liberty,' he said; and again he said it, 'Liberty!'

From some distant steeple two chiming strokes rang out. Hertford halted, turned; and Paget too turned to see the door of the death chamber open.

One of the gentlemen, Master Pugh, stood with his hand on the latch, his head bowed. Hertford approached him.

'The King —'

'— is dead, my lord.'

Into Hertford's hooded eyes sprang a lightning gleam; from his lips, scarcely moving, a whisper, scarcely heard:

'Long live the King!'

SEVEN

On the morning of January 30, at Hertford Castle, where the Lady Elizabeth was at that time living with her brother Edward, she awoke in decided ill humour. She had been 'taken', she informed Mistress Katherine Ashley, her governess, 'with a mortal discomfort in her belly, that she had not closed her eyes until cock-crow'. This being so, and she in no fit case to attend her lessons, would her good 'Kat' make excuse for her to Mr. Cheke? She must lie abed until her trouble, which might keep her there all day, had passed.

To which Mrs. Ashley inimically replied that it was eight o' the clock, and His Highness, with their tutor Mr. Cheke, awaited Her Grace's attendance in the winter parlour.

'Then let them wait,' Her Grace gracelessly retorted; and pushing from her forehead the tousled sandy hair she grinned above the bedclothes. 'Tell Mr. Cheke as I bid you, that I'm sick to the stomach, and unless he'll have me vomit on his lexicon, he had better let me off. Besides, Edward is far behind me in the Orations, so I'll only have to wait for him. What's for my breakfast?'

Mrs. Ashley sniffed. 'If Your Grace is so sick to the stomach, I wonder you care to know what is for your breakfast.'

'Why, stupid, in course I must know, so full of the rumbles as I am that anything I may put down will come up, unless it should be what my stomach can take. A cup of orange water, good Kat, and — yes, a mutton collop. So go see to't. I'll join my brother when I am recovered. Not before.' Then, as Mrs.

Ashley, with a louder sniff, went to her bidding, Elizabeth called after her, 'Have you any fresh news of the King?'

Mrs. Ashley stayed her hand on the door-latch frigidly to say, 'No news of the King, Madame, more than we have heard these three days past, that His Majesty, alas, is slowly sinking.'

'Which means,' Elizabeth reprehensibly retorted, 'that if he's slowly sinking my uncle Norfolk will be sunk.'

'Madame!'

'Well?' Elizabeth snuggled deeper in her pillows. 'We all know what's coming to the duke, and what's come to his son, my cousin Surrey. Him first — God rest his soul! — and now his father. Heads off. Roll 'em down. Spike 'em up on London Bridge. Hooh!' She gave a shiver. 'A grey goose is walking on my grave. Lord save us, Kat, don't stare at me as I were headless, too! Go fetch me that collop and the orange water to drown the repetition,' again she grinned at Ashley's sour face, 'of those stewed eels I ate for supper.'

Meanwhile Edward, that 'little helpless child', was engaged in argument with Mr. Cheke concerning the new system of Greek pronunciation introduced by this inestimable scholar, late Provost of King's College, Cambridge.

'I prefer,' Edward said in his clear precise voice, 'the original pronunciation as used, we may presume, by Paul in the Epistles. For example, here,' he leafed through the well-worn pages of his testament, 'we have it, as Paul quotes in Corinthians I, 15 and 33,' he looked up quickly, 'a similar passage — correct me if I'm wrong, sir — as may be found in Plato.'

Mr. Cheke did not correct him. He held himself in silence, his austerely handsome features masked to conceal his astonishment, not yet staled by daily contact with the precocious mind of this youngster scarce out of the nursery: a mind that, as Mentor to so facile a Telemachus, delighted but also dismayed him. Where would such abnormal intelligence end? In a mad-house? Or as the wisest, most erudite — since Solomon — of kings?

'And that,' Edward meditatively pursued as he pored over the passage in the book, 'might well give rise to doubt as to their authenticity. But, for my part, I believe that Corinthians I, writ at Ephesus in 57, is mainly polemical, while Corinthians II, writ at Philippi in 58, is absolute *homologoumena.*'

'Your Highness…' Mr. Cheke hemmed behind a hand, then removed it to say, 'With every possible respect, that neither I, nor even you —' a delicate sarcasm tinged his words, lost upon Edward who was engrossed with St. Paul — 'are competent to pass opinion or debate upon the authorship of the Epistles as conceived by the greatest moral and spiritual teacher the world has ever known. Paul lends no sanction to theological controversialists who persist in rending Christendom asunder by pursuing the great truths of religion to speculative extremes.'

Edward's small button mouth slanted sideways; he slipped his tutor a look, half sly, wholly sage, as, with a wag of his flaxen fair head, he remarked dreamily: 'Yes … and what, sir, would Paul have to say to this present rending-asunder of Christendom?'

'*Omnia exeunt in mysterium,*' was the obscure answer to that; and, avoiding those wide-apart eyes, now turned full upon him, Mr. Cheke, in haste, added, 'However, we digress from our salient point and Your Highness's — ah — query. The Greek pronunciation, as modified by me,' said Mr. Cheke, with an inflation of his chest, 'is, I consider, more adaptable to English-speaking scholars, than the archaic —'

'Good morning, Mr. Cheke. I trust I have not kept you waiting.'

The Lady Elizabeth, seeming none the worse for her indisposition, stood in the doorway. She wore a dress of amber satin over a kirtle embroidered with green and white flowers, and looked — the involuntary thought may have startled Mr. Cheke — not unlike a flower herself: a flaming crocus, with that hair.

'Your Grace!' He rose, he bowed; Edward, whose feet swung three inches off the ground from his high chair, slid off it, but he did not bow. He stood, and resentfully said, 'You have kept us waiting a whole hour. Why are you so late?'

'Why?' She spread her hands. She was proud of her hands, narrow and long-fingered. Tom Seymour, that blond giant, Edward's uncle, who according to Kat Ashley was the most sought-after gentleman in England — by the ladies — had been heard to say, this again from Kat, that the Lady Elizabeth's hands were 'exquisite', and were she a few years older he would be moved to offer himself for one, or both of them. Which was a monstrous great impertinence, but Tom had always been impertinent — to tease her. So, not unmindful of her tutor's appraisement of herself in her new gown, poised deliberately under the window where the light would catch her hair — she was as proud of her hair as her hands — Elizabeth repeated, 'Why? Because I have been sadly indisposed and slept not a wink for the nightmare. Such a hideous dream.' Rapidly she improvised. 'I was flying through the air up, up into the sky —' more business with the hands — 'and a terrible fire-breathing dragon was after me and on my tail. And, just imagine! As I turned in my flight, hither, thither, like some magnetised desperate moth to wing straight at and be caught in his cruel clutching talons, I saw the dragon's face bearing down upon me, and believe me, Mr. Cheke — it was yours!' And with studied grace she moved to the vacant chair beside Edward, saying rapturously, 'O, but 'tis marvellous — even in a dream — to fly.'

'It may not always,' Edward said, 'be a dream to fly. Some time or some other time, and perhaps in our time, men may well fly in the air. Don't forget Leonardo da Vinci invented, and himself experimented with, a flying machine.'

'Yes, but his invention died with him, and also his flying machine — if ever it flew. What do you think, Mr. Cheke?' This with a flutter of her sandy lashes at her tutor who, manufacturing patience, strove to stifle these irrelevances.

'Madame, I think if the Lord God had intended that man should fly in the air, He would have given him wings. And now may I suggest you bring your attention to bear upon the subject for today.' Opening a heavy volume, bound in red leather and lettered in gilt, he placed it before her, saying, 'I have marked here a passage in the *De Libero Arbitrio* of Erasmus. Will Your Grace kindly construe?'

'But, sir,' with a limpid upward look Her Grace plaintively objected, 'I have already prepared for today the Oration XI on Astronomy.' A statement that was, in part, fictitious, since she had conned by heart this particular oration some six months past, a fact that she hoped Mr. Cheke had forgotten. 'May I remind you, sir, that if you did not wish me to prepare for today the Oration numero XI, I have mistook your instructions.'

And if by this dalliance she contrived further to delay her morning's lesson, a timely interruption served her purpose. The sound of galloping hooves along the drive brought her in a rush to the window.

'Jesu! Here's a company of horsemen —' she pressed her nose to the pane for a better view — 'led by Master Pugh of the household. What does he do here or want with us?' And regardless of Mr. Cheke's attempted protest: 'Madame, this is not the moment —' 'Edward, look,' she deftly intervened, 'there's four of them, or am I seeing double?'

Edward, no less loath than she to seize momentary advantage of respite from a session with Erasmus, joined her at the window. Heads bobbing, he peering and sucking in his underlip, she breathing down her nose, there they stood.

'What,' Elizabeth was pale, 'can this visit mean, so unexpected?' Protectively she put her arm about her brother's narrow shoulders.

He wriggled free, and told her, sulkily, 'It means my uncle Hertford's come. I see him in the rear. Last time he arrived "unexpected", he catechised me for two hours on the Exordium, Narratio, Divisio, and Confirmatio of the Orations, but —' complacently he smiled — 'he couldn't catch me out. If he thinks to put me through my paces now, I'll not be here.' Then, as he made for the door, it was opened by a servant announcing Master Pugh.

In his mud-splashed riding-coat, head bared, Philip knelt to the wondering Edward. 'Your...' A second's hesitation preceded the words, 'Your Royal Highness is requested by my Lord of Hertford that Your Grace and the Princess Elizabeth —' he rose, and with deepest homage bowed, and she caught her breath at that title so long denied her — 'shall be forthwith escorted hence to Enfield.'

It was late afternoon of the following day. In the great hall of the King's manor at Enfield, under the wide stone mullioned window that overlooked the gardens, dreary with wind-driven rain, the two children sat on the high oaken seat, their arms round each other for comfort.

The Earl of Hertford, who in chill, careful words had told of their father's death — which, for reasons best known to himself, he chose to withhold from them and from the people of England for thirty-six hours — had left them there alone. In his presence they had shed no tears. They heard him in cold silence, apparently unmoved. Only when the door closed on his exit, did Edward turn to his sister with the bleating cry, 'They'll separate us now!'

'They won't.' She hugged his thin little shuddering body, and at sight of the slow tears that trickled from his dazed blue eyes, so like their father's, her own tears fell. 'They daren't,' she sobbed. 'It won't make any diff — difference to us. We'll still have each other.'

'We — may not ha-have each other,' blubbered Edward. 'My un-uncle Hertford will see to that.' Then he squared himself, and, with unconscious dignity, drew away from her. 'But I, too,' he said, 'will see to that. I'll have you righted. Honoured, as my sister. I'll put you back in the Succession.'

'Don't,' sobbed Elizabeth, 'talk of the Succession, which can n-never affect me. You'll grow up and be a big strong man and marry and have sons. You'll be a good and wiser, better king than ever he —' Abruptly she stopped herself, swallowing words that must not be spoken; and taking his small slender hand in hers she held it to her lips. 'But you'll always be my own little brother.'

'As you,' snuffled Edward, 'will always be my own Sister Temperance.' His pet name for her; which they both found to be so very touching that their sobs redoubled, until, having wept himself dry, Edward raised his fair head from where he had tucked it under Elizabeth's chin. His tears had wetted her chest that, according to the fashion of the day, was left uncovered. The gold cross she wore suspended from a necklet had marked his soft round cheek. He rubbed it, saying solemnly: 'I've just thought of something. Other than Henry VI, who was a baby in arms when he came to the throne, I'm the youngest king that's ever been a King of England.'

Elizabeth wiped her eyes on her sleeve. 'Are you sure? How old was our great-uncle Edward the Fifth when his wicked uncle, Hunchback Richard, the Plantagenet, murdered him and his brother York?'

'Thirteen,' came the prompt answer. 'Exactly the same age as you.' Then with a giggle, swiftly quenched in his damp ball of a handkerchief, Edward said, 'I hope *my* wicked uncle won't murder me.'

But Elizabeth did not hear him. Her thoughts, like wasps buzzing round a honey-pot, had settled on the promise — or as near as made no matter to a promise — from *Eduardus Rex,* Supreme Head of the Church, Defender of the Faith, and never mind that he was only nine years old: *I'll put you back in the Succession* ... If the King, their father, had not already named her in his will as successive after Mary, and if Edward should not marry — or, if he did, should have no children — and since Mary was far too old at thirty *ever* to be married — then, in the event of Edward and Mary dying without issue and if she outlived them both, then — O glory! — she, Elizabeth, would be Queen.

Her lips parted, her eyes clear and shining, blue as bluest water after rain, fixed in space; her long hands, spread either side of her, whitened and tightened on the oaken window seat.

'What's amiss?' gasped Edward. 'You look so strange. What do you see?' Their father, risen, in his cere-clothes, a swollen horrifying phantom, floating in mid-air, awfully to beckon, or console?

Craning forward shrinkingly, Edward stared ahead, as did she, at the hall screens, behind where might lurk a grisly Presence. 'What,' repeated Edward, clutching at her arm, 'do you see?'

'I see...' and, as she turned to gather him close, that strange rapt look was still about her, 'I see the dawn of a new era, of a great and splendid age, with the coming and the crowning of...' she whispered it, 'of ... you!'

He had come, and he was crowned. Mounted on his gaily caparisoned white palfrey, he rode in procession through the City of London. Every house was hung with tapestries, with pennons, banners, garlands; every window waved its brightly coloured flags; and in the shouting streets a multitude were thronged to see him pass. So very fair, so very small was he, weighed down by the great golden crown, too heavy for a child's head, that the hearts of women swelled at sight of him; men, husky-voiced, God-blessed him as, with a care for that massive emblem of his sovereignty, one hand lifted to hold it from slipping, he gravely acknowledged the deep-throated cheers. And not a man of them who would not have laid down his life for him.

In his cloak of cloth of gold, which swung as he rode to reveal the white-and-silver glitter of his jewel-starred doublet, this sprig of a boy stood for the symbol, not only of a new-sprung monarchy, but of rebirth, a renaissance. The bloodstained tyranny of years had vanished; and now it was as if an orchard, blighted by December's frosts, had miraculously blossomed overnight. He, their child-king, was England's hope, and England's future, raised, in one glorious sun-burst, from the wintered ashes of the past.

So, in 'most royal and goodlie wise', he rode on through his capital to his Palace of Westminster.

It had been a long and trying ordeal to leave him speechless, overwrought, a solemn pale little boy, with no appetite for the Coronation banquet prepared for him in Westminster Hall. There, still wearing the Crown of St. Edward, he sat between Archbishop Cranmer and his Uncle Hertford, who had lost no time in proclaiming himself Lord Protector, Duke of Somerset. And there — we have his word for it in his journal, that, at Mr. Cheke's instigation, he kept for the better part of his short reign, and for posterity — *came in Sir John Dimock, Champion, and made his Challenge, and so the King drank to him and he had the Cup...* Later in the evening were *justs* (jousts) *and after, Order was taken for all his Servants being with his Father and being with the prince, and the Ordinary and Unordinary were appointed...*

Among them Philip Pugh, as Gentleman-in-Waiting to His Majesty the King.

It was evident that Somerset intended to keep his royal charge under strictest supervision, to which means those few of the late King's household had been carefully selected as unlikely to foster dissension with or against the autocratic guardianship of the King, his nephew.

Judicial enquiry elicited that while Master Pugh stayed privately adherent to the older Faith, he was too well-schooled a courtier, or so Somerset surmised, to lead the little king astray from the straight and narrow path of Reform.

As for those others of the Privy Chamber, they were Somerset's own particular toadies and considerably senior in years to Philip Pugh. Tom Wroth, who had got himself married, was no longer attached to the Court, but his father, Sir

Thomas, a staunch Reformer, had been reinstated by Somerset and created a Knight of the Carpet, with some fifty others, on the King's accession.

In February Edward was returned to his studies, not now to be shared with his sister 'Temperance'. Nor, as he had prophesied, would they be allowed to live together. She had been carried off to Chelsea in the care of their father's widow; and to Chelsea, through the spring and summer of that year, went Master Pugh, riding back and forth from the King's Palace of Westminster. That he had always been a favourite of Queen Katherine Parr might well have accounted for his frequent visits, which had surely naught to do with the fact that Mr. Gynkes had gratified his lady's wish for a house, nothing of 'a cottage', yet very much in the country — at Chelsea.

On the last morning in May of that Coronation year, Philip rode to Chelsea Manor with a letter from young Edward to Queen Katherine. She had recently returned from a few days' sojourn at St. James's Palace, ostensibly to satisfy herself that Edward, on whom she doted, was well cared for. There might, however, have been a more personal reason for her visit to London in view of daily calls at the palace, of sundry mercers and mantua-makers, which had given rise to whispers that Her Grace was about to discard her mourning black for colours. Rumour even went so far as to hint that the Queen would soon go bedecked as a bride. What! And Old Harry scarce cold?

Yes, but she'd served him well and kept her head — though she had lost her heart — to be served in her turn by another who had waited for her long enough and was content to wait no longer.

Yet, if any such talk, with bawdy additions and meaningful winks of the eye, reached the ear of the Queen, it did not deter her from buying new gowns nor from her purpose, in the main, to make sure that Edward drank his three pints of milk daily and was not overworked at his studies.

But, despite the love he inspired from those in close contact about him, this strange, self-reliant, self-contained little boy seemed incapable of more than the coolest response to it. Certain it is he was fondly attached to his 'sweet sister Temperance', even though a degree of sarcasm may have prompted his own special name for her. And equally certain is it that while he confessed to 'a liking' for his small cousin Jane Grey, the adoration of his sister Mary left him cold.

But if any deeper emotion were kindled in his dispassionate heart, it was for his page and the friend of his bosom, Barnaby Fitzpatrick, a youngster from Ireland, some two years older than he, and the son of the Lord of Upper Ossory. After Barnaby, a fair second in the running, came Philip Pugh, on whom he relied to carry messages to Elizabeth at Chelsea and to smuggle back her answers, since not only did Somerset keep them rigidly apart, but would not permit them to write to each other. Besides which Master Pugh stood as buffer between Edward and the Duchess of Somerset, his uncle's wife, whom he heartily detested. At her insistence the Protector docked him of pocket money that he had not enough wherewith to make gifts to his servants; also the duchess interfered in the daily routine of his life and the choosing of his clothes.

'She actually,' complained the King to Philip, 'has ordered a tailor to come here and let down the sleeves of my doublet. I've grown apace these last six months, that my fists stick out a good three inches — look.' He showed his thin little wrists protruding from his cuff-edge. 'Let down!' Edward's underlip jutted ferociously. 'What think you, sir, of a king who's not allowed a new suit when he's outgrown his old one? I tell you what —' he came close to whisper — 'you bring me your tailor. I'll order a suit for myself, and let the duchess go hang — the old hell-hag.'

It is unlikely that Philip managed to gain for the King his desired new suit without some heated opposition from the duchess, but the fact remains that a suit was made and paid for, not by Edward nor the duke, but, as we have reason to believe, by Master Pugh.

So it would seem that Philip was in highest favour with the King, and also with the King's nurse, Mother Jack. She too shared the monarch's detestation of his aunt, the Duchess of Somerset, who, as Mother Jack would have it, wore her husband's breeks to over-ride him and another, higher than the angels, she could name. But never in this world would she see her precious ''Ots' put down by a she-wolf in petticoats. No! Not though she be drawn and quartered for speaking her mind, and as for a Protector — what protection, Mother Jack would wish to know, was given to that holy cherub, kept little better than a jailbird and he the Lord's Anointed — and more — as was said at the birth of His Grace that an infant John the Baptist, God-sent, had come to bless them.

These saintly attributes, however, did not restrain Edward from venting, and in no mean terms, his disapproval of Mother Jack's eternal cooings and croakings, her plasters and purges and physics, to try his celestial patience. On such occasions His Majesty would be moved to pipe a volley of right royal oaths, the equal in choice and quality of any bellowed by his father, and improved upon by frequent repetition in his hearing, from the repertoire of his younger uncle, the loud-voiced lusty Lord High Admiral, Tom Seymour. And when Mother Jack dared venture that such language was ill-becoming to His Grace, her precious 'Ots, she would be told with shattering frigidity: 'I am not your precious 'Ots, whatever that may mean, but which I suspect derives in *your* pronunciation from the word *Herz*, as I am so persistently addressed by my good aunt, Anne of Cleves.'

To which Mother Jack would comfortably rejoin, 'God save Your Grace, whatever it may mean is only love. Now come let me change your hosen. They be wringing wet. You've run out in the grass after the rain with that mischeevious Master Fitzpatrick.'

'Mischievous, not mischeevious,' corrected Edward coldly. 'You can't even speak the King's English. And I did not "run out", as you put it, in the grass with Barnaby. I was walking on the lawns with Mr. Pugh.' Then, while Mother Jack knelt to remove his hose and dry his feet, Edward gave a playful kick at her ample bosom. 'Here, is it true — for if anyone can pick up all the gossip of the Court it is yourself — that my uncle Tom Seymour is to marry the Queen Dowager?'

'Now where in the world —' ejaculated Mother Jack, sitting back on her heels and looking sideways and all ways, but never once at the smiling Edward — 'did Your Highness hear such monstrous calumny and lies?'

'That,' said Edward, 'is what I'm asking you.'

'Let the Lord God be my judge,' Mother Jack raised eyes and hands to heaven, 'if I would lend ears to —'

'So,' coolly came the interruption, 'it *is* true.'

'May I be struck dumb,' expostulated Mother Jack, 'if —'

'No such luck,' Edward muttered, 'nor deaf neither.' He slid off his chair and bent to adjust his jewelled garters. 'They're too loose,' he grumbled, 'they don't hold up my hose.' Bending closer to examine, he said, 'These hosen are of coarsest quality.

No wonder they tickle. Who told you to put me in thick woollen hose like any hind?'

'How now, my poppet,' mendaciously soothed Mother Jack, 'they be of finest lamb's wool. My Lord Protector bought half a dozen pair of a journeyman from Norwich.'

'Lamb's wool!' scoffed Edward, as he rubbed one itching leg against the other. 'The thrown-out shearings of a lousy old ram, more like. If I know my Lord Protector,' the childish mouth thinned to an unchildish sneer, 'he bargained for and bought 'em cheap.' And rounding on Mother Jack, still kneeling to tighten his garters, he told her, 'Go fetch me Mr. Pugh.'

Mr. Pugh was fetched, and handed Edward a letter written by the Queen before she left St. James's that same morning. Edward read it through and sighing, said, 'She wants me to stay with her at Chelsea. If I could! But,' dolefully he shook his head, 'I can't. The Duke won't let me.' Then his little peaked face brightened. 'Maybe my Uncle Tom could persuade him, if 'twere only for a week. One week out of fifty-two in the year isn't much to ask.' He glanced down at the closely penned page. 'I'd best reply to this at once. I'll write it in Latin. She'll like that. The Queen was the first to teach me Latin when I was young.'

Philip's mouth twitched. 'Exactly so, Sire,' he said gravely.

'I find it easier to write in Latin than in English,' the King confided, 'because none in this land of mine has taught me how to spell my own language correctly. In fact, none — not even Cranmer — seems to follow any certain rules of etymology.' He shook his head, saying severely, 'I'll have to look into this. There must be boys of my age all over the country, in especial among the lower orders, who can't write, much less spell their own names. I'd like to found schools to teach boys etymology, and I'll call them grammar schools. Yes! That's what I'll call them, King Edward's Grammar Schools, if —' he said, distantly gazing — 'or when,' he added quickly, 'I grow up.'

He crossed to his desk, placed under the window looking out over the river. This desk of his went with him everywhere, from Whitehall to Westminster, and to his country houses. He kept the key always about him, and none but himself was permitted to open it. Covered in black velvet, it held, besides a silver inkstand and two silver gilt sand-casters, a cypress wood box containing his small hoard of treasures, among which were a gold brooch with a centre of white agate; some triangular gold buttons, a lock of his sister Elizabeth's hair, and, most cherished of all, a horseshoe mounted in copper, cast from a favourite deceased and much-mourned pony. Finally, the remains of a stick of eringo — the sea-holly — very stale, surreptitiously pilfered from his Coronation banquet, and this he nibbled while, painstakingly, he wrote to his 'Most Honourable and entirely Beloved Mother':

As I was so near to you and expected to see you everyday, I writ no letter to you but being urged by your request I would not longer abstain from writing first, that I may do what is acceptable to you and now answer the letter you writ me from St. James's, in which you set before my eyes the great love you bear my Father the King of most noble memory —

Having got thus far Edward stayed his quill, glancing up at Philip and round about to see if Mother Jack were near, which she was not, having left the room to dry his wet stockings. And, satisfied that none but Barnaby was present and engrossed in combing the hair of a spaniel pup, a gift to the King from his Uncle Tom Seymour, Edward mysteriously said,

'I don't know what's afoot but I can guess. I tried to get Mother Jack to talk, and though she gave me naught of any matter, she turned so red of face and was so strong in her denial that she wouldn't have deceived a cow. What I really want to know is — *why* should the Queen profess unbounded love for my father four months after his death, which she never has professed to me before — and all this talk of godliness and learning of the Scriptures — as she writes here…' He scanned over the letter and beckoned Philip to come close and read over his shoulder. 'You see? She must have something on her mind that she don't wish to tell me — yet.' He nodded sagely with a sideways look at Philip's deliberately blank surprised stare. 'But I'll have the truth of it, I will.' Another nod. 'So let it bide.'

And, dipping his quill in the inkstand, he wrote:

Cease not to love and read the scriptures, for in the first you shew the duty of a good wife and subject…

Again he paused and called: 'Hey, Barnaby! Bring me a Latin dictionary. I'm stuck for a verb. And do stop currying that pup. You've fetched out half his hairs already. He'll be bald as a coot.'

The dictionary was brought, and the pup, released from his combing, promptly made a puddle on the floor where the rushes had been cleared and a rug from Persia laid, a present to the King from Anne of Cleves.

'Now look what you've done!' cried Edward. 'My new carpet. I *said* not to lay it on the floor. The table is the proper place for it.'

'Faith, then, an is it meself,' retorted Barnaby, who after three years in England had not lost his native brogue, 'that Your Grace 'ud be tellin' has done it? Will I mop it off?'

'You can mop yourself off,' was the grinning rejoinder, 'or stand whipping-boy to the pup.' For Barnaby's duties as Page of Honour included the taking of corporal punishment due to the monarch for misdemeanours as adjudged by the Protector, and which could not be administered to the King's person. So, the mopping-up accomplished under Edward's supervision, he proceeded with his letter:

Wherefore if there be anything when I may do you a kindness either in word or deed I will do it, willingly. Vale, *this thirtieth of May, Whitehall.*

'So, sir,' to Philip, 'I can't say fairer, can I? Will you see if I have made any errors?'

Philip, supernaturally solemn, read it through and returned it saying, 'It is most excellently writ, Sire, and to my knowledge, without fault.'

'Yes,' agreed Edward, 'I'm sound enough in Latin. Not so good in Greek, though, thanks to this new-fangled pronunciation of my tutor. What o'clock is it now?'

'Near upon five hours, Your Majesty.'

'So late? And too late to carry this letter to Chelsea today. You'll have to take it tomorrow.'

So on the morrow Philip rode to Chelsea and delivered Edward's letter to one of the Queen's gentlewomen, Lady Tyrwhitt. She, in common with other ladies of the Court, regarded Master Pugh with more favour than his looks — which none could call handsome — might warrant; and this despite that he appeared to be impervious to invitation or pursuit. What, then, was the secret of the flutters he aroused in the breasts of young maids, old maids, and matrons in attendance on the Royal Dowager? Could it be, as was said, that Master Pugh's affections were otherwise engaged? Or — and here it was whispered — that he cared more for his own sex than for the fairest of women? For why should he stand so politely aloof from, and indifferent to the wiles of, feminine charms? Yet even such as he might be brought to heel, or to his knees. And full-armed with the huntress's equipment of soft looks and toothful smiles, Lady Tyrwhitt, a buxom brunette in her forties, suggested to Master Pugh that he should wait awhile in her chamber, while the Queen wrote a reply to His Majesty's letter for Master Pugh to carry back with him to Whitehall.

To which Master Pugh made answer, equally smiling, that he would return in an hour or two for the Queen's reply. The day was so fair, the air so balmy, he was minded to take a ride across country. He bowed himself out, and Lady Tyrwhitt hastened to Mrs. Ashley with a tale of a certain High-and-Mighty Jackanapes who rides head in air — 'so fair and balmy' — for a fall!

It must be confessed that little love was lost between Lady Tyrwhitt and Mrs. Ashley, due to certain hints dropped by Her Ladyship concerning the Lady Elizabeth's Grace and Thomas Seymour, the King's uncle. Yes, Mrs. Ashley could not readily forgive nor forget Lady Tyrwhitt's tattle of an incident she vowed she had witnessed in these very gardens of the Queen's manor — how the Lord High Admiral had tumbled the Lady Elizabeth that she sprawled on the grass with him a-top of her. Which, without pause or breath, Mrs. Ashley had refuted as a treasonable libel, seeing that the Lady Elizabeth was not only the King's sister but second in succession, and she but a child not yet turned fourteen, and His Lordship devoted to children to fondle and tease Her Ladyship's Grace. As he fondled and teased little Lady Jane Grey, who lodged here in the house with her cousin Elizabeth to be schooled together by this latest of the royal tutors, Mr. Ascham.

'And,' said Mrs. Ashley, sour-sweet as honey laced with lemon, in reply to Lady Tyrwhitt's complaint of Master High-and-Mighty Pugh, 'he *will* ride for a fall, very sure, but — not an he ride a brood mare. A young filly is more to his taste, to mount and to manage and test of her mettle to carry him — and,' Mrs. Ashley expanded, 'such an one, or I'm the whore o' Babylon, is stalled not a hundred miles hence.'

This, the first that Lady Tyrwhitt or any of her kind had heard tell of Master Pugh's fallibility, piqued her interest enough to guard her tongue from the retort, hot on the tip of it, to put this overbearing Ashley in her place. And between the two of them a pretty hotch-potch was set a-boil to burn the ears of Master Pugh, were they not burning hot enough already to the tune of words spoken in farewell on his last visit to Chelsea: 'Come soon again, Philip, I — we — are always glad — so very glad — to see you.' Nor yet was it those words, sweet though they were to hear, that sent his heart soaring high as the lark overhead, as he rode along a bridle-path through a meadow foaming with the flower of the hawthorn. Not those words, but the look that went with them: wistful, haunting, fugitive, as of a note in music.

Crossing Blandel Bridge, used chiefly for pack-horse traffic, and called by Chelsea villagers the 'Bloody Bridge' for its ill repute as a haunt of highwaymen, he sighted a horseman whom he recognised as the King's uncle, Thomas Seymour, now Lord of Suddey, raised to the peerage on Edward's accession. As Philip turned his mare aside to allow the other to pass along the narrow way, he was boisterously hailed.

'Hola, Master Pugh! What do you here? Are you come from the manor? How fares the King?'

The complement of his pietistic brother, the Protector, was Tom Seymour: a magnificent fellow, full-blooded, gold-bearded, and possessed of charm irresistible to women, but likely not so favoured of the men.

Ignoring the first of these three questions hurled without pause for reply, Philip answered the last of them curtly: 'I am happy to report the King is well, my lord.'

'And that is well indeed!' His Lordship's broadening smile showed every tooth in his head. 'But if so be it that the little lad should stand in want of a few nobles — twenty, forty, shall we say? — since my brother, the Protector, sees fit — and rightly, mark you — to keep tight hold on the King's expenditure, you, sir, must acquaint me of His Majesty's requirements, which will be instantly supplied.'

'As your lordship's good intent,' Philip told him hardily, 'will be instantly delivered to the King.'

'But not to the King's elder uncle, who might not concur —' Seymour's smile slipped — 'with my good intent. Good day to you, sir. And what a day! Full of the ripeness of spring's greeting to young summer.' His stallion, fretting at the bit, pawed at the path with a rolling eye for Philip's mare, a fiery, slender-hocked creature, her skin satin-smooth, neck arched and red nostrils a-flare at the stallion's advances. 'A day for courting!' exclaimed his exuberant lordship, 'as my lad here would testify were he free — to make free with your pretty lass.' So they parted; he to the manor house, Philip on to the village of Chelsea.

Giving his mare her head he galloped her over the tussocky turf skirting a meadow carpeted with buttercups and the wild parsley. Honeybees murmured in the long lush grass among the wine-dark clover; bird song was riotous where ash and elm and willow lined the river bank; while, from afar, insistent, came the cuckoo's deepened call to join the choir. 'A day for courting', truly; but the sweetness was gone out of it for Philip, musing on Tom Seymour's fulsome message to the King. The motive prompting that offer of 'twenty — forty nobles,' was clearly manifest as one of many other bribes by which the younger uncle sought to woo and win the confidence of England's crowned child. *A bone between quarrelling dogs,* thought Philip, *each a-snarl, fangs bared to grab the Protectorate prize.* Yet despite his mistrust of the flamboyant Seymour, Philip would have sooner seen him the King's guardian than his hag-ridden brother, dominated by a wife who looked to seize possession, not only of Edward, but of Edward's kingdom. She had already taken to herself the jewels and plate bequeathed by the King's father to Katherine, the Queen, along with her favourite manor of Fasterne. Pity 'twas, reflected Philip, that the boy had none about him, save himself, who was wholly disinterested; for not one of the Protector's Council could be trusted to act for the good of the King or the nation. 'O, but 'tis a world,' said he, 'of shiftless unrealities and villainous corruptions! They who preach of God and murder him in one foul breath are constant to no laws but those they make, to break…' Then he shook his shoulders, as if to shake away the thought of that, reined in his mare to cool her, and turned her head toward the village.

Along the cobbled street he rode, and out again into the highway, where soon he came upon a wooden gate set in a privet hedge. Here he dismounted, hitched the mare's bridle to the gate-post, and walked up a stone-flagged path, bordered either side with every kind of flower.

The house, of irregular frontage, high-gabled, made no pretension to decorative carving as did the house in Water Lane; an old house this, but bearing evidence of recent alteration and improvement in the red-tiled roof and haphazard replacement of half-timbered brick for clay and rubble between the wooden cross-beams.

The front door stood ajar, giving a glimpse of a low-ceiled spacious hall; here, on its threshold, Philip halted, his head turned sharply to the sound of a dear young scolding voice beyond the hedge.

'Jobbernowl! I told you trim it — not *cut* it. A murrain on you for an idle lout! Did you ever see a peacock with so poor a spread? A century has gone to grow this bird, and now you've lopped him of his tail that he looks, poor devil, to be moulting. Give me the shears, I'll clip him myself an he be not too far gone. You go and weed me that bed. There's a mort o' woodbine strangling those larkspurs. And don't you pull a face at me or I'll bash yours to a pulp against yon wall.'

Philip strolled across the strip of lawn enclosed by a hedge, nearly as high as himself, and looked over it. She stood with her back to him, and, towering above her, the dark spreading shape of a yew — 'which,' said Philip softly, 'may well pass muster as a peahen until his tail sprouts again.'

She swung round, her face aglow.

'How long have you been eavesdropping? Did you hear me rate that whoreson? Certes, had I razed his ears with these —' she brandished the shears — 'he'd have got no less than his due for fouling my fine bird, which was planted here when men fought for the red and white rose. Come in, Phil, and give me a hand, if you know aught — which I don't — of topiary.'

'How,' Philip cocked an eyebrow at the wall of box, 'do I get through?'

'Go round to the end of it. There you'll find an inlet.'

But though he found the inlet, and joined her in a formal garden bedded out between broad gravel paths with gilly-flowers, larkspurs, and a wealth of pinks that filled the air with dove-sweet scent, she did not press him further to assist her in topiary.

The noonday sun beat down on her bare head, drew tiny beads of moisture from her upper lip and forehead. She passed her hand across it, saying, 'Warm it is today — too warm for me to spruce up this poor fellow. Marry!' She stepped back a pace or two, considering. 'He sure is translated — docked of his prideful tail by that Satan's imp to turn him hen — as you so rightly have it. Was there not a youth in ancient Greece of whom a nymph became enamoured and prayed the gods to change his sex? Yet why,' Jocosa shifted the shears from one hand to another, 'she should have wished him a woman, I've never understood, nor can I remember his name.'

'Hermaphroditus, son of Mercury and Venus, who bathed himself in a fountain over which the nymph, Salmacis, presided — allow me to relieve you of these,' he took the shears from her, 'or you too will be docked — of a finger. And Salmacis,' Philip airily resumed, 'became, as you say, so enamoured of the youth that she attempted to seduce him, but he would not be seduced. He stayed immune to her desire, until in desperation, she being in such case, poor girl, that she was nigh to frenzy, she prayed the gods that he and she should be united in one body. Her prayers were answered. And so —' his eyes weighed on hers with that in them to bring to her face a warmth not of the sun — 'since ever the world was young, man and woman have been drawn together with just that same longing to be merged in one, a single entity. Thus it was in the beginning, and so it will be until — the end.'

'A … pretty fairytale,' said Jocosa, out of breath. 'Shall we sit awhile in the shade?'

Along a pleached alley to a seat on a grassy mound beneath a sycamore, she led him. There they sat, he humming a little tuneless tune with a smile close about his lips; hers were parted as if to speak, yet no words came. For now, as always, when these two should find themselves together, their words went halt and limping, and their elusive glances, from temptation, fled, as is the way of star-crossed lovers who may speak of everything but love.

So it was all of Geoffrey Pugh and Dame Matilda and of Sprowston, and, 'What of this strife,' Jocosa asked on safer ground, 'that I hear is worsening between the landlords and the tenants up and down the eastern counties, from Norwich City to Lincoln and Cambridge?'

'No worse, maybe, than has always been,' Philip said, 'and long before our time. Strife is bred with us in Norfolk and the Fens. My father has been writing me these ten years of discontent betwixt the overlords and peasantry.'

'He — Gynkes — my husband, has had some later news —' began Jocosa; then she paused, for at that moment a long lean shadow in the grass preceded him who cast it. In his arms he held a little cat, pitifully mewing, its fur wet and clotted with blood.

'O, but see — only see!' Too disturbed to acknowledge Philip's greeting, Master Gynkes recounted how he had chanced on a group of village lads, 'out there,' he gestured vaguely, 'on the green, afore the church, where they had torn down the sacred Image of Our Saviour and were about to crucify this poor innocent on the Holy Tree. And,' said he, tearfully, 'those villains — would you believe? — had nails and mallets ready for the deed, having tied a stone round its neck, and when I came upon them there, albeit half strangled though it was, it fought like a lion for its life. Yes, and they — they cried out against Our Lord with mocking jibes and jeers for what they called idolatry and the worship of plaster images, and —' Gynkes was sobbing now — 'they reviled Her, Our Blessed Lady, God's own Mother. So then I smote about me and cursed them roundly, yes, I did — naming them spawn of Lucifer, but to no avail till I offered them my purse with all it contained, and I took of them this poor one in exchange. They followed me with hue and cry and stone slinging which caught me here — and here —' He bent to his shin bone and ankle, where stains of red had soaked his yellow hose. 'I wonder you did not hear their noise, which followed me all the way home.'

Jocosa sprang up. 'Are they there now? If so, we'll —'

'No,' he shook his head. 'They took to their heels when our men came out to hie them off. Good morrow, Master Pugh,' as if only just aware of him, Gynkes offered a wan smile. 'You must pardon — I've been greatly put about. I'll go in,' he said, 'and tend the cat.'

'And I'll tend you.' Jocosa glanced aside at Philip, who was on his feet.

'Sir,' he said hotly, 'that which you have witnessed is but one more of many like instances arisen from the New Learning that blasphemes the Word of God and of His Son, and puts to the torture innocent victims, not only such as this poor little creature, but men who uphold the Faith of the one and only Church. What of Friar Forrest — he who was priest to the late King's first and lawful wife, Queen Katherine? Did not Cranmer roast him to slow death? Yes! he roasted him alive in an iron cradle over the fire to which he was condemned for adherence to the Pope and denial of the King's supremacy.'

A rash outburst, this, on the part of a courtier who must never too freely voice his opinions, religious or political, but conserve a strict neutrality concerning them. That, as Philip had been schooled, was the order of the late King's day; but now the old order was changed. Under the Protector, free discussion was not only tolerated but encouraged. Somerset's sympathies were democratic; his motive, in principle, humane. His clemency, however, did not prove entirely successful in an age just emerging from barbaric superstition. No sooner had he taken over governance of Edward, than Henry's ruthless laws, the Acts of Six Articles and the Statutes of Treason, were repealed, to result in religious confusion. Released from the tyrant's oppressive decrees, processions of outcast, now jubilant, friars and monks went chanting through the streets, while at every corner their Protestant rivals out-bawled them with the Gospel. It was a bloodless feud between two parties: the one determined to restore the holy images to their mutilated churches with the reading of the Mass, the other equally insistent on the service of Reform by way of Cranmer's Prayer Book.

Thus Philip, who for many years had held himself in, now let himself out with a vehemence which, six months before, might have brought him to the same death as that of Friar Forrest. Then, at the fear-stricken look in the pale eyes of Master Gynkes, and his timid shrinking from this tirade, which he may have thought to be directed at himself, Philip added gently, 'Yet you, sir, are proven valiant in your attempt to crush such sacrilege.'

'No,' Gynkes said sadly, 'not valiant. I am not brave. I was sore affrighted, but less for my own safety than for my little brother's lest he be put to suffer on the cross. There, then, I'll comfort you. 'Tis Friday, there'll be fish…'

Drooling to the cat he went indoors. Jocosa followed, saying low to Philip, 'You, too, go in with us. Poor soul, he'll be mopish for a week in cause of this. You see how it is? When I married him,' she whispered, 'he was inclined, by persuasion or example, to Reform, but now I've weaned him from it and he is as staunch as we are to the Church.'

Later, when his wife had bathed and bound his hurts that indeed were of the slightest, Gynkes insisted that Philip take a cup of wine with him before returning to the manor. A trestle-board with a flagon and two cups was set beneath the sycamore, and seated there, the monkey on his shoulder, his protégé upon his knee, and smelling strong of fish, Master Gynkes treated Philip to a rambling account of a recent visit to Lord Rich, his sister's husband.

This one-time tradesman-cum-Solicitor-General had lately acquired the Chancellorship, grabbed from Wriothesley, thrown out of office as the sole member of the council who had dared protest against Somerset's Protectorate, to get himself the earldom of Southampton for his pains.

'My brother, the Lord Chancellor,' Gynkes announced with naive pomposity, 'is loud in his praise of Duke Somerset. A kindly gentleman, in truth, and an honest, rightly named Protector of the King and the King's people.'

Philip, preserving inimical silence, had one eye on the house for Jocosa; she had excused herself from joining them on pretext of baking a pie. 'Yes,' resumed Gynkes, 'I was saying there are those, my Lord Chancellor no less, who — No, Jeremy, hands off.' This to the monkey that had run down his arm with unamiable attention to the cat. 'Mind your eyes — he'll scratch 'em out an you pull his tail — or is it she? Tis hard to tell at this young age, scarce out of kittenhood. I was saying — now, Jeremy, will you have me slap you? 'Tis a sad knave,' Gynkes supplemented, as he refilled his guest's cup. 'I was saying — Now what *was* I saying?' He knit his brows in an immense effort of concentration. 'Ah, yes, that, as my Lord Rich hath it, the Protector looks to advantage the common folk by endeavouring to lend too gentle an ear to their plaints. Which now reminds — Sir, would you be so good as to change place with me? — Jeremy, you rogue, go to! — or he'll give this little one no peace; I've never known him froward nor jealous of new members of my family. He was always loving-kind and gentle to my bear. You remember my poor bear?' Gynkes sighed heavily. 'He died of his injuries, after all my care of him. If you will kindly take my seat, sir — so — and we'll sit Jeremy aside you, so —'

And when the change of place had been effected, to all save for Philip's content, Gynkes resumed, as if no interruption had occurred — 'which reminds me of some arguefying from my brother's guest at table, a Serjeant-at-law who hails from your county of Norfolk, Master Pugh, with a nonsuch name as of —' He clicked his tongue impatiently — 'a plague on my forgetting! — as some sort of a flower.'

'Flowerdew?' suggested Philip, sidling from Jeremy, now busy in pursuit of fleas.

'Yes.' Gynkes passed his arm through Philip's, gazing close into his face with an earnestness that scarcely warranted the information, 'Flowerdew it was. A winsome name, but not a winsome fellow, sir, believe me. He spoke of — no, I recollect it was the Chancellor who spoke of an Act to be considered — ' he glanced nervously around — 'to do with the branding of vagrants to make of them slaves. Yes, slaves, they said. And this Serjeant Flowerdew was most in favour of the Act, and then did my Lord Chancellor praise him for upholding it and then I said, only they heeded me not, no more than a fly on the wall,' Gynkes smiled, gazing down as he stroked, head to tail, the now purring cat, 'which is the way of these wise ones who know so much and yet do know so little, and think that I know less. For look you, sir,' emphatically he nodded, 'those who keep their ears and eyes open and mouths shut learn more than those who talk. Therefore, did I take note of their remarks as I heard them, seeing that this Serjeant doth hail from nigh to your home Master Pugh, and he made brag of having fenced about and enclosed much common land along the way to Norwich; and did boast also of his despoilment of a certain Abbey Church in that vicinity some years ago. But never tell to living soul,' he laid a finger to his lips, 'one word of this. Have I your promise?'

'Yes, indeed,' said Philip heartily. An easy promise, having gathered but the merest gist of this account since Jeremy's proximity and a consequent itch in that region of his person which, short of stripping himself of his breeks, he would be unable to investigate, was causing him poignant discomfort. 'And now, sir,' furtively he scratched and got to his feet, wriggling his legs, 'I must leave you.'

'What! So soon?' Gynkes, too, was on his feet clutching the cat, as the monkey, in one flying leap, sprang from his arm to a branch of the sycamore. There, by its tail, it swung.

'Sure, the creature,' muttered Gynkes, 'is demoniacal. Nay, now, Jeremy, come down — I say come *down*! Jesu Mary,' he wailed, 'if he's not fixed himself to the topmost height of it, and we've not a ladder tall enough to reach...'

During which diversion, while Gynkes, at the foot of the tree, alternately cajoled, entreated, and threatened the diabolic Jeremy, Philip made good his escape. Avoiding the main exit from the house, he passed by the buttery door and was waylaid by Jocosa, her arms bared to the elbow and powdered white with flour.

'My cook,' she said, 'has taken him a high day to go bury his aunt, the seventh of his family he's buried in six months. I told him an there'd be one more 'twould be himself, and I'd see him quartered first afore he be put down!' Then, joining her laughter to Philip's, she said, 'I had hoped you'd stay to dinner. There's carp, stewed by the cook before he went, and a prime eel pie of my baking. You were always partial to eel pie. Must you leave us?'

Between a second and a second their eyes met.

'Not of my will,' Philip said, low, softly, 'would I leave you … ever.'

Or so she thought he said, but could not be sure since he held his voice on a breath, in-drawn. And not another word was spoken as they walked together through the courtyard to the gate, where she watched him mount his mare and ride away.

'No letter from the Queen in reply to mine?' Standing square before his gentleman, one hand to the jewelled hilt of his trifling dagger, his feet in their black velvet shoes planted wide, his whole pose and attitude was oddly reminiscent of his father's, as was the sullen, small protruding underlip. 'Not a message,' rapped out Edward, 'to the King?'

'Only, Sire, that Her Highness,' Philip evasively replied, 'will write to Your Majesty when —'

'When,' Edward cut in, 'my Uncle Seymour gives her leave to write and tell what I —' he paused, and with a narrow, cold, old look substituted for that 'I' the royal plural — 'what *we*,' he coolly said, 'already know.'

EIGHT

The air was thick with rumours, the town astir with talk soon to be the topic of the day. Like fire the news spread from the manor at Chelsea to the Court of the King. There it smouldered, fanned to conflagration by the fury of the Royal Household's goddess, wife of Edward Somerset, the Lord Protector.

While the democratic principles of this mildest of men may have sprung from his genuine beliefs, his charitable sympathies were prompted by his lady on the assumption that charity must first begin at home. For which purpose she had urged him to demolish three churches and a portion of St. Paul's charnel-house. The material thereby collected was to go to the building of a palace on the Strand for the duke at the instigation of his duchess. Meanwhile they occupied the state apartments at Whitehall; and there, in the sanctum privy to the duke where none but his good wife dared venture, she bore down upon him like a wind-blown galleon weathering a stormy sea.

The late King's will that accorded to Katherine, his widow, precedence above all others as first lady in the land, had ignited in the duchess a flame of indignation, since she as wife — a second wife — to the uncle and guardian of the child-king, herself claimed sole right to that honour. She also claimed descent from the Plantagenets, remote indeed, but sufficient to remind her more lowly born spouse of the fact on any argumentative occasion.

That she had failed to secure the precedence which, by right of birth and rank, she insisted should be hers, snatched from her by a nobody, a Parr, was bad enough. 'But *this* — this latest monstrous, wicked and most treasonable perfidy, this malevolent, unduteous, nefarious disgrace —' filled to overflowing, the adjectival cornucopia poured descending wrath into her husband's shrinking ear — 'is injury past power of belief. Married. In secret. These three weeks. And to her. To *her*!' the duchess frantically reiterated. 'He — your brother Thomas, that libidinous, whoremongering, cuckold-maker, he —' the duchess's voice cracked on a crescendo — 'has *married* her! Do you hear me, Somerset?'

Yes, he heard her, with a movement of his head as if about to duck; and as sundry pages, gleefully jostling for key-hole place outside the door, did hear her.

'God's Passion! That I, of the Blood Royal, should have this insult thrust upon me, and you sitting there meek as a cheese-mite with not one word of protest, you miserable — *aah*!' Raising her clenched hands, the duchess smote the air. Again, instinctively, her paling husband ducked, and murmured: 'Pray, my dearest, do not take this matter so distressfully, I beg.'

'You beg!' his wife vociferated. 'Yes, you'll go beg, cap in hand, to put you wrong and him right. That's always been your way, pelf-licking to pacify and never to assert yourself with him. He twists you — so!' The Duchess wrung a finger. 'How *could* you — you tape-worm, let him go and tie himself to her under your very eyes and unbeknown to you — or so you'll say.'

'I do say,' the duke feebly was moved to retort, 'that what is done, was done unbeknown to me. So how, my heart, could I assert myself if I knew nothing of it?'

'Knew nothing!' was his 'heart's' response to this. 'What do you ever know that should be known, and more shame on you — you disabled weak-kneed cod — not to have made it your duty to have known of this infamous marriage between your kiss-me-breeks brother and a lowly Parr. What a' God's name,' appealed the duchess, 'was she but Latimer's widow, until Old Harry in his lustful dotage took her for his nurse, since no woman worthy of her womanhood would be so debased as to get herself French-poxed by him? And now your pimpish brother who had tried his hand already with both the Tudor bastards, Mary and Elizabeth, has got him Henry's cast-off whore whose head, stuck so high in the air above mine — of the Blood — would have jumped off the block on Tower Green had the King lived a year longer. And what's to come of this venomous marriage? Shall I tell you?' The Duchess came close, her full lips spitting to tell him, ''Tis plain as the nose on your face.' A not unhandsome if somewhat protuberant feature, nervously concealed, at this marked allusion to it, by the duke's trembling hand. 'Those two,' hissed the duchess, 'seek to gain possession of Edward. He's already at her feet. *She* to teach him Latin and preach at him the Gospel, and her knowledge of either no more than'll sit on his codpiece, poor rat!'

The Duchess, her Blood Royal notwithstanding, or because of it, was notoriously forthright in her command of speech. 'And once they've won him over, she with her mealy-mouthed cant, and your brother with his gifts of money — *Buy him this, buy him that* — as so he wheedles Edward's toady, Pugh — Hah! Pugh!' The Duchess pounced upon the name, as a fresh thought struck her. 'I know of these Pughs. They came over the border from Wales with the Tudors. A wild lawless lot, as I've heard tell they were in those days, raised above themselves, endowed with land in Norfolk by Henry, the Usurper.'

Somerset wet his lips. 'I do not exactly follow what young Pugh of the Privy Chamber has to do with —'

'Only that he, in waiting on Edward, is easy game for your brother to bribe, for if he be true to his Welsh ancestry, he'll not be slow in accepting Seymour's largesse to put in his pouch. And what if they breed?'

The Duke blinked. 'If —? Do you speak now of my brother and Pugh?'

'Swallow me, body, soul and guts!' cried the duchess, 'if this clodpate is not lost of his wits. Hearken, you loon, I speak of the Parr and your brother who are so randy hot, the pair of them, that 'tis a marvel she was not brought to bed of a boy on her wedding night, if one's not hidden there already. And Edward, don't forget, will not always be a codling — when, mayhap, you'll see yourself and myself, and your child that even now is stirring here,' she laid a hand against her body, 'put down, that the Parr's whelp be put up!'

So that was the sum of it, overheard by the cluster of pages at the keyhole, delightedly pinching each other's bottoms, until one whispered, *'Cave!'* and they scattered to stand at attention.

To suggest that the door was flung open is to underestimate the exit of the duchess. Had an avalanche crashed upon the frightened pages it could not have caused more disturbance. The lady's billowing petticoats overswept young Henry, Duke of Suffolk, that he staggered and fell on his knees. Before he could pick himself up the duchess swooped to catch him by the collar and drag him to his feet.

'Go you,' she commanded, 'and announce me to the King.' And revolving her gimlet eye on the rest of them, 'What,' barked the duchess, 'do you here? Why are you not at your studies with Mr Adams?'

'B-because, Ma-Madame, Your G-G-Grace,' piped Lord Charles Brandon, the duke's brother, a beautiful child but afflicted with a formidable stammer, 'w-w-we have been exc-c-cused our st-st-studies for today by r-r-request of —'

'Of —? God help us!' cried the duchess, impatient of his hesitancy. 'Whom?'

'The k-k-king,' dithered Charles, 'Your G-G-G-G —'

'Ho! So!' Taking the unhappy youngster by the ear, and with a virulence scarcely conceivable, 'The King, as a minor,' the duchess declared, 'has no authority to excuse you from your studies. I will see to it that Mr. Adams sets the pack of you to memorise and write five hundred lines from the archbishop's new Prayer Book.' Then, rounding on the duke who had slipped a garter in his fall and was striving to adjust his wrinkled hose, she rammed her fist into his back and drove him on, demanding: 'Why, sirrah, do you dawdle? Did I not bid you go before and announce me to the King?'

'Yes, Madame, I —'

'Then go.'

And, stalked by the duchess, he went.

From the huddle of pages watching their retreat, little Charles Brandon detached himself and, collecting a mouthful of spit, he expertly discharged it at the vanishing shape of the duchess.

'The old c-c-c-cow!' was, with deepest feeling, his apostrophe. 'I-I-I'll s-see her p-p-pickled in b-b-b-brine afore I'll r-r-r-r —'

'And so,' cried another to the rescue, 'say we all, afore we'll write five hundred lines!'

Edward, meanwhile, unaware of the racket in and about his uncle's privacy, was writing a letter to his stepmother, the Queen. He had written and discarded three; the fourth and final product he read aloud to Master Pugh for his approval. 'Since,' said he majestically, 'not only do we give this marriage our consent, but we did, in fact, advise and command our uncle Thomas to take the Queen to wife.'

At which remarkable pronouncement Philip's eyebrows went up, his chin down. So the Knave of Hearts had followed his suit of the Queen to play the King and win the hand! A wily trick, and further indication that Seymour had contrived to and succeeded in gaining access to Edward. How? By notes passed back and forth? By bribery of one lesser of the household? There, was a fellow, John Fowler, a foxy individual, recently appointed to the Privy Chamber by the duke. For a consideration Fowler might have been induced to act as go-between; yet Philip could not readily believe that Edward would be a party to a clandestine correspondence unknown to himself. And: 'How came it,' he asked, 'that Your Highness thought fit to advise the Lord Admiral on so weighty a matter as his marriage with the Queen, and, Sire, as I respectfully suggest, with what would appear to be unseemly haste in these early months of Her Grace's widowhood?'

This rebuke, drily spoken, brought an angry flush to Edward's wonted pallor. Avoiding his gentleman's penetrating eye, 'You have no right,' he prevaricated, 'to question me on what advice I choose to give my uncle when he seeks it.'

'Indeed, Sire?' Philip carelessly commented. 'It was Lord Seymour, then, who sought Your Majesty's advice upon this subject?'

Edward's flush mounted to the roots of his primrose-pale hair. His lip bulged ominously. 'Yes. Why not? You should know that none of the Blood — and my uncle is of close kin to the Blood — may marry without our consent.'

And in one of those cyclonic gusts of temper inherent from his father, Edward rose up, his pretty little elfish face furiously contorted. 'I *won't* be dictated to and told do this and that. You take too much upon yourself, Mr. Pugh. I know that you're in league with the Protector and his hideous old besom of a wife, to deprive me of the only — only relative — tears welled in the feverish bright eyes and dried in their own heat — who cares for me or shows me any true affection. My sister Mary — she —' a sob choked his words, but no tears fell — 'she may *pretend* to care, but she cares for nothing in the world save her old Mass, and as for Elizabeth, she loves no one but herself — and *him*. Here —' The momentary storm, so swiftly risen, swiftly faded, as a breath on glass. A faint crow of laughter preceded the information, 'She, Bess, is in love with my uncle Tom, and I wouldn't be surprised, were she old enough, if he would not have taken her to wife rather than the Queen — or, as I also recommended him,' said Edward grandly, Anne of Cleves. She's looking for a husband, too, and she may look! Though it was spread about, and I give it you for what it be worth, that she made the King, her 'brother', an uncle, a year or two before he died.

Philip hid a chuckle in a cough. Despite familiarity with this elderly child, he was never quite prepared for his startling remarks.

'So you see,' Edward sighed, 'I've much upon my mind. 'Tis not all cakes and ale to be a king who's not a king except in name. And, sir,' he plucked at Philip's sleeve to say with coaxing sweetness, 'if I'm sometimes hasty you'll forgive me — yes?'

Who could not? He had charm, when he chose, to melt stones. And taking that small dimpled hand to his lips, Philip bowed over it 'Sire, 'tis I should ask forgiveness if Your Grace has the least cause to doubt me.'

'Never, never, *never,* will I doubt you!' was the emphatic rejoinder. 'And some day or other, when I've the power to assert myself,' he nodded brightly, 'you will have your due in token of my trust. Now may I read you my letter?' But as prefatorily he began: *To the Queen's Grace,'* young Suffolk poked his head round the door pantingly.

'Your Highness —'

Edward slid from his chair, demanding: 'Well, what is it? Come in, Harry. Don't stand there gasping like a landed carp.'

'The Duchess,' mouthed Harry, with a meaning backward look, 'is here.'

'Then I am not,' said Edward promptly; and snatching up his letter, he made for the inner entrance to his bed-chamber, saying hurriedly to Philip as he went, 'Tell her I'm sick or dead or what you will, but don't let her come nigh me, Keep her off!'

How the determined advance of the duchess was kept off and turned to a speedy retreat with her entourage to Greenwich; or that word on bated breath, accompanied by pungent whiffs of vinegar, was wafted through the palace that the King had been confined to his bed as suspect of the Plague, was of less importance than that the Court physicians ultimately, and to everyone's relief, diagnosed His Majesty's indisposition as of no contagious nature. At the same time the learned doctors, so Master Pugh reported, did urgently advise His Majesty a change of air and scene. And what more salubrious environment could be found, or as possibly suggested by his gentleman-in-waiting, than the wholesome country atmosphere of Chelsea?

'Bless his life!' cried Lady Seymour, still known as Katherine, the Queen. 'Tom, will you listen to this? I might be his daughter. Such cheap common paper, too, poor lamb,' she parenthesised. 'Why can't they give him proper parchment?'

And with a smile straying into dimples, the Queen, translating Edward's letter from the Latin, read: *We thank you heartily not only for the gentle acceptation of our suit, but also for the loving accomplishment of the same, wherein you have declared your desire to gratify us ...* 'He has a verb wrong here.' She made a mark in the margin, and went on: *'by the gentle acceptation of our ...* O, but this,' interpolated Katherine, 'is rich! He thanks — he *thanks* me, Tom, for acceding to his wish that we should marry. What seeds have you planted in his mind, you rogue, that he — God save us — declares, *Mine uncle is of so good a nature that he will not be troublesome by any means to you?*'

Her eyes held a look half-quizzical, wholly adoring, as she glanced from the letter to the gold-bearded buccaneer who possessed her heart, her rank, her fortune, and all her young frustrated womanhood to make of her his creature. Three times the widow of old husbands she, with a fourth in her blossoming years, was now at last, and joyously, fulfilled. And, 'Would you believe,' cried Katherine, 'he says, *I give you my written word that I will so provide for you both that if hereafter any grief befall you I shall be sufficient succour ...* Mercy me! And he but nine years old!'

'Rising ten and then but eight to come, before his "written word",' Tom took the letter from her, '*and* my planted seed, bears fruit "to provide for us both". I'll have this, and, by God's Soul, I'll keep it as guarantee. It may prove useful if,' his boisterous laugh drowned his words, 'we should stand in need of Edward's succour.'

'Tom!' Fondly she rebuked him. 'You can't take as guarantee the written word of a babe.'

'He's no babe,' retorted Tom. 'He was born old — Now what are you at?'

She was at a silver button on his doublet hanging by a loosened thread. 'I must sew this on before you lose it.'

The perfect wife, and, as was hinted in Lady Tyrwhitt's parlour, so had she been the perfect mistress. More than that, more harmfully, was hinted between the gentlewomen of the household; how the Lord Admiral had sought to make one higher still his mistress, were she not so already, with him in and out her chamber hot from his wife's bed to hers. Yes! and he dragging off the covers with his hands about her body to tickle and tumble her, until she, screeching like a scalded cat, would leap up and run to her maids who formed a ring to keep him off and laughing loud to split their sides, as brazen as you please. And that went on daily for weeks, until the Queen had word of it and joined them at their jigs to save her face if not the Lady's maidenhead ... A saucy baggage she, king's bastard, king's sister, or nothing, froward beyond her years and still three months short of fourteen.

It was likely, this the general opinion, that Master Pugh had brought the King's Grace here, child though he were, to put a damper on his uncle's wenching, whether she be princess or village bawd, for the Lord Admiral would never, surely, dare engage in wanton misbehaviour with His Majesty's 'Sweet Temperance', and the King here in the house.

'Not so. You have it wrong,' Lady Tyrwhitt put them right 'That young Pugh — he's a dark horse.' Still smarting from 'that young Pugh's' indifference to her charms, Her Ladyship would have it His Majesty had been brought there for a closer purpose than to cook his sister's goose. Hand and glove with the Admiral was Master Pugh to wean the King from the Protector's regency. Had not His Lordship already got for himself the custody of little Lady Jane? It was clear enough to any but a moon-calf that having wheedled the Marquis of

Dorset, Jane Grey's father, into consigning his daughter to his care, the Admiral's next move would be to plight a troth between these royal children.

'This Master Pugh,' Lady Tyrwhitt declared with smiling spite, 'looks to win a goodly share of the Lord Admiral's spoils at such time as the King and Lady Jane Grey, his future Queen, shall be united.'

So the tongue of gossip licked at royal names, but the young Elizabeth, first cause and all unconscious of it, could not know that her childish infatuation was to leave its stain upon her memory and its scar upon her soul, unhealed...

There is a striking contrast between her guardedly un-youthful reaction to the shock of her stepmother's marriage with him whom, to her lifelong undoing, she hero-worshipped, and the characteristic directness of her sister Mary when faced with the deception of her much-loved friend, the Queen.

She did not scruple to give a sharp rap to the knuckles of the aspiring Seymour when somewhat belatedly, he sought her influence to further his suit of her father's widow, 'Concerning which,' was Mary's cutting retort, 'I perceive strange news.' Strange news, indeed, when the secret wedding had already taken place. 'It stands least with my poor honour to meddle,' she continued, 'considering whose wife Her Grace has been of late...' And went on to remind him that, 'Being a maid I am not cunning in these wooing matters?'

Poor Mary, whom love had cold-shouldered, took much to heart the seemingly inconsolable Katherine's haste for consolation. Mary's reply to Tom Seymour was followed, so soon as the 'strange news' had been confirmed, by a letter to Elizabeth urging her to leave the Queen's establishment for hers, so *that we two shall stand before the world united in our disapproval of the match.*

Equally characteristic is Elizabeth's refusal of her sister's invitation. Even at this early age she practised the art of that dissimulation which is the secret of her greatness to make her name immortal, and herself for what she was.

'It behoves us both,' she told Mary, 'to submit to that which cannot be cured. The only thing we can do is to dissemble the pain we may feel at the disrespect with which our father's memory is treated.' And, as excuse for declining Mary's offer of a home, since nothing would induce her to leave Chelsea while Tom Seymour ruled the roost there, 'I shall always submit to whatsoever Your Highness shall be pleased to order, but,' she added gracefully, 'since the Queen has shewn me so much kindness, I cannot withdraw myself from her protection without I appear ungrateful.'

Having written and re-written this to her satisfaction she went to find Edward that he might read the letter before she sent it.

She found him in the garden by the fish-pond with Jane Grey. The two children were seated side by side on the marble parapet of the pool where red-gold carp, like streaks of flame, darted in and out among the water lilies.

Unobserved, and with a jaundiced eye, Elizabeth stood watching those two fair heads bent cheek to cheek over a massive volume spread open and supported on their knees. Her thin lips tightened till she looked to have no mouth. Jane! But naturally. *Jane Grey always in the way,'* she muttered in rhyming ferocity. She had no love for Jane Grey, who had come to live at Chelsea as ward of Tom Seymour and to share her studies under Mr. Ascham, the handsome young tutor, successor to Edward's Mr. Cheke.

Jane, though four years her junior, was ahead of her in Greek, on a par with her in Latin, and prime favourite with

Tom, who petted and fondled her to turn the stomach sick. *Horrid little whey-faced creepy-crawly toad,* she silently commented; and advancing on tiptoe, teeth bared in an ogre-ish grin, she growled in the shell-like ear of little Jane, still unapprised of her approach: 'I'm the bogeyman come to eat you up, skin, bones, and all. Grr — rr — *rrah!*'

Jane's terrified shriek in response to this greeting, and the fright of it, almost toppled her into the pool; only Edward's arm, flung protectively around her, saved Jane, but not the book, from immediate immersion.

'Look out!' yelled Elizabeth. Too late. The volume was sliding — had slid — with a flop and a splash into the pond, to result in a confusion. Jane, who had received a spray of slimy water in her face, burst into tears; and Edward, wheeling round on Elizabeth, stormed at her ragefully, 'There's a thing to do! You did it a'purpose — my book! My Ptolemy. Ruined!'

'I did not do it a'purpose,' rejoined Elizabeth, 'but it serves you right for having pilfered it from the library at Windsor. Who gave you leave to take our father's books?'

'Who gave me — *me* leave,' squealed Edward in open-mouthed amaze at this impertinence, 'to take what is my own? 'Tis *my* book. Everything in Windsor, everything — the whole of England is mine. There's a Beast you are to steal up behind us and push my most excellent Ptolemy into the pond … Jane, don't cry. We'll save it, see? It lies in the shallowest part, scarce ankle-deep. I'll wade in and get it.'

He was for kicking off his shoes in preparation of the rescue, when Elizabeth shoved him aside. 'Let be, you'll only strain yourself lifting it. And you don't have to go in. I can lean over if you'll hold on to me so's I don't fall in after it.'

And while Edward, unwillingly, held on to her, she managed to hoist the sodden volume from the bed of the pond and to lay it, still open, on the grass.

Said Edward, gloomily regarding the drenched pages: 'The text is most dreadfully smudged. And I can't have it reprinted. It would cost too much. I've no money to pay for it.'

'I've a-plenty money,' bragged Elizabeth. 'I'll pay for it or buy you another.'

Edward scowled at her. 'You *can't* buy me another. There's not another extant of this edition.'

'Yes,' chimed in Jane, 'and we were just beginning to construe it.' And then she was in tears again.

'Poor little one,' Edward took her hand to kiss, 'don't cry, my pretty. Are you wet? Yes, you are, and all muddied down your neck. Wait — I'll dry you.'

And as, carefully, with his silken handkerchief, he dried the sobbing Jane — 'Don't cry, my pretty,' mimicked Elizabeth. 'Almost as pretty as a white slug. Cry-baby!' She grabbed Jane by the arm giving it a vicious pinch. 'That'll teach you — my poor pretty-pretty little one, to cry!'

'Leave her alone!' shouted Edward. 'You should be ashamed of yourself, tormenting her — and she but half your size.'

'I' faith, she is — a dwarf!' And with a parting pinch Elizabeth released her, who ran to Edward, squealing: 'She's hurt my arm pinching of me!'

'That's the way,' jeered Elizabeth, 'tell-tale sneak.'

'I'm not,' blubbered Jane, 'a sneak. I didn't — but you — did.'

'O, stop snivelling, do!' Elizabeth gave Jane a poke in the small of her back. 'Go away. I want to speak to Edward without *you* creepy-crawling round us. Go!' She stamped her foot; and Jane, with her knuckles in her eyes, and still snuffling, went — at a run.

'You bitch!' Edward, on his knees beside Ptolemy to smooth the cockled pages, sprang up, his hands fisted. 'You're a bitch to tease her so, poor little Jane. I won't have her teased, d'you hear? I'm going to marry Jane when I come into my own. I'd marry her now were the Protector not so set on my marrying Mary of Scotland, and she only four. But he can't force me into *that* against my will. After all, I *am* the King and can choose for myself, and I've already chosen — Jane. I love — I like Jane,' he corrected, deeply flushed, 'and I'll marry her and make her Queen of England.'

'What, she?' Elizabeth burst into loud laughter; but there was no laughter in her eyes, nor in the rapier edge to her voice that flashed at him, '*She* — who hasn't the guts of a louse? A fine queen she'd make.'

'Yes,' shrilled Edward, in a fury, 'you're right! She *would* make a fine queen, and a better one than some I could name. You're jealous of Jane — that's why you're so vile to her — because she's so much cleverer than you. Why, she can beat you head on at the Classics. I know what I know.'

'*What* do you know?' demanded Elizabeth fiercely. 'That your uncle Tom has talked you into this crazy-mad idea of marrying Jane Grey?'

'No, he did not, then,' Edward stoutly denied. ''Tis my own idea, and a good idea, too. Jane's of the Blood. Isn't her mother our first cousin and third in the Succession? Who else but Jane is a fit and royal wife —' he drew himself up — 'for Us?'

'Yes, who else indeed?' Elizabeth smiled with lips turned down. 'Pity 'tis you're not the King of Egypt, then we could marry each other. The Pharaohs always married their sisters to keep the blood pure.'

'Hmm … yes.' Ever in pursuit of knowledge, Edward thoughtfully digested this. 'But what if the Pharaoh hadn't any sisters?'

'Then I suppose he'd have to marry his nearest of female kin.'

'Which in my case,' chortled Edward, 'would be Mary. No, thank you! Were I Pharaoh I'd be mummified before I'd marry *her*.' Once more he was on his knees beside the book. 'This is most shockingly mussed. No, if I can't marry Jane —'

'I never heard such foolishness!' broke in Elizabeth, wrathfully white. 'A child of your age discussing whom you will or will not marry!'

'Whom I will or will not marry,' retorted Edward, 'has been a topic of discussion ever since I was born. And if it isn't Jane — say they marry her off to someone else while my Protector,' he lifted a nostril as at a malodorous smell, 'has the last word, then I suppose it'll have to be Mary of Scotland, to save the war that's boiling up over the border … The sun has almost dried this now, and it's not *quite* ruined. Why did you wish to speak to me alone?'

'Because,' Elizabeth took from the pouch attached to her girdle the letter she had written to Mary, 'I want you to read this before I send it. Mary has taken such offence at the marriage of the Queen and Tom Seymour, that she doesn't think I ought to go on living here and suggests I live with her.'

'But you won't,' said Edward quickly, 'will you? She'd have you turned Papist and spouting the Mass before you'd been with her a week.'

'No fear of that! I'd sooner die than live with Mary. Look, this is what I say —'

But before Edward could more than scan the page, Barnaby Fitzpatrick came running from the house, breathlessly to tell him, 'Sire! Sir Anthony Browne — by the order of His Grace, the Lord Protector, is come to fetch Your Majesty — away.'

'And I've not been here a week,' grumbled Edward, when, mounted on his cream-coloured pony, he jogged alongside Master Pugh on the road to London. 'I'll stake my Crown the duchess, not my uncle, sent Sir Anthony after me. Trust her to kill whatever smallest pleasure may be mine. I had so much enjoyed,' he said wistfully, 'this short respite at Chelsea.'

So had Philip.

While Edward, in sulky silence, brooded on his wrongs, Philip, lost in memory of one brief interlude, relived its ghostly rapture. Was it but this very noon, or seven thousand years ago, for how to count time's passing in the Eternal Now, to know himself handfasted, sealed, confessed?

He had come upon her in her garden where she sat beneath the sycamore, shelling peas … A smile played about his lips at the remembrance, to see himself again, unseen by her, seated at her homely occupation, a basket at her feet, the sun on her uncovered hair, turning the dark sheen of it to a deep iridescent blue. Long he stood there watching her deft fingers breaking the green pods, and the soundless drop of their pellets to the wooden bowl. Then, as if she sensed his presence, her head had turned. She started up; the bowl jerked, scattering its contents in the grass.

He was all apologies — 'to have affrighted you. I'll gather them.'

'No, no,' she stayed him, when regardless of his fine white hose he would have knelt. 'The birds can have them now. I'll pick some more. They're in their prime for picking. Will you dine with us and eat them with roast duck?'

He regretfully could not. He had come to tell her that His Majesty's visit to the manor was curtailed, and he must conduct the King within the hour to St. James's.

'So soon? I had thought that you —' her voice faltered — 'that he ... the King would be here at least a month.'

'Or a sennight,' he said lightly, 'as His Majesty had hoped.'

'Yes, I too...' And, maybe to avoid the burning message in his eyes, she had stooped to the basket saying, 'There's still some left. I would that you...'

'That I?' And he had neared her, not daring to touch, scarce daring to see the rapid rise and fall of her breathing in the hidden valley of her breasts. 'What would you of me that I must not have of you ... Jocosa?'

At that whisper of her name, her flying glance from under those curled lashes had met his, and his pulses raced again to recall the tremble of her body, that like a windswept flower swayed towards him. He gave way then to take and crush her in his arms. Time ceased to be until, his hunger unappeased by this first taste of that so long denied him, he tore his mouth from hers to say, 'I'm mad.'

And she, 'I love ... your madness.'

That was all; no other word, no parting, no farewell before he turned and left her standing in the sunlight, one hand covering her lips as if to keep and hold his warmth upon them.

But neither he nor she had seen a shadow come and go, nor heard its passing, for the tumult in their blood. Nor did they hear the brittle cry of one who cast himself face down behind the yew hedge among last autumn's unswept leaves. Only a mongrel dog, lost of a foot, saw, heard, and came hopping on three legs, to comfort.

'Master Pugh,' Edward edged his pony close to Philip's mare. 'How strangely you smile to or at yourself. Are you not sad as I am to leave Chelsea?'

'Maybe,' Philip's left hand tightened on the rein, 'I am more sad at this departure than Your Majesty.'

'How so? You are free to return when you wish, which I am not ... Philip?'

'Sire?'

'With marriage in the air and all about us, is it not time that you were married, too?'

Philip's mare suddenly shied. 'Hey!' cried Edward, steadying his startled pony, 'you bumped me! Your mare's in a frisk. What frighted her?'

'A white rag, Sire, in the hedge.' And from that gnomish upturned face and the narrow sidelong look of those pointed eyes, Philip averted his own.

'I saw no white rag, nor did Dominus, but he's always quiet. Nothing frights him except a hedgehog. He abhors a hedgehog. Once when I and Barnaby rode out in Windsor Forest, a hedgehog ran across our path — they can run fast — and Dominus was off like an arrow. I had much ado to hold him.'

'In which case,' Philip said, 'I must request the Master of the Horse that Your Majesty rides always on the curb.'

'No, Dominus, like his name, is masterful. He'd hate to be ridden on the curb, as,' Edward chuckled softly, 'do we all. Marriage also,' again that same uncanny look, 'can be a curb.' And with the persistence of a virulent mosquito he returned to the attack. 'Is that why you choose not to marry, sir? Will you never marry?

'If so be it as God wills and in His good time,' was the evasive answer. 'And here,' Philip added adroitly, 'are we come to the Knight's Bridge across the River Bourne. Would Your Majesty care to turn in at this gate for a gallop in Hyde Park?'

'O, yes!' cried Edward, 'We will. Dominus is fretting to be off. He's had too little exercise and too much corn at Chelsea. If we take the Route de Roy,' he pointed with his whip, 'we may be ahead of Sir Anthony and the rest of them before they reach St. James's.'

So, entering by the main gates of Hyde Manor, they followed the wide sanded way that skirted those vast acres of royal hunting ground, once the property of the Abbott of Westminster; and no more was said of marriage.

Arriving at the chief ranger's lodge on the east side of the park, they came out into a narrow lane, crossed the high road from London to Reading, and so into the park of St. James's. In the distance could be seen the steeple of St. Paul's thrusting a grey finger to the smoke-hazed sky, and beneath it, nestling among a cluster of trees, the thatched roofs of the village of St. Giles. Then, as the walls of his palace rose before him: 'Back again,' sighed Edward, 'to my prison...' Where Sir Anthony Browne with his escort awaited him. 'I wonder,' he muttered apprehensively aside, 'what the duke has in store for me now.'

He did not wonder long.

The Duke, supported by the duchess, put him on the rack of a verbal castigation concerning his visit to Chelsea — 'And in *my* absence,' stressed Her Grace.

Did Edward, probed his uncle, have any prior knowledge of Lord Seymour's secret marriage to the Queen?

To which, always a stickler for the truth and nothing but, 'Not to say for certain any knowledge,' Edward cautiously replied.

'Then how comes it,' from the duchess, 'that you wrote the Queen a letter giving this most shameful marriage your consent? *Your* consent, forsooth! You have not the right, by reason of Your Majesty's minority, thus to —'

'— assert yourself,' daringly the duke took the words from her mouth. 'Allow me, if you please, my love, to deal with him.' Coldly he surveyed the pale little boy, who stood, feet wide, one hand at his dagger-belt, the thumb of the other worrying his lip, a trick of his when nervous. And very nervous now was he, fearing lest he compromise his uncle Tom, or worse, his stepmother, for want of forethought in his answers.

'Edward, what you wrote, if you wrote, or why you wrote to the Queen,' the duke patiently but firmly pursued, 'as I have proof positive you did —' *From that spying sneak Fowler,* Edward inwardly reflected while, cool-eyed, he returned his uncle's scrutiny, who, seeing his dead sister in her child's face, concluded with unease — 'is immaterial.'

'Immaterial!' snorted the duchess. 'What you surely would mean to convey is not the *fact* of his writing such a letter but the motive — malicious, cunning, sinister — that prompted his unwarrantable action. *That* is the point we wish to make clear — in His Majesty's interests solely.' Although this speech was directed at her husband, the duchess addressed herself exclusively to Edward, who, not looking at her, smilingly, said, 'Yes?'

'Yes!'

And on that monosyllable the duchess closed her mouth as if she never meant to open it again. But she did, to demand with avidity: 'Does the King not realise that any such commitment on his part can be construed as nothing short of treason to the memory of his most saintly father?'

Most saintly, my big toe! Edward said to himself; and to her: 'Nothing short of treason, Madame? How?'

'Your aunt —' the duke took up the litany — 'your aunt, in delicacy, Edward, shrinks —' the duchess glared — 'from bringing to your notice that which is necessary now for you to hear. Should a child —' the duke hemmed and glanced uncomfortably away — 'a child have been born unto the Queen, your father's widow, at the time of her marriage to my brother, and within these four months of the late King's death, some great danger might have thus ensued to the ultimate disquiet of your realm.'

Edward pondered over this and came to the logical conclusion: 'But since the Queen has had no child the point does not arise.'

'Not,' said the duchess, significantly, 'yet.'

Edward bowed to her. 'As you say, Madame, and with all respect I say, what may be, will be, and what is now to be, Madame, is an end,' he bowed again, 'to this discussion.'

The Duchess, taken with the flushes, gasped; so did the duke, while possibly in silence he applauded this manoeuvre, since etiquette forbade his wife or any subject of the King, below the Lord Protector, to remain in the Presence when dismissed from it And when, with Medusa-like malevolence, his wife had curtsied herself out: 'That Edward,' the pained duke reproved him, 'was a most ungracious gesture on your part since you should know that your Aunt and I desire nothing but the welfare of your royal person and your State.'

'Yes?'

The gentle repetition of that uncompromising syllable caused the 'Good Duke', so was he named by the commonfolk of England, to redden in his turn, pettishly declaring: 'What with one thing and another, and this unhappy misalliance of your uncle Seymour at which I — and your aunt — are much offended, and a war across the Border pending with the Scots, and agrarian unrest in eastern England, I'd have followed your beloved father to the grave before I would have shouldered the burden of his son and his son's kingdom.'

'The burden of his son and his son's kingdom,' was Edward's calm rejoinder, 'has been shouldered by you, Sir, of your choice; not mine. But if the burden weighs too heavy I'll relieve you of it, gladly. There's no call for you to wait till I'm eighteen.'

A sound, half snarl, half groan, issued from the curled-back lip of the exasperated duke. Jane's son. Little Jane, whose artless — or whose artful — wiles had stolen a march on that black-haired Bullen trollop to capture this boy's father. Jane's milk and water mixed with Henry's red-hot blood had gone to the making of — what? An imp, a changeling, or as some said, genius; or merely an insolent young cub?

Gathering his ebbing dignity about him, 'I see you are already branded,' uttered Somerset, 'with my brother's prejudicial influence. Would indeed that I could wash my hands of him, of his marriage and — so help me, God! — of you.'

But in his journal, and in one brief laconic entry, Edward, always conscientious, records only the sum total of this interview:

The Lord Seimour of Sudeley married the Queen whose name is Katherine with which marriag (sic) the Lord Protectour is much offended…

NINE

It had been a most glorious summer that first of Edward's reign. Every day and all day long the sun poured from a molten sky. The grassy spaces of the royal parks lay parched and shrivelled under the relentless heat that tinged, before their fall, the spinach green of August's leaves with autumn's gold. In London's narrow streets the baked cobbles struck warm to the tread of sweating citizens, the laystalls were black with glutted flies; and, uprisen from the river, that dump of surplus refuse, a stench, like the foul breath of some dying monster, overhung the torpid city.

On a day when, from its dawn, thunderclouds had gathered in the burning blue to hide the sun but not to cool the stifled air, Philip, with John Locke rode along the Strand. Before, behind, a patient slow procession of white oxen drawing wagon loads of bricks, cement, and mortar passed to and fro the site of the Lord Protector's Palace, named for him, Somerset House, and still in process of erection. The voices of bricklayers, interspersed with the raucous commands of their overseers, accompanied the ceaseless hammering of steel on stone, the creak and groan of chains attached to wooden pulleys for the hoisting of heavy weights; while, diminished by distance to the size of ants, the figures of workmen could be seen digging deep in the earth's bowels to make a pleasaunce of the swampy marshes that stretched to the banks of the Thames.

'The Duke's new palace will cost the country more than any war,' John jerked his head at a lumbering cart piled high with iron-wrought gates, extravagantly gilded. 'Gates!' quoth John, with fine contempt, 'and not the main gates, neither. These be but one of a pair to the servants' entry.'

'How can you know,' asked Philip with a twinkle, 'what entry they be for?'

At which John blushed to the tips of his ears that stuck out like a bat's from under his green velvet cap, and looked away to answer, 'So, master, is it said about the town, in taverns and the like.'

'The like,' Philip quizzed him, 'being the door of a certain buttery, mayhap not a furlong from here?'

'I know naught, sir,' John replied, turning, if possible, redder, 'of any such buttery door.'

'Now, as I live!' cried Philip, as if deaf to this remark. 'Talk of an angel —'

'Or a devil,' muttered John.

'— and,' concluded Philip, big with wonder, 'here she comes. Is not this a rare coincidence that she should go a-marketing as we pass by, or more like she loiters with the builders to watch them at their toil and wag her tongue with gossip, brought honey-sweet,' he slyly said, 'to you?'

'Sir,' growled John, ''Tis not in me to lend my ears —'

'They're large enough and burning hot for all that,' again broke in John's master.

'Nor,' doggedly persisted John, 'to gossip with a serving-wench, or any such a saucy piece as that yon baggage, pardie!'

'Ho! So that's the way the wind blows? Full east. But not full east in my quarter for me.' Philip passed a hand across his forehead and ruefully examined the damp spreading stain on the pale perfumed leather of his gauntlet. 'By Cock! I'm sweating like a pig, soused through as I were pickled. I'd liefer the blaze of the sun than this sultry — Ah! good morrow,

Joan.' He reined in his horse to greet a rosy-cheeked damsel with a basket on her arm, a dimple in her chin, and a roving glint in her eye for John Locke, sitting so straight in his saddle that he looked to have a poker down his back.

'And good morrow, sir, to you.' Joan, smiling, bobbed and asked, 'Will it please Your Honour to be calling at the house?'

'It will please my honour,' Philip answered, 'very well — if your mistress be within?'

'Yes, sir, I'll go tell her you are on your way.' And with a flounce of petticoats and the murmured observation — somewhat metaphorically mixed — concerning stuffed images who saw no farther than their stuck-up noses, always seeking for mare's nests in mountains to find molehills, and there was never none so deaf as them what wouldn't see, Joan turned her steps and ran.

Jocosa was at the door when, having walked their horses that Joan might out-race them, Philip and the silent John arrived at the house in Water Lane. Dismounting, Philip gave the reins to his servant and bade him go round to the buttery, where he would doubtless find a welcome awaiting, with a tankard of ale, fresh-drawn.

But no welcome from the mistress of the house awaited Philip, neither in her look that for one instant met and fled from his; nor on her lips that framed the whisper: 'For this once and no more.'

Philip's face lost its warmth, his eyes their light, as he followed her into the hall's shadowed cool that offered thankful contrast to the humid heat without. Crossing to the empty hearth, Jocosa motioned him back as he approached.

'Hear what I've to tell you and then … go.'

'What's this?' He gave an involuntary glance behind him, and to her again, in puzzled query. So they stood gazing at each other without a word, until, very quietly, he said, 'Is this your idea of a jest, to make of me your fool?'

A small tearless sob escaped her, and at that little mournful sound: 'There's not a minute in each hour of the day,' he said, 'that I don't think of you, don't long for you so fiercely that I cannot endure,' he made a helpless gesture, 'the ache of life without you.'

. 'Do you think that I,' she murmured, 'can endure it?' And crossing her hands on her breast as if she hugged some secret there, while her eyes, dark, imploring, clung to his, 'The hurt of it,' her mouth childishly crumpled, 'is pain enough to kill.'

'Pity of Christ!' he breathed. 'If this be so, why — *why* do you not come to me? Must we go on year in, year out, for ever, in this torment? Is it your marriage vows that hold you?'

She shook her head. 'No. Him. He holds me.'

'Do you —' asked Philip in a splintered voice — 'do you love him?'

'I pity him.'

'Pity and love, they say, are of one kin.'

'Yes, but that's not all the reason…'

The pupils of her eyes dilated till their brown was merged in black; her face so drained of colour it seemed the blood in her veins had ceased to flow. Her hands, still crossed on her heart, were trembling now; and Philip, with the acute observance of a man in anticipatory possession of his woman, and who cherishes to glorify her every smallest token, saw, how fastened to her corsage, one red fading rose lipped with velvety dark petals at the whiteness of her flesh. A sigh came from her and a fainting scent, as if that dusky flower at her breast had breathed its last, and, her lashes lowered, whispering, she said, 'He knows.'

'Knows!' Philip uttered a short unmirthful laugh. 'What is it he can know who has the right to know, to have, to hold that which I may not? Does he know I covet what is his, my neighbour's wife, when I have sat with you and him, here in his house, at his board, how many times — two — three — since you left Chelsea? And once with you alone. Do you remember?'

'There is no forgetting.'

Their eyes were joined, but not their bodies, though they stood so near together, and so far apart, each to live again, within the other's memory, that moment of recurrence when he, who never now would leave them, had been called away by his servant on some trivial matter. And they had turned to find themselves, to speak in passion's wordless voice and sight-blind touch of this, their love, that must not be, nor had never, until now, been told.

Why, his mind taunted him, *why should this thing have come to us?*

And she, stealing that thought in answer, said, "Tis no new thing to me. I have been yours always, for the taking.'

'Then,' he lost himself to tell her, madly, 'let me take!'

But she said 'no,' and 'no,' again, that he must pray her in words sprung from the pent flood-tide of his desire, to come with him who had first right to her, defying God and all the world to keep her from him; while with dazzled eyes she listened, and his voice died down in broken murmurs and was silenced in a sudden jarring thunderclap to rock the sky and shake the house, and fling open the door into the hall, where stood her husband.

Emptily smiling, pale eyes wandering, hands rubbing at his sleeves to rub the raindrops from them, he looked neither at one nor the other, saying, 'So ... the storm has broke at last ... to clear the air.'

To clear the air, as may the Lord Protector optimistically have hoped when the threatened storm across the Border broke with a call to arms and gathering of clans.

The adamantine refusal of the Scots to honour the Treaty of 1543, by which their Assembly had promised the baby Queen Mary to the then Prince Edward, now decided the inevitable issue. Somerset, whose persuasive approach to the Scots that they keep to their agreement had proved of no avail, aimed now to bring their country to its knees, their little Queen to Edward, and himself at the head of an invading army.

He, who bowed to no will nor authority other than that of his wife; he, who abhorred all forms of violence and cruelty in an age of semi-barbarism when violence and cruelty were the recognised insignia of might, was none the less headstrong, impulsive, courageous: a curious hybrid of weakness and strength. Part seer and all idealist, he was also intensely superstitious. A firm believer in omens and oracles he waited to strike at the Scots on a Sunday, since, according to the stars, Sunday was his lucky day. On a Sunday he had proclaimed his. nephew king and himself duke, endowed with according lands and wealth. On a Sunday had fallen Wriothesley, his rival, who had opposed him in the council chamber. Again, on a Sunday, after a prayerful session with his God, 'the Giver of all gifts, the Granter of all peace, the Defender of nations, Who hast willed all men to be as neighbours and commanded us to love them as ourselves, not to hate our enemies, and to reform our lives to Thy Goodly commandments', and with a final invocation to 'the Holy Angels that there shall be none or little loss of Christian blood,' he strode forward on his march across the Tweed.

In his journal Edward gave his account of the Campaign, as possibly told him by an eye-witness.

There was great preparation made to go into Scotland, and the Lord Protector went with a great number of Nobles and Gentlemen to Berwick where the first day after his coming he mustered all his Companie and marched on into Scotland ... Then he burnt two Castles and passed a streight of a Bridg (sic) where 300 Scots Light horsemen set upon behind him who were discomfited. So he passed to Musselburg where the first day after he came he went up to the Hill and saw the Scots thinking them as they were indeed 36,000 Men and my Lord of Warwick was almost taken chasing the Earl of Huntley by an Ambushe but was rescued by one Bertiwell, with twelve Hagbuttiers (halberdiers) on horseback and the Ambushe ran away...

Among those 'nobles and gentlemen' who fought with the duke at the Battle of Musselburgh, better known as the Battle of Pinkie, we hear from another source how:

The Lord Protector's aide-de-Camp, Master Philip Pugh, did escort him across the Bridge along a thirty feet wide road and within two bowshottes of the Scottish line, where advancing he did show exceeding valour being wounded in his right arme, yet did he strike as single-handed to hold at bay some twenty Pikemen.

And there Somerset was met by a herald with a challenge from Lord Huntley to stand and surrender or fight out the quarrel to the death, man to man.

The Duke, although he knew himself outnumbered by almost twice his army of eighteen thousand horse and foot, refused. One could not decide a war in single combat. So the night closed in, and, as we have it from Philip in a letter to his father, written from Berwick on the homeward way:

On Saturday morning, September X, our army lay at Pinkie Cleugh 2 miles beyond Musselburg with a Hill called Fawside (Falside) Brae between us and the Ennemie who were far the stronger than ourselves in Foote and Horsemen maugre our support from Admiral Lord Clinton's Fleet standing out in the Forth to the left wing of the Scots. From our Encampment we could see their Cavalrie lined up on the farther banke of the Esk and in possession of a Castle which the Lord Protectour had commanded us advance and seize, spare none.

At 8 o' the clock on the morning of September X we left our vantage point and led by Sir Ralph Bulmer and Lord Grey rode forward to engage, when with much amaze we saw the Scots had quitted their stronghold t'other side the river and did occupy the ground we had marked out for ourselves. They likely believed we would retreat and so escape them and to prevent this they had intent to surprise our Camp and were on their way to surround us but as they came over the Bridge they were checked and mowed down, some 40 or more, by a volley of Cannon from the Admiral's Ship. Then did they halt in much confusion albeit no doubt of their valliance for no sooner did they sight us of the Cavalrie oncoming than they drove full-tilt to meet us who having seized a Hill to the rear had now the advantage of height though not of numbers. Then did we punish them so fiercely that again they halted in a fallow field having in their front a deep wide ditch but our men made little count of that. With Lord Grey to urge them on so did they fall upon and over-ride the Scots. Our horses for the most part cleared the ditch and my roan mare Phoebe albeit she had an arrow in her neck and was bleeding sore took the banke like a swallow. Then as we charged, the Highlanders came at us led by the Pipers with their Kilties, so they call them as might be a Ladye's kirtle cut short and swinginge in the wind up to their naked thighes, and they brandishing their Pykes and Swords and crying strange and wild as so many madmen, Hereticks, ye black-blooded Sacksenacks — or so did I interpret their outlandish tongue and as was I later told by one of them our prisoner that Sacksenack or some such name is how is called in Scottish for an

Englishman, meaning Saxon, they being Kelts as so do they call their
Kilts or Kilties semblably from that name.

It was no easy victorie. They wrenched from us the Royal Standard
which we had a struggle to recover the Staff being broke in twaine one half
of it held by the ennemie and our Bearer killed. Lord Grey was wounded
nighe to death with a sword-gash in his mouth that he was all but choked
with blood in hand to hand contest, our Lances being shorter than the
Scottish Pykes. My Lord of Warwicke was everywhere encouraging
ordering and ranking of his men afresh. On the Scots side Angus bore the
brunt of our attack with his heavy Pykemen from the Lowlands. Arran
and Huntley turned bridle and rode for their lives with us after them to
Edinbro's walls. Arran with what was left of his Companie crossed the
marsh helter-skelter for Dalkeith. Only the Highlanders retreated in good
wise and orderlie fighting to the last. The number of ennemie slaine was
nigh on 14,000 a mighty holocaust of dead and dying the ground strewne
with Swordes, Pykes, Lances thick as rushes on a chamber floor. So was
it ended and my good Phoebe is now well recovered as am I from a scratch
on my arme and will be home with you againe, dear Sir, come Michaelmas
God willing…

But Michaelmas had come and gone before Philip was home
again at Sprowston. Not until a month from the day of the
Battle did the duke, marching south, arrive in London crowned
with glory, acclaimed a conquering hero and intrepid victor,
foremost in the thick of the fight; or so report gave it. Yet
from those, unrecognised, who had shared with him the 'glory',
were heard mutters, below breath, that the Lord Protector had
taken to himself the honour of victory which, for good
generalship and sheet outstanding courage, should rightly have
been Warwick's. Nevertheless the duke declined the triumphal
procession offered him by grateful citizens. Parsimony or
modesty, more feasible the former, may have prompted his

refusal; or, perhaps, as conscience sop expressed between the lines of his Declaration to the Scots, wherein he persisted on the great advantage to be gained by a marriage with their little Queen to Edward, thus joining the two nations in 'Amity, Concord, and Peace'.

It is doubtful if the Scots were so eager to acknowledge 'Amity, Concord and Peace', when they buried their fourteen thousand slaughtered dead and saw their castles and their cottages laid in smoking ruins where amity and concord had fired them to cinders. But they still held their child Queen in safe custody at Stirling until the coast should be clear of Clinton's Fleet, when they could ship her off to France and to the Dauphin.

Somerset, however, had other matters pending of more immediate concern than his failure to achieve a union with Scotland. His brother Thomas, who had refused the proffered command of the Fleet, which was to co-operate with the Protector's army in the recent campaign, preferred, as he put it, 'to abide at home, merry-making with friends in the country.'

Accounts of Tom Seymour's 'merry-making' in the country and with one particular 'friend', were served by the duchess to her duke, and by him received in horror brushed with scepticism.

'How? What! And she but fourteen — a mere child.'

'Child!' echoed the duchess with incalculable scorn. 'So much a child is she as to be *with* child, from what is spoke in common talk as I've had it from one Parry, the cofferer at Chelsea, who was given it *verbatim* by the governess, Kate Ashley, how that when the Bullen's vixen cub lay a-bed so would Seymour come betimes in early morning to her chamber afore the household stirred, and then —' A vibrant pause.

'What then?' the duke faint-heartedly prompted.

'Why, then,' his wife approached her full moist lips to his shrinkingly expectant ear, 'and this ... and thus ... and so ... as told to me by Parry whom I've no cause to doubt, in that he deplores Seymour's cozening ways with Edward, and *he* says, as he had it from Ashley, how your pimpish brother — no!' Virtuously the duchess shook her head. 'I cannot bring myself to tell it.'

Nervously fingering his forked fair beard, 'I beg,' urged the duke, 'that you tell it.'

And she told, while he, inexpressibly shocked, let fly an explosive accompaniment delivered, for all the world, as pellets from a catapult.

'What? No! Slapping of her — *what?* Backside? Upside? In nothing but her —? Never!'

And so much worse to come before his wife had finished that he forgot himself and roundly rated her for bringing him a 'muck o' lies and tattle dished by servants, fit only to be spewed up on a garbage heap.'

Which unparalleled retort from her mild-mannered husband momentarily deprived her of her breath. She stood with fallen lip, mustering her forces to fling at him, 'So much is it a muck o' lies that she, Mistress Mealy-mouthed Katherine Parr, has banished from her house the Bullen's brat.'

'Banished —?' The Duke's attempt at self-assertion in the face of this announcement equally was banished. 'Has she so?'

'She has — so!' spat the duchess. 'Which is proof enough, if proof were needed more than that the late King's bastard and your brother's bawd, carries in her belly, neck and neck with the Parr, what was never there before she went to Chelsea. Take it how you will, I have told you as 'twas told to me.' Sweeping to the door the duchess turned. 'Your brother is a menace to you, to the King, to the State. Think well on this,' she adjured her husband strongly, 'unless you wish to see us plunged in yet another war.'

'War?' the paling duke repeated.

'War, I said and —' Her Grace, in exit, halted, hissingly to emphasise — 'war, or civil war, an you like it better, do I mean. Your brother, in your absence, has made good use of his time not only in whoring but in scheming, low-cunningly, with Edward. I know what you, star-gazing, head-in-air, do not, how Seymour, a son of Belial, has wheedled Dorset, that goose-livered witling, Jane Grey's father, into handing him two thousand gold angels for her board and keep — *and* for her dower to Edward. Hah! That's news to you, is it?' The Duchess presented her husband with a baring of her teeth which on her face served as a smile. 'And this may also be of news to you. Dorset's wife Frances, albeit I abhor her, has voice with me, and an axe —' the duke shied as that word fell from his boiling duchess — 'an axe,' she meaningfully repeated, 'of her own to grind, standing third in the Succession and not joyed to see your brother's way with Edward to name Jane and her sisters before herself in the event, he being puny, of a kingless throne.'

The Duke, still fingering his beard, murmured dutifully into it, 'May God defend.'

'Amen,' was Her Grace's brisk reply. 'But let me tell you, Frances Dorset swears how your brother, at their board, did bellow loud for half the council there to hear him that, "By God's precious soul he would make your next Parliament the blackest that ever was in England." So take *that* now as it be worth, and think it over.'

With which parting shot the duchess left him to think it over, with eventual — and, for Seymour, calamitous — result.

It was a day of mist with a fine drizzle of rain when Philip set out from St. James's on his journey home. He had sent John Locke to the Chepe earlier that morning for some last-minute purchases with instructions to meet him by London's wall at Bishop's Gate.

Since his mare, Phoebe, was out at grass enjoying a well-deserved rest, he rode a young bay gelding bought of Tom Wroth, guaranteed a good pacer and with a mouth of silk, that Philip, while deprived of the use of an arm, could ride him single-handed on the bridle. So soft a mouth indeed had he, and so responsive to the slightest touch, that Philip scarcely knew he had reined him to the right along a certain lane to draw up before a certain house.

One look above at a window, one look below at a door standing invitingly open, decided him. He dismounted, tethered his horse to the gate-post, walked up the flagged path, bordered with late autumn asters ... and was followed.

Not by her, whom for the last three months he had striven, past forgetting, to forget; to crush from his heart the aching thought of all that might have been and the ever-longing hope for that which still might be.

No patriotic compulsion had urged him to serve in the Scottish campaign, any more than his devil-may-care display of spectacular courage was that of the patriot or hero, rather that of the escapist; yet he had not escaped.

Throughout the long trek to the Border, in the first and last heat of the fight, amid that red-stained massacre of its finale, she had walked beside him day by day; had lain beside him night by night when, in his tent, on his straw pallet, weak from loss of blood and in high fever from the poison of his wound, he had raved of unkissed kisses, of love-ecstasies unshared. And, as now he turned, her name unspoken on his lips ready to receive her in the flesh, the spirit, or whatever else of haunting sweet, insufferable torment she might have for him, he saw, not her, but that other, that shadowy third, who had come to be intrinsically as much a facet of their lives as was their guarded secret. And it seemed to him, strangely, that they three were strung together by some spectral cord which, if cut, would cause each one of them internally to bleed. Then, dismissing such fantastic notion as a symptom of the fever still lurking in his veins, Philip gave an answering smile, that felt like the grin of a death's head, to the hesitant, smiling welcome of him who, with tentative compassion, touched his bandaged arm.

'An honourable memento, sir, of your gallantry, of which we have had news, but not a sight of you since your return from Scotland. Come in, come in — and tell us of your doings.' His hands persuaded Philip to the door.

As they entered, the mongrel dog came hoppity to meet them, his ridiculous long tail frantically a-wag, while a tortoiseshell cat, her sides distended with impending motherhood, rubbed herself, loudly purring, round Gynkes's ankles.

'You remember this poor little one?' Still vaguely smiling he bent to fondle her, 'saved from crucifixion and now big with her first litter. If you would be wishing for a kitten, Master Pugh, I'll gladly give … or would the King accept…?' His voice trailed off; his pale eyes went wandering. 'I'm told His Majesty has a love for all dumb creatures.'

'That is so,' agreed Philip, 'but I think His Majesty's affections lie more with dogs than with cats. However,' he hastened to add as he saw his host chapfallen, 'I will submit your offer to present the King with one of this good matron's progeny when I return to Court which will not be until some three months hence, for I am even now upon my way to Norfolk where I shall stay until the year be out.'

'Norfolk?' repeated Gynkes, as in a daze. 'Now that is ... yes, this fadges well with ... He spoke half to himself; and, gesturing Philip to a settle by the hearth where the crackling logs sent forth a fragrance of aromatic herbs, 'Pray be seated, Master Pugh,' he said. 'So you go to Norfolk. We too ... I'll call my wife. She'll be rejoiced to see you, but sad, as am I, that you are injured. Please God you'll soon recover in your native air. 'Tis a sore discomfort to be disabled of a limb and your right arm, too. I, as it haps, by some oddity of birth,' this with a creeping glance aside and a dropping of that one-toned voice, 'am left-handed which is as well, for my right hand,' he held out to Philip a hooked finger, 'is stiffened in a joint and immovable. Will you take a sack possett to warm you on your journey? I trust you are not wetted by the rain?' His balding forehead, from which the pale hair receded, was anxiously wrinkled. 'If so I'll have my servant dry your outer garments.'

'No, indeed, I thank you, sir, but I am dry enough.'

'Then wait you here a moment. I'll tell my wife...' And all the while he spoke Gynkes was edging to the hall-screens. Indeterminedly poised against the dark carved oak in his bright broidered doublet of raspberry doth slashed with primrose satin, his thin stork-like legs encased in yellow hosen, he gave the impression of some gaudy and curious bird about to moult; an impression enhanced by that pale long beaked nose, enquiringly pointed, and a hand, thin and bony as a claw, hovering about his scanty beard.

'Your home, then, is in Norfolk? *Your* home,' smilingly insisted Master Gynkes, 'and not your father's?'

'Yes, my father's.'

'As so was the home of Lord Sowerby, the father of my wife, in Norfolk, which is why...' he inclined his head as if listening. 'I think I hear her in the buttery. I'll go fetch...' And it was as if he evaporated through the screens, so slowly, without sound, did he back and disappear.

Philip stretched his legs to the warmth of the logs, and the dog stretched himself at his feet, both fixedly staring at the fire as if each saw his image pictured there; and to Philip it seemed that the upward leap of the flames was not unlike man's fitful passions, his irresponsible tempestuous demands, that, clutching at each ephemeral delight, were quenched in the smoke of illusion. Was Love of man for woman, then, but a consuming fire to scorch the soul and devour the heart as those Smithfield flames had scorched and devoured a black and shrivelled thing, bound to a stake? No, Love must surely be more vital to man's destiny than a fierce pitiless burning to ashes of all that made life bearable. The shared comradeship of mind and body, lighting a beacon along the years ahead to live, grow old together, and to die and live again, eternally, as one. That could be love as, save for his own mole-blindness, so could he have had it instead of loneliness and hunger that fed on starvation unsatisfied by sordid transitory adventure. Such was the Dead Sea fruit of love, and its taste bitter...

A sigh like a groan escaped him. The dog at his feet looked up; he, too, looked up to find her there. So noiseless was her coming, or he so deep in thought, he believed her yet another of his hauntings.

He stood, and stiffly said, 'I am on my way to Sprowston. I called to know if you would wish me to take a message to my father, or the dame.'

'Yes, give them.' Her face, framed by the dark wings of her hair, was tinged with the fire's glow that sparked a gleam of laughter in her eyes. 'No, give him, your father, my dear love, but not the dame, for between herself and me there's mighty little love to give or take. And you may tell your father also that soon I'll visit him.'

'You will visit him?' His heart jumped.

'Gynkes,' she said, 'has bought my father's house at Drayton. It was for sale, so he heard from Serjeant Flowerdew.'

Philip received this in silence to review a vista of entrancing possibilities. Drayton. Were she there and he at Sprowston, what endless opportunities for contact might be theirs! Mastering elation, and with well-assumed indifference, he enquired: 'Is that so? And did you suggest to your husband he should —'

'I did not.' Swift to dispel that delusion, 'it was his own thought,' she said, 'not mine. I told you, for this long time past, since when we were at Chelsea, he's been watchful. Is it devilment,' her voice sank, 'or saintliness, that seeks, as I feel certain is his purpose, to fling us in each other's path? He will be —' and now a shadowed fear showed in her eyes — 'always asking questions of our early life together; why you so seldom come here, or why I never speak of you who, so he will have it, are close-bound to me as if you were my brother. And he says he loves you as a brother, too. And when he learned that you were gone with the duke to fight the Scots, he was so restless, so disquieted,' she paused, and the crippled dog got up from where he lay and came to her, nuzzling her hand dropped to her side, 'that in his sleep he would cry your name over and over.'

'Must I,' Philip's lips tightened, 'hear your wedded intimacies?'

And at the chill in his face and in his words, the blood rushed to her cheeks and they were back ten years in time's dissolving, her tongue quick to lash. 'Is it of my choice that he and I are coupled? Had you been less of a laggard, my "wedded intimacies", as you are pleased to call his lawful rights, would have been yours. And 'tis only since you cannot have me that you want me — if you do!'

The stab of that riposte struck home to leave him white as she was red. So now these two, who but a second past had, each for each, been pulsing hot, stood in storm-blurred enmity together, until, on a choking breath, he uttered: 'You — you think — you doubt? Then by the Living God,' he swore, 'for that I'll make *you* want me — as much as ever in my life I've wanted you!'

They did not know themselves ridiculous, they only knew themselves in love, while she, tears brimming to her lashes, joy-flushed at his agony, laughed at it and him, and said, 'Is that the way it is with you who once did hate the sight of me, up and ready to damp horns on him, poor soul, who in his fashion loves me more than —' Her eyes left his, were lowered to his sleeveless arm, carried in a sling, and: 'O,' she said, in sighing, 'dear heart, and you so wounded, for me to wound you more.' She neared him then, caressingly to touch the padded wad that bound the splintered bone down to the wrist. 'Does it hurt?'

He marvelled at this swift change of mood that showed her yet to be unchanged, a child still. And when, to soothe her, he assured her that, no, it did not hurt — 'twas a nothing, almost healed — she again, and with a child's naive inquisitiveness, needs must probe him for a full account of the battle, which he would have given just to watch her crouched there in the rushes, her hands clasping her knees, as so often had she sat with him at Sprowston while he would tell her, not unboastfully, of his life and doings at the Court.

'Sit you here,' she forced him back on to the settle, 'you must rest while you may for you've a long ride before you. So, tell —'

But what he had to tell was never told. The entrance of her husband followed by a servant carrying a salver, brought her in a scramble to her feet. Sack was served, and comfits, cakes, Gynkes nibbling and sharing what he ate with the monkey on his shoulder, sliding titbits to the dog, and saying, without a look for Philip or Jocosa: 'An my wife has not yet spoke of my intent, Master Pugh, you will be glad to hear that I have bought her father's house where she was born.' So the talk was all of that; and how Serjeant Flowerdew of Hethersett, 'being of those parts has, on advice of my Lord Rich, with whom he is on best of terms, undertaken to instruct a builder at my orders to have the manor of the late Lord Sowerby of Drayton, father of my wife, put in goodly state for her habitation. I have paid for the house and its lands in her name, the sum of three hundred pounds … No, Jeremy,' Gynkes disengaged the monkey's paw from a jewelled button on his sleeve, 'you mustn't pull. You'll have it off … that in my lifetime and hereafter,' he gave his little empty laugh, 'she shall have her dwelling place in her native Norfolk and nigh unto your home, Master Pugh.'

This smiling monologue, accompanied by spasmodic movements of the head, was the more disconcerting in that it seemed to come not so much from the speaker as from some unseen agency that jerked a string and spoke the words in puppet mime of drama, comedy — or what? — until that toneless voice ran down at last and they three sat in silence.

Philip rose; he said he must be going, it was already high noon, and in these shortening days he must make what speed he could before nightfall; and with a brief 'Farewell, I'll give your message to my father' to her, he found himself outside the door and at the gate, his host behind him asking anxiously, 'Can you mount unaided, Master Pugh?' But before he could lend assistance, Philip was in the saddle, eyes upraised to see a curtain at a dormer window tremble, a face framed in the lattice, and a hand lifted in a gesture that went with him all the way.

The Maid's Head at Norwich was more than usually crowded, even for a market day, when John Locke, on a morning at the turn of the year, pushed open the inn door and sat himself in the only vacant place at the trestle board down the centre of the parlour. He had been commissioned by the dame to buy a drum of dried figs, half a bushel of oysters, twenty pounds of sugar, one dozen dead quails for roasting, a brace of live conies for breeding, and for the dame herself, a thimble.

Having made his purchases, from two gold angels given him by the dame with instructions to see that he received the correct change, and having repeatedly counted the silver left from it to find a different total every time, he was in a pother lest he should have disremembered something. What? Searching through his saddle-bags placed, with the rabbit-hutch and its huddled contents at his feet for safety, since it would never do to leave temptation strapped to his horse in the inn-yard with all these Romanies and ill-conditioned other sort of folk about on market day, he found he had forgot to buy the thimble. Well, it could wait, which his ale, freshly drawn, could not. Stolidly regarding the head of white froth bubbling to the tankard's brim, John, having judged to a nicety the exact moment for consumption, took his first deep satisfying draught, smacked his lips, and returned the half-emptied tankard to the trestle for further contemplation. And while he listened to the gabble of talk around him, he heard, above the comings and goings and the busy clatter and confusion, one voice ring out, spoken by a rubicund stout fellow in a green leather jerkin, and known to John by sight as one John Browne, a cooper, of Old Buckenham. Challenging attention from the company with a thump of his fist on the board, he oratorically addressed them.

'Harken here, my masters. The remedy lies in your hands and yours alone. What boots it to go whining like kicked curs of your complaints to them who suck the blood from your veins and the marrow from your bones? They, who have stolen the birthright of your common land left to you by your forefathers. Ay! And in defiance of the law by Act of Parliament passed in the old King's reign, grandsire of this young one, who —'

A murmurous hubbub broke in upon his speechifying.

'We know naught o' that!'

'Who broke the law, if 'un were passed?'

'Greedy puttocks!' growled another; this a black-bearded giant, swart, unkempt, whose mouthful of yellow fangs lacked two in the upper jaw. 'Caterpillars o' the common weal. *They* be whoam to thank for't, bor'.'

'Which, being so,' said the cooper, who had now the eyes and ears of the whole room, including John, who was sitting bolt upright, his chin thrust forward, his horn cup halted halfway to his face, while he surveyed the rhetorical Browne with a look of mingled repugnance and astonishment. 'Which, being so,' again a fisted thump on the table, 'seek you your remedy. Caterpillars? Hah! That be a good 'un seeing as how them that ride ye feed on your pastures to strip 'un bare, ditched round, enclosed by hedge and fence that none can take nor weed nor root from the soil which be your'n by right o' birth and promise. Yea, sirs, an' if belike a plague o' caterpillars shall fall on to devour your cabbages, lettuces, or what not of greenery — an you have leave to grow 'un in one square inch o' ground outside your door — would you sit by and watch them pests go gorge theirselves nor raise hand or foot to crush them dead? Or would you say to 'em, "Lords, I prithee fill your bellies with these choice fruits o' my labour while I chew road-verge grass, for that be free to all, and thankful am I for even thus much bounty without asking of your Lordships' leave"?'

Some laughter greeted this, while Blackbeard, glaring round at the assembly, and before Master Browne could launch forth again, had put in his word.

'Thankful, yeh! And thankful we should be that we may live — and breathe the common air without askin' by your leave. God's bones! 'Tis deeds we want, not words. For years, since long time back we 'ahve been stuffed chock full o' words enow from suchlike brave fellows as yourseln'.' He grinned to show his reddened gums, and those around the table fell silent, casting sullen eyes at this foul-smelling object in their midst, so evidently of the vagabondage and not fit to rub shoulders with cleanly decent folk, who, no matter they be beggared, yet were honest. But as if unaware of or, from past experience, immune to animosity, 'Yeh, he continued, sliding a filthy hand inside his ragged shirt to ease himself of nesting lice, I mind me how as some time agone when I was stocked on the green at Griston for lifting pigs' swill from a trough to feed my wife in child-bed, and she starvin' hungered, with her milk run sour on her for want of bite nor sup, that the babe sickened and died. Yeh, they stocked me there for petty thievin', as 'twas called, for 'ahvin took what the pigs had left, and lucky were I, so they told me, to 'scape the slicing of my ears — I mind me then how one John Walker did call together some hinds and commons of those parts there on the green where I was stocked, and he did say an so be it ten or twelve good fellows 'ud ride in the night, with every man a bell, and cry in every town they passed, "Pluck down t'enclosures, fill up the ditches and take unto yourseln' what be your own and as many as will not turn to us and render, let us kill 'un even to their childer in their cradles, and when that we 'ahve number enow for to follow us, we will go into their housen and tak' to us all of 'arness and arms that we may find, and vittels for our venture." Which, as this John Walker said, nothing venture nothing 'ahve. But naught did come on't.' Blackbeard, having ceased to scratch, took up his empty cup, stared down at it despondently, and. 'No,' quoth he, 'nor never will, unless one ups with us for leader.'

'Find us such an one then,' cried John Browne, 'and we'll follow him!'

Whereupon Blackbeard, who had raised his head at the opening of the tavern door, jerked it in that direction, saying, 'Such an one is 'ere an' ready up — if I know aught of 'un.'

John Locke slid a look at the newcomer who stood in the doorway and whose entrance caused a stir, with the landlord bowing, the company rising, the cooper advancing, his verbosity flown at a signal from him who demanded peremptorily, 'You, Cooper Browne — those dozen casks you gave promise to deliver at my house yesternoon? Where be they — my twelve casks?'

'I — certes, master, I'll bring 'em to you, sir, the morrow. They be all stacked for delivery, save two.'

'Then you can bring the other ten this day.'

'Ay, master, but,' said the cooper, crestfallen, 'there'll be more than one wagon-load that I must bring 'un back and forth in twice —'

'Bring all you may in once, and make me no shifty sawder for your dallying.' Standing there in the doorway letting in a draught of crisp fresh air, a cold sunbeam lighting his bare head, a whimsical smile lighting his keen eyes, deepest beneath their beetled brows, his glance slowly travelled round the staring company to pinion the sidling innkeeper.

'Sir host, out with your flagons. Give each a stoup of wine. We'll drink,' cried Robert Kett, 'to our good fellowship!'

BOOK THREE (1548-1553)

Arbores serit diligens agricola, quaram aspiciet baccam ipse nunquam.
The diligent husbandman sows trees of which he himself will
never see the fruit.

Cicero

TEN

In the long gallery at Hampton Court a small boy knelt on the deep recessed window seat looking out at a vista of rain-silvered lawns and soaked flower-beds. A month of August drought had passed with the coming of September, and now a beggar's cloak of cloud hung low in the sullen sky to bide all trace of blue ... 'A moody day, a weeping day, most fitting to my miser-ray', he recited to himself, which sentiment he found to be so painfully affecting that it brought a rock into his throat and a rush of water to his eyes. Stealing a glance behind him at the group of pages clustered at the door of his Privy Chamber, 'Silly loons!' he muttered; and to show them that boys of eleven, or near as five weeks to eleven, did not give way to girlish tears even though their tenderest feelings were wracked to breaking point, he pursed his lips in a tremulous whistle to wake his spaniel dozing beside him on the seat. Lifting the dog in his arms, he rested his chin on the satiny smooth head, dolefully to think upon his sorrows.

She was gone, his dear, most kind stepmother Katherine, lost to him for ever, dead of the daughter borne to his Uncle Tom. Another unwilling tear trickled from under his eyelid. The dog snuggled closer, lovingly upgazing. Edward blinked, and surreptitiously kissed the moist black nose ... And the worst of it was, he reflected, whether or no the oversight had been deliberate, he had not been told of her death till after her burial, not in fact until last night; nor had he yet recovered from the shock.

If he had been consulted he would have had her brought to Westminster, laid her in the abbey and would himself have followed the bier as chief mourner; instead, Jane Grey, who for these past few months had been living with the Queen at Sudeley Castle, his Uncle Seymour's house in Gloucestershire, was chief mourner, and as far as Edward knew, Jane would go on living there at Sudeley as ward of his Uncle Tom ... Were he but a few years older he could marry Jane and have her live with him, for there was no reason on earth why Tom Seymour, to whom she was not even related, should be her guardian. Or, come to that, why he, the King, should have a Protector, or in any case such a muddling old jackass as his other uncle, Somerset. For, as his Uncle Tom had told him when, last Christmas Day, he had come to St. James's with gifts from the Queen, 'It was never your father's wish there should be a Protectorate — leastways in the hands of one who bleeds you of your kingly rights to gain his grasping ends. Look at that great palace he is building for himself along the Strand. Whose money goes to pay for the cost of it, running into thousands? Yours. Your money — squandered — so he and his wife may wallow in magnificence while you go short that you must borrow ready cash of Pugh, your gentleman.'

Edward wondered how his uncle could have known of that. Not from Philip, certainly; from Fowler, very like, the snake and: 'God's Soul!' his uncle had roared at him, 'a fine king, you! Little better placed than a jailbird, fed, clothed, decked out in a mockery of kingship — a pawn on the chequerboard of him who would snatch the Crown from your head as your grandfather, the Welshman, snatched it from the head of Crookback at Bosworth.'

It was all most disturbing; nor had Edward much relished this crude reminder of the dynastic upheaval that had raised the House of Tudor from the naked and dead body of King Richard, even though he were the murderer of those two boys, Edward's own great-uncles ... And then there was that other time when the Admiral had brought him a letter to sign and present to Parliament as protest against his over-bearing Protector and those 'kingly' rights denied him, demanding that he, the Admiral, should have the custody of the King's person. But Edward had thought it best to ask advice of Philip Pugh and of Mr. Cheke, his tutor, who told him to have nothing to do with it. His carefully worded refusal, 'If it were my kingly right for you to be my custodian, Parliament would have allowed it; therefore it must be wrong,' had sent Seymour off in a blistering rage vowing vengeance on any man — or brat — who dared oppose him. Quite beside himself he was, which had made Edward wonder if all this interest in him and in his cause were wholly altruistic. Yet he could not but agree with his uncle how grossly unfair it was that the King should have no voice in the ordering of his own life; no word in the governance of his own country, he, whose face was stamped on every new coin <u>mint</u>ed and yet had less money to spend than any one of his own pages.

And, thinking of those new coins bearing the imprint of his crowned head, Edward was minded of something Barnaby had told him; how that streams of base money were said to be pouring out from the Mint at Bristol, of which Sir William Sharrington was Master; and he, so Barnaby declared — trust him to grub up any rags of gossip that might be floating round — this Sharrington, it seemed, had been clipping the coinage, issuing 'testoons', as Barnaby called them, of which two-thirds were counterfeit; and Sharrington was Tom Seymour's bosom friend!

The rain had stopped; a watery sun shaft struggled through the lifting clouds. Edward raised his head and, without turning it, called to the group of boys at the far end of the gallery. 'Barnaby! Is Barnaby there?'

Barnaby was not there.

Little Charles Brandon came forward.

'Sh-sh-shall I go f-f-fetch —?'

'Yes, Charlie, go fetch him,' Edward kindly cut in on the tongue-twisted Charles, 'and the rest of you can leave me. You too, Charlie. Take Corin with you and give him a run. He's not been out to do his dog since first thing this morning, and that was none too good. He's been costive these three days. I'll have Master Vaughan give him a purge.' The spaniel, fastened by a strap to a collar of gold, was led by Lord Charles away.

Edward got up from where he sat and sauntered over to the chimney-piece above which hung the portrait of his father painted some four years before he died. *That,* his son decided, *is not as I knew him, but Holbein always shirks a faithful likeness of the Royalties. Afraid of offending us, I expect.* He glanced at his own portrait on the wall at right angles. *See what he's made of me, I might be a girl dressed up, when I was — how old? Three? As for this* — again he studied Holbein's masterpiece of his father — *there's no bulk here, no monstrous sagging belly; none of that purplish look as of an over-ripe plum; but the eyes, those narrow little pig's eyes, are his — and mine — to the life.*

'You sent for me, Sire?'

'Barnaby,' Edward asked, still gazing at the picture, 'Am I at all like him, do you think?'

'As like,' was the prompt reply, 'as a leprechaun is to a hippopotamus.'

Edward wheeled round. 'A leprechaun? What's that?'

'"Tis a native of my country, one of the small green people who dwell in the hills. The word comes from the old Irish *lu,* meaning little, and *corpan,* a body. I've seen 'um oft-times dancing in a moondrift under the trees at home with a singing as of crickets, but you have to look close to find 'um, their hair being grass-coloured and their jerkins too.'

'Oh? And I presume,' said Edward acidly, 'that you've seen hippopotami dancing in a moondrift?'

'Not at all. But Marco Polo may have seen 'um.'

'We have no evidence that Marco Polo ever went to Africa.'

'Who said he did?'

'You implied it, because — since hippopotami inhabit the African swamps — Marco Polo must have gone to Africa to see them. But I should think it much more likely that Necho, son of Psamatik I of the Saite Dynasty, who, as recorded by Herodotus, explored the north-west coast *circa* 600 B.C., was the first to sight and name them, in as much as the word derives from the Greek *hippo,* a horse, and *potamus,* a river.'

'Imagine!' uttered Barnaby. 'I wonder your head don't burst, so stuffed is it with knowledge.'

Edward shrugged a shoulder. 'Of a sort and of no use to me, who am given nothing that I ought to know and crammed with facts that I don't need to know. Come here.' Moving away from the picture he went back to the window; Barnaby followed and, as etiquette demanded, despite their easy comradeship, he stood till the King, frowningly pre-occupied, bade him curtly: 'Sit.' Then, 'You were telling me,' Edward cast a wary look from one end of the gallery to the other, and satisfied that none was within eye or ear shot, he resumed, 'how when you were in Ireland you heard talk of my Uncle Seymour's capture of the Scilly Isles and something of his traffic there with pirates, so you said, or were about to say when the duchess came in. You remember?'

Barnaby nodded.

'Well, what was it you had in mind to tell me?'

''Tis a long story —' began Barnaby.

'And a high one?' suggested Edward with a grin.

'— as I had it from me father,' Barnaby continued, undeterred, 'who had it from the Mayor o' Cork himself how that the Mayor had seen urn rollicking in the streets there and them lying out in the harbour, and —'

'How,' interrupted the literal Edward, 'could the Mayor of Cork have seen 'them', whoever they may be, in the streets, if they were lying out, as you say, in the harbour?'

''Twas their ships, the pirate ships, lying out in the harbour,' said Barnaby, 'and themselves, drunk and roaring every man of them.'

'But how,' came the inevitable question, 'did the Mayor of Cork from whom your father, as you say, had this information, know that these rollicking, drunken, roaring men *were* pirates?'

'Sure, they were pirates, with the death's head and cross-bones painted on their fronts and backs and them off to the Sallies to link up with your uncle, the Admiral, and himself waiting open arms on the shore there to receive 'um and their booty.'

'I don't believe a word of it!' cried Edward.

'Strike me dead,' Barnaby responded imperturbably, 'if what I tell Your Grace be not the truth as I did hear it from me father. Would I perjure me soul and forfeit all hope of eternal glory for a lie?'

'You'd forfeit your soul — if I know you — for something far less than a lie. Come on, Barney,' Edward coaxed, 'confess. All this is pure apocrypha.'

'Cross me heart, I swear to God 'tis — *cave!* Be easy now,' Barnaby put a finger to his lips, 'here's Charlie. His ears don't play him false if his tongue does.'

Charles, leading Edward's spaniel, handed him back to his master.

'Any result?' enquired Edward.

'N-n-none, your Ma-Ma-Ma-Maj —'

'Then,' said Edward, 'we must send at once for Master Vaughan.' But as Charles bowed and backed he stayed him — 'Wait,' and critically looked his pages over; both were in their scarlet liveries, slashed and embroidered with gold; Edward, too, was dressed in brightest colours. 'Have any orders been issued,' he demanded, 'with regard to Court mourning?'

'None, Sire, to us,' replied Barnaby.

'Then you can take,' said the King, 'this order from me. All my pages, for this next three months, must go in black, and I, for half a year, will wear the purple in deference to Katherine, the Queen.'

Throughout the month of February, 1549, the house in Water Lane was the scene of much activity. Although Master Gynkes had decided to retain his residence in London, certain necessary movables must be taken thence to Drayton.

On the advice of Serjeant Flowerdew he had sold his house at Chelsea, the proceeds of the sale having paid for the rehabilitation of Sowerby Manor. Jocosa, glad of any diversion from the searing monotony of her daily life, busied herself with the buying of materials for bed-curtains, counterpanes, cushions. Gynkes, too, had spent much time and money in shopping expeditions to the Chepe, returning home with a jumble of articles which are listed in an inventory of their household goods as items: *Six saltes, nine goblettes, four covered cuppes, a Spanysshe spice-dishe, and a Barber's bassine.*

'What do you want with another barber's basin?' Jocosa wished to know. 'You have three already for blood-letting, and this has cost six shillings, a mort o' money for a basin.'

'It is of solid silver,' said her husband meekly; and following the suggested train of thought, he added, 'I've a mind to be shorn of my beard.'

'Why?'

'That it may grow stronger.' His wandering glance came vacantly to rest somewhere in the middle distance. ''Tis but a sorry growth, not having recovered its full strength since I took the smallpox before that we were wed. Yes, and,' he nodded brightly, 'there be other reasons for't as advised by my — by one whom I consulted in a certain cause.'

'Fie, Gynkes, you are mighty mysterious. And what,' she asked, less to satisfy her curiosity than to humour him, 'is this certain cause?'

'I'll tell you sometime, and in the meantime,' his eyes shifted from their focal point and travelled to her glossy head, down-bent above her tambour frame, 'let this one reason satisfy. I think you care more for shaven men than bearded.'

'And why should you think that?' She was accustomed to this verbal game of battledore and shuttlecock, light as feather-down between them and as trivial; yet she must always fear a stealthy insinuation in such toneless commentary as now, when he made answer, 'Because he — your kinsman and friend of your youth — he has no beard. Maybe his beard, were it to grow, would be as weak as mine.' And from that fixed, pale stare Jocosa turned away to rummage among the skeins of coloured silks on the stool beside her. She was embroidering a length of crimson damask for a bed. On the death of her father his property had been seized by one of his creditors, John Green, Lord of the Manor of Wilby, who, while confiscating and enclosing the Sowerby lands, had allowed the house to fall into decay. The title deeds of the sale included a moiety of the furnishings and the bed on which Jocosa was born.

'That,' Gynkes said, watching her re-thread her needle, 'will be a handsome piece of broidery when it is done. For what purpose will you use it?'

'As a tester for my bed at Sowerby.'

She heard the crack of his knuckles and knew his hands were clenched together, the fingers intertwined in one of those unconsciously tormenting tricks of his. '*Our* bed,' he gently corrected, 'the bed I bought for you, which was your parents' marriage bed. Serjeant Flowerdew reports it of great worth, although worm-ridden and in sad neglect. I'll have it cleansed and put in order before we lie there.' The rushes, freshly strewn, hissed to his step as he neared her. 'When would you wish to go from here?'

'So soon as it may suit your conveniency, sir.'

'My conveniency, sweeting, is yours.'

'Then it were best we wait till after Eastertide, when the roads are easier for travel They'll be hock-high in mud till then.'

'An it please you, wife, I am content.' A pause. 'Mayhap Master Pugh will travel with us should he be visiting his father at that time.'

'I do not know if —' a tensive muscle moved in her throat as she swallowed — 'if Philip be returning to Sprowston in the springtime.'

Again his knuckles cracked, and at that sound she caught her underlip beneath a tooth to halt a scream, but steadying her voices her bitten lip released: 'He — Philip,' she said dearly, 'prefers, I think, to be at Sprowston nearer Michaelmas, which is his birthday.'

'So? His birthday? Then you and he are almost of one age.' He stood over her, so close that she could smell the pungent musty odour of him, underlying the perfume with which he soaked himself 'Brought up together as brother and sister, sharing your pastimes and all of your young lives since ever you were codlings. It must have been a sorrow for you to part from him, and he from you. I wonder he does not take him a wife. What is it you look for?'

'My needle.' She was down on her knees in the rushes. 'It slipped a thread.'

'You'll not find it.' He gave his little empty laugh. 'Searching for a needle in a haystack. Yet he's still young enough to marry as at your age, but two and twenty. Of what age were you when you left the convent to live with him at Sprowston?'

'Twelve years,' she answered wearily, 'as I have told you many times. Nor were he and I at Sprowston together, save when he came there on vacation from the Court.' She lifted a flushed face. 'You are right. I'll never find it,' and got upon her feet. ''Tis no matter. I am short of silks and must send out for more before I can go on with this.'

Gathering the twisted skeins she placed them in a casket of carved ivory inlaid with pearls — one of her husband's many gifts to her — and taking her tambour frame stowed all away in an oaken chest that stood between the windows. Gynkes, still standing by her chair, followed with his eyes her every movement.

The hall darkened to the wintry dusk; the logs spluttered and flared, casting a flickering red light on panelled walls, struck fiery gleams from the bediamonded hilt of his dagger and the jewelled buttons of his doublet. Suddenly: 'Your beauty,' he said in his colourless voice, 'is like that fire's flame. It burns — it burns me — here.' He touched his chest. 'Does he not say that you are beautiful?'

She closed the drawer and turned; her face, warmed by the fire's glow, became for a moment very still.

'He? Of whom do you speak?'

'Of whom should I speak?' His eyes widened that their whites looked to be merged in the pale irids, giving almost the impression he was sightless. 'Of whom — but of my brother? For since he is your brother in all but name, he must be my brother too. I love him as I would were he my brother, and I grieve he comes not more often to visit at my house. So rare are his visits that I ... I can only see him in my dreams. Last night again I dreamed...'

He approached her. She backed from him till she stood pressed against the wall, her hands spread behind her clutching at the moulded ledge. 'Yes, last night,' he told her softly, 'I dreamed that he and I were together in some open place, with a great noise of men around us and the clash of arms as if a battle raged, though I saw none save him and I — the rest were shadows. And it was as he and I were joined in a fierce struggle one against the other, or in my dream as in a close embrace, until I saw myself and he were drenched in blood — his blood — that gushed in a red vomit from his side to drown me, that I —' he cracked his knuckles — 'that I cried out. And then,' his mouth stretched to a smile, and he giggled, 'then I woke.'

'You,' she made her lips firm to tell him, 'ate too much and too late of roast pig for your supper, lying heavy on your stomach that you rode the night mare.'

'Yes,' he said, and 'Yes,' again, with awful eagerness. 'I rode the night mare, as always I ride her. A gaunt red mare she is with tossing mane that I dread to sleep lest I be carried off so far I'll not return, which is likely why I cannot hold my water, so I wet my bed o' nights.'

Jocosa closed her eyes, shutting out the sight of him and of that smile. 'I'll go tell the cook to stew you a sheep's heart stuffed with marjoram, which they say is beneficial for incontin … ence.'

And how she got away she did not know.

Behind the screens she waited, her heart drumming at her ribs, her ears strained for any sound from that close heavy silence where she had left him standing. Then, her mouth covered to hush her noisy breath, she heard the whisper of his footsteps in the straw, and the mutter of his voice: 'The moon … when the moon be at the full, then shall I be full and ripe … to sow.'

A chilled sun shaft crept through the window of Jocosa's chamber where Joan had laid ready on the bed the gown of apricot satin, the petticoat of cloth of gold, the ruby velvet headdress with its beading of pearls and the emerald fur-lined cloak. In the harsh unsoftened light, enhanced by the silvery glare of the snow lying thick on the gables of the house just building in that country lane across the way, those jewel-garnished colours took each a gayer, deeper hue to dazzle the eye and call forth fulsome admiration from the handmaid.

'Marry, mistress! There'll be none, I'll warrant me, so fine as you at the Lord Chancellor's banquet this night.'

Seated at her toilet table spread with a miscellany of pots and flasks of perfume, Jocosa dipped her fingers in a jar containing a cream of the Flower-de-Luce; this she applied to her face with particular attention to her nose. 'For,' said she, 'the frost will bite it off if I give it no protection.' And turning from her silver mirror, 'Come now, unbraid my hair,' she glanced aside, 'and shut that door into your master's chamber. It brings a draught.'

All the rooms on this floor communicated, with a second door giving access to the gallery that ran the whole length of the hall. As Joan made fast the latch of the door to Gynkes' room, his voice was heard calling to his wife: 'Sweeting, I've a rare surprise in wait for you.'

'Another of his pretty gifts, madame. There never was,' Joan rhapsodised, deftly unbraiding the thick plaits, 'so generous a husband. Scarce a day in a week but he does not bring an offering of some sort from a posy to a necklet, or this gold comb for —'

'To scalp me!' Jocosa snatched it from her. 'Look what you're about. You've pulled out a handful. Stand away. I'll comb it myself.'

Joan stood away to watch her mistress pass the comb down the dark shining curtain of her hair that hung straight as rain to her knees. 'Never,' gushed Joan, 'did I see the like of it! A mantle of black satin. Faith, mistress, should you go naked with such hair as this for cover, you'd be warm. My Lady Rich —' whom Joan had served before she came to attend on Jocosa — 'Her hair! Why, madame, if I tell you — did I comb, brush, curry or oil it whatever, it still would be a spider's web.' A dimple reflected in the polished mirror encouraged Joan to further confidence. 'Madame, today I met Margaret, my Lady Rich's woman, in the Chepe and great with news concerning the Lord Admiral. She too was buying hosen for Her Ladyship, but not so good a quality as those I bought for you, her lady having priced her to the limit of one shilling, and no hosen fit for gentle wear can be bought at such a meanly cost. Yet it is known the Lady Rich was well endowered — rich, he-he! —

well named, yet as I can vouch for't, she looks to every groat which is not as with her brother, my dear master, who would give you sun and moon, were they —'

'What,' cut in Jocosa, 'of the admiral?'

'Certes, madame, I'm telling you. They fetched him from the house of his mother, the Lady Seymour, which is far distant down in Wiltshire, for my Lady Rich's woman she hears all from her mistress — him being of the council and Lord Chancellor to boot — and they do say as how my lord, the admiral, has been brought to the Tower and held there on a charge of treason.'

'Treason?' Jocosa swung round. 'He, the King's uncle — in the Tower? Girl, you rave!'

'Madame, an I rave,' Joan said, enjoying herself hugely, 'may I be drawn and quartered and my head stuck on a pike. I speak the truth, as 'tis the talk o' the town how that His Lordship grieves not for the death of his wife nor wears no speck o' mourning for her who was the Queen, but goes decked in brightest colours to woo, forsooth, the second lady in the land which is, they say, to set her right who has been wronged with child by him and — Ow, Madame! Mistress, pray!' Joan, loud squealing, ducked, but not in time to save her a clout on the ear.

'Clack-tongue!' blazed Jocosa, 'that'll teach you to cry treason. Open your blabbing mouth again to puke filth at one so high above you as a star is to a crab-louse, and I'll have you on the cutty-stool, if not at the cart's tail. Now dress me quick.'

With loud sniffs to punctuate a *sotto voce* dissertation concerning trodden worms that would never turn to answer back on those they loved no matter how abused nor cuffed though wild horses dragged them to the gallows but would from this moment evermore be dumb, Joan dressed her lady, quick. And when perfume had been sprinkled on the corsage, the head-dress adjusted, the last gold bodkin skewered, and Joan, her vows and ill humour forgotten, pridefully surveyed her handiwork — 'O, mistress, short of heaven there never was such glory —' the door of the master's room opened.

In preening complacence and a doublet of carnation satin, one hand to his hip, the other raised palm outward, he stood posturing. His face, reflected in the silver mirror, shone white and hairless as a bone.

Joan uttered a piercing shriek, followed by a loud guffaw, while Jocosa sat petrified; then, turning to see her maiden in the chokes, she was herself convulsed.

'Oh, mercy me! Oh, sir!' gasped Joan. 'Was I ever so affrighted? I mistook Your Honour for a corpse.'

His smile broadening — their laughter was infectious — 'Well, wife?' Gynkes slid a finger round his chinless jaw, 'I warned you to prepare for a surprise and here it is. I — my man — has shorn me of my beard. I knew as it would pleasure you.'

'Lord! Lord!' Joan held her sides. 'I'll surely burst.'

Gynkes lost his smile. 'You have forgot your manners, wench. Tell her,' said he fretfully, 'to go. I'll have her whipped. A saucy piece.'

'Go, Joan,' she was bidden; and in the giggles, hastily, Joan went.

Fumbling in his pouch, Gynkes took a something from it, and approaching, timidly, his wife, said, ''Tis no vain whimsy, sweet, that I am shorn of my beard, but done a'purpose on advice of a wise man, an astrologer-physician whom I had reason to consult in cause of my bad dreams and night trouble — being born under the sign of Aquarius, and also in cause of — but that's no matter. Howbeit he told me that men who are shorn of their beards and other more intimate hairs of the body save only the hairs of their heads which, as with Samson of old, doth render them weak, so will they find their potency increased in that the strength of their hair's growth shall pass into their male organs and their loins be girded up. He also gave me this potion,' he opened his hand to disclose in its palm a thin crystal phial, 'for you.'

'What,' she asked faintly, 'would I want with a potion?'

'That you and I,' he came close to whisper, 'shall breed.'

For a full minute she sat as if palsied. He, too, was silent, watching her. On the wide brick hearth the piled logs spluttered and flared, giving out a cheerful warmth; but she was icy cold.

''Tis seven years or more,' said he, 'since we were wed, and no stirring in your womb yet of a child. But as the soothsayer doth foretell … And verily 'tis a wise man of whom the King's late Majesty did seek advice when wedded to Queen Anne Boleyn and to Queen Jane, that both were proven fruitful. So drink this tonight,' he took her hand. 'Why, dear love,' he said, 'how you are chill,' and closed her fingers on the flask. ''Tis a rare compound brewed by the wizard in my presence and, that there be no trickery, he did recite me the name of each simple as one by one he dropped and stirred them in his cauldron. *Nota bene* —' His pale forehead wrinkled in the effort to remember, ticking off the items on his thumb. 'The milk of a woman, the rennet of a lamb, a bullock's spleen, the testes of a horse — and what more? Ah, yes — the heart of a unicorn, the pizzle of a stag — a virgin's wax — and the skull of a man killed by a violent death. All of which,' he smiled at her, nodding, 'is ground to a powder and mixed with the urine of a he-goat.'

'A savoury brew,' she strove to speak lightly, 'but nothing to my taste.'

''T'will be much to your taste, wife, I promise you.' He leaned over her; she saw his blackened teeth and her gorge rose; his breath was high. Repressing a shudder, she turned from him. 'For this is a potion,' he told her, 'in especial for a woman be she barren. For myself, I have also here a potion distilled from the liver of a hedgehog, dried and beaten likewise in a powder and which, if taken in wine one hour before a man shall couple with his wife, his reins shall be strengthened that when he go in unto her she shall conceive.'

'How,' she calmed her voice to say, 'can you believe such moonshine?'

'Moonshine! Yes.' He fell on his knees beside her. His face, a stranger's in its unfamiliar nakedness, was exalted; his eyes glittered. 'Yes! Moonshine, as 'tis tonight when the moon be at the full, which the soothsayer did tell me is the most proper time to test the worth of these elixirs. So, wife, I pray you of my heart, to drink of these magical waters compounded for you by his wizardry. Look, I'll break the seal.'

She shrank back, crying, 'No!' and 'No!' again. 'I won't,' and was at him in a frenzy to claw his hands that fumbled with the stopper of the flask; and at the drive of her nails in his flesh he gave a yelp of pain, forcing back her fingers to free himself.

'Nay, let be!' Whimpering, he clambered to his feet. 'Why so shrewish? See! You've drawn my blood.' He showed her two reddening crescents on the back of his hand, and clapped it to his mouth to suck. Tears welled and dribbled down his nose. 'I never thought,' he blubbered, 'to be so beshrewed by one I cherish. I'm in no mind now for the chancellor's banquet — branded as I am — by you.' And peevishly tongueing his hand, 'I'll have to go in gloves,' he said, 'to hide these scars.' He glanced down at his soiled knees, 'and I must change my hosen too, for they be sullied.'

'Yes,' she said, 'go change them.' And followed after him to latch the door. The phial lay where it had fallen, half concealed in the rushes. She took it up and hurled it at the fire. It hit a log and fell in a glassy shower on the hearth. From its spilled contents rose a fearful stench to make her retch. And then she called for Joan.

The maid came running, still rosy-cheeked with laughter.

'Madame, the master! He is sure possessed — and skewbald. For look you, mistress, so long has he gone bearded that his face is of two colours — Why, mistress, dear, you're so white as a sheet! Are you sick?' Gingerly sniffing Joan stared about her. 'And what's this that stinks so foul?'

'I let fall a phial of physick. There's glass splinters on the bricks among the ashes. You'd best sweep them lest the ape comes grubbing there to cut itself. Give me my cloak.' And as Joan wrapped her in it: 'Bring your pallet to my chamber here tonight,' Jocosa bent to peer in the mirror, pinching her cheeks to restore their colour. 'I am chilled. I have a rheum. I do not wish —' she spoke in jerks — 'that your master lie with me lest he should take it.'

'Madame!' cried Joan, concerned. 'You shiver.' She held her hand in both of hers to chafe. 'And cold, too. You sure are taken with an ague. You should not venture out this bitter weather.'

'I'd liefer go out than stay in.'

'Well, then, mistress, I'll have ready a posset against your return and a foot-bath of mustard and water as hot as may be to draw the rheum from your head to your feet.'

'Joan.' Jocosa gripped her arm. 'Tonight, tomorrow night, and all nights while the moon be at the full, so must you sleep here in my chamber. Joan — you will?'

'Yes, mistress, surely I will,' Joan replied in wonder; she made as if to speak again, but at sight of her lady's shrunken face and that dark haunted look in her eyes, she closed her mouth and shook her head, and said no more.

The Lord Chancellor had gathered to his house in Cloth Fair by St. Bartholomew's a distinguished company. This banquet, prepared by his good wife within the narrow limits of expense allotted by her lord, whose passion for economy surpassed even that of his model, the Protector, served a dual purpose. Ostensibly to celebrate the birth of a fifth son, it also combined a long-deferred return in hospitality to certain fellow members of the council to whose support he stood beholden for hoisting him on to the Woolsack.

Bullet-headed, rodent-mouthed, spare of build and balding, he, dispenser of justice and punishment meted by torture, did the honours of his board with a marchioness and countess either side of him. Lips politely framed to honeyed platitudes, the Chancellor managed to convey to the Ladies Northampton and Warwick his unbounded delight in and admiration for their none too considerable charms, the while his pricked ears registered all likely tags of talk wafted to him above that multiloquent babel.

'Thirty-three charges!'

'Stands fast by his denial!'

'Not so! He admits to the first three of them.'

'I tell you, he rightly refuses to answer except he were brought upon trial.'

The Lord Chancellor's eyes, like slits of steel, rested on the Marquess of Northampton — Lord Parr of Kendal, brother of the late Queen Katherine — the last speaker, whose voice rang out in a momentary hush.

His wife, a vapid little creature, turned a nondescript face to her host. ''Tis to be hoped, my lord, that the Admiral will be acquitted of these shameful accusations. Such a handsome gentleman, and courageous as a lion.'

The Chancellor slanted her a look. 'There is no doubt, madame, of His Lordship's courage. Of his acquittal,' he gave a shrug, 'we can but hope.'

He had placed her on his right hand although she had no legal claim to precedence above the wife of Warwick, in that her marriage, as decreed by the Protector, must remain unrecognised on the grounds that Northampton had a wife still living whom he had divorced for adultery; for which anomalous pronouncement, in view of the late King's marriages, Northampton nursed a bitter grievance against Somerset. Rich, however, who always inclined to the more politic course of 'hunting with hounds, to run with the stag', gave all deference due to the Lady — never mind she were pseudo — Northampton.

The Chancellor's stiletto glance around the table stayed to linger on the Earl of Warwick. Nothing of the dauntless man-at-arms in that so seeming gentle fate, those velvety eyes, dark and melting — truly, yes! — as the eyes of a stag. But a stag when brought to bay can, none the less, be vicious to deal a mortal wound before the kill. A thin smile dragged down the Chancellor's lips to the shape of an inverted V. He turned to Lady Warwick, and scooping up in his fingers a tasty morsel from his dish, he placed it on hers. 'Larks' tongues, madame.'

His tone smooth, mellifluous, was akin to a caress to put her in the flutters.

'Larks' tongues!' She nibbled at a scrap between her fingers, 'Delicious.'

They were not; nor were they larks' tongues, but the scuts of rabbits, boned and spiced with cinnamon and cloves. Servers passed a boar's head glazed and stuffed with pigeons' breasts and raisins of the sun. Again the host served the ladies, and beckoning a page bade him, 'Call for music.'

The minstrels, hired from a tavern in the town for this occasion, left their seats below the salt and sheepishly filed up the staircase to the gallery. The Chancellor, picking his teeth with his thumbnail, grown long for that purpose, followed their going with his eyes. As shabby a threadbare set of knaves as ever he did see. And when from above came a tuning and scraping of fiddles followed by a dirge-like wail of tabor and pipe, the Chancellor banefully addressed his wife seated between Lords Warwick and Northampton: *You — you scrag of mutton! Why bring me this scurvy posse of discordance to split the ears with a yowling as of amorous cats?* But this he did not say aloud: what he did say, rising, bowing, lifting his goblet to his lady with a hearty assumption of marital bliss and the pride of a paterfamilias, was: 'My lords and ladies join with me, one and all, to drink to this happy event and to her whose worth, as it is spoken, is priced above rubies —'

'Yes,' muttered Warwick aside to his neighbour, Lord Paget raised to the peerage by Somerset, 'at the price of a fortune in cheese.'

'— and who blesses me with yet another lusty son.'

'Four already, and ten daughters,' twittered Paget.

The company was on its feet, the hostess, too, on hers, all smiles till she saw her husband's look, sharp as knives upon her, and the stab of his downward gesture as indication that she, the toast, must sit, not stand.

She sat, her smile fixed, her hands interlocked beneath the board, while the guests politely seconded her loving lord's appeal. A hen-faced woman, lean as a rod and, from perennial child-bearing, sickly, she much resembled in form and feature her brother. That the two recently ennobled gentlemen on her right and left had maintained a lively conversation exclusive to themselves with not a word to her throughout the meal, neither chagrined nor dismayed the Lady Rich. She was well accustomed to such disregard from her husband's associates. Raised to highest rank by the condescension of her godly spouse, she went effaced, as it were, in a nimbus of perpetual apology not only for her own inadequate existence but for her humble origin as the daughter of a grocer which, from constant reminder, she could never, even were she so inclined, forget. Nor did the fact that her lord and master also carried the insignia of trade, equalise their situation. Two generations divided the Lord Chancellor from a former Richard Rich of the Company of Mercers from whom he was descended.

And now, having performed his duty to his very lesser half, His Lordship called for a toast to the ladies. Cups were replenished, the musicians twanged their lutes, the fiddles squeaked, and boys' voices sang:

'Bring us in good ale
And bring us in good ale,
For our Blessed Lady's sake,
Bring us in good ale...'

The company, turning convivial, joined in the chorus, and, as the drink circulated more freely, so did the guests change their places at table to sit where they would. The younger people, Lord Rich's sons and daughters and the Dudley boys, sons of Lord Warwick, clamoured for a dance. The tables were cleared, the trestles borne away. The elders dispersed, some to their homes, others to talk together in scattered groups about the hall. Lord Rich, his face wreathed in smiles of husbandly affection for the benefit of all who cared to see, sought his wife, bitingly to tell her, 'The capons were burned to cinders, the boar's head was raw, the fish stinking, and why —' the eyes of His Lordship rolled up to the rafters — 'why in the name of all that's unholy comes your hoddy-doddy brother to disgrace my board in the mask of a new-sheared ram?'

'Not,' his wife faltered, 'a mask … I think it…' She had the habit, most vexatious to her lord, of never finishing a sentence; or if by chance she did, she would then repeat it twice, of more.

'And who,' broke in the chancellor with a grinding of his teeth, 'is that apple-faced young gentleman whose arm he paws so lovingly?'

'I — is he not one of the King's … whom I understood your lordship did …'

'Ptchaw!' or some such sound issued from the sorely tried Lord Chancellor. 'Did *what?*'

'Invite,' breathed out his lady in a tremble, 'as so your lordship said when … yesterday you said … but not the name. You said … all of the King's gentlemen, but only one … you said … that only one would likely …'

'Go,' snarled His Lordship, 'and mingle with my guests. Don't stand here mopping and mowing at me like a zany. Have you no sense of your duties as hostess or — God help me! — as my wife? Why —' again he raised his eyes in supplication — 'why was I so cursed as to take unto myself this chinless gibbering ewe to saddle me with sucklings once a year? But this'll be the last o' them. I'll find me a bawd.' He may have found one already since he was the father of another four sons, unacknowledged. 'She'd cost me less and give me better service than you with your litter. Fifteen!'

And having delivered this graceful speech, still accompanied by the tenderest of smiles, the chancellor strutted away.

His lady uncertainly followed. She had a buzzing in her head and a weakness in her spine; her legs, too, were behaving in unaccountable fashion. The doctor had warned her and her husband to postpone this banquet until she be fully recovered from her long protracted labour; but she ... he ... her husband had agreed that the doctor's opinion was, as her lord had rightly said, not worth the shilling he charged for each visit and which, unless she wished to see him, her dear lord, a beggar, God forbid ... but her milk had dried too soon and the babe, her little one, so frail as a snowflake for all that he had almost killed her and for which she loved him more ... he took not readily to ass's ... a foster-mother costing far too dear ... And now the walls were in a curtsy and the hall was in a spin and she in a cold sweat, groping her way blindly to a settle. She must not ... no, she must not ... But she did.

'There, then, there! All's well.' An arm supported her; a pomander was held to her nose, a cup to her lips. She tasted and gratefully swallowed a drop of mulled wine, gazing up into a pair of eyes, dark and kindly.

'Jo ... Joco...?'

'Yes. Take one more sip of this.'

One more sip was dutifully taken; her head cleared. 'I ... so foolish ... I would not have my lord see how ... would he have seen how I...?'

'None saw, and you're not foolish. The hall is overcrowded and too hot with these great fires. So, madame, you are recovered, yes? Can you walk or shall I send for your woman?'

'If Your Ladyship permits —'

Another there beside her; and sense, of a sort, returning, he whom she recognised as that same young gentleman of the King's Privy Chamber, described by her husband as apple-faced. He was; and of an open countenance and courteous, with such steady eyes like bits of bright blue...

'Sir, I think...'

He raised her up. Her brother, too, was hovering.

'You should consult my astrologer-physician. He will compound you a magical potion to cure all ills and weaknesses. I myself have —'

His wife interrupting, said, 'Sir, go tell that page — no, I will.' And she darted off. And now, O, heaven! A lady, large and handsome, was bearing down upon her.

'I am indeed concerned to see Your Ladyship thus overcome.'

So she had been seen. Disgraced. And from her lord would never hear the last of...

''Tis naught, madame ... I ... 'tis nothing. The hall...'

But the lady was neither listening nor, thankfully, looking at her now, being full of smiles for Master ... the King's gentleman, whose name had slipped her memory if ever she had known it 'Come aside, sir, I would speak a word —' such a charmful voice the lady had, soft and cooing as a dove's — 'alone, with you.'

The young gentleman appeared to hesitate, glancing from the lady to his hostess who told him hastily, 'Yes, sir, indeed, pray leave ... I would not wish to incommode ... my brother, he will...'

The young gentleman bowed. 'My duty, madame.'

Yet still he seemed in two minds whether to go or to stay, but when Lady Rich implored him, 'Sir, indeed, I beg...' he submitted to be drawn, albeit it seemed unwillingly, away.

Left to themselves, brother and sister watched them pass in and out of the dancers, but not to partake in that merry-go-round: to sit apart, heads close together; he, serious and silent, she speaking rapidly and drooped toward him that her hair bright and glittering, as if gold-dusted, touched his cheek.

'Is not she who went with Master Pugh,' Gynkes cracked his knuckles, 'the wife of Sir Thomas Browne?'

'I do not ... my lord commanded me invite so many, I cannot recall the names of...'

'It is she,' her brother nodded. 'I remember when I was at Court how that my Lord of Surrey did name her Geraldine the Fair, but 'twas not her rightful name, she being Mistress Elizabeth Fitzgerald.'

His retentive memory had always been a source of wonder to his sister, and of hope, to encourage her belief that the doctors, whom her parents had consulted when he was a boy ... he not having found his speech until his seventh year ... might have been mistaken in that ... not quite as others of his age. Yet see how he had overcome his backwardness to buy himself, on her dear lord's advice, and for a largely sum, a place at the late King's court, for which she must be forever grateful ... and then his happy marriage with, that dear good...

He was saying, 'You should certainly visit my astrologer. He lodges hard by here t'other side of Bartholomew's. 'Tis a wise man who will brew you a potion that you suffer not from weakness after childbirth. It was he caused me to shave my beard and to drink of his waters so my loins be girded up that I and my wife, we now shall breed.'

'Your wife?' His sister roused herself. 'Is she … your wife, with…?'

'Maybe,' he nodded eagerly. 'Or if not this month, then when the moon comes full again which is why my beard is shorn. Do you like me better as I am or as when I was bearded?'

'I like you,' she stroked his sleeve, 'howsoever you may be, and as you … are.'

Twelve years his senior, they two were the sole survivors of ten children; and he, the youngest, whose coming had cost their mother's life, had turned to his sister for the only love that he had ever known. And gazing at him, her eyes damp, 'With all my heart,' she murmured in her small, sad voice, 'I wish…' But what she would have wished she did not say.

Over by the hall screens the Chancellor, who, while fully aware of his wife's indisposition, had turned his back upon her sooner than embarrass his guests by drawing attention to her fantods, had been buttonholed by Warwick.

'Your lordship has been in audience with the King today?'

'I have.'

The chancellor's keen glance measured top to toe this latest of Somerset's 'new lords sprung from the dunghill', thus did the Protector pleasantly describe his chosen members of the council, forgetful of the fact that he also was one of the 'new lords'. True, he could boast a more distinguished ancestry than most of them, unless it were John Dudley, Earl of Warwick, who claimed Plantagenet descent from a bastard son of the Fourth Edward. It had become a fashion among these 'dunghill lords' — and some of their ladies, not excluding the Protector's wife — to claim Plantagenet descent, if only in defiance of 'these upstart Tudors'; yet despite his, alleged, royal lineage, the father of Dudley had been a lawyer of none too savoury repute. As Henry VII's personal attorney he had, by fair means or foul, amassed for his miserly king a vast fortune, running into millions, with some substantial pickings for himself. His son John, whom he sent for a soldier, was destined for a remarkable career. Honour after honour had been heaped upon him from the age of twenty, when he had gained a knighthood for valour in the fight against the French. Turning to the study of naval warfare he served with equal distinction at sea as on land, to become Lord High Admiral at forty. When, at the rise of the Protector, he stepped down from this appointment that Tom Seymour should step up, he was given nominal command of Somerset's army to further his series of meteoric triumphs with that outstanding victory at Pinkie. Eulogised by a contemporary as 'a man of parts, a consummate soldier and the ablest diplomat of his time', he was regarded by his fellows in the council — and Lord Rich — as a potential force against which it were best to go armoured.

So these two, both 'men of parts', took each the other's measure; the one rat-mouthed, sharp-eyed, and, disadvantaged by his lack of height, somewhat aggressively pompous; the other, graceful, tall, delicately featured, with nothing in his dress, elaborate almost to effeminacy, or his person, to suggest the dauntless intrepid campaigner. Never an oath nor coarse-worded jest had been heard to pass those womanish full lips that, despite their sensitivity, looked to have been grafted upon steel. And, lifting to his nostrils a fragile gold ball suspended from a slender chain, he languidly inhaled its spiced contents.

'I take it then,' said Warwick, 'that His Majesty is now acquainted with the facts as laid before him by yourself?'

'As laid before His Majesty and corroborated by the Lord Protector,' the Chancellor cautiously replied.

Warwick flicked him a look and then away to the centre of the hall where young couples in a cloud of dust, kicked up from the oaken boards, were dancing the cavolta. And, his eyes straying to rest upon Henry, his son, who partnered Winifred Rich, the Chancellor's daughter, 'I can guess,' smiled Warwick, still sniffing the pomander, 'how exactly Somerset corroborates your own and the council's opinion of this "so sorrowful case, yet his bounden duty to the King and the Crown of England doth weigh greater with him than allegiance to his blood and his own brother".'

The Chancellor stiffened; there was more than a hint of mockery in the uplift of this 'new' Earl's lip and that almost verbatim repetition of the Protector's words spoken privy to the King in the Chancellor's presence, both having deemed it proper that His Majesty be prepared with a preliminary rehearsal of the pending debate before the council. Had this pawky fellow a second sight or a third ear?

'The King,' pronounced Rich warily, 'to whom the Lord Protector did outline, with restraint and due deference for his tender years, the most heinous of the Admiral's offences and — Hem!' Behind his hand he gently coughed.

'Not omitting,' Warwick suavely supplemented, 'his conduct — or shall we say misconduct — with the Lady Elizabeth's Grace?'

The Chancellor inflated his chest. 'All that it were necessary for our child Sovereign to know concerning the Admiral's offences have been presented to His Majesty, who is persuaded he must give his consent that the Bill of Attainder be introduced into Parliament.'

Warwick's upper lip revealed two almond-shaped front teeth with a narrow gap between them; and to the Chancellor came reminder, gleaned from some old gossip's tale harking back to his nursery days, how that he whose teeth were widely spaced would never want for money: which, Lord Rich reflected, might well apply to Warwick. Money to burn, and for his heir to inherit along with an earldom. And now his glance chased after his daughter.

'They make a handsome pair,' said Warwick lightly, 'your pretty young maid and my son.' And circumventing the chancellor's eager assent to that, since this was not the moment to discuss the minimum price he would demand as dower for Lord Rich's not-so-pretty-young maid, he reverted to the more absorbing case in point.

'I am informed that the governess, Ashley, and Parry, the cofferer, who, as your lordship is aware, are detained in the Tower, have given some incriminating evidence.'

Roused from rapid calculation regarding the maximum sum of five hundred pounds for his Winifred in exchange for her possible rank as a countess, the Chancellor turned sharp about.

'My lord, we tread on egg shells —' Warwick quirked a smiling look at Rich's feet, shod in dust-covered black velvet, planted square in the fringe of rushes swept back from the centre of the floor — 'which,' said His Lordship in a louder tone and not caring for that look, 'one false step can too easily crush.'

'I saw,' said Warwick idly, 'my Lady Browne at table. Did not the princess Elizabeth — set me right if I am wrong — request that Lady Browne be appointed in waiting during the detention of Mistress Ashley?'

The Chancellor's face became decorously grave. 'I have heard some such talk, doubtless promoted by the Admiral before his arraignment. One pays small heed to rumour, yet I believe it to be common knowledge that Lady Browne and the Lord Admiral were, at one time —' A tactful pause.

'Thick as thieves?' suggested Warwick pleasantly.

'I was about to say —' his host arrested the passing of a page bearing a salver laden with goblets of wine — 'will your lordship take a cup of Muscatel? Canary? No?' And to the boy aside, in a sibilant whisper, 'Serve citron water, not wine, to the dancers. I was about to say, my lord, in view of the — ah — reputed friendship between Lady — between the Admiral and Sir Thomas Browne, the lady's husband —'

'Who,' again came smiling interruption, 'is twice her age and sickly.'

The chancellor held himself in patience. 'Your lordship appears to be better acquainted with the age of Sir Thomas Browne than am I, which — an I were permitted to suggest — is not of paramount importance more than that the state of Sir Thomas's health has impelled Her Ladyship to decline the post.'

'Meanwhile Lady Tyrwhitt is in command at Hatfield, that she may send report to you,' the pomander slid from Warwick's fingers and swung from its chain to click against a silver button on his doublet, 'of this latest inquisition?'

'Latest?' The Chancellor's never too firmly closed lips fell open. 'The enquiry,' he stressed the correction, 'has been judicially conducted, and if all the evidence be proven as offered by Parry and Ashley, under —' he hemmed again.

'The rack?' suggested the smiling Warwick.

'My lord!' The Chancellor expressed profoundest shock. 'No, indeed. Such methods are preserved solely for heretics. Every leniency has been shown, and more than is deserving, to Her Grace's servants, whose respective testimonies when both were independently examined, do agree, and from which one conclusion only can be drawn.'

Warwick's eyes returned to his son and Rich's daughter. The dance had ended, and the two young people were quenching their thirst from a shared cup.

'My lord,' Warwick quoted softly, 'these be shameful slanders, for beside the great desire I have to see the King's Majesty, I do most heartily desire your lordship that I may come to Court to shew myself there — as I am.'

'God's Life!' burst forth the shaken Chancellor. 'How come you to know of that letter from Her Grace to the Protector?'

'As you did come to know it,' Warwick was still following the movements of Rich's daughter and his son who had now paired off together, hand in hand. 'Our good duke,' he murmured, 'torn between avuncular duty and brotherly love, revolves like a squirrel in a cage around the Privy Council seeking advice from all in turn, and yet will not heed when 'tis given. Ah, yes, I see her now, the Lady Browne, over there by the hearth-side,' he screwed an eye at her, 'whose beauty with the passage of — how many years since Surrey's fall? — is somewhat over-blossomed.'

And she whom Philip, at fourteen, had adored to distraction, was tenderly cooing close into his ear: 'So, sir, you will intercede with, the King on Her Grace's behalf that she be allowed a hearing from His Majesty to let him know, as she is so desirous to do, that there is no word of truth in these base rumours. For God alone can say,' the lady histrionically declared, 'what vile imputations against Her Grace's honour have been brought by knavish tattle to our innocent young king.'

She pressed nearer, her shoulder touching his. Her satin petticoats submerged his padded breeks; and, from across the rift of years, Philip glimpsed himself as once he was, in panting palpitation at the very sight of her whose charms, viewed at such embarrassing proximity and in the light of bought experience, were none too delicately savoured. Her skin had coarsened and was pitted as an orange; her hair, orange-coloured, too, dropped glinting flecks of gold upon his sleeve. The perfume of amber and roses, emanating from her corsage, mingled with the warmer riper scent of her armpits.

'Madame, the King,' said Philip, carefully, 'has been told nothing detrimental to the Lady Elizabeth's honour. Moreover, all letters from Her Grace to the Lord Protector denying these scandalous reports have been shown to and read by His Majesty.'

'Yes, but...' The lady heaved so deep a sigh that the scant concealment of her low-cut bodice exposed more than was meant to be hid, and from which Philip, a trifle red in the face, glanced, not very quickly, away. 'Ah, me!' Another sigh, and, 'Oh!' a somewhat belated adjustment of the corsage, 'these modes — so shaming,' yet her languishing look as she pressed closer to him still, betokened nothing of shame. 'I was present,' she confided, 'when Sir Robert Tyrwhitt came to Hatfield to examine her. She — Her Grace — stood there defiant,' cried the lady with emotion, 'as a leopardess. But for how long can she stand against these monstrous accusations? She begs, she implores that the King, her brother, shall know the true facts of the case.'

'The true facts of the case,' Philip said eyeing her straight, 'are already known to those who may best deal with them.'

For an instant the lady's dove-like mask slipped from her as, with caustic venom, ''Twas that fool of a governess,' she hissed, 'who stuffed her full of Seymour's love for her. A pack o' lies! She told Tyrwhitt herself, as I did hear when in attendance on Her Grace, how Kat Ashley had said, voice went in London that Seymour would feign have married me —

her, which is to say — before Katherine, the Queen. Marry *her*, that chit — that child?' the lady hastily corrected. 'No such intent, I'll swear, had he in mind. As if he'd dare aspire! And all these abominations the result of a young girl's delight in his prankish high humour. So you see, sir,' she appealed, 'how I am placed? The princess has none but myself for her comfort, since she has no faith in the loyalty of Lady Tyrwhitt. And now that my husband is sick unto death that I must be at his bedside and no longer in waiting, I came hither tonight in the hope I might meet with one of the King's gentlemen and report to him the Lady Elizabeth's words to Sir Robert Tyrwhitt lest some falsifying of the same be brought to His Majesty. Were the truth, the *whole* truth as I heard it, be carried aright to the King before it be distorted by lying tongues, such truth should clear her utterly, and him. And him!' To her eyes, with care for the kohl on their lids, she applied a shred of handkerchief. 'He, who goes in deadly peril from these infamous indictments. 'Tis false, shamefully, wickedly false, that he did offer himself to her as husband. He did not, as I can vouch for't — he did *not!*'

It may have crossed Philip's mind that behind this display of dramatics lay a more personal interest than that which concerned the princess.

'So, sir, if you would do this thing for me — for the Lady Elizabeth's Grace — that the King shall be moved to receive her, you will earn not only her unbounded gratitude but —' she seized his hand to kiss and say — 'but mine.'

Philip's smile was a little sideways. Disengaging, he rose from the settle and bowing, answered noncommittally, 'I am, as ever, madame, at your service.'

'As once upon a time, indeed, you were!' She wagged a playful finger. 'I remember how you were wont to send me red roses — which they say is an emblem of love — when we were young together.' She was forty now, at least. 'Have you so soon forgot?'

'How, madame, were it possible I could forget?'

He bowed again and backed; but she had not yet done with him. 'So for our youth time's sake, sir, will you not take me to dance?'

'Madame does me too much honour,' Philip said; and, within himself he groaned; From limpets, from she-porpoises, howso they be sprightly, Lord deliver us! Then, as he led her out, the minstrels in the gallery sang:

'My love he loves another love,
Alas, sweetheart, why doth he so?...'

Long into the dawning Jocosa lay awake watching grey fingers of light steal through the chinks in the window curtains. At the foot of her bed Joan slept and intermittently snored. From behind the closed door of her husband's room came sounds of muffled steps, vague mutterings, with here and there a word or two distinguishable. 'Moon ... the moon.' And, 'O, the Plague!' And at last a silence. He too must have slept; but she did not.

Superimposed on shadows, dimly lit by the dying embers on the hearth, the night's pageantry passed and re-passed before her. She saw herself a mote, a speck, discarded amid the colourful mosaic of the dance, when, having consigned Lady Rich to the care of her maid, she returned to the hall. And then ...

But why should she care? What was it to her that he had been so deeply engaged with a lady of redundant charms, that he could not even glance in her direction nor seek exchange of word with her the evening through, but had sat gazing, eye to eye, and speaking, almost, mouth to mouth, with one who in age could be his mother? No accounting for a young man's fancy, yet it seemed he had been faithful to this fortyish — fiftyish, maybe — first love.

Jocosa recalled how that long ago at Sprowston he had burbled of a sonnet, or a poem or a something, and in a moment's expansion had read it to her who peeked over his shoulder and had seen its dedication, 'To the Fair Geraldine'. Huh! So fair as a blackamoor under the paint... And turning on her right side and then upon her left, for the bed was hard as bricks and she as cold as stone in it, despite the warming-pan had raised a blister on her heel, she was reminded how Winifred, her husband's niece, a gawky girl, who would insist to call her 'Aunt' as she was sixty, had cornered her to say that Harry Dudley, the Earl of Warwick's son, had confessed himself. So those two were in love now, and would soon be wed if their respective fathers gave consent. All this was excellent, and Jocosa, stiff with smiles as a favoured 'Aunt' should be, had expressed herself delighted until Winnie ceased her raptures to ask: 'Is not that young gentleman close in talk with Lady Browne, your cousin, Master Pugh?'

'A very distant cousin,' Jocosa had replied; and was shattered to hear, 'Sir Thomas Browne, her husband, so old as nigh on eighty, is like to die. She'll soon be free to wed again with one of her own choice, which,' said Winnie with that neighing laugh of hers, 'is evident for all to see. *She'll* lose no time. Look, how she tweedles him, kissing hands, and now to dance...'

Pleasant hearing, this! And: *'My love, he loves another love,'* most aptly sang the choristers. Huh! As much love in him, Jocosa snorted to her pillow, as may be in an oyster, maugre his vows that life without her could not be endured; yet it would appear he could very well endure his life without her. Jerking up her head she turned viciously to thump the pillow that felt as it were stuffed with flint, not feathers; and then reversed it, seeking a cooler place to lay her cheek and finding none, for the drenching sweat that she was in, she flung off her shift and lay nude. Having feigned a sickness to be left in peace tonight — much peace for her, she'd say! — she now in truth, and miserably, had sickened.

She shivered and was hot, burned and was cold, with her head in a whirl like a spinning top; and this a judgement on her for inciting Joan to lie, that he, poor moonstruck soul, be kept from his right to her bed and her body. A wickedness indeed to deny him the hope of a child, yet were there any honest magic in his stinking potions then it would have been her duty to grant him of his wish ... O God, not that! No, never that, since a child misbegotten by such ill-conditioned means would be, for sure, a monster. Joan, however, had performed her part as she was bid, standing there on guard at the dividing door to drive her master out as he came in hugged in a fur-lined knee-length wrap and nothing more to hide his nakedness, but not his spindle-shanks...

'Prithee, sir, my mistress sickens. Keep away, 'tis — Lord 'a mercy — the Plague!'

'The Plague!' The candle-shine had revealed his face with its high-boned cheeks and that pale vanishing chin. His eyes, white as the eyes of the blind, went searching for her where she lay with the bed covers drawn up to her nose; and, play-acting, she had moaned and snuffed and gasped for breath while he, though terror-stricken at the thought of that which all must fear, did not, at once, turn tail. Cracking his knuckles nervously, he said, 'Go fetch the doctor.'

'What, sir? At this hour of the night and in this snow? There's a drift three yards high down the lane into the Strand

and no ways else to reach the doctor's lodging.' Another bare-faced lie. 'I'll attend my Lady until morning.'

'But you —' his fingers as precautionary measure, were pinching the tip of his nose, that he spoke in a voice like the squeak of a puppet — 'you'll be infected.'

'No, sir, for see you, I did take the plague when at my mother's breast — God rest her — who did die of it,' Joan told him, glib as a pedlar, 'and I am thus protected. But you, master, are not. I pray you, sir, be gone and smell a lemon and bid your man to bathe you well in vinegar. Nor come you here again, sir, at your peril.'

With which Joan had shut the door on him and bolted it.

And now it was nigh morning and the household astir. She could hear the maids with their besoms outside in the gallery, and from afar the sound of wheels and hooves on frozen cobbles; the cry of a sweep, a water-carrier, and the clink and rattle of a milkmaid's cans as she turned from the Strand into Water Lane. Jocosa listened to her footsteps crunching the crisp snow as she passed by to the postern at the backside of the house. She must have a cup of fresh cool milk to ease her dry, sore throat.

'Joan,' she called softly, and got out of bed feeling sick enough now, in all conscience, to die. What vengeful visitation had come upon her as a punishment for her unwifely and undutiful deceit?

Her teeth a-chatter, all her limbs aching, she tottered barefoot to rouse Joan, who sprawled, fully dressed, on her pallet.

'Madame!' Rubbing the sleep from her eyes Joan started up. 'What is't o'clock?'

'Full morning, and I — not a wink,' Jocosa said, hoarsely, 'have I slept. Joan, I have been most wrongfully at fault, and am now judged as I deserve.' She laid cold hands to her hot forehead. 'Joan, dear Joan, go leave me. Souse yourself in vinegar, for your words have tempted Providence to strike me that I now in truth am taken with — the Plague!'

'Jesu!' Joan, who had opened her mouth preparatory to scream, received a none too gentle pinch.

'Quiet. Do you want the whole house in a scare? Run for a doctor. Refill the warming pan. Give me to drink. My throat — Mass! How I ache and am cold, but I'll be colder before this day is out, when I lie stiff and —'

'Madame!' Recovered from her panic, Joan was on her feet to take command. 'Get you back into your bed this minute, or stiff you'll be before nightfall, no question, mother-naked as you are.' She searched about and found a tinder-box and candle, lighted it, and, hustling her mistress to her tumbled couch, proceeded to explore her groins and armpits.

'Never,' she muttered, 'praise be, a sign of buboe.' And peering at her lady's chest, 'Why, madame, you are covered with a rash o' spots which never is a symptom o' the Plague nor of the Sweat, for if I know aught of sickness,' Joan told her, much relieved, 'and so I should, as eldest of my mother's six who did not die, God forgive me, of the Plague, but of a fit. You have nothing worse, though bad enough yet naught that can't be cured, more — or I'm a Frenchman — than the measles!'

ELEVEN

The measles it was, and a severe attack that confined Jocosa to her bed at doctor's orders for two weeks. Not until her convalescence did she hear from Joan a garbled version of the talk that had set half London by the ears, for: 'As I did tell you, madame, as was told me by my Lady Rich's woman which this latest news confirms, the Lord Admiral has none but himself to thank for what's to come.' Joan had it pat how that Lord Seymour had admitted his intent to gain command of the young king's person, and had bribed His Majesty's attendants...

'Which of His Majesty's attendants?'

Jocosa raised her head from the cushions where Joan had placed her on a settle by the hearth.

'Nay, madame,' Joan made haste to assure her, 'not Master Pugh. You should know him surely as above suspicion.'

'Who,' Jocosa closed her eyes, 'is above suspicion in this cesspool of a Court? What more have you heard of the Admiral? Though I'll dare swear whatever it may be, the truth on't is no greater than a mustard seed in a whole field of such.'

But if Joan's recording of the case, passed from mouth to mouth in taverns, at street corners, and throughout the town were sifted to its barest facts, the main fact still remained, statutable and stark, that Lord Seymour, the King's uncle, stood, by evidence sworn, condemned to a traitor's death.

He had refused to be examined by the council, insisting he reserve his defence that he be tried before a tribunal. Whereupon Somerset called his Chancellor and council in debate, which the boy king was impelled to attend, and to hear of nefarious intrigues and crimes ascribed to his uncle Tom: he, who had always been so generous with his gifts of money. And now that, and a host of other offences, had been charged against the Admiral; his traffic with pirates, his seizure of Lundy and the Scillies; how he had encouraged the plunder and wrecking of merchant vessels; this Edward found hard to believe. He, himself a sailor, to sink a good ship, fully manned! Bad enough and likely to involve the Admiral in a heavy fine and possible long-term imprisonment, but never surely treason under penalty of death.

Worse, however, was to come. He had gone about sowing discord against the Protector and the Parliament of His Majesty, the King; he had mustered to his side ten thousand adherents with the purpose of establishing an opposition party … Well, argued Edward to himself, why not? This catchpenny Parliament was nothing of *his* choice, and as for that rat-faced old Chancellor — a pity he and the whole scurvy lot of them hadn't been sunk to sea-bottom instead of those brave merchantmen.

His glance wandered away to Lord Warwick, who lounged on a front bench, lost, as it seemed, in admiration of his legs encased in crimson hose stretched out full length before him. He was sniffing at a gold pomander. Certainly the hall was stuffy and it stank: of men's bodies over-heated in their velvet fur-lined robes. Edward, too, was overheated and sweating from the weight of his heavy Crown and mantle. And, as if conscious of the child's stare, Warwick raised his head; his eyes went searching to meet those of the pale little king, with a smile and a reassuring nod. And Edward recalled that this was a very gallant officer and gentleman who had fought with such success against the Scots at Pinkie, but the honours of the victory, which should have been his, had gone to the Lord Protector.

And now what was this? Edward perked his pointed ears.

'A letter has been drafted from the Admiral.' The Chancellor's slimy voice was, Edward thought, like a snake's, if a snake could speak; and as he had spoken when he had primed the King with the form of answer he must give to any questions put before him by the council. 'A letter demanding that His Highness should take over the governance of his own realm, and the Admiral the custody of the King's most royal person.'

Edward's face whitened; his thumb was at his lip. *Yes,* he tried to say, *but I didn't sign it. I refused to sign it* ... Better not. Least said soonest mended. 'All of this he hath admitted...' And so on and on again, an interminable series of offences, much of which was repetition and nothing irrefutable; yet he whom they named 'the accused' had made no attempt to refute them.

At last the dreary business was nearing its end; and the Protector, for the first time directly addressing the King, said, 'Your Majesty must know how sorrowful a case this is to me, yet in view of the charges brought against my brother, the Lord High Admiral, I must uphold my bounden duty to my Sovereign and the Crown before allegiance to my brother and my blood.'

From his seat among the Lords of the Council Warwick cast a look at him who stood to deliver, very sorrowfully indeed, and with a quiver in his speech, the ultimatum: 'I therefore cannot refuse the request of the Lords, in so far as the Admiral will not come hither to answer more than these first three charges relating to Your Majesty.'

Every eye was turned on the pale boy on his throne-like seat, the crown weighing down that small drooping head. This was his cue: he had his answer prepared. The words were etched at the back of his mind in letters, glaring white on a black walk Clutching the gilded arms of his chair, his piping treble quavered through the council chamber: 'We do perceive there is great things which be objected and laid to my Lord Admiral, mine … mine uncle, and they …' the childish voice faltered and sank, that it was scarcely audible … 'they do tend to... treason. We perceive that you require justice to be done and we will that you... proceed according.'

But while they did 'proceed according', not one word at the debate was said concerning the charges brought against the Lord High Admiral of England, and Elizabeth, sister of the King.

And what of her, that young royal girl, whose life and future greatness must go clouded in the shadow of suspicion cast by the passing of the first and perhaps the only man she ever loved? Friendless, deserted, she faced her accusers to deny the evidence of Ashley, her once trusted governess, and her cofferer, Parry. Their confessions, describing in odious detail Seymour's visits to her chamber and their romps together on the bed, were repeated verbally, *ad nauseam,* and confirmed by letter.

Those letters, written and signed by her treacherous servants to save their skins, were brought to her at Hatfield. Yet, though stricken, shocked, and herself in deadly peril of her life, she stood her ground to defy these 'shameful slanders', with a flash of that same indomitable spirit which in after years was to defy the might of Spain.

Just so much and no more under Tyrwhitt's examination would she admit to those charges made *against my honour and my honesty, which be these — that I am in the Tower and with child by my Lord Admiral Seymour.*

In the Tower. That, on the face of it, so utterly, ridiculously false, must have given rise to doubt regarding the 'confessions' of the governess and Parry. And then her masterly trump card flung in the face of the Protector.

I most heartily desire your lordship that I come to Court and shew myself there as I am. And insist, if needs must, on a medical examination. And this from a girl of fifteen.

Somerset, staggered by that blow to take the wind out of his sails, was still further deflated when, with imperious insolence, she coolly adjured him: 'Issue a Proclamation throughout the country declaring these tales are lies, lest it make the people think you and your council believe such rumours spread of the King's Majesty's sister.'

After which they dared not touch her; a leopardess, indeed! And one who stalked to spring with feline cunning at their throats. The 'King's Majesty's sister'... and God alone knew if she, in whose veins ran her mother's evil blood, might not yet gain access to the King's most precious person, working mischief to incite His Majesty against his guardian and Protector of his realm, and so divide the country, already taking sides for or against the decree of the council and that council's Chief.

Their fears were groundless. She had done her part, and won her day at the close of his whom she was powerless to save.

He wrote to her and to her sister Mary the night before they brought him to the block. He contrived a pen from an 'aglet', the tag of the cords that laced his hose; and made ink 'so craftily and of such workmanship as the like hath not been seen…' Thus Bishop Latimer, preaching before the King at Westminster after the deed was done. He hid the letters in the sole of his shoe and gave them to his servant to deliver. They never reached their destinations; his man was intercepted, the letters seized and read, in secret, by the council; and what he wrote in that cold dawn of his last day was never known.

During the weeks that followed the passing of the Bill of Attainder, Edward suffered silent agonies of self-reproach. None guessed, unless it were Philip and Barnaby, how this sorry business had preyed upon the child's mind so that when he took one of those feverish colds to which he was subject it laid him low. Vainly Mother Jack would strive with every kind of tasty dish to tempt his appetite; he had no wish to eat, nor to practise at the butts, nor to play at rovers with his pages. He would sit nursing his dog, his eyes grown too big for his face; and over and over again he would ask himself, 'What else could I have done but tell the truth?'

His uncle *had* given him money, *did* say he should be sole ruler of his kingdom with his Uncle Tom as guardian only of his person, not his realm. And all other sort of things had the Admiral said, which he would never have admitted had they not dragged it out of him. What must his uncle have thought when he heard how he had been betrayed by his own nephew? Yet you couldn't, Edward insisted, call it betrayal to answer fairly questions put to him by his council or to give his consent to the passing of a Bill. He owed that much duty to his Parliament if not to the Protector.

They said it took three strokes of the axe to kill him.

'I will say if they ask what I think of his death,' shouted Latimer, a wiry whippet of a man, with a sharp — some said coarse — sense of humour. 'I would say he died dangerously, irksomely, horribly. God left him to himself.' The Bishop pointed a skinny finger at the little king sitting huddled in his high-backed chair. Died. Horribly. Three strokes of the axe … 'His God had clean forsaken him. What would he have done if he had lived still? Well, he is gone, he knoweth his fate by this. He is either in joy or in pain…'

Not pain, prayed Edward. *God! not pain …*

'For wheresoever the tree falleth there shall it rest. By the falling of the tree is signified the death of man; if he fall in the south he shall be saved.' *Why the south?* wondered Edward. 'For the south is hot and betokens charity and salvation; if he fall in the north, in the cold of infidelity, so shall he be damned. And this surely was a wicked man.'

No! Edward cried within himself. *'Tis I that am wicked. I am the King. Had I spoken as a king and not as a cur, I might … I might have saved him.*

The Bishop's face was patterned with bars of blood-red light filtered through from the stained-glass window high above him. 'Now before he should die,' thundered Latimer, 'I heard tell he had commendations to the King and spake many words of His Majesty. All is 'the King, the King'. Yea, *bona verba* …' And the King would never know what was in the mind of him 'who', again the Bishop's finger pointed, 'was a man the farthest from the fear of God which ever I knew or did hear of in England. I have troubled Your Grace too long'.

But not so long troubled as was the Protector. He may have been equally fretted by splinters of remorse concerning the end of that same 'wicked man'. Nor did his wife's incessant trumpet-cry — 'In future, you'd be well advised to heed what I say, for see how all has come about as I did warn you' — give much ease to the festering reminder that he had sent his brother to his death. Moreover, the raggle-taggle followers

Tom had rallied to his side with his free distribution of largesse and his hearty camaraderie, were the first to sling mud at their 'Good Duke', and to howl at him when he rode out from or rode in at London's gates.

'Unmerciful! Unjust! What manner o' Protector is this who names himself Friend of the People, yet will hack off the head of his brother as one hacks off a branch from a tree and without a fair trial to speak for himself. Fratricide!'

The sunny sky of the Protector's reign was heavy with the storm clouds of unrest ... The People's Friend! Yes, in all ways had he striven to be that, whose first effort to improve conditions among the lower orders, and in particular the peasantry, had been his famous Proclamation against enclosures.

'Having care to the good of the realm that by enclosing of lands and arable grounds in divers places, many have been driven to extreme poverty, wherefore a speedy reformation shall be made so ye shall put away all fear of landlord or master. Yea, with all my heart I will do good unto my country.'

That was his message to those who had suffered hardship from starvation, deprived of their livelihood by misappropriation of their pitiful small holdings. And he had kept his word to them. He sent a body of commissioners to investigate their grievances, and had even established a Court of Requests in his own house to hear the complaints of those who had found neither sympathy nor justice in Westminster. Report had come to him how that his representatives in town and village were met with rapture as they were celestial messengers. 'The world of iron rule is ended, a new, a golden world is given unto us ...' And now this hideous domestic crisis, dropped from a blue sky to submerge his 'golden world', wherein 'all private profit, self-love, and such like devil's

271

instruments', so had he promised and such was his aim, 'shall be destroyed.'

That he had taken to himself much 'private profit', at the Revenue's expense, in his great treasure-house still building on the Thames, may have accounted for the loss of his people's faith in him and in his works, that he must stand before them execrated, damned: a 'Fratricide'!

Those premonitory thunderclouds came nearer, ever nearer, borne on the wings of revolt. All over the country threatening mutters were heard against the duke, his Protectorate, and his new-fangled fashion of prayer, prompted by Archbishop Cranmer. From Devon, Somerset, and Cornwall, news was brought of mutinous attempt to re-establish the Old Faith. Once again in village churches the Mass was said in Latin by officiating priests in cope and vestments.

The harassed Protector called a meeting of the council. Such defiance must be quelled, by whatever drastic means, before it spread. And quelled it was, with a rounding up of the Faithful, a hanging of their priests from church steeples, and the threat that all insurrectionists 'would incur damnation everlasting in the fires of Hell'.

But neither threats of interminable roastings down below, nor the grim sight of those bodies above, swinging to their slow awful deaths in chains, could stem the sporadic retributive storm-clouds, rolling up from the western to the eastern counties to break in the blast of rebellion.

The King and his Court were at Oatlands when, on a day in July of that disastrous summer, Philip Pugh was surprised to receive a summons to wait upon His Grace, the duke of Somerset What could this mean? Hitherto the Protector had ignored his existence other than in curt acknowledgement of his presence when in waiting on the King, at such time as the duke should call to enquire of His Majesty's tutors how his studies progressed, or, as afterthought, and rarely, of his nephew's health. And now this imperative command that Master Pugh attend forthwith upon the duke at the Palace of Whitehall.

Ushered by a page into an anteroom, Philip was abstractedly greeted by Somerset, seated at a table with Lords Rich and Warwick on his either side as if they were heraldic symbols supporting; and certain he looked as in need of support.

This was the first time since Seymour's execution that Philip had seen the Protector at close quarters, and he saw him greatly changed. His finely featured face, always pale, had yellowed, save at the tip of his nose which had ever been dyspeptically pink. His eyes, still of a startling blue, were sunk in their sockets and circled with a network of fine coin-like markings. In the lank moustache, shaped like a horseshoe, straggling down to meet the forked fair beard, some silver threads were visible that never surely had been there before. A sick man, decided Philip, and one who looked as he went haunted. He was aware of a subdued tension in the duke's hesitant gesture that wordlessly bade him to sit; and his side glances, unreturned, at those two beside him. Warwick, languid and elegant in buff-coloured sable-edged velvet, was staring down at the back of his hand: a long sensitive hand with intelligent tapering fingers. The Chancellor, pompous and fidgety, eyes up at the rafters, tapped an impatient tattoo with his toe as if unspokenly saying, *Get on with it, do!*

And the duke did get on with it, further to mystify Philip. 'I understand you to be, sir, a native of Norfolk?'

'That is so, Your Grace.'

'You are wont to take your yearly leave of absence for three months in or about October?' And without waiting for assent to this, 'Your father —' again the duke glanced aside, with a pettish pucker between his brows, at Warwick still engrossed in contemplation of his hand, which Philip now perceived to have an occupant: an infinitesimal insect. 'Your father,' said the duke, pointedly glaring at Warwick to recall his errant attention, 'owns some considerable property in the neighbourhood of Norwich —'

Now what in the devil? wondered Philip.

'— which being so, Mr. Pugh, you may have heard somewhat of complaints and grievances lodged by the peasantry against the lords of the lands thereabout?'

'All my life, Your Grace,' Philip answered coolly, 'for so long as I remember, and as my father before me can remember, there have been complaints from the peasantry against the landlords, and not only those of Norfolk.'

'Yes, yes, as well I know.' Mounted on his hobby Somerset launched forth on an excerpt from his pet Proclamation: *The land which has been tilled and did keep divers families in good work and labour is now gotten by insatiable greediness of mind into one or two men's hands, that the force of the realm is weakened and Christian people driven from their houses, eaten up and devoured of brute beasts.'*

And Philip, his gaze fixed on that delicately chiselled face with its beautiful mild eyes, thought, *He goes through life mistaking glow-worms at his feet for stars in heaven … What* is *all this?*

'Great rots and murrains lately sent by God which should not so soon fall. Therefore, as I do see it, these people have a just cause for lamentation, which it is my earnest wish to remedy and so —'

'A money-spider,' murmured Warwick.

'What?' The Duke turned on him sharply. 'You said?'

'A money-spider,' repeated Warwick, simply. 'I have been watching an exquisite example of the Creator's workmanship in this so perseveringly insistent a small creature. Look how it spins itself a fairy cord that it may descend from higher spheres to explore these nether regions. With what temerity it forges through an impenetrable forest, the hairs on my hand, that it may —'

'My lord!' The Chancellor, with a murderous look, crashed in on these flights of fancy. 'May I remind you that this is no occasion for irrelevancies? Your Grace,' he deferentially inclined his head, 'would say?'

'I forget what I would say,' sulkily rejoined the duke. 'I am put out.'

'Was it not,' prompted Warwick, who had now induced his molecular visitant to crawl along his forefinger, 'Your Grace's intention to enquire of Master Pugh concerning one —'

'Kett!' The Duke snatched the name from him, spitting out the word in repetition, 'Kett. Robert Kett, Squire of Wymondham.' *Pronounced Wyndham,* Philip silently corrected. 'Are you, sir,' interrogated Somerset, 'acquainted with this Kett?' And to Philip's brief affirmative, 'What manner of man is he?'

'An honest man and one whom I believe to be,' said Philip, 'of integrity.'

'A man,' the Chancellor treated the King's young gentleman to. a look of the utmost disfavour, 'who breeds discord and disunion among the lower orders. A man of infinite malice.'

'A man,' was Philip's cool rejoinder, 'who, an I dare to differ from your lordship, has less of malice in him than of good intent — misplaced'

'How,' asked Warwick idly, 'misplaced?'

'In that, my lord, he is inclined to let sentiment play havoc with his reason.'

'Yes,' mused Warwick, 'sentiment … the hair shirt of the hypocrite.'

'Master Pugh.' The duke's eyebrows met across his high-bridged nose; but his frown was not for Philip. 'Since, as I was about to say, you are used to take your vacation in October, it would suit our purpose better,' he often used, unconsciously, as may be, the royal plural, 'if you would take your leave of absence now.'

Philip bowed. 'As Your Grace wishes.'

Somerset relaxed his fretted forehead. 'The fact is, Mr. Pugh,' he leaned across the table confidentially to say, 'We have had certain knowledge of disturbance in the neighbourhood of Wymondham. Do you know of this village, or small market town of Wymondham?'

'I do, Your Grace. My home lies within ten miles or so of Wymondham.'

The Duke fingered his beard. 'So, this Win — how do you call it — Windom? — has become, we hear, a centre of disturbance, doubtless resultant on the recent revolt in the western counties. Revolt is contagious, or, should we say, imitative? As one may see a herd of beasts, cows, sheep, or such, peaceably grazing, whereas one will be stung by a wasp to turn it rampageous, so then will all stampede. Thus do we feel it expedient,' the duke permitted himself a wavering smile, 'to take the bull, as it were, by the horns.'

'The bull being, in this case,' drawled Warwick, 'a sheep, on which a tax of one penny is levied should it feed on those common lands that are not yet confiscated by the overlords … Go, spin your web,' he lifted his hand from which the diminutive spider dung suspended by its flimsy thread, 'so you may ensnare whatever smallest weakling fly shall come your way.'

The Chancellor gave a rageful grunt, and, folding his arms across his chest, resumed his devil's tattoo with his toe.

'And yet,' the Protector was biting at his nails, 'despite my earnest endeavours on their behalf: they rise —' a faint flush crept through his beard to his cheek-bones, deepening the permanent pink of his nose — 'these scum, these ignorant malefactors, they rise against me — I — who have —'

'— made history,' Warwick smoothly intervened, 'with your incomparable Proclamation.'

Philip passed a hand across his mouth to hide a twitching there.

'But you, as with all great reformers from time immemorial,' said Warwick, spreading unction, 'may not reap your harvest in your lifetime. Men's deeds, their aspirations, their greatest of achievements, live after them. So as it was in the beginning with Our Lord Himself, so will it be with Your Grace unto the end.'

And, as Philip's glance swerved from under raised eyebrows to meet Warwick's, he saw the lid of the Earl's eye farthest from the duke, unmistakably, tellingly, lowered; and again he masked his mouth.

The Chancellor was saying fussily, 'Have I Your Grace's permission to give this gentleman your instructions and the data of the report I — we — have received from Serjeant Flowerdew?'

Philip's head went up. Now, at long last, having beat around the bush, it seemed they had come to a clearing.

'Yes.' The Protector nodded agreement in evident relief. 'I will leave you with Master Pugh to tell him all that you deem proper he should know.'

He rose from the table; the other three stood. The Duke motioned Warwick to the door and followed; there he turned.

'My Lord Chancellor, we desire,' again the royal plural, slightly emphasised, 'that Master Pugh be put to no pecuniary disadvantage in any undertaking wherewith he be commissioned. See to it that all and sundry expense incurred in our service is charged to — the Crown.'

On the morning of Philip's departure for Sprowston came a letter from his father crossing his sent by messenger two days before to prepare them at home for his arrival. His father's crabbed scholarly hand, at the best of times no easy task to decipher, had been rendered almost illegible.

... these misfortunate events which for (indecipherable) *come to fall upon and devastate our lands. It was a sennight gone that talk went hereabout how the men of Attelboro', Eccles and Drayton did fill up the ditches and pull down the fences ... to John Green, Lord of the Manor of Wilby whom you may recall did take possession of the house of my kinsman Lord Sowerby deceased and hath sold it to the husband of his daughter Jocosa. Sobeit yester'een when was ended the annual festival of St. Thomas Becket held in the Chapel at Wymondham dedicated to the Saint of blessed memory whose name was (struck out of the Calendar) by King Henry VII sundry persons did set about to throw down the fences at Hethersett where Serjeant Flowerdew hath enclosed much common land. Whereupon Master Flowerdew to save his property and at the same time... Squire Kett being his long-sworne enemie did incite them to desist from despoilment of his land and turn their purpose upon Kett's enclosures for, saith Flowerdew, he who is the first to speak* (fair?) *words in your goode cause hath worked to wrest from you your* (rights?). *Moreover Flowerdew did offer the sum of 40d. if they would do to Kett what hath been done to him. So seemeth evil forces are abroad led by Sathanas himself that fearing*

of most dire consequence and on advice of your Grand-Aunt Matilda have I set a watch upon the gate-house for as Ovid hath it Qui non est hodie, cras minus aptus erit. *He who is not prepared today will be less so tomorrow.*

Vale. Quid vesper faret incertum est …

Having made what sense he could of this in one hasty reading, Philip re-read it in the privacy of his bedroom in the inn at Hoddesdon where he and his attendants lay the first night of their journey. Closer application to the rambling contents of his father's letter had sent him off at break of day besieged with a host of misgivings. Nor did John Locke's churlish reception of the two couriers who rode with them to carry messages to and from the Protector, serve to decrease Philip's distaste for his mission, *which,* he told himself, *take it how you will, smacks something of espionage.* Yet he was bound to bear in mind the Chancellor's last words to him: 'If this disturbance in East Anglia be of so grave a purpose as reported' (*by Flowerdew?* had been Philip's silent query) 'then no time must be lost in the investigation thereof, that a force, if need be, shall be sent to maintain peace and order.'

The day was fair, the going good. Some rain had fallen in the night to lay the dust of the roads and refresh the thirsty earth, burnt to a dark ochre from long drought. The sun had lowered in a warm red sky when they rode into Wymondham. The Festival of St. Thomas Becket, Wymondham's great annual event, terminating in a Mystery Play performed for two days in succession, was over; but the houses were still festooned with garlands of faded flowers, while here and there among the townsfolk could be seen a down-at-heel jester in cap and bells, a bedraggled minstrel, his lute slung across his shoulder, a pedlar with his empty tray, hangers-on from the fun of the fair held beyond the town in celebration of the Saint. Outside the Green Dragon Inn, which before the Dissolution had been the guest house of the abbey, groups of men and some women were gathered, not, or so it seemed to Philip, as by haphazard but rather as if by some common accord. And in the marketplace he saw a body of men who stood in marching formation of four or six abreast. He reined in, and turning to John who rode beside him: 'Go you on to Sprowston with those two,' he jerked his head at the following couriers, 'and tell my father I'll be with him later. I'll stay here awhile and see what's to do, which may be much or little.'

'Master,' John urged him, ''tis not for me to cross your ways but shall you stay here so will I, and send the duke's men on without me to the Hall. God's Body, sir!' John had so far forgot himself as to swear an oath, 'I do mislike a concourse such as this, full o' low mutterings that bode no good, and of black looks as ne'er I saw in my born life in Wymondham's men and scarce one among them that I know, as they most look to come from places afar — Suffolk, Cambridge, Lincoln too, it seems.'

'Having come from afar,' Philip reminded him, 'for the Feast of St. Thomas of Canterbury.'

'As may be,' John said doggedly. 'But yet methinks there's more than meets the eye and ear in these sinistrous faces and so quiet spoken, sir, and orderly, which comes not nat'ral to Wymondham folk which is free and outright of their speech. Master, I mislike the looks on't and would know what's more a-foot afore I'll leave you, for I mistrust this —'

'What you mistrust or do mislike,' cut in Philip tersely, ''is naught to do with me. All you've to do, sirrah, is as you're bid. So, on to Sprowston. See to it the duke's men be well fed and lodged. Here, wait —' A second thought had struck him.

Glancing round his shoulder, he dismounted. 'Take my nag to the Green Dragon. Have him stabled, and tell Dick, the ostler — if 'tis the same old man as ever was — that I'll be back to fetch him before nightfall.' Then as John made no answer to this more than with ill grace to take the bridle rein of Philip's horse, he was ordered: 'No, get you down and come aside with me.' Beckoning one of the couriers he told him, 'Hold the horses till my man returns. Now, John, quick, along this alley here.' And John was hurried away, in a huff.

Once well out of sight of the crowded street, 'Give me your hood,' Philip snatched it from John's head, the cords having been left untied for coolness; and pulling it well down over his hair and forehead to his eyebrows, he fastened it under his chin; then with a quick survey around and up at the gabled windows of the houses abutting on the alley, to satisfy himself that none was there to spy on him, he took off his doublet of fine embroidered cloth and handed it to John, saying, 'Give me your jerkin and take you mine. It will fit you seemly, myself being broader in the chest than you, who are longer in the back than I. Come on, you grouchy buzzard —' Philip danced impatience — 'would you have the whole town at our heels?'

The exchange of headgear and doublet was effected without further parley from John, whose silence, however, during these manoeuvres, spoke volumes.

''Struth!' Philip gave a hoot of laughter, 'if ever I saw a pimple on a pumpkin so it is my cap on you.' And leaving John to swallow that he sauntered out into the marketplace.

The crowd had increased and formed into columns of as much as eight abreast, stretching far along the main street where still a few loiterers, yokels and children, stood in gaping wonder, while at almost every window the heads of women bobbed, and faces peered; but the doorways of their houses, Philip noted, were fast shut.

'What is't about to do?' he enquired of a bearded ruffian in a leather jerkin so tattered and stained that its original colour and texture were wholly submerged in its dirt.

'About to do?' echoed the fellow, who appeared to be rounding up and checking the crowd as a shepherd's dog rounds up a flock of sheep, 'why, bor, lend ears to your sight and — follow on!'

Even as he spoke there rose from all sides a tuneless chant, the signal for that straggling column to surge forward on the march; some with long strides, some with short, but each man, and a smattering of women, yelling as they went to burst their lungs:

'Cast hedge and ditch in the lake
Fixed with many a stake
Tho' 'twere never so fast
Yet asunder be it wrast...'

So this, Philip thought, *is what's to do!* And tacking himself to the tail of that vast company, which now must have numbered some hundreds, he marched with them. Bearing left, on the outskirts of the town, he saw they were making for the house of Robert Kett since his was the only habitation along that way; but before they reached his door he had rode out to meet them. Pulling in his horse he raised his hand with a stentorian cry of 'Halt!' At which the decisive tramp of feet died down to an uncertain shuffling; and the whole crowd of them spread fanwise in a semi-circle.

On either side lay pasture lands, criss-crossed with ditch and fence that when Philip last had visited Kett's house he was positive he had not seen. In the golden evening's distance men and boys toiled through the last of the light, pitch-forking the stooks of the harvest on to the oxen-drawn wains. Nearer, yet less distinctly patterned against the greying green, spectral flocks of sheep grazed, along with heifers, cows, and herds of steers.

'Stay, ye men of Wymondham!' Loud and clear rang out Kett's voice. 'I know for why you come.'

A low concerted growl was the ominous answer to that, accompanied by furtive exchange of looks from scowling faces.

Holding John's hood over his face to hide all but his eyes, Philip elbowed himself forward, dodging taller men and pushing past those shorter than he, until he could gain a closer view and hearing. He saw also that those in the forefront of the column went armed with bludgeons, rakes, staves, billhooks, the purpose of which was defined in Kett's next words.

'You are come,' he told them, 'to pluck down my enclosures, to fill up my ditches — at a price. A poor enough price too, I'll warrant me. Flowerdew!' He trailed a jeer of laughter to that name. 'Your lawly Master Serjeant, while so well about it, might have set a higher value on his minions than forty pieces of silver, which, shared among the lot o' you — and fine numbers here, I see — would not go to buy one sheep a-piece. No, nor not one mutton-shank.'

''Tis not mutton-shanks nor sheep that we be after!' spoke up an isolated angry voice, passed unheeded by Kett, who went on.

'Yet 'twas only *thirty* pieces o' silver as was offered for the sale of God's Son.'

This was followed by blacker looks and rising mutters.

'Blasphemy!'

'Harken to the whoreson sacramentary!'

'Heretic!'

'Fools!' Kett's voice went up to shout them down. 'Off you go confusing of your issues. I'm no sacramentary, no, nor heretic. We of Norfolk cling to the Old Faith, but I'm not here to talk o' that. Let each man worship as he will and the devil take the hindmost — as he has done already down in Devon.'

A guffaw of approval greeted this. Philip saw Kett's teeth parted, white-gleaming in his grizzled beard, and with the throw-back of his head, his red arched palate as his boisterous laugh joined theirs. But still that same voice of one unseen was heard again, sullenly insistent: ''Tis more'n sheep we be after —' a chorus of assenting 'Yeas!' — ''Tis justice we be after.'

Philip saw and recognised the speaker now as one John Browne, a cooper from Old Buckenham, well known around those parts. 'Justice, and the rights of men to live and have their being and their state soever small it may be in our own native land —'

'So we may live — not starve!' shrieked a tousle-headed woman with an infant sucking at her shrunken breast 'That our milk runs dry for want of food more'n can fill us from the flesh o' snails, pigs' droppings, and a handful o' sneaked grass.'

'What feeds *your* sheep, *your* kine, so they grow fat on the lands that be our'n!'

It was the black-bearded Goliath who now thrust himself forward, threateningly to brandish a fist above the heads of them all while he yelled out in strong dialect: 'Where be your promise made to 'un thick'ee year a-gone that you be for and not agen us? And now what's come o' your garnderin'? That you ha' done as all them others do to fill your belly on our midderns wrast from us.'

'Ay!' A single-throated roar went up. 'We're here to tak' and hold fast to our own!'

'Surely!' Kett capped that roar with one louder. In the day's dying light his head, outlined against the sky, dove-coloured now, was ringed with gold from one down-thrust bar of amber; and, breaking in on stray uprisen murmurs: 'Friends,' his hand went out to them, 'hear me! Give me leave to speak *your* minds, that I speak for and with you as of *my* mind, you and I.'

'And I!' Another had ridden up to join him, whom Philip saw to be Kett's elder brother, William, a big brawny man in his sixties with a mass of silvery hair and a face like a large red smiling moon. Halting his horse alongside Robert's he called out, 'I am with you, staunch as is my brother here whose purpose is that we all stand in one purpose — together.'

A stillness fell on those pressed close to Philip, nudging shoulders, straining eyes to stare and ears to listen with an eager fixed intensity to Kett's words, borne on that heavy breathing silence.

'Friends, know this! That I am and will be ready, at all times, to do whatsoever I can to crush the power of those that ere long, so as you repent your painful labours unto them — shall they, these great ones — repent their crimes. You have suffered and endured with patience many wrongs and miseries of cruelty and covetousness in all sort, that you seem to have been hated and accursed of God. But this I promise you — and before God take my vow on't — that the hurts done unto you in seizure of your commons and your pastures by the lords of our lands shall be revenged.'

'Revenged!' A howl of universal elation soared up in echo from five hundred throats. 'Yea! Revenged!'

He had them now in the hollow of his fist, all doubt, all hostility fled. They were with him to a man, when solemnly, quietly, yet in a voice that reached to every ear: 'Take me,' he said, 'if you will, in this great work as lies before us, not only as your comrade, brother, friend, but as your captain and your leader.'

A shout went up at that to hit the sky while still he spoke. 'Friends! Brothers! This, moreover, would I say, that whatsoever lands I have enclosed —' he stood in his stirrups spreading his arms in a gesture to embrace his dusk-gloomed acres right and left — 'shall again be made common unto ye and all men, and these own hands of mine —' he held them out — 'shall first perform it.'

Another shout stormed up as they rushed forward to surround him in a frenzy of cheering. His horse reared; Kett's knees gripped the saddle and, as he caught the reins to steady his startled beast, his brother turned his horse aside saying over his shoulder:

'I'll be off now, Robin. 'Tis well done.'

Well done! So Philip in his heart acclaimed Kett's overture, even while he saw the danger of it.

Mutiny.

Lips pursed in a soundless whistle, he slipped away unnoticed in the falling dark, lit now by a star-pricked sky, where a slender young moon lay on her back in a halo of bronze.

A fine homecoming, was his thought as he rode in at the gatehouse of Sprowston, where Jake, old Andrew's son, hailed him with a growl of, 'Who goes there?'

Philip leaned from the saddle. 'A friend.'

'Why, young master! Is't you?' Skew-eyed with wonder, Jake lowered the club he held ready. 'Why come you so late and in this guise?'

'I took a toss,' Philip told him airily, 'into an open drain, and was so befouled I made shift to change my suit, and then,' he called behind him as he clattered on into the yard, 'I fell in with some good company — at Wymondham.'

TWELVE

The removal from London to Drayton in the spring kept Jocosa busy throughout the summer months. The measles had left her low-spirited, listless, with such loss of weight and appetite as to convince her maid Joan she was in a consumption. But the ordering of her household at Sowerby gave her more to occupy her mind than the state of her health and discontent. This latter, although she would not have confessed it, was largely attributable to the fact that Philip had not once called at the house in Water Lane to enquire how she did, for he surely must have known of her illness, since, as Joan informed her, she had met with his man John in the Chepe during the week that she sickened. 'So, madame,' Joan had said, 'I doubt me not Master Pugh will fear to come nigh you lest he take it.'

'As so should he fear,' retorted Jocosa. 'He who goes in constant attendance on the King would never risk carrying infection to a child.'

'True enough, madame, but he could have sent that fiddle-faced long John of his to ask after my Lady, or to bring you flowers, fruit or some such gift as does the master daily, for your cheer.'

'Fine cheer for me would be a gift from him!' rejoined Jocosa, sharp as knives. 'I've known him long enough to know that any gift he's like to give will be given to none but himself.'

'And one other,' Joan said slyly, 'a buxom widow she be too, as so I hear from Margaret, my Lady Rich's woman, who had it from Mistress Winifred, that Lady Browne, now her husband's dead and buried — high time, too — goes handfasted soon to wed with our Master Pugh who's had his eye on her since — ouch! *Aah!* Madame dear, be not so curst — I'm black and blue!'

'And you'll be black and bluer afore I've done with you.' Reluctantly Jocosa detached her thumb and forefinger from a vicious pinch applied to her handmaid's fleshy underarm, 'you lying jabberjaw. What's it to me if he should wed with whomsoever, be she widow-woman, Jenny-ass or milch-cow, for which so be it *that* one Lady Browne, she well could pass. Or should his taste be for a Sultan's harem, let him take them all to wife and welcome! Would I care?'

'Only, madame,' Joan made answer tearfully, rubbing her bruised arm, 'seeing as how he, Master Pugh, is your cousin —'

'Twice removed and nothing far enough removed,' Jocosa said, 'from me...'

She was thinking back upon that talk when, on a July morning at Sowerby, she had come to watch the dairymaids busy at their churning. So warm the day, so full of sun, no cooler place was to be found than the dark-shaded dairy with its high arched roof and stone-flagged floor.

Seated on a milking-stool, her hands hugging her knees, she paid small heed to the girls' chatter, until: 'There 'e be, as like the Living Christ himself with the light o' heaven round his head — so the tinker swear'd to't as was there along to hear 'un. "I'll be your captin," says 'e, "to lead you an you'll follow." So then they ups an' goes with 'un and —'

'They?' Dragged forward to a present dimmed by a more vivid past, Jocosa roused herself 'Who is "he"? And who are "they"?'

The speaker, a plump, rosy-cheeked fifteen-year-old, turned holly-berry red in the sudden silence fallen on the three of them. Then: ''Twas Squire Kett o' Wymondham, mistress,' said she with a nervous giggle and a side look at the other two, who were beating away at the thick leathery folds of cream as if their lives depended on the butter-making.

'And what,' demanded Jocosa, 'of him?'

'Why, mistress, that he goes for to make some great stir hereabout, as was told to my father by a tinker from Bungay, as Squire Kett comes to give us — which is to say me father an' all such as goes so poorly beggared of the common land what has been seized as of their lawful rights.' And now there was a glint of challenge in the girl's large bovine eyes. 'Which was how my father heard it from the tinker.'

'So that's the way it is!' cried Jocosa, up-sprung in a fury. 'All's the same the world over, tittle-tattle, tale-telling. First my girl, Joan, with her big mouth, "*she* said, and *she* said" — and now you with your "*he* said". A tinker — be damned!'

And out of the dairy she dashed.

That the gossip of a country wench should have occasioned this hot outburst, may have caused as much surprise to her as to the three she left there staring.

Certes, she told herself, *I'm in such tetchy mood of late one would think I were bedevilled — and for why?*

Why indeed? As they in the dairy may have asked, and in particular she who had borne the brunt of her young mistress's attack. Heads together, whispering: 'There's ill-doings hereabouts,' they said, 'and omens of no good, for look you, see how she lets fly at us as if the evil one had bit her —'

'Or a serpent,' the spokeswoman said darkly. 'Did you not hear how Mistress Kett, the squire's wife, riding whoam from market yester'een was bit in the breast —' the tinker again, who had much to say on that — 'Yes! bit by a snake that leapt

290

at her from the old oak tree that stands midway between Wymondham and Hethersett.'

'Ah! And see how the butter be so slow to come. Sure sign o' Satan's work, or witch's work, or somethin'.'

The noon glare of the sun shimmered white hot in the courtyard where a group of serving-men stood in a huddle, their voices a-buzz as the honey-drugged drones in the hollyhocks, peering over the south wall of Jocosa's privy garden. At sight of her the men slunk back into the kitchen, but she had no eyes for them. Shading her face with her hand, she gazed under it up to the red-tiled roof of the granary where the white fan-tails from the newly stocked dovecote, preening their snowy plumage, bowed and strutted at their love-making.

Jocosa pushed open the granary door to scoop up a fistful of grain, and, palm outstretched, she waited. Not yet tamed to come at her call as would those in the dovecote of her London house, they still could be coaxed to feed from her hand; and soon, very cautiously, a prim young hen, her coral red toes clawed under, winged down to snatch, and then was gone. Another and another followed, gingerly to peck; and presently a dozen were picking at the scattered grain around Jocosa's feet. One more courageous than his fellows, his fine fan-tail reared, his chest proudly pouted, flew up to her shoulder, billing love into her ear, until the clop and clatter of hooves startled him and the rest of them away.

He, who had sent them flying, rode into the forecourt under the arch of the gatehouse, with no greeting for her more than a long-held look, as wordlessly answered; but the rush of the blood to her face from her heart, in that half second's pause, spoke for her — to him.

He dismounted; and she, coming forward, said confusedly, 'I didn't hope … did not expect you would be at Sprowston till October. The men … I'll send one to take your horse.'

'No need. I'll hitch him here.' Philip slipped the reins through an iron ring attached to the granary door. 'He'll stay quiet. 'Tis old Crispin, aged twenty now. You remember him?'

'I do, but he looks no older than when…' She stroked the soft dark nose, and her composure recovered, 'Will you,' she invited, 'come into the house?' Through the buttery she led him with politest chill apology. 'An you'll excuse this shorter way than the longer way round to the main entrance, sir?' Nor did she see his eyebrows quirk at that.

Pausing at the screens that divided the domestic quarters from the great hall, she turned; and still, with ice, she said, 'I have to offer you my heartiest felicitations on your betrothal, or by this time, maybe, marriage to the Lady Widow Browne.'

'My —? God's Life!' He was shaken, unamused; and fierce as she to take her words and fling them back at her, 'Who has dared to couple me with that —' he checked himself — 'her name with mine to falsify it?'

'Huh!' The well-remembered hunch of her shoulder gave her to him once again, aged twelve. 'There's never smoke, they say, without a fire. Search rumour and you'll find stuck deep in it, a spark o' truth to spring into a blaze.'

'Not in such rumour smouldering in ashes of burnt refuse, puked from lying talk —' Then, at the light that flooded her face and eyes, 'Sweet,' he closed with her to say, 'why do you receive me as I had come to steal — as so I have!' And she was in his arms, her mouth possessed; and all those petty, thorned anxieties of self-tormented lovers were dissolved in that one moment's sweet appeasement, which never could appease.

'See,' she whispered through his long throbbing kiss, 'how I am foolish — mad.'

'As I am — hunger-mad — for you.' His lips strayed to her lowered eyelids. 'Love, my love, I taste your tears. Why tears?'

'For me. For us. I listened to my woman's babble but …' She drew away from him. 'I was hurt that you came never near me, nor to ask if I were sick or dying — dead, after the measles.'

'The measles! What more foolery is this?' For so unaccountable is the way of love that, even in this snatched second's comfort of reunion, they must seize on such a trifle to magnify the pain of it beyond all sense. 'How —' incredulous concern loudened his voice — 'how should I know of the measles?'

But she, with a scared glance about her, hushed him. 'I thought I heard — no matter. All's one and all's forgotten. Come into the hall.' Yet inconsequently, as she went, she said to him behind her, 'Did not your man John tell you, or has my woman lied? If so —'

''Tis John, who is so near of words and chary of repeating them or any spice of hearsay, that unless that he be driven he would never speak at all.'

And now they were together in the great vaulted hall with its open, brick hearth, wide enough to roast an ox, where ferns and tall grasses had replaced the winter's logs; and there Gynkes' monkey crouched, its small hairy fingers scrabbling in a comfit box, its black lips sugar-powdered. 'The devil!' cried Jocosa, 'It's ate a pound of marshmallows to sick up all over — go on, away with you!' It leapt to a stool and sat malevolently glaring at her with its wicked little human eyes. 'All animals I love,' she said, 'but not this one. 'Tis sure possessed with Satan's mischief in it.'

'Jocosa,' Philip took her hands and drew her to him, saying urgently, 'I am come to bid — implore — that you leave here so soon as may be. This very night were it possible.'

'Leave here — leave Sowerby? Why should I?'

But as he made to tell her why, a faint bleating sound followed by a shuffle of steps, turned them both to see her husband in the doorway.

At sight of Philip he halted. He was holding in his arms a very young, small lamb; and, while he caressed it, his glance slid from his wife to Philip with a pale blank stare.

'I saw a stranger's horse in the courtyard,' he said, 'I did not know that you ...' Limply he took Philip's hand; his touch was damp. 'Since when did you arrive?' And without waiting for reply, 'Look, wife, what I have found, lost of its mother, an ewe lying dead out there in the grazing, undiscovered by the shepherd. Her babe sucked at her dried teats and she was ... dead.' His fixed smile and cold empty look at her, and then again at Philip, sent a shudder down Jocosa's spine.

'Philip,' she told him, 'is come to give us news of — of what,' she asked, 'were you about to tell when —?'

'Sir,' he turned to Gynkes, who had come nearer to stand between him and Jocosa. Under his beardless chin he held that pitifully bleating mass of wool. 'The Commons, led by Robert Kett,' said Philip hardily, 'have risen and are marching on to Mousehold, to pillage horse and victuals from all the manor lords along the way. Sir, I beg you for your wife's sake, persuade her she must go from here. The whole of East Anglia is up and in revolt.'

'Yes, my men out there,' Gynkes gestured vaguely, — 'speak somewhat of such doings. Wife, go fetch me a bowl of warm milk for this little orphaned one — an infant ram. I must feed him that he suck of my finger milk-wetted, as it were his dam's udder.' And as Jocosa went he ran a hand around his jaw, saying in that one-toned voice of his, 'I am not shaven this morning. My beard grows fast in summer weather that I must shave at night when its growth be strong. And tonight at the full o' the moon it will be stronger. Do you shave once or twice a day, sir?'

'Will you,' Philip said abruptly, 'heed me what I tell you? Your wife must go from Sowerby at once, and —'

'No,' the other interposed with a glitter in his eyes and that set smile stretched back skull-wise across his yellow teeth. 'No,' he sidled nearer. His breath, foul-smelling, was hot on Philip's face. 'Where she, my wife, is, there will I be beside her. And where better than under this roof which was her father's? Should the Commons rise —'

'Do I not tell you,' cried Philip, 'they *have* risen! This is war between us — the landlords and the people. Your shepherd who no longer guards your flocks that they die —'

'Pooty-pooty diddly-poo!' crooned Gynkes, nibbling at the ear of the tiny struggling creature. 'Don't cry, then, sweeting. We'll not run into danger. My wife and I, we will advance to meet it. Sir, I thank you for your thought of her, but I, her husband, must have first right so to decide. I'll go find her, and look now to this little starven one.' He wandered off; but at the screens he turned and said with awful quiet: 'Sir, know this. My house and all that's in it is well guarded, watched from evil-doers, robbers, vandals, sneak-thieves, friends, or … brothers. All is guarded here and watched. By me.' And in his soundless ghostly way was gone.

At sundown the next evening Jocosa, in her garden, attended by her page, filled her basket and his with flowers for the house. The beds had just been watered, and the drooping roses lifted grateful heads to enrich the air with fragrance. But, as she stooped to a red damask bloom, relishing the scent of it, she drew back startled by the nearing sound of horse and foot, and a man's shout, 'Hola, there, give way.'

'Boy!' she called to him who set down his basket and ran to her.

'What, mistress,' he panted, 'is come?'

'How should I know till I see?' Taking him by the arm she dragged him with her to the high wall of mellowed brick where peaches ripened. 'Bend down,' she said, 'that I may mount you.'

'But, mistress —'

'Ssh!' She clapped a hand over his mouth. 'Hold your tongue and do as you are bid. Get down!'

And down on all fours he went in the moistened earth, but not without whines of protest: 'Madame, my fine new hosen what the master bought for me in Norwich this last week — they'll be mussed and —'

'I'll muss you,' hissed Jocosa, 'if you pip at me. Keep still.' And, setting first one foot and then the other lightly on his back, she hoisted herself to the top of the wall, and there by her hands she clung. She still could see nothing, but heard enough to know of a to-do about the gatehouse. 'Such fools we were,' she muttered, 'not to put a guard upon it.'

'Mistress,' wailed the kneeling page, 'what'll I do if the master sees how I have mussed my fine new hosen?'

'Up with you!' Jocosa kicked a heel at him. 'Go tell the men come out and meet what's here. Let them bring whatever arms they can lay hands on. There's dirty work out there beyond the gates.'

And as the boy made off, she, clutching the wall-top, pulled herself head and shoulders higher, cursing her petticoats, grazing her palms on the rough bricks until she gained enough purchase to swing her legs over with an eight-foot drop below. As she slithered to the ground her kirtle caught on a nail. Wrenching it free to leave a jagged tear in its silk, she fell head foremost in jarring contact with the flinty cobbles of the court to scrape her chin. But with no thought for that she was up and on her feet again, alert for the commotion heard but still not seen; then even as she strained tip-toe for some first sight of it, they came storming through the archway.

Their leader, a stout florid fellow with a rough reddish beard, his capless head covered with a thatch of hair, bronze burnished, shouted to those behind him, 'Halt!' and mock-gallantly, he bowed to her who stood puzzled, pricked by some elusive memory of that face and voice. 'Madame, loath as I am to disoblige beauty, yet if beauty will disoblige me, I must regretfully issue command to my men to take that which I may not be given.'

'Ho!' Jocosa faced him hotly. 'This is as I was warned. You and your whoresons come from Kett of Wymondham. So what would you have of my obligement?'

'Sweetness,' he flashed her a wide white grin, 'yow to ask me that? An I dare to answer in what way you may oblige me —'

'An you should dare,' she blazed, 'who dares enough in impudence to hang you! I know why you are here — to take and plunder. Go!' She raised her fist. 'Go out the way you came. I'm not alone. My men —' below her breath she damned their tardiness — 'will lay about you quick, to skin you of your scurvy hides if you —'

'God's Bones!' His forceful interruption stayed her words. 'Is it — is it not? It *is*!' he cried, with over-boisterous delight. 'Jocosa, grown to blossom from the bud as I first knew her!'

She knew him then. Will Kett! And he was saying, wonder-struck: 'But what do you here? This is — or was John Wilby's house.'

''Tis my house now — my father's house as used to be — bought for me by my husband.'

'Your —? So you're a wife. Whose wife?'

Insolent his look, more than insolent his eyes, with admiration glowing, feigned — or not? The same Will Kett, and all his youth's hot-blooded promise fulfilled in manhood.

'The wife,' she said, 'of none whom you would know.' Then, lest he might mistake this slight digression for a truce, she told him, sharp, 'You'd best be gone, you and your followers, lest mine do throw you out.'

'Is this,' he asked, exaggeratedly chapfallen, 'all you can offer me for friendship's sake across the bridge of — ten years, is it? Twelve? A churlish reception, i' faith! And more than I did bargain for, since I can't take by force what I would have from you or,' he hastily amended, at her frown, 'from your husband, whosoever he may be. But, as between friends, I will ask you the favour of some vittals for my men and fodder for my horses, that I may not be bound to rifle your larder, nor,' he gave a glance aloft at the fluttering pigeons on the red-tiled granary roof, 'your dovecote for a winter's store, should the manor lords and commons be at cross purposes or cross-bows for — shall we say — the next six months?'

'You devil's spawn!' she cried, her temper up at this last piece of impudence. 'Empty-handed have you come and empty-handed shall you go. Not a crumb for your men, not an oat for your beasts nor feather from my birds shall you take with you, unless it be over the dead bodies of my guards.' *May they rot in hell, and where the devil,* she asked herself, *were they? Ah, here, at last!* Three, at most four, shuffling, hang-dog, through the buttery and out into the yard.

'Up and at them, fellows!' she turned on them to shout. 'These be Kett's ruffians — to rob what I'll not give.'

'Nor what I'd take,' Will insinuated with a twinkle, 'having sampled long years past a taste, too bitter-sweet, of your refusal.'

And at the lightning gleam of reminiscence held, with laughter hidden, in her eyes, 'Sweetheart, spare your fears,' said he, with an answering gleam and contemptuous look at the huddled lackeys and her white-faced husband cowering behind. 'If these few cravens here be all you have for your support, then take my word in honour bound that neither you, your house, nor aught within it shall be troubled. For I'd not demean myself to come at grips with such as — that!' He swung round, jerking a thumb across his shoulder at the backing group, and giving out a great laugh, 'Right about,' he told his men, 'we'll not waste our good time here, nor this gentle's neither.'

Well!

Flattened close against the wall, she watched them crowd out through the archway where, at the gatehouse, stood a company of horse and foot, and the most raggety-taggety down-at-heel bobtail crew she ever had seen.

Briefly, Will Kett spoke to them. She could not hear his words but she saw, as he sprang into the saddle, that those who were mounted followed at the gallop and the remainder, by his stirrup, at a run.

The reports from Philip Pugh of the Norfolk rising created in Westminster a considerable stir. First the western and now the eastern counties in revolt, and scarcely had the one been dealt with than another had arisen, still more formidable, headed by this dangerous agitator, Kett.

Back and forth along the King's highway rode the couriers, their numbers now trebled, their steaming horses no less blown and exhausted than were they in their haste to bring all news to the Protector.

He, poor man, found himself in sorest straits, and the council unanimous in holding him responsible for faulty weak administration: he, who had 'liked well the doings of the people,' and had denounced 'the covetousness of the gentry which had given them reason to rise', saying, 'it were better they, should perish in their cause than starve to death...' And see now what had come of his much-vaunted Proclamation, and of himself as the 'Friend' of the people, to raise their hopes by granting them inches that they must ravage for ells. See what his fine promise to them of a new 'Golden World' had brought! Rebellion. And that fire-breathing Kett, with his rant of treason prompted by the 'Good Duke's' vision of Utopia. Hah! Utopia! Remember the end of Thomas More who had envisioned a Utopia? And now we have this Kett, perched in an oak tree on some common land around or near about the city of Norwich ... What! An oak tree? Yes. An oak tree. Called by him, forsooth, the 'Oak of Reformation'. Stealing the very name from the new religion. And the peasantry come from far and wide to hear him and follow at his beck in support of his challenge to the King with his infamous 'Rebels' Complaint'. Pages of it.

And then the final gauntlet flung: 'We will have Liberty, Equality in all things or these tumults and our lives together shall be ended.' Liberty. Equality. Words fed them by their 'Good Duke'. And this only a beginning. What would be the end?

Master Pugh, himself a Norfolk man, gave it that his father and a certain Master Gynkes, a kinsman by marriage to Lord Chancellor Rich, these and others of the gentry were likely to lose their lands if not their homes. The numbers of Kett's following had swelled from some few hundreds to five — ten thousand — rebels, while day by day, and night by night, more and more of them flocked to Kett's call from all quarters of East Anglia. This vast insurgent army must be victualled. But how? By raids, by plunder, by the lifting of horses from the stables of the landlords, and of cattle from their byres, by threats and by invasion? They had taken possession of Mount Surrey, once the home of the poet Earl, on Mousehold Hill; but mansion though it was, it could not house Kett's army. They must have huts; and in an incredibly short time huts they had, of thatch and wattle, 'come out like a rash of boils on the Heath' — so, from his window at Sprowston, Philip saw them.

They had thrown down the fences of the ancient Close of Norwich, were, swarming like locusts in the city's common pastures, first step to their 'Individual Freedom', as proclaimed by Robert Kett from his rostrum in the Oak.

But more ominous even than these aggressive overtures, was the apathetic attitude of the Norwich citizens who offered little or no resistance to the rebels; and not in Norwich only but in the land around where the lords of the manors, cowardly, had fled, leaving their households and their acres to the mercy of Kett's men. And, strangely, they were merciful, those homeless, starving thousands, in utter subservience to the orders of their 'Captain', whose command was to seize, but with no rough usage, all of food and fodder they could find. So as they went they took, holding prisoner any who attempted to resist them.

One who did resist them has been floated into legend in those parts: Sir Roger Wodehouse. The council knew of him by name, his brother Thomas having been about the Court for many years. But of all who read through Master Pugh's report, only Warwick hid a chuckle in his hand.

And now, my Lord Protector and my Lords of the Council, it doth seem that this gentleman, a near neighbour of my father and of Kett's and much esteemed in the County did summon his servants and with one wagon load of provisions and two more stacked with caskes of oure good Norfolk ale, Sir Roger set forth for Eaton Wood where Kett hath struck his Camp on his march to Mousehold Heath. There did Sir Roger, his servants and his wagons, come upon him pleading on the grounds of good friendship and neighbourly that Kett should disband his insurgents and take as peace offering his giftes of food and ale. Maugre which persuasion as I have it on evidence of my man Locke whom I did send to reconnoitre, Kett, nothing pacified in truth the more incensed by this advance did order his rebells to fall upon Sir Roger known hereabout for his short stature as the Little Knight. And they did strip him of his clothing and caste him in a ditch by Hellesdon Bridge and but for our servants' timely aid Sir Roger might have suffered savage injury and this, my Lords, despite their captain's order which thus far but for how long is no bloodshed. Then did these two, John Locke and Edgerley, Sir Roger's man, put up a sturdie fight to save him and did drag him naked from the ditch and from the rebells, who had robbed him of every stitch of his apparell that he escaped at the last with his bare skin. And the insurgents made right merry cheer with his good ale...

Two houses only were passed unmolested, notably Sprowston Hall and Sowerby at Drayton. Those other manor lords, not excepting Serjeant Flowerdew, who had been plundered of their food, their cattle, horses, and who had not fled the county, went in hiding, servantless, their domestics and farm labourers having joined with the insurgents.

Word went about among the sufferers of vandalism that the homes of Squire Pugh and Master Gynkes, the newcomer at Drayton, had been spared solely on account of a youth-time friendship between Kett's son, Philip Pugh, and Pugh's kinswoman, Mistress Gynkes of Sowerby. Since Will Kett was in command of the victualing of his father's rebel army, the deduction to be drawn from his clemency was obvious. None the less, Master Pugh, more foe than friend to any Kett, was hot on the track of the rioters.

Their numbers had now increased to twenty — some said thirty — thousand, all flocking to the camp at Mousehold. And, mounted on the rostrum in the Oak Tree on the road that crossed the common land between Hethersett and Wymondham, Kett, self-styled 'Captain', took command, issuing orders, dispensing justice and punishment to malefactors who had robbed the manor houses but would not render up their spoils for the common weal. Yet despite those tens of thousands planted thick as hops on the Heath north-east of Norwich, the trade of the city went on much as usual. It was the landlords on whom revenge for long years of oppression must be wreaked; not on honest citizens or shopkeepers. That Thomas Codd, the Mayor, with his predecessor Alderman Aldrich, certain of the clergy and Master Philip Pugh who, it was understood, held a watching brief in their cause on the part of the Protector, had met in conference together, gave the citizens of Norwich to hope that these abortive doings would soon be pacifically ended.

They were unduly optimistic. All efforts to make Kett see reason served only to make him see red. Within ten days of the Feast of St. Thomas, the rebel camp at Mousehold unfurled on high its banner of revolt, with beacons blazing and bells pealing from the hill-tops to spread the tidings through the length and breadth of Norfolk, in every village, hamlet, and rural outpost of the county, that their Great Day of Freedom had come.

A week or so after Kett's latest outburst of defiance Philip received a request from the Mayor of Norwich to attend a meeting at the house of Alderman Augustine Steward. He, a wealthy merchant and much respected citizen lived in Tombland, a spacious square fronting the two main gates into the Cathedral Close.

Philip found the Mayor, Master Steward and old Alderman Aldrich already there when he arrived. The day was warm, and their velvet robes of office hung about with golden chains and much befurred, seemed scarcely conducive to comfort. All were perspiring freely.

The Mayor, at the head of the table with his Aldermen on either side of it, graciously waved Philip to a stool at the foot and began a preamble to do with a 'Bill of Requests and Demands' sent by Kett to the council.

'Such threats as these, such insolence,' puffed the Mayor importantly, 'cannot be permitted to pass.' And taking a parchment from a pile of documents before him, 'I will read you, sir,' he said, 'a few extracts from — now where are we? Ah, yes...' He appeared to be in a considerable fuss searching through the pages to find what he sought; but even as he cleared his throat as preface to his reading, Philip made bold to intercept.

'Sir, I too have received a copy of the Bill of which the main purport may be summed up in its final significant statement, that "all bondmen be made free as God did make all free with

His Precious Blood shedding", which is, on the face of it —' he paused, 'an ultimatum.'

'You —?' The Mayor's lips rounded in a voiceless O. 'I was not aware that you —'

'That I,' Philip spent a long cool look on the now much perturbed Mayor, 'am also acquainted with Kett's "Demands"? I take it, then, that unless he withdraw them and his rebels from yonder on Mousehold, you intend to use armed force against him. Yes?'

'No.' Tom Aldrich, grown greyer, thinned with age and edentulous since Philip had last seen him, answered for the mayor, whose mouth still stayed dumbly spherical, 'we are not empowered to use force until permission be granted by the Crown. But this Bill of Requests from Kett's Commons listing their grievances,' the affable old gentleman offered Philip an exposure of toothless gums in an ingratiating smile, 'will, surely, have all due consideration from the council, as from us.'

'Since you, sir,' said Philip, equally as affable, 'and you, too, Mr. Mayor,' he glanced up directly at him who seemed to have shrunk beneath the weight of his heavy gown, 'have affixed your signatures to the Bill with that of Kett.'

At which announcement, startling as it was unexpected, a shocked silence fell upon the three, broken at last by a tremulous 'Y-yes,' from the Mayor, who folded his ringed hands on the table, and, avoiding Philip's eyes, blinked nervously his own. 'It — it was thought advisable that we show ourselves —'

'Unbiased?' suggested Philip helpfully.

'Exactly so,' agreed Tom Aldrich with a heartiness that belied his anxious glance at the wilting Mayor. 'We deemed it wiser to endorse Kett's petition rather than incite him to further and more drastic means. At all costs must we avoid a clash of arms.'

'Which,' said Steward, speaking for the first time and sententiously, 'is our sole aim and purpose, Master Pugh. I cannot but approve this manoeuvre on the part of our good Mayor and Master Alderman Aldrich,' he bowed to both in turn. 'We should not at this juncture be seeming too antagonistic to the Commons and their plaints.'

'Not that we hold with Kett's infamous proceedings,' the Mayor lifted his sunken chin from the enthrottling grip of his fur collar, 'yet we are agreed 'twould be impolitic to show ourselves ill-favouredly inclined to him, lest we — lest —'

'— lest others,' Steward suavely supplemented, 'should bring us and the city out of frame.'

And what the devil, Philip wondered, *can he mean by that?*

Although his contact with and experience of civic officialdom was of the briefest, he had learned enough to know that integrity and loyalty to any given cause were but a lagging second to personal greed and ambition. Though what these worthies hoped to gain by sitting on both sides of the fence or, more aptly, of the city gates, he could not for the life of him conceive, unless it were that hope sprang far-seeingly high to claim their share of spoils from the manor lords in event of a local disturbance infecting the whole country to bring about — good God! — a civil war.

He shifted his seat for more comfort on the stool; his leg had gone to sleep, as had seemingly the Mayor and his two Aldermen, so pregnant their silence, so downcast their eyelids, so motionless the three, until a gentle preliminary cough from Master Steward roused them from their torpor.

'Sir, we invited your attendance here today that you, acting as intermediary between ourselves and the duke —' Master

Steward drew his fingers down his forked beard as if measuring his speech which was slow and his words which were wary — 'that you may know the City Elders have, on their part, elected to send an emissary to the Lord Protector to acquaint him with the gravity of our situation.'

Philip's eyebrows shot up. *So that's the way it goes!* These pillars of civic authority resented that he, representative of the landlords, the majority of whom had left them to sink or swim on the tide of revolt, should have communication with the council denied to themselves.

He offered his blandest smile to the sweating three. 'A wise precaution, sirs,' he said. His eyes reverted to the Mayor, who was plucking at the marten-bordered sleeve of his gown. A shaft of light from the stained-glass window cast pools of colour on the table's oaken board and on the Mayor's black and rather dusty velvet cap, clamped down on his forehead. He took it off and waved it back and forth before his face, that now shone with a sickly dew. 'I pray you, sirs, forgive me — the heat —'

'But,' continued Steward with scant regard for Master Mayor's discomfort, 'should the rebels take the offensive against us we then will be driven to attack We have therefore considered it advisable that His Majesty's Council send us forthwith men and arms, which request Master Sotherton, one of our most respected burgesses, has carried to the duke on our behalf.'

'And when,' enquired Philip, still gazing at the window where a bluebottle buzzed against an amber-tinted pane, 'did this Master Sotherton set out upon his journey?'

'These three days since. He should,' stated Steward, 'have arrived at Westminster by this time.'

'Three days,' smiled Philip, 'too late.'

'What!'

'Yes, gentlemen —' that simultaneous ejaculation from the trio was smartly countered — 'yes, too late! My report, to the same effect, was received by His Grace last week And as I did intend to tell you at this session, were I,' his smile broadened, 'given opportunity to speak, York Herald is on his way to Norwich and, failing interception, will be here tomorrow.'

In the market place, below the frowning walls of Norwich Castle, a multitude had gathered to greet the King's Herald as he rode through the city and out at Bishop's Gate to the rebel camp on Mousehold Heath.

The sun glinted on his gold-and-scarlet tabard, bearing the device of the King's Arms; and on the silver broidered saddle-cloth and armoured head-dress of his horse, whose trappings were scarcely less magnificent than his. The glitter and the glory of this Royal Messenger, his entourage and trumpeters, gladdened the citizens to an outburst of cheers to hit the highest turrets of the castle as he circuited the city accompanied by the Mayor and Aldermen, and followed him all the way.

Those few who were mounted rode behind, others on foot, ran beside him, jostling for place to touch his golden spurs, his silver stirrups, hailing him their saviour in the King's Most Gracious Name. So immense the crowds, so voluminous the din that Herald's horse, chosen for docility and therefore somewhat spiritless and aged, took unexpected fright. York, riding on a loose rein, bowing right and left, and quite unready for the sudden rearing of his placid steed, was thrown violently forward on his horse's neck to crack his nose. The consequent pain, to say nothing of the bruise spreading half across his face and which a trifle dimmed his dignity, may have been a factor in his impolitic approach to Captain Kett.

So, with pennons flying, trumpets blaring, the procession came to Mousehold.

'*Oyez! Oyez! Oyez!*'

That proud triumphant trumpet cry rang out across the heath, drawing echoes from the hollows and mounting to the hills. And, from their tents and rough-hewn huts, Kett's hordes, like scuttled beetles, rushed forth in their thousands on the sun-drenched, gorse-emblazoned green. Heading them in measured slow advance came Kett, his son and brother, to hear the Royal Proclamation read, declaring: 'The King His Majesty's most gracious pardon to all of ye that will most humbly submit themselves and depart quietly, every man to his house.'

That vast company, attentive, maybe a little chastened by this royal magnanimity, listened in uninterrupted silence; and when those last resounding words died down, up went a clamorous shout: 'God Save the King's Majesty! God save our good King Edward!'

It is likely York did not anticipate such immediate and loyal demonstration; and what with the excitement of the crowds, the hurtful bump on his nose and the general confusion, he made his fatal and tactical error. Instead of leaving it at that, he needs must take upon himself to enlarge on his official message and harangue Kett, as: 'You, Captain of Mischief! And you many others as are present, give ear. You, who have wickedly cast yourselves into open conspiracy and rebellion against your country, should rightly receive punishment for your evil doings; yet, so great is the kindness and clemency of the King's Majesty that of his singular and incredible favour he will preserve your safety if forthwith every man lay down his arms and forsake this den of thieves. Then, and then only, shall you obtain your pardon. But —' raising his hand on high, York threatened them — 'should you hold fast to your present evil mind and purpose, the King His Majesty will bring his just revenge to bear upon ye for your villainies!'

Ominous mutters rose up on all sides from the rebels, in answer to this. Kett, highly indignant that he and his followers whose campaign was to them a crusade, should be lectured as if they were a gang of urchins caught in the act of robbing an orchard, now stepped forward to fling back a contemptuous retort.

'Kings and princes pardon the wicked, not the innocent. We are guilty of no crime. We despise such speech as yours — high-flying to fall low, and which gives naught to us nor to our duty as true subjects of the King.' Then, turning to his men, he called in a voice that roared above the clink of harness, the stamp of restive hooves, the scandalised murmurs of the civic company, and the loud cheers of his own: 'All of ye — stand fast! Heed not this babbler and his talk. Mind ye only of the cause that binds us here in brotherhood.'

A storm of applause went up from that ragged host, gathered round to hoist him on their shoulders; while York backing his horse, again frighted and ready to bolt, commanded John Pettibone, Sword-bearer of the city: 'Arrest this man!'

Another false move on Herald's part, since arrest was not within Sword-bearer's province; nor could the Mayor, armed with nothing but municipal authority, attempt the capture of Kett with an incalculable army behind him, out for blood. So, after some hurried discussion with his colleagues, it was decided to return into the city leaving Kett still master of the field.

However, once inside the gates of Norwich, Codd, acting on advice of his aldermen, ordered watch and ward to be kept at every post All hope of peace was now abandoned, the city under arms, and cannon bristling from the castle moat in challenge of the enemy camp on the hill above.

And that same evening came the first heavy bark of Kett's guns, followed by prompt retaliation from the city, but with more noise than damage done on either side since the distance was too great for the range of cannonballs, falling harmlessly short of their targets. And all through that night, while the interchange of fire shook his windows, Philip in his room at Sprowston was writing his account of the day's events to be carried, with a warning, by his couriers to Somerset.

...To Your Grace I submit that it is now imperative the city be defended by sufficient armed support. Such small ordinance as we have at our command is spent to little purpose for want of skilled gunners, albeit Kett hath contrived to obtain ammunition from I doubt me not the City gunsmiths or from afar as Lowestoft brought up to vantage point on the Heights above the City ...

Although not in the direct line of fire, Sprowston was near enough to Kett's guns on the Heath to suffer the incessant din of bombardment. Only one of the household, Dame Matilda, went undisturbed by and slept through what she took to be, and insisted was, a thunderstorm.

Now in her eighties and deaf in both ears, but still straight as a ramrod, she looked at least twenty years less than her age. When Philip, next morning, urged her to leave Sprowston, she determinedly refused to budge.

'Here I am and here I stay. When Cromwell, the late King's disciple and devil's familiar, hounded me and my sisters from

God's sanctuary of Carrow, I was powerless against their combined forces of evil. But I'll not be driven from your father's house by any Kett or his ruffians. No! You tell me what I heard last night was cannon fire — and I tell *you*,' retorted the redoubtable dame, 'that I know the voice of nature when it calls. I saw the lightning flashes. I say it was a thunderstorm, as six bowls of cream souring in the buttery bear witness. Go, boy, and tell your tale to the village simple who'll believe it. I will not.'

Philip knew better than to argue, but — what to do with her? He had hoped he might have persuaded her to take refuge with the Princess Mary at Kenninghall. He had already despatched a messenger, praying Her Highness to receive his aged aunt, Dame Matilda Graby, late of Carrow Abbey; and by return had come a gracious answer assuring him that 'any of his kinswomen, and his father too, would be her welcomed guests and held in safety till these dangerous embroilments be passed.'

Whereupon he sent John Locke to Jocosa at Sowerby with a copy of the Princess Mary's letter, and renewing his entreaties that 'she take advantage of Her Highness's good grace, and go forthwith to Kenninghall for his own peace of mind if not for hers.'

But John came back with a long face and longer tale, his tongue for once unloosed, to tell how he had been met by the lady's husband at the door, who, knowing him to be his master's servant, 'took the missive,' quoth John, 'from my hand. Then did he look close at the seal and in his halting fashion he did say, "Here be a stag's head with horns." Yes, sir, and he did repeat it,' said John stolidly, 'with horns — misplaced — for 'tis *my* crest should carry the horns. I could make nothing of such talk, sir, for he did wander in his speech and looked so sinistrous, and pale as a bone that I did fear me for his reason, and when he had read the letter through he tore it in snippets, savage-like, to throw about, saying, "Whatever danger lies within my house I am the master of it to protect mine own. So take you this from me to Master Pugh. I thank him for his thought of her, my wife, but I, her husband, am her rightful guardian as before all other of her kin be he brother, friend, or the Princess Mary. And whereas this is my home and hers, by God's Holy Rood I swear that none shall enter it to thieve from me and mine." Then in my face,' said John, nor moved a muscle of his own, 'he slammed the door.'

More disturbed by this recounting than he cared to admit, and since events in the city were rising to a head, Philip rode out that night to Sowerby. He had heard how three of the rebel envoys — Ralph Sutton, a hatter, Isaac Williams, a tailor, and the cooper, John Browne — had been sent from Kett to the Mayor with a flag of truce and the demand of a free passage through Norwich that provisions be brought to the camp. And, 'Should right of way be refused then would their Captain bring all the force at his disposal to lay siege to the city of Norwich with resultant destruction and death.'

Which deprived the mayor of whatever little courage he possessed; and, sooner than risk the fulfilment of such dire threats, he might have agreed to Kett's high-handed proposal; for until the council should send him men and arms for his support — and slow enough were they in coming — the city, save for some half dozen obsolete cannon, lay at the mercy of those overwhelming rebel hosts. But his aldermen, of stouter heart than he, would have none of this timidity. Together they sent an extravagantly worded reply to Kett, signed but not written by Mayor Codd.

You, Kett, and your rebels, most wretched traitors all, who have despised the King's Majesty and committed so many intolerable villainies shall be shut, not only of the city, but at no distant period ye shall meet with the punishment your madness and folly have drawn unto yourselves...

The fat was in the fire, and all night the fire burned with the cannonade of Kett's retort. But still the balls fell wide. So, finding artillery useless, he called his leaders together to decide by what other means they could force the city gates.

It was during this temporary lull in the bombardment that Philip rode over to Drayton. Dismounting in the lane that led to Sowerby, he hitched his horse's bridle to an out-jutting snag in the hedge and made his way on foot to the gatehouse. All there was in darkness; no stir within, no sound without, no light of moon, no star-prick in the sky, overcast with cloud.

Removing his shoes, and, as he stepped noiselessly under the archway, he heard from the porter's lodging a series of slow unmistakable snores. But although this evident somnolence served his present purpose, it gave him little ease of mind. Much guard for Jocosa was here!

Skirting the back of the house he stood gazing up at the darkened windows. Which was hers? Prowling, soft-padded as a cat in the dew-wet grass, he came to the main entrance. Above it, in an oriel, a hair's-breadth gleam filtered through the drawn curtains. This, then, must be her chamber. Shared? Savagely he thrust from <u>him</u> scarifying visions conjured by the thought of that.

Long he stood there sending up to her his silent message wherever she might be. How to bring her to the window? Not a sign of human life beyond that puny thread of light. Would she come? Could she hear his spirit calling her? Or — Jesu

314

Mary! — was this her woman's room and he wasting his soul's strength on that clatterpate Joan. He had best be gone. But still he stayed, holding breath to listen, straining eyes to see … nothingness. Mayhap she was away, or the Princess Mary might already have summoned her to Kenninghall. The princess had known her mother as she had known Philip's. Both, before marriage, had been maids-in-waiting to the Lady Mary. Or mayhap Gynkes had considered his warning and taken her to London. If only that were so, to lift from him this awful burden of anxiety, for God alone could tell what those rebels, running riot with unaccustomed drink and feasting, might not do to her, despite Will Kett's forbearance; nor could Will keep watch over all of them at once … By this time he had worked himself into a frenzy to fall on his knees, praying intercession of the Holy Mother to bring her to that unresponsive window. And then … the miracle.

Most Merciful Beloved Virgin! A thousand candles offered to Her Blessed Shrine in the secret chapel of his father's house could not suffice for this beneficence.

Cautiously the curtains opened. He saw her face, like a white flower, framed there, peering out. If he could climb to her! No foothold in that wall, no loosened brick, no beam, no helpful creeping plant, not one nailed shrub nor tree. A wall. Some twelve feet from her window ledge, and he but a despised five-foot eight inches here below it. O, if one more miracle could make of him a giant!

Ineffectually he leapt into the air, his hands clutching at that unrelenting wall to find no grip of any sort; then down again with curses on his wretched lack of height. But were he *ten* feet high he could not have reached her.

Narrowly the casement opened. He could see the movement of her lips, heard her laughing whisper: 'What clown's antics are these? Do you practise for the high jump?' And then to sink him, 'Go.'

'Sweet life!' His voice breathed up to her, frantic in its urgency. 'Come! Come with me — now. Out — out on the sill. 'Tis you must jump, not I. I'll catch you in my arms. You'll not be hurt. I'm taking you pillion, straight to Kenninghall. The princess has sent word she would receive you. Dear love, for my love's sake, I pray you, come.'

He saw the shake of her head and the loosened fall of her hair on her shoulders; her teeth glistened to her smile and her answer, soft, still whispering: 'I can't hear a word you say, but don't … don't speak aloud.'

He groaned, *'Miserere mei,'* and with impatience danced, repeating: 'Love, for God's sake, come!'

'Ssh!' She put a finger to her lips, cast a hurried look behind her and back again to him; and even in that moment's poignancy the gleam of her held laughter, like a sun-flash in an April sky, lighted her shadowed face. 'He — Gynkes,' she leaned across the sill to tell him, 'is in the armoury. He has found some rusty coats of mail of my father's and has been at them polishing all day. He swears he'll take his part if called on to fight the rebels. You —' and now her lips were in a tremble, 'you — will you fight?'

'I'll do whatever rightly must be done, only that you, dear heart, once more I beg —'

'No, no!' She mouthed the words, waving both hands in a hurried gesture of dismissal; and, drawing close the curtains, shut him out. But she had left wide the casement, and her voice, speaking to one within, came to him standing there.

'I opened the window to listen for the guns, but could hear nothing. There's not a sound. All's still.'

And in that stillness Philip turned, and as silently as he had come he went.

THIRTEEN

In his library at Sprowston, Geoffrey Pugh — engrossed in his latest work, a transcription from the Greek into Latin of the Socratic dialogues — stayed impervious to and unaffected by Kett's army, stationed within sound and far sight of his house. For, if truth be told, the roaring of the guns, that with intermittent pauses went on day and night, disturbed the squire less than did Dame Matilda's frequent appearance at his door with a catalogue of various complaints.

Item: Half the servants had fled to join the rebels as alternative to capture.

Item: Sundry of Kett's demoniac tribes had rifled the dovecote and carried off at least three dozen score of pigeons.

Item: The goose-girl had been raped and not, it seemed, unwillingly, by one or other of those villains or Will Kett himself.

Item: The shepherd, Richard Page, had been handing out the half-grown lambs *ad liberatum* to the rebels, being, semblable, leagued with them; and, finally, was nephew Pugh aware that the enclosures of the rye and barley fields had been uprooted and carried off to Mousehold for firewood?

Then, perceiving that 'nephew Pugh' had paid no slightest heed to all of this, 'Will you,' his aunt sharply recalled him, 'put aside your script, sir, and attend to me? Your son is in a pother to have me sent from here and into hiding. I'll not go. Am I a hare to run from these hounds? No. But that you safeguard your house and your dependants and keep a watch on their stealing which I, unaided, cannot do, nor be in half a dozen places at one time, I do adjure you — pray, sir, what is it you seek?'

The squire, who had risen from his desk, was short-sightedly peering at the row of bookshelves ranged along the wall behind it. Light from the window fell on his head where the once flaxen hair, now silvered, receded from that high-domed mild brow.

'The second book of — ah, here!' Reverently he took down a massive volume. 'I think,' said he, his head aslant to listen, 'that the guns have ceased their fire,' and he returned to his desk and oblivion.

The Dame stalked to his side and stood over him. 'Sir, will you heed me what I say? Your house and all within it is in danger.'

'Sublime! Sublime!' rapturously murmured the squire, leafing the vellum pages. 'With what delightful wit and sar-sardonic satire he chastiseth his disciples.'

'I am but mortal,' his aunt stated, 'and have but mortal patience. Grant, O Lord,' she prayed, 'O, grant me more.'

Her face, ivory tinted beneath the broad white band of her coif, showed a delicate tracery of wrinkles like the veins of a skeleton leaf. Her teeth had fallen out and her mouth had fallen in, but her shoulders, mantled in that same black habit she had worn for the better part of her whole life, were still unbowed. As a stone monument carries the time-honoured weight of years, so did Dame Matilda carry hers.

'And not,' she went on in the shrill-pitched voice of the deaf, 'your household only but your son's life is in danger down there in the city, now besieged. One of our men has come back from market bringing with him naught of my commissions, for all trade is halted and the citizens in hiding behind locked doors with the rebels sacking shops and houses, as thus much did I gather from his shouting in my ear to break my drums, and — so he told me — they are battering the gates.'

'Yes, this is as I have it, and not as — not as Doctor Cheke in his —' the squire turned another page, took up his quill, dipped it in ink and began rapidly to write.

'Nephew,' crossing her arms inside her ample sleeves the good nun, who despite her prayer for patience was fast losing it, said, 'will you listen to this tale of disaster? The city — if I did hear aright — is like to fall, and may even now have fallen into the enemy's hands. The Mayor, one Codd, so your man conveyed to me, has been captured by Kett's rebels and is —'

'What!' In greatest agitation the squire started up. 'My son — my son is captured? No!'

'Yes,' the dame asserted vigorously. 'Captured. Taken. Bound in chains. Stoned. Mocked. In ribaldry. And now perchance you will bestir yourself, for what is done to him may be done to you or any one of us.' She crossed herself, murmuring, *'Deus misereatur nobis.'*

'But how —' The squire ran distracted fingers through his scanty hair — 'how,' he cried, 'to rescue him? I could — yes, I will! I'll go to the camp and appeal in per — in person to Kett, my *quon* — my *quondam* friend for his release. I cannot believe he would wil-wilfully harm Philip for whom he has always professed an affection. Dame, do you mean to say — do you know for cer — for certain,' he approached his lips to the nun's inclining ear, 'that he is captured?'

'Yes. Captured. Imprisoned,' shatteringly stated Dame Matilda, 'so take warning. *You* may be their victim next.'

And between the two of them this cross-purpose might well have continued until midnight, with the squire in equal fear for the fate of his son as for his cherished manuscripts and books. Having decided that these latter must for their safety be buried in the ground, he was about to summon his men to bring spades and set to work, when Philip burst into the room.

He was filthy. Sweat shone through the smoke-blackened grime on his face; he had a cut on his forehead, a rent in his jerkin and from head to foot was powdered grey with dust.

'My — my son!' His father rushed to embrace him. 'God be thanked! But how did — did you escape?'

'Escape?' echoed Philip, disengaging. 'There's no question of escape. The city is still ours. I bring good news. Northampton with a force of men and arms is on his way to Norwich. Augustine Steward who, since the downfall of the Mayor yesternoon, acts as his deputy, is waiting to receive the Marquis at his house. Mass, am I weary! I've been firing the cannon. Three of our gunners are wounded and —'

'And you,' his father broke in, 'you too — you bleed!'

"Tis nothing. I was overblown,' grinned Philip, 'knocked out, to graze my head in falling, not being skilled in the humoursome tricks of big guns. Good Dame!' he shouted to her who concernedly was examining the blood oozing from the slight wound above his eyebrow, 'I've had nor bite nor sup since dawn. Is there a hank o' mutton, beef or aught to eat in the house?'

'Yes,' the dame nodded. 'Pus — in plenty. I'll fetch a bowl of vinegar.'

'Holy Saints!' yelled Philip. 'Food! I asked for *food*.'

'A little is cured with a little,' said the dame; and out she went.

Later when cleaned, reclothed, his forehead in a plaster, Philip sat at table, wolfing pickled pork washed down by a tankard of ale, he related to his father how the mayor had been seized by the rebels, 'Who,' he said between mouthfuls, 'have done with their cannon and taken to the long-bow which frights the citizens a deal more than the guns. But we gave 'em back good measure, each a quiverful for those who had climbed the gates and were inside the streets fighting with bare fists, failing other sort of weapon. Even their boys, half-naked and unarmed as they are — and this I saw with my own eyes — did pluck out our arrows that were sticking in their flesh and handed them back, all dripping with their blood, for the rebels to use against us.'

'Most — most distressful,' murmured Geoffrey while the dame, contentedly smiling from her tower of silence, replenished Philip's dish. Then:

'But the heartiest cheer,' chuckled Philip — 'no, good aunt, no more, prithee! I'm stuffed full to bursting — the heartiest cheer and best of all was when they rounded on the Mayor, for I hold no brief for him who I'm inclined to think shares the City, Corporation and the townsfolk between himself and Kett, as hand to glove, playing for *his* safety. Yet that game won't save his hide. Not content with capture, the rebels rallied round to mock him with howls of 'Oyez!' in mimicry of Herald, and a play on his name that I laughed myself sick, "As many as will come to the camp tomorrow shall buy a cod's head for a penny!"'

'A cheap price for fish,' said Dame Matilda whose better ear had seized upon this tag. At which Philip, in the act of drinking, laughed again to choke himself, and was patted on the back by the dame with injunctions to, 'Look up. Count ten. Hold your breath.'

And when, still laughter-shaken, he had spluttered and whooped himself quiet, his father said mildly, 'Boy, of my love and for — and for myself I ask it, do — do not be rash to run into danger. Remember as Seneca has it, *Potentissimus est qui se habit in potestate.* I'll go now and bury my — bury my books.'

The situation in Norwich, deliberately minimised by Philip in his account of that morning's events, was far more serious than he had led his father to believe. For, with the capture of the Mayor, trussed like a turkey and carried off to Mousehold amid a hailstorm of stones and jeers, Kett's desperadoes, encouraged by this first success, returned to their attack.

The inhabitants, horrified at the humiliation suffered by their honoured Mayor, and terror-stricken lest they should be similarly victimised, lost what little heart they had, and, as the rebels poured down from the Heath dragging their cannon with them to bombard the city at close range, those few who were guarding the gates abandoned their posts and fled. One John Bacon, a grocer, in charge of the cannon at Bishop's Gate, stuck to his gun as long as he dared, but at sight of that savage mob plunging in the river to swim across and clamber up the near bank, bearing down in their hundreds on the walls of Norwich and his isolated gun, he too gave up and joined his fellow citizens in flight.

From Steward, the Deputy Mayor, Philip had obtained a cross-bow and quiverful of arrows. This inadequate equipment, however, was soon spent. But when he found the cannon at Bishop's Gate deserted, and made attempt to turn it single-handed on the enemy, only to be flung down by the recoil, he deemed it better to go than to stay and court certain capture — or death.

He had left his horse stabled at the Maid's Head where a number of scared citizens had gathered to revive their sunken spirits with red ale and hope, born of the rumour now in circulation, that the King's troops were marching to the rescue of the city. And, even as Philip mounted his mare in the inn yard, one of his couriers, hot speed from London, came galloping in. 'Sir, I passed —' He could hardly speak with his

323

breath in gasps, so blown was he, and his horse no less, streaked black with sweat, foam-speckled — 'I passed my Lord Northampton with some fifteen hundred strong — on the road — from Cambridge. They'll be here afore nightfall.'

'God send,' muttered Philip. 'We'll need every man of them against those devils yonder. They've got the Mayor, they've got the gates, they'll have the city too!' Then seeing the courier spent and drooping from his saddle, 'Go you in,' he said, 'and order of mine host a bed and board for a night's rest, well deserved.'

But there was no rest for Philip. Back at Sprowston and so soon as he had written his report of events to date, 'I doubt me,' he told John, 'that I'll be home tonight. If not, you can tell my father, for his ease of mind, I'll be lodging at the house of Master Steward.'

'Sir,' John's eyes, with the look of a suffering spaniel's, sought his, 'am I not to be along with you,' he jerked his head, 'down there?'

'No. You must stay here on guard. All may be over by the morrow, for once inside the city, Northampton's men, trained soldiers all, will make short shift of that mob even though they be a hundred more to every man of ours.'

'Master,' John asked stolidly, 'do you not go in armour? 'Tis not safe to cross Mousehold with never so much as a breasplate for guard against them bowmen.'

'I don't cross Mousehold, thankee!' Philip told him. 'I'm taking the longer way to come in by St. Benet's. I don't fancy myself chained to Mayor Codd in Mount Surrey. Nor would I let those devils have sight or smell of Phoebe. They're partial to good horseflesh — rot their guts!'

'Amen to that,' John answered, glum. 'But, sir, I'd feel more peaceable an you'd go armoured.'

Philip grinned in his long face. 'The suit I wore at Pinkie don't fit me now I've broadened.'

'There's a mort o' suiting,' John tightened a saddle-strap, 'that'll fit you in the armoury.'

'God's Tongue!' cried Philip, 'am I your Jemmy-Jessamy that you'd pack me up in harness lest I be pinked by their archers — and none of 'em can aim but cock-eyed. And would you have me go about the city clank and rattle like a tinker? Phoebe, bless her, is their mark, but if there's more street fighting yet to come I'll send you word to bring what's needful for us both. And see to it,' he swung into the saddle and called over his shoulder, 'that our men keep those hell-hounds from the stables, for if any should lay hands on my old Crispin I'll string him up and hang him — on Kett's Oak!'

And with a laugh he was off, lying forward on the mare's neck, riding short. John watched him turn westward along the turf-track that skirted the yellowed fields of rye and barley where the fencing stakes had been uprooted by the rebels. John watched his master put the mare to a hedge, a brook, a ditch, and on again full tilt, her satin flanks agleam in the last pouring gold of the sun that dazzled John's vision and misted his eyes … till he could see no more.

Philip found the city in a tumult of excitement. Heartened by the news that the King's troops had arrived, the now-jubilant citizens came out of their hide-holes to give them rousing welcome as they entered by St. Stephen's Gate.

At their head, in full panoply of armour, rode Northampton led by Norroy King-at-Arms. A company of nobles, knights, and squires followed after, with a body of Italian mercenaries bringing up the rear.

The deep reddened glow of the westering sun flashed fire from helmets and lances and pikes; from silver harness and chain mail; from Norroy's crown and sceptre: a brave sight. No sign now of panic, nor of rebels, who with the coming of Northampton had retired to their camp on Mousehold Heath.

Leaving his mare at the Maid's Head, Philip elbowed his way through the shouting crowds in Tombland, to the house of the Deputy Mayor where the Marquis and his entourage were lodged. After a modest meal of meat, bread, fruit, and wine charged to the City Chamberlain's account at a none too modest price, Northampton called the Deputy Mayor, the Aldermen and City Elders to a meeting in the marketplace. A deal of talk ensued, some speechifying from the Marquis, and much cheering from the onlookers — most of whom were in a state of celebration — before it was decided to ask for volunteers to guard the gates; a suggestion that brought with it roars of approval but lamentably few volunteers. Then, expressing profoundest regret at the compulsory absence of the Mayor — more cheers and some snickers, sternly hushed by the absent Mayor's Deputy — 'I give you,' quoth Northampton with a flourish of his steel-gauntleted hand, 'my promised word to take all care of ye unto myself in the fervent hope that ere long the spirit of violence wherewith so many are inflamed shall be suppressed, and —'

This declaration was met with such yells of applause that not another word of it was audible. Whereupon the Marquis and his gentlemen returned to Steward's house, and the townsfolk to the Maid's Head there again to toast the King's men and, right rollicking, to drink the cellars dry.

Philip, at Steward's request, stayed behind to set the house in order for the comfort of Northampton and his officers. The Deputy Mayor, who had hurried home in advance of the

Marquis, was in a rare taking. 'For,' said he, 'I have but little knowledge of the requirements due to the nobility. Nor can my house accommodate one half of the number quartered here. I was prepared for a dozen at the most, and here am I planted with near upon two score, and but four beds to offer them.'

'If I know aught of the nobility,' said Philip, 'fill 'em up with wine and they'll not ask for beds. They'll bed themselves where they fall — in the rushes.'

The Deputy Mayor shot a dubious glance at the smiling young gentleman who lounged against the chimney breast eating an apple pilfered from a dish of fruit placed on the sideboard by Master Steward for the delectation of his guests, and which, to judge from the cores strewn about the feet of Master Pugh, looked now to be sadly depleted. Nor did Master Steward much relish the notion of more wine to be offered, since the City Chamberlain's maximum estimate of three shillings and eightpence per meal for the party, with a pound of sugar extra at fourteen pence — a luxurious commodity in which only the rich could afford to indulge — was already much exceeded. The Chamberlain had made it clear that the balance of surplus expenses, if any, would be Master Steward's own responsibility. To his relief, however, the gentlemen were more disposed for sleep than for food or drink. Those who, with their host's profound apologies, must go short of a bed deposited themselves and their armour in the hall, the gallery, or wherever else they could find space to lie.

The Marquis was sole occupant of the guest room. Lord Sheffield, Sir Thomas Cornwallis, Sir Thomas Paston, and Sir Richard a Lee, on assumption of first come, first served, made a dash for the three remaining beds and there, in possession, they stayed. Philip found a corner in the hall, but what with the concerted snores of his companions and the stifling airlessness of the night, he, although bone-weary after the day's exertions, could not sleep. He was beset with a lurking disquiet as result of Northampton's review of the situation while he pored over the plan of the city and its defences, drawn up by Philip and with him discussed at more length than purpose.

What, fumed Philip to his inner man, could such a one as William Parr, a Westmorland squire turned Court parasite and councillor by reason of his sister's marriage to King Henry, know of military tactics? He, who had never led an army nor fought in any war was no match for a Kett. Mettle should meet mettle, not a jellyfish prinked out as a crustacean! And scarce a man above his ilk among his officers, other than Sheffield, Cornwallis and Paston. As for the rest of them, trust the Protector for picking the wrong man with the right one at his elbow. Why not Warwick? Warwick, who had smashed those fighting Scots and, by God, were they fighters! Warwick would know how to … how to smash … and…

Here he fell into a doze from which he was aroused, as it seemed, five minutes later, by a clanging of bells, a beating of drums and the cries of the watchman, 'To arms!'

The gentlemen sprawled about the hall, startled to wakefulness, got upon their feet, and with yawns and oaths, went searching each among the piled armour for his own. Philip, who had none and no weapon other than his sword, snatched it up from where it lay unsheathed beside him, and was out through the screens and into the street while the knights and squires were still haggling as they sorted their harness.

In the marketplace, where the soldiers were encamped, a bonfire had been lighted against surprise attack in the dark of the night and in a town to which all of them were strangers. The leaping flames revealed a scurry and flurry of halberdiers, arquebusiers, bowmen, and one shouting through a trumpet orders which were lost in the thunder of the castle guns, pounding away at the enemy's camp on the Heath. But, as before, the balls fell wide, either overcharged in their loading or deliberately levelled too high, since for the most part they were manned by the city gunners many of whom were suspected of being, or known to be, in league with Kett.

By this time Northampton and his officers, still half asleep, and in half armour, had arrived; all seemed uncertain what to do or where to go. In the light of torch-flares held aloft by tradesmen and prentices, who had rushed from their shops in their shifts ready to panic again, Philip caught a glimpse of the Deputy Mayor. In his robes of office, very hot, very red in the face, he was striving to make himself heard above the racket and the roar. With his hands circling his mouth he shouted through them at top of his voice: 'My Lord Marquis requests that Sir Anthony Denny, Sir Thomas Cornwallis and Sir Richard a Lee shall take each six men for watch and ward at the Gate of St. Benet's. My Lord Marquis requests —'

'God's Passion,' muttered Philip, 'no!' and dashed up to him, 'Sir, surely not. St. Benet's needs no guard. Every man we can spare must be put to Magdalen, Pockthorpe and Bishop's Gates — that's where they'll come in, east and north of the city. Not the west.' As so he had already warned Northampton.

But Steward, submissive to higher command, and having collected Cornwallis and Denny, continued to bellow: 'Sir Richard a Lee! Where is Sir Richard a Lee?'

Sir Richard a Lee was sitting cross-legged on a market stall among vegetables left there to rot, and of a mighty stink.

A short, snoutish, paunchified young man was Sir Richard a Lee. In the haste of his dressing he had put on his breast-plate back to front, and taken not his own but another's pair of greaves and thigh-pieces, which being much too tight for his ease he had discarded. He had also forgotten to fasten the points of his hose, and these had slid down and hung over his sollerets, the shoe-like casings of steel for protection of his feet tucked under him where, tailorwise, he sat.

Screwing an eye at Philip, dimly discernible in the waning light of the bonfire: 'Crucify me!' he ejaculated, 'if 'tis not Philip Pugh. How come you here? You were not with us on the march.' And when Philip told him his home was in the neighbourhood and he here on vacation, 'Pardie!' snorted Sir Richard, 'I could name a better way of spending a vacation.'

'As,' suggested Philip, 'sitting on your rump among the cabbages. And wherefore?'

'Wherefore? Why, a'cause,' rejoined Sir Richard, 'I prefer to sit than stand — stiff as I am from a hundred or more miles in the saddle and but six hours' sleep in four nights. And now to come into this stew!' Disgustedly he stared about him. 'Look at our fellows yonder, herded like sheep without a shepherd, and no dog to harry 'em. Hi, there!' Rising from his mailed haunches he called to a cluster of halberdiers. 'Go take your stance t'other side the castle. That's where the rebels will —'

'They won't,' rapped out Philip. 'They'll come in at —'

But his words were halted by a sudden fearful uproar and shouts of 'Every man to his arms!' as a down-rushing stream of insurgents from Mousehold poured into the city at Bishop's Gate.

Leaving Sir Richard to detach himself from his stall and readjust his armour, Philip dashed away. To the soldiers standing uncertainly about him, 'Come,' he cried, 'all of you — up and follow me! Come on!'

One, a grizzled veteran, but light of build and wiry, sprang to attention, waylaying him. 'Sir! Captain Pugh — who led me of your company at Pinkie. Do you remember?'

'Faith! Well do I remember.' He did not, but one quick over-glance decided him that here he had a useful second-in-command. So, 'Bring up your men and come on — on! *On!'*

Cheeringly, with shouts and yells, he urged them forward where he led. It had worked at Pinkie and it worked again; for he, to whom a fight was the best of all sport — and little enough, as king's gentleman, did he get of it — had that about him when flung into a fray which must infect others with his own exhilaration. So it served; and within a matter of minutes he had two hundred or more halberdiers and pikemen at his heels. In the fitful light of a harvest moon riding high on a hurry of a cloud, their weapons shone silvery and fierce as a river torrent in full spate. Still leading, and unhampered as he was by harness to outrun them all, he met with and dodged a rain of arrows from Kett's archers who had gained the city wall. And as he felt the leather of his jerkin ripped — 'God blight me!' — roundly did he curse himself for not heeding John's advice, that he now must go unshielded, his chest a target for the first clear shot. But luckily Kett's men were better put to it with axe and club than with the long-bow.

The walls at Bishop's Gate were a hurtling mass of rebels, almost indistinguishable in the dark of the night from the stones and bricks at which they hacked and hewed to force a passage through whatever crumbling breach would take them. Those of Philip's company who, unquestioning, accepted his command, fought hand to hand with halberds, pikes, swords or, lost of battle-arms wrenched from them when wounded, they still fought, iron-fisted, till they dropped.

Savagely relentless on both sides was that struggle; for, while Kett's hosts outnumbered Northampton's by some twenty thousand to fifteen hundred, his were trained soldiers and Kett's but a hooligan rabble; yet all endowed with that same undaunted spirit to do and to win, or to die.

Throughout that night the battle raged and still the city held, defended by a mere handful of the King's men against Kett's overwhelming forces, who, beaten back, were fighting for their lives a losing game.

Dawn was in the sky when those few rebels left inside the city gates dragged themselves on hands and knees, through their own and other men's blood, to strike one last blow for their cause before they too were driven back, battered but not broken … yet.

At the break of that day Edmund Gynkes rose up from his bed beside his sleeping wife, and crept like a thief from the house.

His man had his orders and was waiting in the forecourt to buckle him into his armour and mount him on his horse; but with his legs encased in steel he was sore put to keep his seat, and told his servant: 'Loose me of my thigh-pieces. Breast and back plates will suffice.'

'Shall I, sir,' his man half-heartedly offered, 'go with you?'

'No. I go alone. I go to meet my friend, that we shall stand and fight together, he and I.' And at the smile on his master's face, so greyly white beneath the lifted vizor, at the blind stare of those pale eyes as he dug spurs to his horse and went clattering out of the court, the man crossed himself and mouthed into his beard a Paternoster; for old customs, despite the New Learning, died hard.

The casualties among the King's men were light compared to those of the rebels who, with scarce a suit of harness between them, fought in their rags or rough jerkins, small protection from the arrows of trained archers.

Much to the Deputy Mayor's content, since his cook and most of his servants had fled in the night, Northampton, with his officers, and Master Pugh, did not return to breakfast at his house. They had all trooped into the Maid's Head where a gratefully beaming host, confident that the Lord Lieutenant had crushed the rebellion, ransacked his larder to serve them of his best. Only a few of the gentlemen were wounded, and none, save Sir Richard a Lee, put out of action.

Lying face downward on a settle — he had been 'sliced in the buttocks by a brutish bearded giant of a fellow' — so to a grinning audience Sir Richard, with a great to-do of groans, recounted, 'who came at me with a hatchet —'

'To attack you in a rearguard action?' solemnly suggested Lord Sheffield amid the cachinnations of his brother officers. For, confessedly, Sir Richard had not been conspicuous for leadership during the worst of the fight, and was seen in full retreat before the end of it. But the barber-surgeon, called to tend the injured, ordered him to his bed for three days at the least. At which mine host of the Maid's Head offered him his choicest guest room, accepted by Sir Richard with alacrity; and there, posteriorly stretched, he submitted, not without screeching protest, to the surgeon's probe. He was, however, sufficiently recovered to partake, right side up, of the broiled fowl and wine provided by the landlord, more sympathetically inclined than were his fellows.

Philip, meanwhile, having done hearty justice to a breakfast of stewed carp, sheep's kidneys, rye bread, and a tankard of ale, wrote his report of the battle and gave it to the courier who had his horse saddled in the courtyard and himself ready to be off. Philip handed him the sheet of parchment saying, 'I have writ the barest facts of this last night's encounter, since I've had no time for a more detailed despatch. But I've made it clear, I hope — if not you must impress upon my Lord Protector — that although we've won the first round we're in urgent need of reinforcements. When they've done licking their wounds they'll be up and at us again with half the citizens behind them, believing there's safety in numbers. And, by Cock! they've got the numbers — all of Norfolk, most of Suffolk, and over the border into Cambridge.'

The courier, a sturdy youth but light of weight for speed, had, by the look of his blood-spattered doublet and the raw gash across the knuckles of his sword hand, taken his good part in the doings of the night. He slid Philip's despatch into his leather bag, snapped the lock, and said, 'I've heard talk among the townsfolk, when I sat at breakfast in the parlour, that they've catched and hanged an officer of the Italian mercenaries.'

'Yes, curse them!' Philip folded a fist. 'Another nail in Kett's coffin, though not of his own driving. He fights clean. It was the city watch on Magdalen Gate that let pass the Italians, and they, not knowing the lie of the land, fell into the trap of Kett's men out there on Magdalen Hill, who'd likely been warned of their coming. These pariah curs of the city who lick at Kett's breeks while they yap at his heels, are a worser enemy than he, for back face, front face, one knows not friend nor foe. So, hot haste with you now to Westminster, and not much rest, I'll warrant me, did you have yesternight.'

When he returned to the inn parlour he found the Deputy Mayor and three burgesses in earnest consultation with Northampton, Sir Thomas Paston, Cornwallis and others. The remainder of the gentlemen, whose injuries had been treated by the surgeon, lay about on settles or the rush-strewn floor to rest their aching limbs and snatch what sleep they could. The surgeon, a sprightly little robin of a man, was attending Lord Sheffield's broken wrist, 'Your lordship,' he chirruped, 'will find this balm most soothing, composed of horehound bruised and boiled in an old hog's grease.'

'A murrain on your old hog's grease!' retorted young Sheffield. 'How'm I to wield a lance with my dexter wrist in splinters?'

'Not in splinters, my lord —' for His Lordship's cheer the surgeon achieved a little joke — 'but in splints. As when I strap you — so,' he produced from his bag a strip of wood, 'and bind you — so,' in a trice he had Sheffield's arm in a bandage, 'that your lordship will be free from pain and right as a trivet. 'Tis a simple fracture, merely — so!' And round Sheffield's shoulders he fastened a sling in less time than it took him to tell. 'And now my lords and gentlemen, who's next?' None was next. 'Then my lords, Sir knights and gentlemen,' he sidled to the door, his bright beady eyes peering hopefully at each in turn, expectant of a fee not apparently forthcoming, 'I will bid you a very good day.'

Philip, seeing him crestfallen, said, 'If you will wait upon the Lord Lieutenant at Master Steward's house, you'll receive due reward for your attention,' to send him off in a twitter of thanks.

'Mr. Pugh,' Northampton hailed him, 'how think you of this proposal? Our Deputy Mayor suggests we make a second approach to Kett with an offer of pardon. You are, I believe, acquainted with this Kett. Is he likely to listen to reason?'

'To reason, yes, my lord, but not to threats.'

'Which being so,' Northampton said, 'here is the message I am sending him by Norroy King-at-Arms.' And from a parchment he read: *'Go you your ways and declare unto your company from the Marquis of Northampton, Governor of the King's forces, that the King's Majesty doth command and admonish you that you all do repent of your misdoings and so put an end to the outrages which you have committed. If you will do this then shall you be safe and free from peril and no man among you shall be charged with the crimes of which he may be guilty.'*

'That,' Northampton looked up and around at the listening faces, 'should fetch them. It is more than the traitor Kett deserves — a free pardon and no penalty. Remove the fear of the hangman's rope, or worse,' his thin lips parted in a snicker, 'and he'll come to us crawling on his belly.'

Not, said Philip silently, *if I know Robert Kett.*

Steward stood up. 'I will go with Norroy Herald an you permit, my lord.'

'By all means, do. But,' Northampton rolled the parchment to strike at a cruising wasp, 'best not go nigh the camp to run your neck into Kett's noose. Make your approach at one of his outposts. I'm told there's some four or five hundred of them beyond — is it Puck — Pockmark — or some such gate?'

'Pockthorpe, my lord,' Steward corrected him. 'So, sirs, we are agreed?'

The burgesses in one voice were agreed; and when Norroy, with full pageantry, and the Deputy Mayor, had departed in state, Philip laid himself down in the rushes and slept, but not for long.

Once again from all quarters came the warning cry, 'To arms! To arms!' For Kett's myriads, stung to desperation by the rout of the previous night, had stormed the city at its weakest point: the undefended meadows of the hospital.

While Northampton and his officers, heedless of their injuries, set to and buckled on their armour, Philip dashed up the stairs to the room of Sir Richard a Lee, who, reclining at ease supported by pillows, was gnawing at the remnants of his fowl.

'Your harness!' cried Philip. 'I want it.'

'My — ah, yes,' Sir Richard pointed. 'Yonder, by the clothes press. You can have it. I'm done for,' groaned the wounded knight. 'Would that I could move but leg or arm to take my part in—'

'There's only a breast-plate here,' broke in Philip. 'Where's your back-plate? No matter. I can make do without. I'll have this —' he took up a lance — 'and this.' And, ramming Sir Richard's helmet on his head, was gone from the room, down the stairs and out into Tombland within seconds.

There, opposite Erpingham Gate, the bulk of the King's men were gathered, and almost all unmounted; for this, as Philip saw in one brief summary, would be a hand-to-hand fight with overpowering odds against Northampton's meagre force.

And there, like some volcanic tidal wave, uprisen from deep undersea eruption, Kett's countless thousands crashed down on the King's hundreds to flood the open square confronting the cathedral. It was a multitudinous frenzy of sight and sound; a writhing massed convulsion of gorilla-faces, staring eyeballs; of maniacal arms in tossing rivulets of steel, red-stained; of battle cries, of yells and oaths and the agonised shriek of a horse.

Philip's lance was lost, wrenched from his hand in that sweeping onward surge. Blood was in his nostrils, in the air. Blood dripped from brandished weapons, from shreds of flying flesh that, like great crimson butterflies, alighted fantastically on helmet-peak or spear-tip.

Striking blindly left and right, Philip, the merest dust-speck in that human hurricane, was borne along, stumbling over severed limbs and the bodies of men lying limp, not dead long enough to stiffen, and then he saw … and even in that hellish maelstrom knew the face of one, grotesque and palely smiling from its armoured frame beneath its lifted vizor. He saw, and, in a second's swift temptation, would not see another, of some evasive memory, whose black thicket of beard was red-dyed from a gash in his cheek; whose froth-flecked lips roared a gibberish of dialect, while with his upraised arm he swung a battle-axe in gleeful, half-demented anticipation of the death blow about to fall on that feeble, nodding head. One second only, and Philip was himself again to whip out his steel and drive it stark through that murderous arm, slitting it bare to the bone.

With an animal snarl of rage and pain the killer dropped his axe and, in tortured savagery, sprang, to be struck down by a passing halberdier; and over and above his dying howl, above the clang and clash of metal upon metal, the stamp and clatter of plunging feet and hooves, Philip, most fearfully heard, pressed close into his ear, an elfin whisper: 'Friend … brother. This is as I have dreamed, and this … and this!'

He was, absurdly, pinioned in a fierce embrace of clinging arms; but even as he struggled free, he felt the sharp grinding stab of a dagger thrust up to its hilt between his hinder ribs, and the warm rush of blood in his mouth as he staggered and fell.

By noon all was over, Northampton in full flight and the rebels in possession of the city. The casualties suffered by the King's troops were reported to be considerably more than those of the previous night. Several of the officers had been killed, among them Lord Sheffield, Northampton's second-in-command, flung headlong from his horse during a charge in the thick of the fight and hacked to death. That was the turning point of the battle. Dismayed and discouraged by Kett's torrential force, plunging down from Mousehold in ever-increasing strength and numbers, the rank and file, lost of heart and leaders, forsaken by their Lord Lieutenant, sought escape from the shambles through the city's shattered walls and gates. So, seeking cover from pursuit in lanes and woods and ditches, those who had not fallen by the wayside footed it to London.

All that day, and for weeks of days to come, Norwich swarmed with exultant rebels, sacking shops and houses deserted by their owners who, likewise, were fled or in hiding. And, as they went, the rebels, cock-a-hoop, joy-drunk with victory and the wine of their spoils, set fire to whole streets of houses — and a strong wind blowing.

From his bedroom window, Augustine Steward, no longer Deputy Mayor, watched the flaming tongues lick merrily at the thatched roofs of Holmes Street nearby. *Rain,* he prayed. *O, God, send rain!*

And rain, in answer to his prayer, or coincidentally, was sent 'within the hour to quench the conflagration before its hold had gained upon the city.

Sick at heart, Master Steward looked on the smoking ruins around Tombland. His mercer's shop, of which his wealth derived, had been rifled, his goods stolen and, although he could not see, he guessed that it, too, had been fired. Bitterly did he regret that, while Norwich stood divided in its loyalty to King or Kett, he, against his shrewder judgement, and, as a respected statesman of the city, had in duty bound supported the Crown and the Lords of the land — to his undoing. He had offered my Lord Marquis, Commander of His Majesty's miserable little force, and to his nobles, knights and squires, the hospitality of his house and board at great personal expense, never now to be refunded. And see what woeful end had come of it; deprived of his office, the prey of vandals, and his servants gone. Wiser than he, they had backed, every one of them, the winning side to join the camp at Mousehold. And here was he, undefended, alone in the house save for the barber-surgeon who had called upon the Lord Lieutenant for his fee a few minutes before the first alarm was sounded, and since he could not get out in the midst of the battle he had stayed. Then, while at his open casement Steward stood, his eyes smarting with smoke, his mouth gritted with cinder-dust, he heard a great shouting, the beat of a drum, and cries of: 'Hola! Open door to us in the name of our King Kett! Open, or we will break it down!' And a battering and hammering of iron upon oak.

'"King Kett" … Holy Grace!' muttered Master Steward as, with more prayers on his lips and fear in his heart, he left his stance at the window and, clinging to the stair-rail, for his knees were weak, he went down into the hall. The barber-surgeon, all colour drained from his wontedly robin-red face, cowered in a corner by the empty hearth. 'What now,' he quavered, 'is come?'

A squad of rioters was come to search the house for the Marquis, as excuse for further plunder, and to threaten Master Steward with a traitor's death unless he revealed the Lord Lieutenant's whereabouts.

'He lies not here,' Steward falteringly told them. 'How should I know where he be hid? I give you my word for it.'

But his word for it, so faintly given, was not taken. They shoved him aside and went seeking from room to room, hewing at the furniture with clubs and hatchets, throwing open cupboards, chests, to seize upon their contents, pewter, silver dishes and whatnot of his household goods. Then they stripped him of his robes of office, demanding his money or his life.

Trembling, swooning, bereft of half his clothes and all his dignity, the wretched ex-Deputy Mayor handed over a purseful of gold; and then — only then — was he quit of them.

'Jesu,' he blubbered as they went, 'have mercy on us!'

'And all this,' gasped the surgeon, 'has come about — with the battle fought and lost — in three hours. What,' and he was weeping now, 'is become of my wife and children whom I left at my home in safety — as I thought?'

'Thank God,' groaned Steward, 'that I have neither wife nor child. Both dead long years ago.'

'See — see there!' The surgeon had crept to the window and was craning his neck to peer out. 'More of Kett's men — but these look to be routing the rioters. See!'

Down below, among the scattered dead and dying, one in broken harness sat and fondled in his arms the body of 'my friend,' he called him, 'friend…' while a ring of rowdy urchins jabbed at him with the points of daggers and a lance-head pilfered from the aftermath of carnage.

Steward came to look over the little surgeon's bald head.

'If I be not mistook,' said he, ''tis Kett's son there who gives those knaves a trouncing.'

And vigorously, too, did Will Kett trounce some half-dozen youngsters, lads in their early teens or less who, with cat-calls and hoots, baited their victim while he, foolishly mowing, told them: 'Yes,' and 'yes! As I did unto him, so do to me. See how I bleed as did he when I stabbed that the red vomit flowed.

But it flows not now. He is my friend. I love — I loved — *a-aah*! that pains me well. Give — and give me more.'

'You whoreson whelps!' Will lunged and grabbed from a tormentor's hand the blade of steel to lay the flat of it about his stern, shouting, 'Go! Get you gone, you green-toothed rat, before I skin you raw — and you! and you!' to send them scuttling with howls; and to his men: 'Take this.' He touched his toe to the pitifully gibbering crouched creature. 'No, wait. First let's see the damage done by those young fiends.' But when he had peeled him of his hauberk Will found his hurts to be no more than surface pricks. 'His mind,' he said, 'is injured, not his body. Take him to the castle. This one here —' he turned him over, and: 'Mother of God!' he whispered; and was on his knees to raise him up, looking long into that cold, ashen face.

Unfastening the leather jerkin Will set his hand inside it to find the quiet heart.

Then: 'Carry him,' Will said, 'to Steward's house hard by. I know — I knew — this man. He also was my friend.' And baring his head he murmured low, '*Requiescat in pace,* Philip Pugh.'

FOURTEEN

The King was at Windsor when he heard of Northampton's defeat, duly recorded in his journal:

The people sodenly gathered together in Norfolke and encreased to a great nomber against whom was sent the Lord Marquise Northampton with a nombre of...

The King paused from his writing and called across to Barnaby, deep in a game of chess with Harry Suffolk. 'How many did my uncle Somerset say were sent against this Kett? Was it one thousand and sixty horsemen?'

'Yes, Sire,' answered Barnaby, moving a pawn but not his head. 'Check ... As so I understood it to be.'

'Then he couldn't —' Edward nibbled the tip of his goose-quill and pondered — 'he couldn't have counted the Italians. I thought it was fifteen hundred, all told, but I'd best put it down as he gave it.'

And in his beautiful, decorative hand, that always had bettered his spelling, he wrote:

With 1060 horsemen who winning the towne of Norwiche kept it one day and one night and the next day in the morning with loss of 100 departed out of the towne, among which was the Lord Sheffield slaine. There was takin divers gentlemen and serving men to the nombre of 30 with wich victorie the rebels were very glade...

343

'Beasts!' The King spat out the word on a labial breath, and for some minutes sat idle, his thumb teasing his lower lip, his brows drawn frowningly to meet above his small, snub nose. On the terrace below his window some other of his pages played at leapfrog; and at the sound of their shrill laughing voices, he reached over furiously to slam the casement shut. A hundred lost, but only Sheffield named among the killed. Who else? And what of Philip? He may not have been in it. The messenger who had left Norwich on the morning of the battle had been the last to see him ... Alive? Still, no news, good news.

He got up from his desk and strolled over to watch the chess players. 'Your king's in danger,' he told Barnaby. 'You should have brought up your castle, not your knight.'

Suffolk murmured, 'Check.'

Edward bit from his thumb a shred of hanging skin. If only he could know the names of those hundred lost. Slain. Not all of them, surely not *all* of them? But ... a handful fighting in a street brawl against some twenty thousand, so the courier had said. *What a fool,* he cried inwardly, *what a crass, weak-kneed, pretentious fool is this Protector of mine — save the mark! — to send that popinjay Northampton to quell a revolution. That's what it is, revolution. And like to infect the whole realm.*

'Checkmate,' said young Suffolk.

And Barnaby, 'I'll play you again for my revenge.'

Edward left them to it and went back to his desk, but not to sit; to stand, gloomily staring at the window full of waving tree-tops. The sky was banked with rain clouds. Rain had come, or so had been reported, to put out the fires lit by those devilish swine. An Act of God? And this Kett naming himself 'King of Norfolk'

'Yes!' Edward whipped round on his pages, shouting, 'and here are we with half England in flames, the French king at Boulogne, war certain with France, and my Lord Protector sending Warwick — Warwick! the only man of our council worth his salt — sent off to Scotland for another invasion. What do *you* care, you couple o' beetle-headed peascods, if we and our kingdom are — checkmate!'

And in one of those sudden rage storms of his father's heritage, Edward dashed across the room to sweep the chessmen from the board. They fell clattering and bouncing on the polished oak to knock off the head of a bishop.

'That for an omen,' muttered Suffolk, red of face, as he gathered up the pieces to re-set them.

'But,' the King with a tight little smile said, soft, 'it may not be the head of a — bishop.'

'Ah, now, Your Grace, be easy,' soothed Barnaby, whose quick glance at his fellow page was anything but easy. 'Wait till my lord of Warwick gets his teeth in 'um. He'll rout 'um good and proper.'

'Don't I tell you,' and Edward squared his underlip to tell him, 'that our uncle, the Protector, has sent Warwick off to Scotland?'

'Sure then,' said Barnaby, 'Your Grace must fetch him back.'

And Warwick was fetched back; not directly, maybe, at the order of a king still a few weeks short of twelve years old; yet despite his tender youth, or because of it, may have been endowed with a sixth or sounder sense than he who ruled him: that instinctive perspicacity which so often is the complement of precocious childhood. And this particular child was outstandingly precocious.

The 'Good Duke' must have had an uncomfortable quarter of an hour when faced by a small, determined boy with feet wide planted, one hand in his jewelled belt, the other fingering his gold-hilted dagger; and in those narrow eyes that same coldly meditative look of his father when crossed, or when considering which of the more drastic penalties should be passed as sentence on offenders who had dared oppose him.

It is possible that the gentle-voiced insistent question, 'Why? But why did Your Grace suggest first yourself, then Northampton, and not Lord Warwick, to take command of a relieving force in Norfolk? Why?' may have been too forcible a reminder of a similar, if more ominous insistence, prefaced by a replica of that thin, close-lipped smile and that same repetitive, *Why? Why do you not?* or *Why do you?* Always the more gentle-voiced when at his most merciless, so did Edward Seymour, Duke of Somerset, remember the sire of this very gentle little boy.

Great was the discomfort of the Lord Protector at that interview, and no less when he found himself confronted in the council chamber by that same question, 'Why?' from rows of hostile interrogators. 'Why do you not send Warwick into Norfolk?' Nor did his indecisive answer, 'Yes ... Warwick could, were it necessary, be recalled ... or he may not yet have started on his march to the Border,' convince the council that not even now did Somerset realise how critical was the present situation. With his usual obstinacy, and against all advice, he would continue to take the line of least resistance in order to avoid inflicting on the masses, his disciples, more severely remedial methods. Look how he had offered free pardon to the rebels if they would lay down their arms and repent. A free pardon! 'What a confession of weakness' — 'or treason!' — so from mouth to mouth behind their hands went the whispers of the council. Surely such pandering to murderous outlaws might be interpreted as enticement to further a nationwide revolt? At all costs, though it be to the loss of his nephew's Crown and kingdom, must he uphold his much-vaunted Proclamation by which he had declared himself 'Protector', not only of the King but of the people and their 'Rights'. And this Norfolk Rebellion and one in Yorkshire threatening, was the result of his liberal dogma so arbitrarily pursued. True, the council had granted him almost unlimited power, and heartily now did they regret it. For, see how he had misused and mishandled that power. *And in a short time had become so haught and arrogant,* thus the statement of the council, *refusing to hear any man's reason but his own, that he stickt not openly to taunt such of us as frankly spake their opinions.*

Past and present molehill grievances rose to mountain-height, capped by accusation of more sinister portent. Had not the Protector of the King's person and realm seized on Church lands to build and name for himself a palace at vast expense — not to him, but to the Crown? And had he not handed indiscriminate endowments, peerages, estates, to his chosen? And latterly, look how on all occasions he used the King's Royal Stamp and Seal to his own signature. Was it not evident that this Protector of their child-Sovereign purposed to gain supremacy of the very throne?

It must at last have dawned on the star-gazing Somerset that his position was decidedly invidious, wedged between the Scylla of his democratic principles and the Charybdis of his councillors' mistrust. Yet, despite their ill-concealed disfavour, Somerset, perversely, still stayed undecided as to whether he or Warwick should command a second, stronger force against the Norfolk rebels. Not until more than two weeks after Northampton's retreat did Warwick receive his orders:

Few gentlemen of Norfolk who had fought in the Battle of Norwich were in fit state to repair to the 'said Earl', when he set out on his eastward march. Those of the Norfolk squires who still retained their freedom came to meet him at Wymondham. Those others who would have been only too eager to join him lay imprisoned in the castle; and some lay at death's door.

As were the majority of Norfolk houses, so was Sowerby bereft of servants, with exception of Jocosa's page and her woman Joan. The rest had fled — 'to Mousehold, I'll warrant me,' Joan said when she and her mistress watched the last of them take to his heels.

'Ay! And if all's righted and they come slinking back, the white-livered chuff-cats,' declared Joan's lady, 'so may they stew afore I'll give 'em house-room.'

Since the morning her husband had left Sowerby, 'armed and in full harness,' as reported to Jocosa by his servant, she had heard no news of him, although word ran like fire that the city was fallen to the rebels. Then, one morning, Joan burst into the kitchen where her mistress, now the household's cook, was rolling pastry.

'Madame! John Ball from Yarmouth, as so ever them Balls being staunch and loyal to the gentry, have brought fish back and forth to Norwich as in ages past, and Mousehold too —' more obscurely voluble than ever was Joan in her excitement to tell how John had supplied fish to 'those devils — may they rot! — and the castle for the warders, not the prisoners, I'll swear —'

'Well?' cried Jocosa, as Joan paused for breath.

'Why, madame, so I'm telling you that while I took what was left of his herrings and mackerel, him having no smelts, John Ball did say as how among the gentry lying there in chains but well and lively is our —'

'He!' Jocosa's hands leapt to her heart. 'Dear God be praised.'

'Yes, madame, indeed. Not killed as we had feared, never having word of him since he left home but now we have it certain sure the master's in the castle along with other of the squires hereabouts.'

'Who...' Jocosa asked in a dwindling voice, 'what others?'

'Sir Roger Wodehouse, Serjeant Flowerdew, Squire Corbet of Sprowston whose dovecote was sacked so John Ball said but not ours, thanks to —'

'Did he say ... is Master Pugh ... among the prisoners?'

'No, madame, he said naught of him. But is not this gladsome news that the master he be saved?'

'Yes.'

'And when I for one as had it in my bones he'd ne'er come back so weakling he but brave withal to take his share o' the fight against the rebels,' Joan chattered with false cheer as she saw her lady's shadowed face and the tremble of her lips. And to herself Joan sighed and said, *Poor pretty she be pining — not for him that's her husband, but for the one that should ha' been, and God forgive me pity 'tis that t'other's spared and not himself, for if ever two did eat their hearts out in love wasted so did they. And now she'll never see him more, nor I his fiddle-faced long John...'*

'So, madame,' she said brightly, 'we'll be well stocked with fish until next week an I pickle the fresh herrings and souse the mackerel that they'll not turn high and we've still half a mutton and three bacon flitches in the larder and with eggs a-plenty we'll not want.'

Jocosa, who was pale, said, 'Hot it is today for baking.' And she opened the oven door to shove in a pan of caraway cakes; then back to the table and up to her elbows in the mixing bowl, while Joan gutted the fish and gave her mistress further news she'd gathered from John Ball. 'He did say, madame, as how that Kett and his brother have been come and go to Yarmouth to stir up the townsfolk that they join with him and his Satan's army, but they'll not move finger to his beck, not they! From the fishermen down to the last herring, Yarmouth — as so John Ball did say — is hot blood for the King, and'll not turn traitor though they be drawn and quartered — there you are, then.' Joan flung a couple of fish heads to the mewing cat. 'And this for you.' She dropped a herring roe into the slavering mouth of the crippled dog, sitting up on his hind legs to beg. 'He misses his master,' said Joan; and her knife, poised to slit a mackerel, was stayed in mid-air at the sound of a galloping horse at the gatehouse. 'The rebels,' she gasped, 'come to sack us!' And down on all fours she went to duck under the table.

'Get up!' Jocosa shot out a foot at her damsel's plump behind. 'Cowardy! 'Tis naught but one horseman. I'll go see.'

'No, madame.' Joan crawled from her shelter. 'I'll go.'

But Jocosa was already at the door and in the court, there to be met by her page.

'Mistress, a man is come from Sprowston. He asks to speak with you.'

'Sprowston? Who...?' voicelessly she questioned, and was answered by a cry from Joan who had followed her out.

''Tis John! I see him through the archway. John … John Locke!'

John Locke it was. Dismounting, he led his horse into the yard where the two women waited; the one, her face joyous, her hands outstretched to him who, although he took and held them, looked past her to that other from whose face all colour faded, whose eyes were wide and searchingly on his.

'My master,' John said.

And she, whispering: 'Is — is he —?'

'No, madame.' John bowed his head. 'As yet he lives — and asks for you. The doctor who attends him bids you come. 'Tis a case of life or — death.'

'I thank you,' she said, 'John.' And to her page, 'Go, saddle me the bay mare. Joan, my riding habit. And I'll be with you, John,' she said, 'directly.'

On the way to Sprowston John told her how Will Kett had come upon his master in Tombland lying in the shambles among the dead and wounded, and had brought him to Master Steward's house and left him there, 'believing him to be,' John said stolidly, 'a corpse, as so he would have been but that a surgeon happed to be with Master Steward and did find a spark o' life. The lung,' John stared between his horse's ears, 'is pierced. Then was word sent to the squire who himself did go into the camp to speak with Kett who gave him a free pass to the city that Master Philip be brought to Sprowston in a litter, when at such time he might be moved. 'Twas six days agone afore they brought him home. I did warn him as he should ha' gone in armour, but he'd ha' none o' that.' John waited a second, swallowed, and went on: 'When later in the morning I went down into the city with his harness — the battle — it was over.'

'What doctor,' Jocosa asked, stiff-lipped, 'is he who attends him?'

''Tis a physician sent for to Cambridge by the squire. And yesterday when Master Philip roused up from his stupor and for the first time spoke — he spoke of you, madame, and called your name in frenzy like, him wandering with the fever — the physician he advised that you should come. All in human power,' John said with a plum in his throat, 'as may be done for him, is done. What now may hap is in God's hands, not our'n.'

'Yes,' said Jocosa. 'I ... yes.'

Dame Matilda received her at the door of Sprowston Hall. She had evidently been awaiting her arrival. The old nun's finely chiselled features, her eyes undimmed and ageless, betrayed no sign that day and night for near upon a week she had kept unremitting watch by Philip's bedside. Without wasting words beyond a curt ''Tis well you are here. He is restive but quieter now,' and with the air of a general marshalling his forces, she conducted Jocosa to the door of Philip's room and left her there.

With a coldness in her hands and a dryness in her mouth, Jocosa lifted the latch and went in. Geoffrey Pugh rose up from where he sat on a stool by the bed. His cheeks were shrunken; he looked haggard, worn. He took her hand in his, murmured something unintelligible, and to another in the room, 'My kin — my kinswoman, Mistress Joco —' he said; and to her, 'This is Doctor —' She did not catch the name of the grave-faced, grey-haired gentleman who told her, quiet-voiced but with a reassuring smile, 'I think, madame, that you will prove to be a better physic for my patient than any I have yet prescribed.' And he followed after Geoffrey Pugh.

Jocosa was alone with him who lay inert, unstirring, his face carven in a strange transparent immobility. His hands, outstretched on the coverlet, looked to be transparent, too. So colourless and so wan was he that her heart fainted to see him. Did he see her? His eyes were not quite closed, showing each a thread of blue.

She knelt and whispered: 'Love, my love … I'm here.' O, his eyes, not closed, not open, as if he had no strength to lift those pale lids, yet he had asked for her. He must have had the voice to ask for her. 'Speak,' with all her soul she willed it, 'speak to me. You mustn't go. You mustn't … Say that you'll not leave me.'

And then she saw his lips make the smallest movement, the very shadow of a smile, to bring a rush of tears to her eyes, as from his heart to hers he answered on a whispered breath: 'I called you and you've come … so I'll not … go.'

For the next few weeks while the rebels held the city Jocosa stayed at Sprowston to share in the nursing of Philip, not without strong opposition from the dame. Nothing would induce her to give up possession of the sick room, which she regarded as her rightful province and Jocosa a trespasser therein. Tussles between the two resulted in a grudging compromise. Jocosa should take the watch at certain intervals by day, and — a great concession, this — from each dawn till morning.

'Three hours at the most,' Dame Matilda decreed, growing always a little more gaunt, more grim and more determinedly resolute.

When not resting, which was seldom, or sleeping, which apparently was never, she would busy herself in the still-room brewing simples, mixing unguents — 'of more worth,' she told

Jocosa, 'than all the doctor's physic. The seed of the mustard, boiled in white wax and dissolved with gum arabic in rosewater, will disperse all humours and ease pain.'

'Yes,' said Jocosa, 'to raise him a blister.'

'A clyster? No,' emphatically denied the dame. 'If he be costive, rhubarb.'

And Jocosa, casting up her eyes, went back to Philip.

His recovery was slow. For days he lay semi-comatose, rarely speaking. Only his eyes spoke for him: eyes that were childishly large and blue, so much bluer for the dark-ringed hollows round them, gazing up at her who was always with him, when not driven from the room by the dame. But the doctor, now returned to Cambridge, had made light, for her comfort, of his lassitude. 'He is weakened; once he is about again…'

When, she wondered, would he be about again? And sometimes she wondered if ever, so quiescent, so waxen was he to fright her, having no appetite for food, gradually thickened from liquids to solids; no interest in life, save when she was with him, his hand in hers. So would she sit for hours, not moving, only watching, while he slept; waiting till he woke to hear his voice say faintly: 'You … still here? You'll not leave me?' And she to tell him, 'Yes, my soul, I'm here and I'll not leave you.'

If only it were so, that she might never leave him!

Not until five weeks had gone by, and when he was allowed to sit up for a while during the day, did he begin to question her. 'What news of the rebellion?'

'Lord Warwick,' she told him, 'is on his way to Wymondham.'

'Warwick!' He half rose from the settle where John had placed him, with cushions, by the window. 'And only now — after all this time! How long is it since Northampton's —' She saw his face contract and guessed he could not bring himself to say the word 'retreat'.

'Long enough,' she said lightly, 'and too long for our peace.'

'Yes.' And then, his eyes on hers, compelling, 'I fought another battle here,' he said, 'and single-handed. That is so, isn't it? The doctor from Cambridge gave me up for lost.'

'But you were found again.' She slipped from her stool to kneel beside him. His hand came out to touch her hair.

'Found, brought back to life by you, but not — for you.' He lay watching the distant slopes of Mousehold where, heat-hazed in August mist, the hosts of Kett's army were scattered, too far to distinguish more than an isolated sun-gleam on canvas tent and armour; and presently: 'Your husband — what news of him?'

She told him what news of him: a prisoner in the castle and uninjured.

'That,' he said, 'is well — so they do treat him well.'

'Yes.'

But his head was turned from her and he did not see her hands were clenched that their nails dug into her palms.

And that same day once more was heard at Sprowston the thunder of the guns. For Warwick's last attempt 'to quench this flame, so dangerous and dreadful, without slaughter and bloodshed', thus his message delivered by a herald at St. Stephen's Gate, had failed.

John Locke, who was permitted to make use of Squire Pugh's free pass to and from the city bringing what was needful for the household, reported how the Earl, 'at the head of a great band of men and cannon, now in numbers more than equal match for Kett, had forced entry into Norwich on the threat that war would be declared upon the citizens thereof unless the gates be opened to the army of the King.'

The very sight of that vast cavalcade of infantry, horse, and ammunition, brought the townsfolk and Deputy Mayor Steward from their bolt-holes. Those few of the rebels left within the walls stayed to hear the herald's proclamation. The rest, at the order of their captain, had retired to their camp. 'So now,' said John, 'they stand at a deadlock.' Warwick's offer of pardon had been refused — 'with curses on him,' quoth John, 'when great routs of rebels came flocking down from Mousehold. So hugesome was the crowd there by the gate near the camp that naught could be seen but a thicket o' men shouting rageful at Herald and calling on him for a traitor, to give them fair promise o' pardon which was worth nothing more than barrels filled with rope and halter.' And then. as witnessed by John Locke, had come Kett himself 'to stop their yowling that they might hear Herald's speechifying. And those who could not hear him being too far off and for the press o' people round about, Kett did bring him forward by the river, when one o' them young vagabond knaves rushed out at the King's Herald with such play o' filthy gestures and words not to be repeated before madame —'John flickered a look at her who sat by Philip's couch, her lips apart, her eyes wide on him who, as a granite image could it have spoken, gave his account of what he'd seen. 'And then,' said John stonily, 'one of the King's archers, standing nigh to Herald, took his bow and shot the boy straight through the heart that he fell dead.'

'So,' Philip said, 'the fuse is lit.'

John nodded. 'Sir, it is, to explode all hope o' peace with Kett. For, as like a carpet did his runnions come spread around him who I'll swear did doubt his mind — as I saw when I followed out at the gates — would he or no accept Lord Warwick's pardon for his rebels, even though that herald made it clear there'd be no pardon but a traitor's death for him. And

I did see them pesky devils come grab at Kett's arm, while there he stood uncertain like, pulling at him this way, that way, calling, Whither go you, Captain? Whither? Where? Will you forsake us? Stand fast. Trust not his word, nor Warwick's. And then —' A terrific crash of gunfire from Mousehold drowned the rest of it.

Philip lifted his head from the pillow. 'And that,' he said, 'is Kett's answer. He'll not forsake them. So — what now?'

What now, at noon on that August day, was the fiercest fight of all in the battle for Norwich. Warwick had undertaken more than he could hold against Kett's army, to suffer a disastrous setback. The drivers of his gun-wagons had mistaken the road into the city, and, passing on and out through Bishop's Gate, found themselves surrounded by Kett's hordes who captured them and almost all their ammunition. Yet Warwick still retained the great bulk of his horse and infantry, drawn up in Tombland prepared for the offensive. Moreover, he hourly expected reinforcements of fourteen hundred German mercenaries, the Lanznechts.... If he could only keep the rebels at bay till they came!

From his window at Sprowston Philip watched the distant fire-flash of guns but did not know those guns were Warwick's, seized and served by Kett's men; he saw the storming of the rebels down the hill and chafed at his inertia — 'Tethered here, unfit to take my part in it!' He worked himself into a fever again to be up and at them, and was only quieted by a dose of something mighty bitter tasting, poured down his throat by Dame Matilda, which put him sound to sleep and Jocosa in a fright lest he would never wake.

'He'll wake,' said the dame, 'when my brew, distilled from poppy juice, has done its work. I can't have him up and down as he were full of jumping beans to burst his wound and bring about another blooding. Let him be.'

Jocosa let him be, and watched beside him for the better part of all that day until, toward evening, he came to and more than ever in a state of jumping beans', when John, returned from Norwich, brought word that the German reinforcements had arrived!

This joyful news called for liberal draughts of metheglin, in which all, not excepting Dame Matilda, took their share. And while Warwick's tired troops, equally joyful at the coming of the Lanznechts, made merry at the Maid's Head; and while the earl and his officers were likewise wined and feasted at Augustine Steward's house — and this time go hang the expense! — Kett made his fatal decision.

With the great advantage gained by the capture of Warwick's artillery, he determined to disband his camp at Mousehold and hurl the full force of his army and his guns in one great offensive from the low-lying plain of Dussindale beyond the city's walls. And in the late afternoon of the following day:

'Look!' Philip called Jocosa to him where he stood at the window, for he was now allowed to walk about the room though not yet about the house. 'They're firing the camp.'

Volumes of flame-shotten smoke belched up from the timbered huts and canvas tents, blotting out the distant hill in a false night darkness, deepening to copper-red the golden evening sky.

'What,' gasped Jocosa, 'does it mean? Has Warwick —'

'No, I think not Warwick.' Philip closed the casement. ''Tis a fearsome blaze to choke us. No,' he said again, 'not Warwick, for if so there'd have been noise of it. We've heard no sound of guns. This is Kett's doing, but God alone knows why.'

'John went again into Norwich this morning,' said Jocosa. 'Maybe he'll have somewhat to tell us.'

What John had to tell was of Warwick's final ultimatum: a free pardon to all, save their leaders, on an unconditional surrender. 'But,' said John, 'as they stand fast, so will they fall.'

Thus, in a moment's disastrous misjudgement, did Kett forsake his stronghold on the Heath for the valley below. He, who had hitherto proved himself a master of strategical command, may have been urged to this last desperate manoeuvre by his peasant rebels. In full confidence of victory, as prophesied by local superstition, Kett's followers went shouting through the camp the age-old rhyme:

The country gnoffs, Hob, Dick and Hick
With clubs and clouted shoon,
Will fill the vale
Of Dussin Dale
With slaughtered bodies soon.'

But the slaughtered bodies in Dussin Dale were not of Warwick's men.

In the low level plain around Sprowston, Philip at his window, his arm about Jocosa, watched the awful devastation of Kett's army, caught in the trap of the dale. Under the terrific charge of Warwick's cavalry and the disciplined trained force of the Germans, firing volley after volley of shot from bow and matchlock, Kett's front ranks, like blown dust-devils in a storm, were driven back, and, for their lives, they turned and fled.

Those who were left of the thousands killed and wounded on that blood-soaked battlefield laid down their arms and surrendered. Their fight for liberty was lost, their leader crushed; he, too, a fugitive and flying for his life. His day was done.

He had sent his wife and son ahead of him to make for the coast, there to take ship for Flanders, and were now, he prayed, on the high seas.

The summer dusk was closing in with shadows when, avoiding pursuit by devious ways, the one-time 'King of Norfolk' came to Swannington, a hamlet some eight miles beyond Norwich. He could have gone farther but his horse could not. The poor beast, who all that day had carried him through the blinding dust and deafening noise of battle and whose flank was bleeding from an arrow shot, sank to his knees, half-dead. Kett dismounted, got him up and led him through a gate into a nearby farmyard, where two men were loading hay on to a cart. They looked sharply round; and looked again, and to each other mouthed the one word: 'Kett!'

And when he would have darted up a ladder placed against the wall below a hay-loft, they came at him with their pitch-forks, for the men of Swannington were not of Kett's persuasion, being true and loyal to their king. Then they fetched a rope and tied him hand and foot, and went to tell their master, a farmer of the name of Richards, of their capture, that he might send word of it to the Lord Lieutenant.

Early the next morning twenty horsemen of the Earl came to Swannington where the rebels' captain lay, locked in a room at Richards' house. He had been given meat and drink, his bonds unloosed that he might feed, but he had made no attempt to escape.

He heard the heavy tramp of feet on the stair, and, when they burst in on him, he gave himself up quietly, saying, 'All's one — and all's over. See to't my wounded horse be cared for. Any farmer's lad can have him, so he be treated fairly.'

Then they bound and took prisoner Robert Kett of Wymondham, in the name of His Majesty the King.

An ironical twist of fate it was that he and Edward, Duke of Somerset, should be held captive in the Tower, both at one and the same time; both in their misguided idealism champions of that which they believed to be a just and righteous cause; both doomed to die a traitor's death. But the 'Good Duke' had yet a year or more to wait before his end, while contention in the council chamber and throughout the country strove for and against his interim release; for the other no release, no trial, save the hollow form of such; and no defence from either of the brothers Kett, each of whom had pleaded guilty.

It had been full summer when Robert Kett, for six weeks, held rule in Norwich City; it was midwinter when he and his brother were returned in fetters to the scene of their brief triumph to be flung into the castle's dungeons. Their imprisonment was short, their end unmercifully long, with the same awful penalty pronounced on each, that:

Robert Kett, in obedience to the King's command, be drawn alive from the ground up to the gibbet placed on top of Norwich Castle and there his body to be hanged in chains. His brother William to be taken also and to perish alike being hanged on the Church tower at Wymondham.

High above the city, from the steeps of Norwich Castle, a tattered scarecrow swung. For weeks it had been swinging there to strike terror in the hearts of those, who, on the day they hauled him up, had come to see and to revile, with howls of execration, their one-time 'hero', their brave 'King Kett'; he, who had promised that 'the hurts and sufferings done to them by the wicked lords of the land should be revenged. Before all things else will I strive,' so had he sworn, 'for your deliverance and welfare, and in and for your cause I will spend my very life.' Fair words. Fair promises. Yes! he had spent his life and they too, some thousands of them, had spent theirs down in Dussin's Dale of Death. And a hundred more at the rope's end, here in the market place. So much for his promises; and they who lived, returned as dogs to their vomit, slaves once again to the lords of the land.

Day by day and night by night, that which once had been a man fluttered its rags as it hung in its creaking chains; or when storm-gales yelled about those grim-faced walls, it would kick its legs and, airily, would dance; or it would spin, like a capon on a spit, fast and faster, round and round, the drollest sight to see, that even the children, no longer scared of it, would pause and laugh and upward point at 'old Kett' swinging there.

Skulking dark birds circled to peck at its empty eye sockets; rains soaked it, snows shrouded it, and still it hung, until its fleshless bones slid from the iron grip that long had ceased to torture.

So passed Robert Kett, nor never knew that four centuries after him his promise of 'Welfare' to those for whom he died would be fulfilled.

But his Great Rebellion and this bitter end of it is coolly dismissed by the young King in his journal:

The Earl of Warwick overcame them in plain Battel .... takin Ret their Captain who in January following was hang'd at Norwich Castle and his head hang'd out.

The King had more to worry him than a revolt of peasantry in Norfolk, defeated by the Earl of Warwick in one day.

Philip Pugh, his gentleman, had been wounded nigh to death and would not be well enough recovered to resume his duties for some months. Bad enough, but it might have been worse for, as Edward later heard, Master Pugh was out of danger. He must therefore wait in patience until Philip should come back; and in the meantime he had none but Barnaby to whom he could unburden the latest of his troubles concerning the behaviour of his Uncle Somerset.

'Either he's run mad or so shall I,' confided Edward to his henchmen, 'if my uncle comes again to drag me out of bed at all hours of the night as twice last week he did at Hampton Court — and me stuffed silly with a cold — to go down to the quadrangle and address a crowd of people there outside the gates. "I pray you be good to us and to our uncle." Me! The King!' fumed Edward. 'What think you of that?'

'Sure, I think,' rejoined Barnaby, darkly, 'Your Grace is right. The Duke must be at his wits' ends.'

'If —' said Edward with a chuckle and a sneeze — 'a curse upon this rheum! — if my precious uncle was possessed of any wits to end. Could you have seen him as he stood there beside me at the gates, and the wind like a knife cutting at my chest, that now it hurts me every time I cough — could you have *seen* him looking like a moulting buzzard with his bald head and his beaked nose, croaking at that crowd of village folk, 'I'll not fall alone,' he shouted loud and wild. 'Or if I'm to be destroyed, so will the King and the Kingdom be destroyed.' Threatening the people with destruction to my kingdom and to me — to me!' jerked out Edward, rubbing his sore chest, 'if they would not stick fast to him for their "common weal". Never mind me and *my* weal. Oh, no. So what think you of *that*?'

What Barnaby may have thought of that he did not say. He was anxious for his little king who coughed into his handkerchief to stain it red.

''Tis only from my throat,' said Edward quickly. 'It often bleeds when I start coughing.'

But not, thought Barnaby, *before himself did fetch you from your bed when you were in a fever.* Barnaby, who had not been in attendance on the King that night, had heard from others of the pages how Mother Jack had minced no words to tell the duke the King was sick and in no state to be got up — 'or at Your Grace's peril', so Mother Jack had told him; but in such haste was the duke to be gone he would not heed her, nor his old hag of a duchess screaming out that he must wait for her until she'd packed her jewels. He had bade her follow in a barge downstream to Kew, and hustled the King away, mounted on his pony to ride shivering and coughing through a pea-soup fog to Windsor. And, wondered Barnaby, for why? What could have driven the duke to such extremes that he would risk the King's dear life and all. For why?

Edward, too, was asking why, nor would he readily forget or forgive his Protector that uncomfortable journey, and the blow to his pride that he should be made to go a-begging of a crowd of yokels outside his palace gates 'Be good to me and to my uncle....'

Yet when spring danced again on the green lawns of Hampton Court to a fanfare from daffodil trumpets, the King, for the first time in his short reign, had come into his own; a king at last. His 'Protector' had fallen, and the people, to whom the duke had appealed as 'Friend', were for the most part turned against him; nor did the leaflets he scattered broadcast 'in the name of God and the King to defend His Majesty's Lord Protector against certain lords and gentlemen who would depose us', bring more than a tepid response. Their 'Protector', despite his high sounding talk of Liberty', and his avowed dedication of himself 'to the service of God and the State', had done little enough for the State. Nor — so those who adhered to the older Faith declared — for God. Thus went opinion over ale cups in taverns. For look you, when leaders like Robert Kett did make attempt to rise with all power of support at his elbow — look what's come to him and to those who battled with him for their rights, to do them wrong! They were sick to death of promises, *and* of a Protector. What they wanted was a king. Why, old Harry, tyrant, adulterer, fornicator and great-poxed for his sins though he were, had always been hearty, hail-well-met with the best or worst of them. Nothing so prideful as this one, climbed up on his sister's shoulders by way of his nephew's throne. But Warwick who had brought him low was still to bring him lower while he enjoyed to play a game of Cat and Mouse with the once powerful Duke of Somerset now humbled, imprisoned, disgraced in the eyes of the world. Violent charges had been laid against him as of 'devilish and evil purpose to enrich himself and his satellites; and of arbitrary misuse of his trust as Lord Protector.' Sufficient pretext to throw him in the Tower and threaten him with death unless he signed a full confession of his guilt.

In terror of his life, the abject Somerset would have signed anything to save it. Then, after having sunk him, deprived him of his wealth, his dignity, his state, Warwick raised him up again, restored to him his property, his seat upon the council, gave him length of rope enough to hang himself … and waited.

The downfall of his uncle brought for Edward 'a release', he told his council, 'as from prison'. Warwick, while tacitly understood to be the Governor of the King's person, assumed no title of Protector nor of Regent. True, he had in mind to take to him the Duchy of Northumberland, at such time when he should deem it opportune; which was not yet; and in the meantime he must set about to woo the little king. He had already won his confidence by his approach, not as autocratic guardian but as counsellor and friend. He realised that Edward could be led but never driven; and so tactfully he led him and on so long a leash that the boy might well rejoice in his new freedom. He had been given, besides other royal prerogatives hitherto withheld, the choice of his attendants and the handing out of honours to his favourites. So, when Philip returned to Court, he found an eager bright-eyed lad, grown taller, though still not tall enough for his twelve years, narrow-chested, and less pale than his wont; yet the fitful flush in those thinned cheeks was, to Philip, a thought disquieting. And then that cough! A little dry, harsh cough that tore his slender frame and interrupted his warm greeting.

'We have — we've missed you,' Edward said. 'They told me you —' he turned to cough again, and his flush deepened — 'have been sore wounded in our cause. I prayed for your recovery. God heard and answered me. He always does.'

'Your Grace —' Philip bowed his lips to that small, hot, outstretched hand, with something caught in his throat to halt his speech. But when he would have risen Edward stayed him, 'Wait,' and to his watching pages he bade one, 'Bring me a sword.'

A sword was brought by Barnaby. Edward took it from him and lifting it with both hands, for it was heavy, laid it on the shoulder of his kneeling gentleman.

'Now rise — Sir Philip,' said the King.

FIFTEEN

On a May morning in the following year, the Princess Elizabeth rode from Hatfield to visit her brother, the King, at Whitehall. It was a marvellous fair day, the trees just full, the birds at song, and the air fragrant with the wind-loosened flower of the hawthorn.

Mounted on her white long-tailed palfrey, her green velvet habit almost trailing the ground, she went attended by the ubiquitous Ashley and an escort of gentlemen, who, having been promoted to her household by the odious Protector, or, as she suspected, by his duchess, were remarkable neither for their comeliness nor wit.

This was Elizabeth's first emergence from her retirement at Hatfield since her name had been involved with that of Tom Seymour to bring about a *scandalum magnatum*. She had held herself aloof from the world and from gossip, immersed in her studies with none but her tutor, Mr. Ascham, to admire her scholarly achievements and extol her charms in Greek and Latin verse, that, from constant repetition, had ceased to entertain. She was in fact, at seventeen, ready to embark upon fresh amorous adventure, not to be found in the hermetic seclusion of Hatfield.

As she passed through the villages of Barnet and Highgate she graciously acknowledged the bobbings and cheers of the cottagers, glad to know that she was not forgotten nor mistaken — awful thought! — for Mary, who often took this road to London from her home at Hunsdon. No. They could not possibly mistake hers for her sister's wizened, old, pinched face. Why, Mary was well in her thirties, a proper old maid...

Elizabeth had brought with her a present for Edward: her portrait, in miniature. He had asked for it and she had written him a gushing letter, expressing her delight at 'Your Majesty's desire for a thing not worthy of desire. My picture, I mean; for the face, I grant, I might well blush to offer, but the mind I shall never be ashamed to present...' *Or to speak,* she might have added; yet she had not spoken when her mind had been distorted and her heart wrung out of shape by the death-blow to him on whom her first young love was spent. Had she then been given leave to speak her mind with Edward, she might have stayed his hand from signing his uncle's life away. But that was over, buried in her past. Her future?

She stared ahead at the twisting tree-lined lane where the searching sunlight probed through interlacing branches to pave her path with gold. And to herself she smiled, with closed lips. Her teeth were not her greatest beauty; uneven, inclined to decay. She had learned not to show them by practising her smile before her looking-glass. And other things than that did she practise to her mirrored self: her poise and posture, the movement of her long white hands while she recited extempore Latin speeches to imaginary ambassadors, come from France, from Spain, from Austria, to woo her for their princes. For if, at seventeen, she didn't begin to think of her marriage, certainly no one else would.

Which, if truth be told, was the reason of her visit to Edward: that she should be seen and admired, not by that moonish sentimental Ascham or her own dreary gentlemen, but by Edward's Court which was entirely a bachelor establishment; and well established too, as she had heard, since Warwick had taken over reins of governance, where no woman, now that the curmudgeonly old duchess had been put down, would be put up … unless it were the sister of the King. And again she smiled.

So in high good humour Elizabeth arrived at her brother's palace. Deceived by his bright colour, she told him he looked in exceeding good health.

'I am, but for this tickling cough,' he said, 'which I don't seem able to shake off.' He admired the miniature, and politely added, 'But it doesn't flatter you.' It did; yet she was none the less flattered to believe him. He had certainly improved both in manner and appearance, and was surrounded by a group of courtiers all seemingly enraptured at the sight of her, but all a trifle too young for her taste, with exception of Sir Philip Pugh, on whom, since he was known to be a confirmed misogynist, she would not waste her wiles. Then, when she had been offered and accepted wine and comfits, she glanced aside at the gentlemen and pages near about, and satisfied they were tactfully removed from earshot, 'What,' she asked her brother, 'is all this I hear of Somerset's attempt to raise a following in London? They say that he's inciting the citizens in revolt to seize you and take possession of the Tower. Is it true?'

Edward's eyes narrowed. 'As likely true as not. He's done for himself this time.'

'How?'

'I'll tell you how — although I shouldn't. And don't you dare repeat it to any living soul. Promise?'

'Cross my heart.'

'Well then,' Edward dropped his voice and leaned nearer to her where they sat together on the window seat. 'Warwick has got wind of a plot hatched by our good uncle.' His upper lip was folded back and his nose wrinkled as a puppy dog about to bite, but not in play.

'And so?' urged Elizabeth. 'Go on.'

'It's past belief, yet,' Edward said, 'we've damning evidence enough and witnesses to prove it. He's so desperate he'll stop at nothing to get hold of me again — not even murder.'

'Not —' Elizabeth paled; her hand came out to grip his knee — 'not you?'

Edward, coughing, shook his head. 'No, not me. Not yet. Warwick and others of the council first and then...' He rubbed his chest. 'But they, or rather Warwick, uncovered it in time, and aptly, on St. George's Day, when one Palmer — I don't think you know him, Sir Thomas Palmer, knighted in the French wars, a close friend of Warwick's — came to him in his garden at Ely Place and told him on no account must he attend the banquet to which the duke had invited him for the following night. It seems —' Edward locked his hands together and looked down at them — 'it seems our excellent good uncle had arranged that a dozen or more hired assassins disguised as lackeys should kill Warwick and others of the council while they sat at his board, ate of his food, his honoured guests.' And unclasping his hands, he picked at his thumb, softly saying, 'Quite a Machiavellian conception, don't you think?'

Elizabeth released a breath. 'Have they taken him?'

Edward nodded. 'And this time there'll be,' his small mouth hardened, 'no escape.'

'So he,' Elizabeth lowered her eyes, 'is the second uncle whose death warrant you will have signed.'

'Yes.' His thin closed smile answered hers; but her face was bleak.

A thousand men at arms were massed on Tower Hill, come to keep order among the multitude of common folk assembled there to see the execution of their 'Friend'.

His brother, whom he had sent to that same block where now he stood, died 'irksomely, horribly'. Not so Somerset, the 'Good Duke' to the last.

He had dressed himself in splendour as for a State occasion. He was calm, his greying beard carefully trimmed, his brow placid. As he turned and formally bowed to the officials circled round him on the scaffold in the icy stillness of that January morning, a universal sigh, like the rustle of dead leaves falling, shivered through the silence. Then, bare-headed, he addressed the crowd in words so dispassionate, so simple, and devoid of any dramatised self-pity, that almost all, save those accustomed to such scenes and speeches, were in tears.

'Masters and good fellows, I am come here to die. I am content to die for as a man I have deserved at God's hands many deaths. It has pleased His Goodness thus now to visit me and call me to this present death, as you do see, where I have had time to remember and acknowledge Him, and to know also myself...'

He was still speaking when a thud of tramping feet, as of an approaching army, crashed through the silence to create a sudden panic. With shouts and cries of 'The soldiers! Break! Break!' the crowd scattered in all directions. Their alarms were groundless. Although indeed a company of soldiers had arrived, and a few minutes later than the hour they were ordered to attend the execution, the noise of their coming was caused by a last-minute race to be in at the death on Tower Hill. But so great was the confusion and the spectators so hysterical that when one, mounted, forced his horse through that surging throng crying: 'A pardon! A pardon from the King!' all were thankfully ready to believe him. But the duke was not deceived. He knew his Warwick too well. He stood, cap in hand, until the excitement died down, and waving back those who rushed forward to the scaffold, clambering upon it as if to seize and carry him away, he called strongly to quiet them: 'No, good people! No! There is no such thing as a pardon for me. My time has come.'

Then, with methodical precision, he drew his rings from his fingers and handed them to the executioner. He unfastened his cloak, let it fall at his feet, unbuckled his sword, and, with another bow, presented it to the Lord Lieutenant of the Tower.

A chill sun-gleam glanced through the leaden sky to light his face and eyes, upraised as he knelt, and said, low-voiced, 'Lord Jesus save me.'

Three times he said it before the axe was raised, and in one swift stroke descended.

There followed a wild demonstration. Those who had come to watch and to applaud a traitor's death remembered only that he, whose severed head rolled from the block, had vowed to love and befriend them, their 'Protector'. Some, unrestrainedly sobbing, fell on their knees; others swarmed around the scaffold to cup in their hands the slow red drops as they trickled down into the straw.

'Of all things in the world I most desire,' said the King, 'is to see the world.' He stared out of the window where, between the level marshlands of Greenwich, the river glided on its ceaseless way. 'Not this little world of mine, but a greater, wider world still to be discovered.' On his desk, drawn close to the casement, he sat poring over a map spread across it. 'Look, Philip, here is the route you will take,' Edward told him, 'as good old Cabot gives it.'

And with his forefinger he traced the course of the north-east passage through ice-bound seas, yet unexplored, to

Cathay. So, for days during these past few weeks, would he sit; or when, as often of late, he was too tired to sit, he would lie on his couch engrossed in geographical and astronomical studies; of the stars, the tides, and the enthralling variations of the magnetic needle in which the veteran navigator, Sebastian Cabot, had instructed him. For this year, 1553, was to mark the greatest event in his short reign, when the company of Merchant Adventurers were to undertake their voyage of discovery in search of a trade route by the northern coast of Russia to the Far East. And Philip had asked for, and been granted, leave to join the expedition.

Since the release of Gynkes from his imprisonment in Norwich Castle, Philip had been faced with the bitter knowledge that all hope of life with Jocosa was lost. Her husband had been returned to her incurably, though harmlessly, insane. And she on whom, in his infantile idiocy, he was now a helpless dependant, could not — would not — be persuaded to desert him.

They had met, she and Philip, when he went home to Sprowston in the autumn of 1552. They had stood together in the orchard at Sowerby under the apple boughs heavy with fruit. The sun, slanting through a silver green lattice of leaves, brightened her dark uncovered head and all her loveliness, his for the taking ... if she would give.

Was it, he urged, her early cloistered upbringing that imposed on her this fettered martyrdom in mockery of marriage? Why should she deny herself and him their right to live for and in each other — 'As by all the laws of nature, we were meant,' he said, 'to live.'

'But not,' she answered him, in so cold a stillness that he thought her heart had died, 'by the laws of God.' And seeing her unmoved, unmovable, he lost himself, madly to plead with her: 'No God of love would sanction a marriage such as yours! I am your mate. I! And I defy God, man, or imbecile, to part us. If you cared, if you loved, if you hungered as I do, you could not so destroy me — for a shadow. If you could know the truth —'

And in a flash he saw again that awful moment when this same shadow which haunted their lives had clung to him in its death-embrace — to kill. If she could know! But she must never know.

He heard her say, 'Would you have me do to him what he would not, even now in his mind-sickness, do to one of his dumb creatures? Can I leave him, lonely, lost, untended, he who looks to me for all his needs as his crippled dog does look to him?'

His face was turned from her that she might not see his eyes, and him, unmanned. And so they stood together in a silence a long time, until, 'If love were all,' she said, 'I would go with you. I'd follow you to the earth's ends — if love were all. But it is not. This which has come to us of parting and of pain may be,' she said, 'a privilege, God-sent. I think He would never give the worst of us a burden greater than our spirits' strength can bear.' He heard the catch in her voice, and his face came round to hers; he saw her tears, unfallen, and the tremble of her young ungiven body that yearned for his as he for hers, and yet must not be joined. She took his hand and held it to her lips. 'You would not love me half so well,' she said, 'if love were all.'

He gathered her into his arms; he kissed her hair, her eyes, her mouth, and told her, 'While I live and though I die, I am yours utterly. For always. And hereafter…'

So they closed a door upon their dream within a dream, that lay beyond desire; beyond life.

'I am losing all my gentlemen,' said Edward sadly; for Barnaby was gone to France, but he had been recalled. Harry Suffolk and his brother, Charles Brandon, too, were gone and. could never be recalled. Both had died, within a few days of each other, of the sweating sickness that in the previous year had fallen, on the country, mercilessly to strike at young and old. And seeing the boy's underlip squared to steady a shake in his chin, Philip said hastily: 'Sire, if Your Grace would have it that I stay and do not go on this expedition, I will gladly —'

'You will not!' cried Edward, ''Tis my wish you should go, and the ship that shall take you is — the *Edward Bonaventure*.' So, for himself, had he named the finest, best equipped of that: small fleet of three, and the pride of the Merchant Adventurers.

All through this joyous spring it seemed to those about him that the King had taken a new lease of life. A few months before, an attack of measles followed by the smallpox had laid him low, but in a letter to Barnaby in Paris, six weeks later, he wrote: *We have now shaken that quite away.* And then *While you have been occupied in killing your enemies* — for Barnaby had taken his part in certain minor skirmishes against the French — *we have been occupied in the viewing of faire countries...*

On the map that was ever beside him where he lay watching the tireless river flowing past his window; watching the bright painted barges and wherries trailing their coloured shadows; hearing the homely sound of field and farm; the lowing of cows at milking time; of rooks cawing, gulls mewing, mingled with the distant ring of hammers from far timber-yards borne on the down-stream winds. So would he watch from his window in his palace on the Thames, until he saw the dawn of that long and eagerly awaited day when the willowed banks on either side the river were thronged with excited spectators; the day that his three gallant ships would set out on their perilous voyage through frozen seas to the lands of the midnight sun.

On London's wharf, below the bridge, a privileged cluster of women, mothers, wives, and daughters of the crews, were come to speed their menfolk on their way, with the ripe raw jests of Wapping on their lips and brave laughter in their tears. 'See!' Whispers, nudges, peerings, tiptoeings, signalled the approach of the ships' officers, headed by their Captain General, Sir Hugh Willoughby. They all knew him; for months he had been back and forth among them to London's Pool and shipyards.

In their sky-blue doublets, slashed with gold and silver, glinting in the sunlight, they stepped briskly down the gangway. No women clung about their necks; their farewells had been said in private. Only the last of them paused, swung round on his heel and stayed rooted, his hand shading his eyes that travelled from one woman's face to another's as if he sought and could not find; or listened for a name unspoken, or a word unsaid...

Then, his head flung up, he turned, and following his shipmates, came aboard.

On the roof of Greenwich Palace flags were flying, pennons waving, cheer upon cheer rising, falling, echoing from bank to bank, when the first of those three ships was sighted in the river's bend. And as she skimmed the sun-flashed water, ruffled in a thousand wrinkles by the dancing breeze that swelled her proud white sails outspread like the wings of a swan, the young king leaned from his window, his face flushed, tears springing, his frail boy's voice calling, 'God send you safely home to me, my *Edward Bonaventure*!'

AFTERWORD

The King did not live to see the return home of the *Edward Bonaventure* and her two sister ships, the *Bona Esperanza* and the *Bona Confidentia*. He died on July 6, 1553, eight weeks after the Arctic expedition sailed, in the seventh year of his reign and the sixteenth of his life. But the story of that voyage to the Arctic, with Philip Pugh's part in it and subsequent adventures, is yet to be told.

Although numerous historical characters appear in this book it is from first to last a novel; yet, while Philip and Jocosa are imaginary figures, the pageant of events in which they participate are entirely authentic.

The scenes of Kett's Rebellion are reconstructed from the wealth of documentary material and accounts of eye-witnesses that have been handed down to us. All who fought on either side in the Norfolk rising are real persons, even to Sir Richard a Lee, who when the rebels first stormed the city, was, as we are told, discovered *sitting on a stall in the marketplace and in half-armour.*

The house of Augustine Steward stands much as it was when Lords Northampton and Warwick used it for their headquarters. Mousehold Heath is now a widely developed area, and Sprowston a suburb of Norwich, but the ruins of Carrow Abbey may still be seen beyond what were once the city walls; and in the list of names given of the nuns, or Dames as they were called, who were at Carrow at the time of the Dissolution, we find that of Dame Matilda Graby.

Lord Chancellor Rich did marry a daughter of a grocer, Elizabeth Gynkes, or Jenks, who bore him fifteen children, but there is no evidence that she had a brother Edmund.

It is interesting to note that in 1949, the fourth centenary of Kett's Rebellion, a tablet was raised on the walls of Norwich Castle to his memory, not as a traitor, as a champion of freedom and justice.

And finally, if you take the road from Wymondham to Hethersett you will see by the wayside, standing as it stood four hundred years ago, Kett's 'Oak of Reformation'.

I am gratefully indebted to the chief librarian of Norwich Public Library and his assistants, who have so courteously aided my research.

Doris Leslie

BIBLIOGRAPHY

Kett's Rebellion in Norfolk, The Rev. William Russell, 1859

Robert Kett and the Norfolk Rising, Joseph Clayton, 1912

Kett's Rebellion, S. T. Bindoff, 1949

History of England (Reign of Edward VI), J. S. Froude, 1909

Mediaeval People, Eileen Power, 1924

Mediaeval English Nunneries, Eileen Power, 1922

Lives of the Queens of England, Vols. IV, V, VI, Agnes Strickland

England in Tudor Times, L. F. Salzman, 1926

Literary Remains of Edward VI, Roxburgh Club, 1857

The Journal of King Edward's Reign, written with his own hand, from the original in the Cotton Library, privately printed for the Clarendon Historical Society

King Edward VI, Sir Clement Markham, 1907

Henry VIII, A. F. Pollard, 1913

England under the Protector Somerset, A. F. Pollard, 1900

Itinerary, J. Leland, Ed. L. Toulman Smith, 1906-10

London in the Time of the Tudors, Sir Walter Besant, 1892

London, Sir Walter Besant, 1892

English Social History, G. M. Trevelyan, O.M., 1944

Carrow Abbey, W. Rye, 1889

Machyn Diary, Ed. 1848

Sermons of Hugh Latimer, Bishop of Worcester, Collected Edition, 1926

The Complete Herbal, Nicholas Culpeper, M.D., 1653

A History of Everyday Things in England, M. & C. H. B. Quenell, 1938

Survey of London, John Stow

Dictionary of National Biography

A NOTE TO THE READER

If you have enjoyed this novel enough to leave a review on **Amazon** and **Goodreads**, then we would be truly grateful.
Sapere Books

Sapere Books is an exciting new publisher of brilliant fiction and popular history.

To find out more about our latest releases and our monthly bargain books visit our website:
saperebooks.com